Bradshaw h
in English, "*Duck!*"

Bradshaw didn't question the voice. He immediately hit the dirt, falling on his right side as he covered his head with his hands. A split second later, the sound of suppressed gunfire filled the alley, followed by the signature *thud* of bodies hitting the dirt. Bradshaw poked his head out and glanced. The two officers bled out from wounds in their throats and faces, the blood mixing with the puddles on the asphalt.

He glanced up to see who had warned him. Both of them wore leather gloves, black M65 field jackets, cargo pants, and black ski-masks with skulls printed across the front. Judging from what was displayed through their eye holes, one of them was more than likely a white man, while the other was definitely Asian.

The white man offered Bradshaw a hand. "Get up. We've gotta move."

Other works by Steven Hildreth, Jr.

Forsaken Patriots
#1: *Fault Lines*

The Ben Williams Series

The First Bayonet
The Sovereigns
The Ronin Genesis

FORSAKEN

PATRIOTS

NIGHTMARE EXODUS

STEVEN HILDRETH, JR.

First edition June 2019
ISBN 978-1-09778-922-1

NIGHTMARE EXODUS

Printed by Kindle Direct Publishing, an Amazon subsidiary.

"We only have two choices: do nothing or do something."
-Tony Kirwan, founder and president, Destiny Rescue

"Slavery is a weed that grows on every soil."
-Edmund Burke

Dedicated to the over 40 million victims of human trafficking worldwide.

CHAPTER ONE

Washington, D.C.
15 September 2018
22:19 hours Quebec (16 September 02:19 hours Zulu)

He could barely remember the redhead's name. Amy? Aileen? Andrea? It was irrelevant in the end. She was a disposable pleasure, an intern to the junior senator from Kentucky. Starry-eyed and, more importantly, both fit and curvaceous. When he had spotted her across the room in the Nixon Room at the Capitol Lounge, the fabric of her black blouse and gray skirt was strained in all the right places. That was the catalyst that spurred him to approach her and initiate a conversation.

Why, yes, he *was* Greg Lambert, the one at the White House. No, he wasn't there with anybody, just having a drink to take the edge off after a long day. Yes, the heinous murder of four federal agents was absolutely disgusting. Absolutely, the socialists of the Democratic Party did not appreciate law enforcement for what it was. Could he buy her a drink, no strings attached? Maker's Mark? Good choice. She had to come from money to be drinking in the Cap Lounge, so she certainly could afford her own drink, but Lambert was nothing if not an old-fashioned gentleman scoundrel.

After the first round, the conversation shifted to politics. Her favorite President was Reagan, a fairly standard answer. Lambert preferred the room's namesake, Richard Milhouse Nixon. The man's longevity in the political game and sheer determination to stay in office was nothing short of extraordinary. That was when Lambert launched into an abbreviated dissertation of, in his opinion, American politics' most misunderstood figure: G. Gordon Liddy.

Predictably, she immediately brought up Watergate. Lambert walked her through Liddy's life. Jesuit educated, a commissioned officer who unfortunately missed the call to combat due to medical issues. After a stint as an FBI agent, Liddy was a lawyer, then worked in the Nixon administration in varying positions. That alone was an impressive résumé, but it didn't stop there.

That was when Lambert delved into the reality behind Watergate: much like the President in 2018, there were elements within the administration actively working against the Man to bring him down and usher in an age of cultural Marxism and big government. Liddy was tapped initially to plug the leaks, but the mission eventually became to protect Nixon and guarantee his reelection. In Lambert's eyes, the only thing Liddy did wrong was hire amateurs to do the black bag job at the Democratic National Committee's headquarters. There was no shortage of former special operations veterans who would have been better suited for the job. Instead, a hodge-podge group of locksmiths, former CIA assets, and political flunkies were the ones who were discovered by a working-class security stiff.

Liddy didn't snitch, though, and that was key to Lambert. He did his time standing up. Jimmy Carter did one good thing in his administration, and that was commuting Liddy's sentence. *Will* was written, followed by a movie, and acting gigs and speaking engagements. Lambert confided in What's-Her-Name that the signed copy of *Will* in his study was his most valuable possession.

The young intern hung to every word. She was hooked, so when Lambert suggested they go back to his place after six rounds, she was more than game. The Uber picked them up outside the bar, and it was a 25-minute drive to his house on Florida Avenue. He took the hint when she started leaning against him and letting her hands wander. His hand slid up her skirt to work its magic surreptitiously. By the time they arrived at his place, she was begging for it.

When they stepped inside the spacious four-bed/three-bath brick row home, What's-Her-Face was stunned that he could afford it. That told him that while she might have come from money, she wasn't in his tax bracket. Still, that wasn't applicable to the evening's proceedings. They made their way to the bedroom, where their carnal activities would have brought a blush to an adult performer's cheeks. They fell asleep for a spell, then woke up for round two.

That brought Lambert to where he was in that moment: a lit Montecristo in one hand, a tumbler full of Johnnie Walker Blue in the other, and the woman's nude form sprawled beside him. A combination of the alcohol and a diligent thrashing had done a number on her. A smirk crossed his face as he sipped on the whiskey.

And they call Republicans sexually inhibited. Pfft.

Lambert pulled on the cigar and blew thick smoke rings towards the ceiling. Random pickups were about the thrill of the hunt, but they were only occasional. He had no designs for settling down anytime soon, though he was sure at some point he would, if only to prepare for his entry into the political spotlight. A trophy wife and an obligatory child for the voters in more traditional areas…but, that was well down the road.

At that moment, Greg Lambert, Ph.D. was a senior adviser to the most powerful man in the world, a brash and revolutionary man that would correct the damage inflicted on the nation by an unconstitutional progressive over the opening years of the 2010s. Power was what drove Lambert. It was an element far more intoxicating than sex: the knowledge that his words and ideas influenced the 326 million citizens in his domain, as well as billions across the globe. American exceptionalism was back in fashion, and Lambert was a key figure in shaping its return.

Lambert's Samsung smartphone sounded off with Inner Circle's "Bad Boys." He leaned over to the bedside stand, set his tumbler down, and picked up the phone. The caller's identity was obscured, the call being routed through the RedPhone app. He swung his legs from beneath the covers and walked out of the room, leaving the anonymous redhead to sleep off her buzz. Once he was in the hallway, Lambert unlocked the phone with his thumbprint, then watched as his phone shook hands with the caller. Once the call was encrypted end-to-end, he lifted the phone to his ear.

"Jeremy," Lambert said. "What's going on?"

"Bradshaw slipped the net, sir," Jeremy Hawthorne said.

Lambert rubbed his temples. "How do you know?"

"He's not dumb. He knew the moment he killed my men, his only option was to flee. He had a head start, and I'm certain Rivera helped him. Doesn't help that he's trained in evasion and urban surveillance."

"I see."

"I can start shaking the trees. Arrest Rivera, bring in anybody tied to Bradshaw, start trying to draw up a target packet."

Lambert inhaled deep through his nostrils. "It doesn't matter," he said. "He's on the run without resources. The red notice will leave him few hiding places. He'll either do the smart thing and find a rock to crawl under, or he'll pop his head up and the Russians will smash it."

"The Russians?" Hawthorne asked, perplexed. "I thought we were going after him, sir."

Lambert reflexively shook his head. "We can't risk that exposure, and your unit's not combat ready. We still have work that has to be done here at home. You need to replenish your personnel before we can look forward."

"He knows about the Russians. If he hasn't put two and two together, he will soon."

"Let him. The Russians served their purpose. Tensions are high. The lefties are getting rowdy. We've got pretense to start locking them up. Anybody sees the correlation, the blame is laid squarely at the Russians' feet."

Hawthorne hesitated before he responded. "Yes, sir."

"Jeremy," Lambert said, "you've done a great job so far. We've accomplished so much in so little time. Giving scum like the White Resistance Movement a nudge was necessary to cut out the cultural rot in this nation."

"I agree, sir," Hawthorne said. "I just wish it didn't require losing my men."

"Bruce, Phil, Lucas, and Garrett were patriots," Lambert said solemnly. "They gave their lives for a better America. We honor their sacrifice by rebuilding the Boat Crew. There are still leaks to plug in the White House and irritants that need addressing."

"Yes, sir," Hawthorne said. "Derrick and Robby are already on their way back to DC with the bulk of the gear. I'm wrapping up procedural issues with the Phoenix office and I'll be back on a red-eye."

"Good. When you get back, get your men together. Let's do lunch and have a strategy meeting."

"Yes, sir. Looking forward to it."

"Me, too," Lambert said. "See you then."

Lambert killed the call and locked his phone. He glanced at the framed photo of him with G. Gordon Liddy from 2012, Liddy with a stoic smile and Lambert beaming with his freshly signed copy of *Will* in hand. Lambert pulled on the cigar once more and blew rings at the picture, then turned back towards the bedroom.

When he reentered, the redhead was stirring, rubbing her temples. "Who was that?"

"Work," Lambert said. "Nothing major."

"Work's no fun," the woman said. She crawled to the edge of the bed and took him in her hands. "*This* is fun."

Lambert extinguished the cigar in the bedside ashtray as the redhead took him in her mouth. He leaned his head back, closed his eyes, and smiled.

Long live the king.

Manzanillo, Colima, Mexico
16 September 2018
16:45 hours Romeo (21:45 hours Zulu)

JACK BRADSHAW'S LOWER back was tense. Aside from the necessary refueling breaks, their only detour had been a six-hour break at a rest stop. Bradshaw had pulled guard while his chauffeur—Ramón Perez, a philanthropic *coyote*—slept and recharged. Perez hadn't been kidding when they grabbed breakfast and fuel in Heroica Nogales. They were going to drive as hard and as fast as they could to reach their destination. The terrain had shifted from the rugged expanses of the Sonoran Desert to the luscious, vibrant greens of the rainforest in Colima State. It would have been an enjoyable drive were it not for the stiff, unaccommodating seat.

Despite the discomfort, Bradshaw didn't blame Perez for the approach. It didn't take a criminal mind to know that to remain stationary and in the open for a prolonged period of time was unwise, particularly if the package being ferried was a fugitive from justice.

In Bradshaw's case, it especially didn't help that he was wanted for the murder of four federal agents. It didn't matter that said federal agents had entered without a warrant, or that their suppressed weapons declared their intent. Those inconvenient facts were omitted when the "murders" were presented to the press.

There was no turning himself in to report his side of the story. If they were willing to break into his apartment to murder him in his sleep, it was not beyond the realm of possibility that they would engineer an "accident" during transport to a detention facility. The only option was to run, and Bradshaw knew that remaining in the States was ill-advised. It would only be a matter of time before law enforcement closed in on him. In that circumstance, Bradshaw's Army Ranger background and his public cop-killer label would guarantee the law would come in shooting.

Bradshaw's expression soured as he reflected. As much as he lacked remorse over killing Jeremy Hawthorne's secret policemen, there was no way he would drop the hammer on an honest peace officer acting on the information he or she was given.

That left one option: an international exodus.

The nuts and bolts of the transport were handled by Perez, but he and Bradshaw were connected through the former's niece. Gabriela Rivera had been Bradshaw's principal on a bodyguard assignment. Bradshaw had saved her life twice from a white nationalist group which had been infiltrated by a Russian intelligence operative named Kazimir Merkulov.

Bradshaw knew Merkulov was Russian intelligence prior to his unmasking in the press. While serving with the 75th Ranger Regimental Reconnaissance Company in Afghanistan, Bradshaw and his men fell victim to a firebase attack. The perpetrators were Taliban insurgents advised by what appeared to be ethnic Europeans. Bradshaw had put a bullet in Merkulov's chest during the base defense, but one of the Talibs had dragged Merkulov from the battlefield during a tactical retreat.

While canvassing the battle's aftermath, Bradshaw witnessed one of Merkulov's fallen comrades speak his dying words in Russian. The whole incident had been covered up by the highest levels of the chain of command, which had driven Bradshaw from the Army. In retrospect, that event foreshadowed darker things to come.

Bradshaw's mind drifted back to Gabriela. It was far too soon after meeting her to use words like "love," but he would have been lying if he denied their shared connection. Bradshaw entertained the notion of prolonged commitment, something he thought he would never do again after his failed marriage. Gabriela compelled him to reconsider with her brilliance, charisma, and her robust work ethic. It was hard not to like her, and even harder not to fall for her.

That potential future had been snuffed out the moment Bradshaw had pulled the trigger on the rogue peace officers. Each time his mind wandered, he saw her face, a reminder of what he'd had…and lost. Equal parts sorrow and rage welled inside his chest, and he fought to maintain control.

Thankfully, Perez's voice cut through Bradshaw's reverie and brought him back to the present.

"Hey," he said. "We've arrived."

Bradshaw grabbed his go-bag from beside him. "I left the weapon and ammunition in the compartment. Dispose of it for me, will you?"

"You've got it," Perez said. He glanced over his shoulder. "You know which dock you're headed to?"

"Yeah," Bradshaw said as he slung the bag over his shoulder.

"Most of these guys speak English. It's an international port. If they don't, there'll be somebody nearby who does. You'll blend in. Just don't linger."

"Got it." Bradshaw reached forward to shake Perez's hand. "I owe you my life, sir. Thank you."

Perez gripped Bradshaw's hand and shook it. "You're a good man. I would trust you with my niece, were the circumstances different."

Bradshaw let out a heavy exhale as he nodded. "Thank you, sir."

"Know this, though," Perez cautioned. "She's got her life to live. You've got more pressing items on your plate. Focus on what you need to do to stay alive. Should the circumstances change to where you can come home, don't be surprised if she's moved on."

Bradshaw shook his head. "I'd never begrudge her that, sir." He sighed again. "Thank you, again."

"*Vaya con Díos,*" Perez said.

Bradshaw stepped out of the Chevrolet pickup and shut the door behind him. Perez pulled out and guided his truck back to the highway. The first thing Bradshaw noticed was the crispness of the oceanside air. Overcast skies made false promises of precipitation. The temperature was in the mid-80s, but his clothing had already started to soak in sweat, courtesy of the outrageous humidity.

I'm already missing Arizona, Bradshaw groused internally.

The port was bustling with activity. Men and women of every nationality and ethnic origin scurried about the docks, either looking to board or disembark a ship, or searching for cargo.

The stacks of shipping containers off to the right caught Bradshaw's eye. They came in various colors, though red and blue seemed to be the most popular. They were marked in a variety of languages and bore the flags of several nations. A yellow crane moved in position, lowering its claw around one of the containers and slowly lifting it up.

Bradshaw adjusted the sling to his go-bag and let out a heavy sigh. *Well, no time like the present.* With a dutiful nod to himself, Bradshaw marched forward towards his destination.

CHAPTER TWO

The Port of Tanjung Priok was responsible for over half of Indonesia's maritime commerce. It moved millions of 20-foot equivalent units in cargo per year, which in turn provided goods for the residents of Java, the world's most densely populated island. The port was bustling, with cargo ships coming and going at all hours.

Ajij Mentari was one of three shift managers for the general cargo terminal. A 17-year employee of the state-owned Indonesia Port Company, Mentari had started fresh out of secondary school as a dock worker, largely securing ships that arrived in port. Mentari was ambitious, largely due to being newlywed when he secured the job, and he quickly took on collateral duties while acquiring additional skillsets. Safety inspector, cargo inspector, team leader, and section supervisor all came Mentari's way in a 12-year period. Three years later, Mentari attained the coveted shift manager position. It came with a considerable pay bump, commensurate with the added responsibility.

As the short and wiry Mentari patrolled the container rows, he allowed himself a moment to bask in what his position truly entailed. The port—and the operation thereof—was a machine. When it was well-oiled and maintained, it was a source of commercial lifeblood for Java, and in turn for Indonesia at-large. Were it to come off the rails, it wouldn't just be the corporate entity or the Indonesia Port Company that would feel it. Shortages in essential imports were a real possibility. It was Mentari's running of a tight ship, as well as the same from his colleagues on the swing and overnight shifts, that kept the nation running.

Mentari reached his destination. The container ship was a feeder, more than likely delivering cargo to Malaysia, the

Philippines, or Papua New Guinea. Feeders were far less tedious to load, but they were still a time-consuming matter, even with a competent crew. Agung's team was the one assigned to work on the feeder when the day crew came on. Loading had taken up the bulk of the past two days, and Mentari knew that Agung's team would wrap it up by the end of the shift.

Agung walked down the gangway, clipboard in hand and his team in tow. Mentari checked his watch as the short and stocky Agung reached the docks.

"Cutting it close," Mentari said.

"Still beat the deadline," Agung said with a smile. He handed the clipboard to Mentari, who accepted it and began to inspect the paperwork. Mentari pulled a pen from his breast pocket and signed and initialed where necessary. Once he reached the back of the stack, he nodded, took the papers, and returned the clipboard to Agung.

"Well done," Mentari said.

Agung gestured to the man immediately behind him. "You can thank McCloud for that. The man is a caffeinated monkey. He just doesn't stop."

Mentari glanced to the foreigner. Unlike most of the manual laborers, who were either locals, Malays, or Filipinos, "McCloud" was clearly ethnic European. He was lean and tall, standing a full head over both Agung and Mentari.

"That's the fifth double shift you've worked in the past week, McCloud," Mentari said. "You know you're not getting paid any extra for it. Don't you have a life outside of work?"

Jack Bradshaw removed his yellow hard hat, the dark man-bun falling loose from beneath. He wiped his brow with his forearm, the accumulated sweat collected by the long sleeve of his blue T-shirt. A smile emerged from beneath his thick beard. "No, sir," he said in heavily accented Indonesian. "I just don't like unfinished work."

"It won't be unfinished," Mentari told him. "The next shift will pick up where you left off. Why don't you just do your eight hours and go home?"

"Just need to remind Intan's team that day shift pulls their weight," Bradshaw said, his grin widening.

Mentari chuckled. "You're something else, McCloud, but your work ethic is admirable." He gestured over his shoulder with his thumb. "No overtime tonight. Go home and *rest*. I'll see you bright and early."

Bradshaw nodded and offered an informal salute. "Yes, boss!"

Mentari shook his head and smiled as Agung led "McCloud" and the others back to the dock entrance. He put his hands on his hips and sighed. The "Canadian" was polite, professional, made an effort to learn the local *lingua franca*, and was eager for work. Mentari figured he could fudge the books and get him paid for his extra work. While he understood the budget manager was strict, Mentari felt it'd be a shame not to reward initiative and motivation.

A SILENT SIGH fell from Bradshaw's nostrils. Something he'd learned when he ran his first patrol in Tal Afar back in 2007 was that most cities bore a similar aesthetic. Aside from the toll that four years of war had taken, the city had resembled several of the "rougher" areas he had seen in Tucson and other metropolitan areas. The more developed the nation looked, the more the city resembled places in the States. Of course, every city had its peculiarities, but the same features persisted: paved roads full of vehicles, traffic signals, billboards, and skyscrapers.

Bradshaw took in the scenery from the backseat of the taxi. Jakarta reminded him of a slightly dirtier version of Manhattan, which he had visited once on mid-tour leave. Even the signs possessed a hint of familiarity, as the Indonesian alphabet used the same 26 Latin characters as English. It was the character arrangement that was foreign.

Jakarta hadn't been on his travel bucket list before, though he could see why it would make the list for others. In Bradshaw's case, his motivation for selecting the city was pragmatic: it was the largest city in Indonesia, a non-extradition country. He was a drop in a bucket, and with the right precautions, he would remain off of local law enforcement's radar and out of reach of Jeremy Hawthorne's task masters.

He noticed the pavement gradually deteriorate in quality, the tell-tale sign that they had reached the Warakas boundary line. Bradshaw scratched his beard, then ran his hand through his thick mane. For a moment, he thought about a haircut and a beard trim, but he decided against it. It was better to save that for the inevitable day where he'd need to bug out once more.

Hope that's not any day soon, Bradshaw mused. *That'd break the bank.*

"Here we are," the taxi driver said from the front, in English. He wore a concerned face. "You sure you want to be dropped off here?"

Bradshaw smiled. "You're new here?" he asked.

"Yeah, first week," the driver said.

"I see," Bradshaw said. He nodded and said, "I'm fine here." He extended a wad of *rupiah* towards the driver. "Thank you. Keep what remains."

"Thank you, sir," the young driver said with a smile and a nod.

Bradshaw walked the streets, his duffel bag slung on his back. He had given the driver a location a few blocks away from his apartment. Grocery shopping was in order, and there was a fish shop within walking distance.

It took two minutes to reach the shop from the drop-off point. Bradshaw had discovered the shop shortly after moving into his apartment. They sold a catfish that he found was especially delicious in *woku* sauce made from scratch and mixed with fried noodles to create *mi goreng*. He had taken to the cuisine rapidly, being a fiend for spicy foods.

The shop itself wasn't much. Like the other buildings in the neighborhood, the state of the brick walls suggested that the building greatly outdated Bradshaw. The one-story edifice was used for storage. Commerce was done under a veranda that shielded several merchant kiosks.

A light drizzle fell from above as Bradshaw entered the veranda. He gave a nod to the proprietor, who returned it. Chatter continued around Bradshaw as he perused the selection. It took him a minute to find the catfish, and another couple of minutes to select the cuts. As he reached for it, Bradshaw felt eyes on him. Slowly, he turned around to see who had taken an interest in him.

The girl didn't look a day over fifteen. She was thin, bordering on emaciated, with matted shoulder-length hair that framed her gaunt cheeks. Judging from her ratty hand-me-down shirt that was several sizes too large, filthy jeans, and sandals that had well exceeded their recommended mileage, Bradshaw figured that meals might not be a weekly event, much less daily.

It was the fear in her dark eyes that twisted a knot in his chest. Bradshaw was familiar with the look. He had seen it in the eyes of men, women, and children throughout Iraq and Afghanistan. When Bradshaw saw the look in the eyes of malefactors, he fed on it, but when it was presented by those to whom he'd never do harm, it never failed to do a number on his conscience.

Bradshaw offered the girl a smile and a wave. "Hello there," he said in Indonesian.

The girl chuckled uncomfortably as she held up a hand to wave, unsure as to how to process the pale foreign giant addressing her. Bradshaw kept his distance and made his way across the shop with his selections in hand.

There was a small stand at the edge of the shop that contained wrapped *dodol Garut*, a popular toffee-like confectionary. Beside that was a cooler with a variety of drinks. Bradshaw grabbed a handful of *dodol Garut*, then selected a bottle of *es selendang mayang,* which he found to be a local equivalent of the *horchata* rice milk he enjoyed back home.

With his selections in hand, Bradshaw made his way to the proprietor. After a brief assessment of the purchases, the proprietor quoted a price, and Bradshaw produced the necessary *rupiah*. Bradshaw had the fish put in one bag, and the candies in the other. The girl was still there when he approached her slowly, holding out the bag of candy.

"Here," he said. "For you."

The girl stared between the bag and Bradshaw, attempting to detect underhandedness. Eventually, she stepped forward, accepted the bag, and quickly retreated as if Bradshaw would change his mind. It wasn't the most nutritional fare, but that was a concern for those fortunate enough to live outside of poverty.

"What's your name?" Bradshaw asked.

The girl deliberated answering him as she unwrapped one of the *dodols* and stuffed it into her mouth. She chewed, swallowed, then chased the confectionary down with a mouthful of the sweet, iced drink. Her eyes bore into Bradshaw's, searching for a hint of ulterior motive. When she could not find one, she spoke, her voice meek yet raspy.

"Citra."

"I like your name," Bradshaw said. He smiled, then placed his free hand on his chest. "My name is Neil."

"Neil." Citra said it slowly in an attempt to comprehend it. The way she said it, it sounded more like "nail." Bradshaw nodded as she said it.

"You have a home?" Bradshaw asked.

Citra shook her head. "I'm an orphan."

Bradshaw touched his hand to his chest once more. "I am sorry." He sighed and said, "If you see me around here, you can ask me for food. I will also try to give you new clothes."

Citra eyed him skeptically. "Why do you do this? Are you a *preman*?"

Bradshaw had learned about *preman* early in his Indonesian stay. Historically, *preman* were gangsters associated with a variety of clans and syndicates. Over the past 20 years, the majority of them had transitioned into strongmen for political parties, defending national, ethnic, or religious honor. A sizeable minority remained tied into the black market trades, primarily human and narcotics trafficking.

A couple of weeks after Bradshaw had settled into his apartment, a group of young, harsh looking men had attempted to shake him down. When Bradshaw refused to capitulate, the group's leader had produced a knife. Bradshaw had taken the knife from the young man without much of an effort, and warned him that the next time he drew a weapon on him, he would bury that weapon someplace dark and damp. He followed the threat up with a warning for whomever led them: he had no interest in disturbing their racket, but he also had no desire to be party to it. If they left him alone, he would do likewise. Bradshaw hadn't been disturbed since.

Bradshaw shook his head emphatically. "No. I am not a *preman*. Just a person who likes to help others."

"Then that would make you the first," Citra said, her voice brittle. "Nobody does anything selflessly."

Bradshaw opened his mouth to comment on how her cynicism was unbefitting of her age, but he thought better and bit his tongue. Without parents or anyone to care for her, he could only imagine what she had done in the interests of surviving the streets. He would have been surprised if she ever dreamed of a future. With a sigh, he produced more *rupiah* and extended them towards her.

"Get a hot meal. It is my gift to you."

Citra accepted the money and stuffed it in her pocket. "I am grateful, though you should be careful. Your compassion may harm you one day."

"Perhaps," Bradshaw said. He smiled. "As long as *you* don't harm me, I think I'll live to see another day." He gestured down the street. "I'll see you around."

"Thank you, Neil," Citra said. She offered him a tight-lipped smile, then turned and hurried down the street.

Bradshaw sighed. Seeing the destitute abroad had always served as a reminder of how good he'd had it in the States. In that moment, it also served as an indirect reminder that he couldn't return home. He pursed his lips, then turned in the direction of his apartment complex.

THERE WAS NOTHING special about the studio apartment. Wood constituted the majority of the floor paneling, with tile for the kitchen and bathroom. Bradshaw had put a lot of work into it his first month there. The walls and floors were scrubbed clean to Ranger standards, the lights were replaced with energy-efficient LED bulbs, and every surface was restored as close to its original state as possible. When Bradshaw finished, it almost resembled the average studio in a decent neighborhood back home.

Bradshaw sat in a lawn chair as he scooped the last of the catfish *mi goreng* from his plastic bowl. His Acer laptop—the only thing he'd carried with him from his previous life—rested on a folding table directly in front of him. He'd gone over the laptop several times prior to his arrival in Indonesia, ensuring it was clean of spyware. Not wanting to rely solely on his admittedly limited technical skill, Bradshaw had also subscribed to a virtual private network service and took care not to utilize any services he had frequented in the United States. Given that he avoided social media, that left only his Amazon account and his e-mail, and their absence was barely noticed.

In the background, the Windows Media app played "Immigrants (We Get the Job Done)" from *The Hamilton Mixtape* on low volume. A Daily Beast article filled the screen's forefront. Things were heating up in Venezuela between the government of Nicolás Maduro—Hugo Chavez's successor—and Juan Guaidó, who had been selected by the National Assembly to be the President after the previous year's election results were declared invalid.

A Swedish journalist named Annika Hernroth-Rothstein, who had been in-country covering the protests, was abducted, beaten, and threatened by *colectivos,* militias formed by the late President Chavez to enforce his will.

"Hmm," Bradshaw grunted. *Wonder if the Russians have their fingers in that pot, too?* He had always paid passing attention to world events to remain minimally informed. Since his flight from the United States, Bradshaw's focus on the topic had intensified. The study of Russian active measures had become a hobby in the wake of his falling victim to such activities. Besides the obvious power moves in Ukraine and Syria, Bradshaw had noticed potential activity in central Africa and a hand in the yellow vest protests that had gripped France since the previous November.

Bradshaw finished reading Rothstein's article on her experience and let out a low, long exhale. He knew many would retreat into solitude's safety in the wake of such an experience. From what he'd read, she fully intended to brush her shoulders off and move forward. *Ballsy,* he thought. *Gotta give her props.*

He closed the article and made his way to Google. Once there, Bradshaw searched "gabriela rivera twitter." He didn't have an account himself and couldn't remember the address off the top of his head, so he resorted to Google leading him to the account. Bradshaw clicked on the first link, which took him to Gabriela Rivera's Twitter. He was greeted with a professional headshot where Rivera smiled wide, along with a banner that read "#Resist."

Rivera's Twitter feed had been largely reduced to retweets since the previous September's Rally for Humanity in Tempe, Arizona. Bradshaw had noticed that she had only given four interviews since then. Out of those four, only one had been televised, conducted via Skype. He chalked that up to her wanting to keep a low profile.

The background song ended, and the media app shifted to the next song: "War" by Bob Marley. Bradshaw had drafted the playlist from an interview Rivera had done prior to their meeting that focused on her personal side. It was an eclectic mix of traditional Mexican music, rap, reggaetón, and old school reggae. None of it was Bradshaw's standard musical fare, but it brought him closer to Rivera.

Bradshaw clicked on the profile picture and watched it fill the center of his screen. His fingers traced a line along the image of her cheeks. Looking into her eyes, he could almost feel the warmth they'd held the last time he had seen her, standing in the driveway of her *tío's* Nogales home. He clenched his jaw and forced a long exhale through his nostrils.

God, I miss you, Gabby.

Not for the first time, he considered making an account to reach out to her. The notion was shot down a moment later. Bradshaw knew that if he truly cared about her—*Or loved her, even?* he wondered—then he needed to stay off-grid.

It didn't lessen the sting of being robbed of the opportunity for a life spent with her, or that they only had a handful of shared memories, or that he didn't have a picture of the two of them together.

Bradshaw closed the browser window, powered down the computer, and glanced to the one personal accoutrement he'd obtained. It was a cork board, pinned to which were various mementos of his recent forced travels. There was a matchbook he'd picked up at a gas station in Hermosillo, a coaster he'd lifted from a bar in Panama City, a tourist brochure from Tangier, a Sphinx-theme postcard from Cairo, and a patch of the Socotra dragon tree he'd bought from a street vendor in Aden.

It was hard to believe he'd accomplished that much travel in six months. At the same time, Bradshaw had been more worried about being recognized as an international fugitive than about sight-seeing. Still, he'd allowed his inner tourist to peek out a smidgeon, a reminder of how far he was from home.

Bradshaw realized he had been running his thumb along the red-on-black paracord bracelet affixed to his right wrist. For obvious reasons, he had left behind the KIA bracelet memorializing his best friend, Logan Fox. It was comforting to know that Gabby was holding onto it for safe keeping, but he found three months into his journey that he was bothered by his naked wrist. Bradshaw had paid a coworker aboard the cargo ship to order the necessary materials and had constructed the bracelet during their stop in Cairo. It wasn't as good as its predecessor, but it helped put his mind at ease.

With a sigh, Bradshaw rose from the chair and made his way to the cot that served as his bed. He stripped down to his boxers, then lowered himself to the cot and wrapped himself in his poncho liner. The melatonin would hopefully be kicking in any second. Bradshaw had been forced to increase the dosage to seven milligrams just to force himself to sleep.

As fatigue's warmth washed over him, Bradshaw hoped that the chemical assistance would be enough to keep the nightmares at bay.

CHAPTER THREE

Tanjung Priok, North Jakarta, Indonesia
14 March 2019
16:05 hours Golf (09:05 hours Zulu)

The off-brand MP3 player was loaded with songs that Bradshaw had pirated via a YouTube to MP3 converter. It was a mix of his Gabby playlist and the music on which he'd grown up. Being an unskilled stevedore was physically strenuous and soporific work. Bradshaw approached it like he'd tackled the more menial tasks dealt to him as a young Ranger: he lost himself in the music.

At that moment, Johnny Cash's "God's Gonna Cut You Down" filled his ears as he worked on cinching a CONEX to the cargo ship deck. The Man in Black's later discography shifted focus to tales of judgment from higher powers and the innocent being condemned for crimes they didn't commit. In the wake of the previous year's events, Bradshaw found deeper meaning in those songs than he had in days past.

Bradshaw finished the last tether, then glanced out towards the Java Sea as he wiped his brow with his forearm. Storm clouds gathered on the horizon. He sighed as he pursed his lips. *Looks like rain.* Tropical climes seemed to be the standard for safe haven on the lam, but people often failed to account that those environments were dense with precipitation.

Goddamn, I miss the desert, Bradshaw thought. Another sigh filtered through his nostrils.

A voice cut through Johnny Cash's rich baritone voice. "Oi! *Barat!*"

Bradshaw turned around to find several men gathered on the deck. The man at the front, Intan, was the evening shift leader. Bradshaw glanced at his watch, then chuckled in surprise. He removed one of his headphones and said, "Huh. Lost track of the time."

"Yep," Intan said. He gestured over his shoulder with his thumb. "We'll take it from here."

"No complaints from me," Bradshaw said with a smile. He made his way to the edge of the CONEX and climbed down. When he reached the deck, he made his way to the gangway. "Thanks for the relief."

Intan put a hand on Bradshaw's chest to halt him. He involuntarily tensed and inhaled deeply to control his reaction.

"Take it easy with the work," Intan said. "You're making the rest of us look bad."

Maybe you should pull your weight, then, Bradshaw mused. He put on a smile and held up his hands. "Sorry," he said as apologetically as he could muster. "Not trying to rock the boat. Just wanna earn my keep."

"Uh-huh," Intan said. He motioned with his head towards the gangway. Bradshaw took the hint and made his way to the docks. His work gloves came off and were tucked into his back pocket.

Note to self, Bradshaw thought. *Turn it down a notch, but not enough that the boss man notices me slacking. Gray man, Jack. Gray man.*

Bradshaw walked the streets of the same vendor district he'd visited the day prior. This time, he stopped by a local barbecue shop he'd passed several times during his meandering trip home. He had seen the racks of *cha sio* hanging in the window of the small meat vendor, and his mouth had watered. Bradshaw had been thinking about the Chinese-derivative barbecued beef since lunch time and he had made the decision to splurge.

With his selections in hand, Bradshaw began to make his way toward his apartment. Even through the paper bag, he could smell the blend of hoisin, honey, five-powder sauce, and soy sauce.

He almost didn't notice the girl from the day before approaching, a smile on her face and her hands clasped at her waist. It took him a moment to remember her name.

"Hello, Citra," he said pleasantly.

Citra beamed. "Hello, Neil."

"How was dinner yesterday?"

"Delicious!" She pointed to the bag in his hand. "What do you have there?"

"*Cha sio.*" He opened up both the outer paper bag and the inner plastic one and extended it towards her. "Would you like some?"

Citra shook her head emphatically. "Oh, no," she said. "I can't."

"C'mon," Bradshaw said. He smiled. "I hear it's pretty good." She paused, and he reached into the bag for a beef strip. "Let's try one together."

Citra's eyes flickered between the piece of meat and Bradshaw's eyes. She couldn't detect any deception, and she reluctantly accepted. Bradshaw pulled out a second strip for himself and took a bite. As he chewed, a content moan competed for space with the meat. He swallowed, then looked at the half-bitten strip.

"Holy hell, that is *amazing*," he said. Bradshaw put the rest of the strip in his mouth and chewed, holding his hand away from his face. Citra giggled at Bradshaw as he savored the barbecued meat.

"Thank you," she said as she took another bite.

Bradshaw grunted as he chewed the rest of his meat and swallowed. "Of course." He licked his fingers clean and vocalized his approval once more. His eyes glanced skyward. "Looks like rain tonight."

Citra sighed as she chewed. "Yes. It does."

"Do you have a poncho or something to keep you dry?"

"No," Citra said. She quickly added, "It's okay, though. I'll find a way to stay dry."

Bradshaw reached into his pocket and pulled out some cash. "I'll tell you what," he said. "There's a clothing store a few blocks away from here. I think I saw a poncho in there." He presented the wadded bills to her. "Get yourself a poncho. You can use the rest for food tomorrow." When he saw the look on her face, he said, "It's like I told you before. I like to help. No strings attached. You'll make me feel better knowing you're dry and fed."

After a moment's hesitation, Citra accepted the money. In a serious tone, she said, "You truly are too kind."

"I'm just doing what I can," Bradshaw said with a small grin and a nod. "I'll see you tomorrow?"

"I'll be around," she said. Citra stuffed the cash into her tattered jean pocket with one hand and lifted the piece of *cha sio* to her mouth with the other.

"Stay dry, now," Bradshaw said. He gave her a parting smile before he stepped around her and began to make his way down the street. *Sweet girl,* he thought. *A survivor. I wonder what she'd be had she had the good fortune to be born into better circumstances. She's got a good head on her shoulders.*

He made it another four steps before he heard Citra scream.

Bradshaw spun on a dime and immediately scanned the street ahead. Others looked towards the source of the screaming as well, but none of them were spurred to action. Bradshaw couldn't see Citra, but he was sure the screaming was coming from the right-hand side of the street—

There! Bradshaw recognized the weathered jeans as Citra lashed out at one of her attackers with flailing kicks. The counterattack was to no effect, as the group of young men dragged her into an alley. A scowl formed on Bradshaw's face as he sprinted forward. As he reached the alley's mouth, he dropped his duffel and his *cha sio*, then peeked around the corner.

There were three of them. From profile, Bradshaw recognized one as one of the *preman* that had accosted him months earlier. They were struggling to get Citra to the other end of the alley, but she scratched, clawed, and kicked to impede their progress. The thugs were speaking too quickly for Bradshaw to keep up, but he caught a few epithets being shouted. A loud *crack* reverberated throughout the alley as one of the *preman* struck Citra with an open hand.

Ice water hit Bradshaw's veins as he steeled himself. With a short, forced exhale, he rounded the corner and marched forward, his hands at his side. His footfalls were silent, and he said nothing until he was within a meter of the trio.

"Oy! *Goblok!*" Bradshaw shouted.

The three heavies spun to look at him. For a moment, fear filled their eyes, and Bradshaw smiled icily. The fear was quickly replaced with the faux confidence utilized by predatory types worldwide. Two of the three *preman* advanced slowly on Bradshaw, and he mentally nicknamed them Tweedledee and Tweedledum. The one holding Citra tight against him was christened Tweedledweeb.

"Oh, looky-looky," Tweedledee said in English. "*Meester* fucking shit tits American!"

Bradshaw took a small step to his right to better position himself for the fight to come. "I'd say your English is shit, but I've been butchering your language for the past few months, so at best, we're even."

Tweedledee produced a karambit and moved his hand in a figure-8 motion in front of his face. "You want butcher? We can do butcher, American!"

Bradshaw sighed, his eyes locked on the curved blade in Tweedledee's hand. "I told you back in December, I'm Canadian. And nobody has to get butchered. Just let her go and I'll forget you pulled a knife on me again." His eyes hardened. "You remember what I promised if you repeated that mistake?"

"I'm gonna cut you up, *Meester* American cunt!"

Bradshaw stopped moving and reverted to Indonesian so there was no miscommunication. "Bring it, *perek.*"

Tweedledee let out a war cry as he rushed forward, the karambit held high over his head. Bradshaw waited until he was within range, then lashed out with a push kick that knocked him back into a wall. Tweedledum let loose with a haymaker, and Bradshaw ducked beneath it. He spun and went to work, his fists connecting at full power with Tweedledum's ribs. With the third strike, Bradshaw heard a muted *crack*. He then stood to full height as he drove his fist into Tweedledum's chin. The uppercut lifted the *pre-man* off the ground, and he fell on his back, stunned.

Bradshaw turned to Tweedledweeb and marched forward. The heavy threw Citra out of reach and readied his hands. Citra took the opportunity to turn and sprint for the alley's mouth. As Bradshaw approached Tweedledweeb, he heard the sound of hurried footfalls against pavement. He turned in time to find Tweedledee sprinting back in the fray, and side-stepped to avoid the knife slash. Bradshaw was too slow, and a sharp, hot pain stemmed from his upper right arm as the blade broke skin. Tweedledee spun on a heel and slashed once more. Bradshaw leaned back, the karambit's tip fractions of an inch from tearing through his larynx.

Tweedledweeb materialized from the left and drove his foot into Bradshaw's ribs. Bradshaw stumbled back, his arms clutching his ribcage as he struggled to catch his breath. *Little fucker kicks hard*, he allowed himself to think before he recomposed himself. He stood up straight and reassumed his fighting stance. Tweedledee was to his right, and Tweedledweeb squared up in front of him. All three men eyed each other, looking for who would flinch first.

Bradshaw broke the stalemate with a feint towards Tweedledee. The knife-wielder flinched backward, and Tweedledweeb rushed forward. Bradshaw turned his attention back to Tweedledweeb, stepped forward, and drove his knee into the groin without breaking stride. Tweedledweeb hunched over at the waist. Bradshaw grabbed Tweedledweeb by the shoulders, struck him on the bridge of his nose with a headbutt, then tightened his grip and pushed him forward. Tweedledee had rushed forward and lunged with his karambit, and the steel buried itself square in Tweedledweeb's back.

As Tweedledee's mouth dropped open at what he had done to his friend, Bradshaw pulled Tweedledweeb back and tossed him aside. He stepped to Tweedledee, grabbed his knife hand, and drove it forward. The blade was buried in Tweedledee's abdomen, which elicited a piercing shriek from the *preman*. Bradshaw grabbed the blade handle with his right hand, yanked the knife free, and spun Tweedledee around.

Bradshaw pinned Tweedledee to the wall face-first, leaned forward, and growled in Indonesian, "I warned you." Without delay, Bradshaw plunged the karambit into the base of Tweedledee's skull, severing the brain stem. A fountain of blood squirted from the jagged wound, and Tweedledee collapsed the moment Bradshaw ceased to hold him up.

With a heavy sigh, Bradshaw dropped the karambit to the floor and surveyed the carnage. One dead, one grievously wounded, and a third with serious injuries. He glanced down. Blood stained his button-down shirt, jeans, and boots. He could feel specks of blood on his face, and he was certain he'd gotten blood in his beard, as well. Bradshaw winced as he breathed in, suddenly re-aware of what were likely bruised ribs.

"Shit," he breathed. "Goddamn it." With his arm wrapped around his midsection, Bradshaw ran as fast as his injuries would allow to where he'd left his duffel. He'd worn out his welcome in Indonesia, and the window was closing for a clean getaway.

AT THE OPPOSITE end of the alley, Kirsana Nirmala leaned back around the corner, her hands trembling as she held her Samsung smartphone. She brushed a lock of black hair out of her eyes as she opened her Video app and replayed the footage she'd just recorded. The picture was shaky and a bit blurry from her having utilized her camera's zoom feature, but there was more than enough usable footage in the two-minute video.

"My God," she breathed. The fighting was unlike the action films she'd watched in days of boredom. It was aesthetically unpleasing, brutal, and crude, and yet breathtakingly effective. When she had heard the screams through the cracked-open window, Nirmala had ordered her cab driver to stop, then got out and rushed to the source. She was certain the foreigner was going to be eviscerated, and yet he emerged victorious. He did not stay around to give a statement to the police, instead fleeing the scene.

Who are you? Nirmala thought. The question circulated in her mind as she brought up her contacts, found the number she wanted, and dialed it. After two ringback tones, the other party picked up.

"Kirsana, this had better be good. You're interrupting dinner."

"I'm sending you a video," Nirmala said. "We need to run with this on the website."

The other party sighed. "Send it over. I'll take a look."

"Okay," Nirmala said. She terminated the call, then attached the video to a multimedia message and sent it. Nirmala looked up, glanced around, and saw her cab had abandoned her. A frustrated sigh fell from her lips, and she began walking briskly down the street. She needed to hail another cab and get home quickly. It was going to be a long night of phone calls, Google searches, and staring at a blank document until it was filled with her words.

As Nirmala scanned the streets for a cab, the question replayed once more: *Who are you?*

CHAPTER FOUR

Bekasi, West Java, Indonesia
14 March 2019
19:01 hours Golf (12:01 hours Zulu)

The mansion was three stories tall, built a couple hundred meters to the northwest from the shore. It afforded those opportune enough to spend time on the master bedroom's balcony an incredible view of the Java Sea. To describe sunrises and sunsets with that particular backdrop as "picturesque" would be inadequate. Even the roughest of men with the coldest hearts felt *something* when they witnessed Nature's canvass in the Javanese skyline.

The festivities had started early that day for Suparman Guntur. He'd cracked open his first bottle of Drum Green Label shortly after waking up, and a new pair of whores were brought to service him. The day had been a drunken blur of fine foods, amazing sex, and the belly warmth brought on by good whiskey. Guntur and his whores had christened every room in the mansion as the hired help did their best to ignore the lewd displays. Even if they were bothered, they were powerless to protest. The power derived from the act was an aphrodisiac, serving only to worsen his thirst for pleasures of the flesh.

Just before six in the evening, Guntur had allowed the whores to rest themselves for the night ahead. He'd put on a silk robe and proceeded to the balcony. He brought with him a bottle of Drum Green Label—the fourth he'd cracked open that day—along with a tumbler and a Montecristo to watch the sunset. He was a rough man, his heart frozen through years of abuse, violent trauma, and Machiavellian underworld politics. Nonetheless, were Guntur capable of tears, he would have shed them while watching the sun slip beneath the horizon.

It wasn't just Nature's glamor that cut deep and moved him. Guntur saw the view as representative of everything he had worked for over the past 36 years, everything he'd sweat and bled for, everything he'd killed to achieve. His ascent from being the bastard son of a whore in the slums of North Jakarta to his dominance of Indonesia's underworld had been violent, often murderous, and rife with duplicity. The sunset was the daily reminder that he had made it, and that those who'd written him off were either dead or in his employ.

There was a knock at the balcony door, and Guntur looked over his shoulder. It was Sharif Aditya, his second in command. He towered over Guntur and most Indonesians at 1.83 meters, and was model handsome, despite living an existence that was rougher than Guntur's in many ways. Aditya had been his enforcer when Guntur was a lieutenant in the Syndicate. When Guntur had ascended to the chief *preman*'s billet, Aditya was rewarded for his loyalty by being named his adjutant.

"Join me, Sharif," Guntur said. His eyes remained locked on the horizon.

"I have news," Aditya said quietly.

Guntur glanced over his shoulder and looked Aditya in the eyes. The expression on his face told him the news's bend. Guntur stared out at the ocean, clenched his jaw, and pushed an exhale out through his nostrils.

"Who?"

"Elang."

Guntur's pulse heightened at the mention of his brother's name. "How?"

"A foreigner, in Warakas during an unscheduled pickup. We're putting out feelers."

"Are we utilizing the police?" Guntur grabbed the tumbler and poured the contents down his throat, punctuating the gulp by sucking air through clenched teeth.

"Not yet," Aditya said. "I assumed you wanted to handle this in-house."

Guntur shook his head. "Reach out to Nyoman. I want this piece of shit brought in."

Aditya hesitated. "Nyoman will want more money to make him disappear from the books."

Guntur whipped his head around and glared at Aditya. "Then *pay him.* I don't give a damn. Find the motherfucker and bring him to me."

Aditya nodded and offered a half-bow. "It will be done." He turned and marched back inside.

Guntur looked back to the sea. His breathing intensified, and he scrambled to grab the Drum Green Label and pour himself another double. He needed numbness, not to stave off tears, but to keep his rage from running murderously wild. The employees were loyal, and the whores asleep in his bed were merchandise. To hurt either one would be to hurt himself.

It wasn't that he was surprised by the news. Elang had always been brash and aggressive where Guntur had been quiet and observant in comparison. Guntur knew that Elang was bad for business, that he lacked the necessary vision and demeanor to work in Guntur's circles. It had been only a matter of time before a line was crossed.

That didn't change that Elang had been his first criminal partner, ever willing to follow Guntur's lead.

It didn't change that Guntur and Elang had shared a birth mother, and that each was the only family that the other had.

A knot tightened in Guntur's chest as his accelerated pulse thundered in his ears. He slammed the double, then stood up and threw the glass at the deck as hard as he could. As the glass shattered, he balled his fists, looked to the sky, and let out a howl that grew in crescendo, the motion gripping every muscle in his body.

Warakas, North Jakarta, Indonesia
14 March 2019
19:09 hours Golf (12:09 hours Zulu)

WHEN BRADSHAW ARRIVED at his apartment complex, he found a hiding spot and watched his front door as he caught his breath. As the adrenaline wore off, the pain in his ribs intensified. They were definitely bruised. He pressed his fingers against his ribcage, internalizing the pain as he probed. There were fortunately no tangible cracks, but he'd definitely need to ice and wrap himself.

Later, Bradshaw thought. *First, time to bug out again.*

After a few minutes, Bradshaw saw no sign that his abode was under surveillance. He walked briskly across the street, took the stairs to his second-floor apartment two at a time, then marched to his door. The keys were in his hand by the time he reached the door, and he disappeared inside.

Bradshaw moved to his cot and moved it away from the wall. He took a knee and ran his fingers along the wall until he felt the indentation. His fingers wedged behind the false panel and pulled it free. Bradshaw set the panel down, reached inside the hole, and removed a waterproof bag. Within were a change of clothes, a knife, and what remained of his money.

Bradshaw replaced the panel, then set the bag on the cot and started his hasty inventory. He had been taking a couple hundred dollars or Euros per fortnight and converting them into *rupiah* for the best of both worlds: local currency with which to buy necessities, but high-value currency in the event that he had to run.

He finished the inventory, then buried his face in his hands. The last that Bradshaw checked, the Euro was close enough to the dollar that he could consider them 1:1 for rough calculations. With that in mind, Bradshaw had a little over four grand left in his bug-out fund. The Ace McCloud identity was burned, which meant he couldn't take a cruise or a plane. He doubted that he had enough money to cover a new set of papers, and that was *if* he could locate a quality forger.

You really fucked yourself now, Jack, he thought. *So much for 'power extreme.'* Bradshaw removed the knife from the bag, then threw the bag into his duffel. It was a simple kitchen knife, sharpened to a fine point, and encased in a crudely constructed cardboard sheath. It fit down the front of his pants for appendix carry. It was a testament to both Bradshaw's adaptability and his lack of criminal knowledge. A real-deal operator would have known how to find a black marketeer and get their hands on a firearm. Even in a nation without a gun culture, there was always a demand for hardware and someone willing to provide the supply.

Better than nothing, Bradshaw mused. He took a deep breath in through his nostrils. *Focus.* The important thing was escaping Jakarta. Once he was clear, he'd have some breathing room.

Running. Again. *Does it ever stop?*

Bradshaw started for the door, then stopped suddenly in his tracks. He strained his ears to identify what had made him freeze. After a moment, a familiar realization dawned on him.

I can't hear anything. It's too quiet.

Crouched low, Bradshaw crept to the window adjoining the front door. His hand reached for the blind and slowly pulled it back to peek outside. The men advancing on the apartment were dressed in a woodland-style splinter-type camouflage pattern, with black ballistic helmets and tactical vests. They carried an assortment of Pindad SS1-V1 clones of the FN FNC, Steyr AUGs, and Kalashnikov-type rifles with black polymer furniture. Bradshaw scanned both ways and found that both ends of the street were blocked off by marked squad cars, with figures standing beside each vehicle.

"Oh, shit," Bradshaw breathed. He slowly released the blind, then bolted for the bathroom. He locked himself inside, then climbed on top of his toilet. Bradshaw reached for the window, popped it open, then unslung his duffel and pushed it through the window. It took some effort, but the bag cleared and fell to the ground 12 feet below. Bradshaw slipped his legs through the window first, then held on to the edge as he lowered the rest of his torso through the opening. He gritted his teeth as he strained to avoid contact between his ribs and the windowpane. As his head cleared, he heard the signature sound of wood splintering as the assaulters made entry. He glanced downward, exhaled, and then released. The impact stung the balls of his feet, but he was on the move a moment later, his duffel in hand.

Bradshaw was light on his feet, his footfalls concealed by the rain. The knife remained sheathed. At this point, he no idea if these were honest officers looking to bring him to task for murder or if they were on the take. Until he knew more, Bradshaw would give them the benefit of the doubt. That left two options: total evasion, or non-lethal techniques. Both were long shots, but the odds weren't getting any better the longer he remained at ground zero.

The rain picked up a notch. Bradshaw cinched the duffel bag's strap tight so it remained flush against his body. He prowled to the end of the alley, where a rifle-wielding police officer was posted, his back turned. Bradshaw surveyed the ground in search of any loose item. An empty beer can was at his feet, but he ignored it, unsure if it would have the weight to maintain flight in the weather.

Shit, Bradshaw thought as he continued to search. Most of the trash was too light. He forced a silent exhale past his clenched teeth. Committed, Bradshaw slinked forward, his knees bent, his breathing controlled.

When he was within arm's reach, Bradshaw lashed out with a hard right cross to the back of the target's head. Taking advantage of the sucker punch, Bradshaw spun the officer around, slipped beneath the officer's right armpit, and wrapped his right arm around the officer's throat. Bradshaw's left hand clenched his own bicep to lock in the triangle choke. The officer slapped Bradshaw's arm to no effect, and a few seconds later, he went limp.

Bradshaw quickly took the handcuffs from the officer's duty belt and used them to bind his wrists at the small of his back. He patted the officer down and found a handkerchief in his pocket. Bradshaw fashioned a gag out of the handkerchief and tied it tight around the officer's mouth.

He dragged the officer behind a dumpster and relieved him of his weapons.

Bradshaw now possessed a Pindad SS1-V1 rifle with a single 30-round magazine, a Pindad P1 clone of a Browning Hi-Power with three 13-round magazines, and a collapsible baton. Bradshaw folded the rifle's stock, removed the magazine, and stuffed it and the baton into his duffel. The two spare P1 mags went in his front-left pocket. He did a press-check to see that the pistol was loaded, then dropped the magazine from the well to ensure it was full. Once that was done, Bradshaw carefully slipped the P1 down the front of his jeans, hammer back and safety on. He knew he was one bad accident away from shooting himself in the groin, but that was outweighed by the necessity of getting the gun into play immediately if it came to that.

He considered taking the man's radio, as well, but Bradshaw's barely conversational Indonesian didn't include the National Police's lexicon. Instead, he turned the radio off and removed the battery from the receiver. In the event that the officer slipped the cuffs, it would buy Bradshaw a few more seconds before the cavalry was alerted.

Bradshaw glanced both ways at the alley's mouth and saw it was clear. He jogged across the street, his head held low. Bradshaw willed himself to be invisible, knowing full well if an officer saw him at a distance, they'd immediately advance on him. Warakas was not a known expat area, and being a six-foot-tall white man had once more become a novelty, much to his chagrin.

The invisibility lasted about five seconds. From behind, he heard a man shout, "You there! Stop!"

Bradshaw launched into action, moving as quickly as his feet would carry him and doing his best to ignore the stabbing, throbbing pain in his side. As he ducked right into an alley, he heard the unmistakable *crack* of a round fired past where he had been standing a moment earlier, punctuated by the unintelligible shouting of a superior berating a subordinate. He put it out of his mind and shifted his focus to the alley in front of him. A couple hundred meters down, Bradshaw hooked a right into a perpendicular alley, making his way towards the vendor where he had bought the catfish the day before.

The pain in his side intensified. He growled through clenched teeth as he redoubled his focus. *C'mon, Ranger, suck it the fuck up!* Move!

As he neared the end of the alley, two camouflaged officers appeared, one with a Pindad SS1-V1 and the other with an AUG. Both barrels were trained on him as they advanced slowly. Bradshaw immediately froze in his tracks.

"Hands up!" they shouted. "On your knees!"

Bradshaw pretended not to understand and raised his hands to shoulder level. His eyes frantically traversed between the two men. If one of the officers got close enough, he could certainly disarm them. He severely doubted he could disarm both at once, at least non-lethally. One of the officers had taken a shot at him, but that wasn't evidence of being on the take. It could have just as easily been a jumpy officer.

"Let's just shoot him and get it over with," one of the officers said.

"No," the other said. "Aditya said Guntur wanted him alive."

Bradshaw had no idea who Aditya or Guntur were, but given they had discussed summary execution and had failed to inform him he was under arrest, the idea that these officers were just doing their jobs was fading faster by the moment. However, they were well trained, with one of them moving ahead of the other to set up an L-shaped box on Bradshaw. Both had angles on him and could drop him if he tried anything.

Fuck me.

In that moment, Bradshaw heard a voice shout in English, "*Duck!*"

Bradshaw didn't question the voice. He immediately hit the dirt, falling on his right side as he covered his head with his hands. A split second later, the sound of suppressed gunfire filled the alley, followed by the signature *thud* of bodies hitting the dirt. Bradshaw poked his head out and glanced. The two officers bled out from wounds in their throats and faces, the blood mixing with the puddles on the asphalt.

He glanced up to see who had warned him. Both of them wore leather gloves, black M65 field jackets, cargo pants, and black ski-masks with skulls printed across the front. Judging from what was displayed through their eye holes, one of them was more than likely a white man, while the other was definitely Asian.

The white man offered Bradshaw a hand. "Get up. We've gotta move."

Bradshaw knew better than to ask questions. He accepted the hand, sucking air through his teeth as he stood. The Asian positioned himself to Bradshaw's right, setting up another L-shaped. That told him they were professionals taking a calculating risk that he would be amenable to…whatever it was they were doing.

Bradshaw jogged with the masked men to the alley's mouth, where the possible white man hooked a right to a parked silver Toyota Alphard. The Asian hopped into the driver's seat, while the other one rode shotgun. Bradshaw climbed into the back, slammed the door shut, and braced himself as the Asian spun the van around and raced out of the neighborhood.

"Can you slip the dragnet?" the shotgun rider asked.

"Rah!" the driver said.

Bradshaw held his side and winced. "Whenever we get where we're going, I'm gonna need an ACE wrap and an ice pack."

"Let's get clear and then we can work on fixing your boo-boos," the passenger said. "Tracking?"

The last word confirmed that the man was prior American military. Bradshaw wasn't sure whether that reassured or scared him. He felt better knowing the Pindad P1 was down his pants.

"Oh," the passenger added. "We did you a courtesy by not locking you down. Do us one and keep your hands where we can see them. I'd hate for there to be a misunderstanding."

Bradshaw exhaled as he rested his elbows on his knees and clasped his hands in front of him. "Tracking." He sighed. *At least they're not talking about taking me to mystery men, and if they'd wanted me dead, they'd have just shot me in the alley.*

Fuck it, Bradshaw concluded. *Let's see what happens.*

CHAPTER FIVE

Cengkareng, West Jakarta, Indonesia
14 March 2019
20:27 hours Golf (13:27 hours Zulu)

It took an hour and change to make the trip across town. Bradshaw glanced out the rear windshield every so often, half-expecting a squad car to pull up behind the minivan. Thankfully, the most dangerous thing they had to deal with was the late-night traffic congestion. The shooters up front had removed their masks, but Bradshaw still couldn't get a good look at their faces. They utilized side roads to avoid tolls, which made tactical sense as the toll roads were monitored, but did absolutely nothing to ensure a faster trek.

Their final destination was a warehouse that over-looked the Mookervaart River. The Asian pulled the Alphard to a stop, and he and the white man disembarked.

"Stay here," the white man said. "We'll be back for you."

Bradshaw said nothing as he watched the two men walk into the warehouse, presumably to clear it. He kept his head on a swivel, searching for anybody staring too long at the vehicle. He had to presume the National Police had put out an all-points bulletin, and the locals would fall over themselves looking for him if they offered a sweet enough reward. That wasn't the full extent of his worries, either: it was only a matter of time before the US Embassy's legal attaché received the APB. If they got a hold of his fake passport photo, the legal attaché—a federal agent, usually FBI or DEA—would put two and two together and sound the alarm. From there, Bradshaw knew he'd only have days before Tier One pipe hitters from Bragg, Dam Neck, or Harvey Point came looking for him.

Finally, the door opened, and Bradshaw got his first good look at the Asian. He was slight of stature, but the way he moved and carried himself screamed a military background. The Asian addressed him in fluent, lightly accented English.

"C'mon," he said. "We're clear."

Bradshaw grabbed his duffel and followed the Asian across the lot to the warehouse entrance. The edifice was three stories tall and largely hollowed out, though the concrete floors were dry and well-swept. The Asian led Bradshaw to a threadbare but well-illuminated office within, equipped only with an empty desk and some chairs.

He got his first solid view at the white man, who was seated on the table. He had curly auburn hair that was thick on top and trimmed on the sides, pale skin, and narrow blue eyes. His jaw line was square, and his lips were thin, protruding from beneath a circle beard. When he spoke, his voice was gravelly, with a hint of a Southern accent.

"Jack Bradshaw," he said. "You're a long way from home."

Bradshaw's blood froze, but he kept his hands in plain sight. He could see a pistol holstered on the man's hip, and something about him told Bradshaw he could draw and fire well before Bradshaw's procured weapon cleared concealment. He took a deep breath and fixed his eyes on the speaker.

"You know who I am."

The man smirked. "Anybody with an internet connection knows who you are. You killed four federal agents, then slipped out of the country."

Bradshaw scowled. "That's one version of events."

The white man clicked his teeth. "I almost didn't recognize you. Grew your beard out. Grew your hair out." He wagged a finger at Bradshaw. "I also knew something was fishy about the official version of events. The guy they portrayed on the news would have dropped those cops." A pause. "You're definitely not plugged in down here, or you would have known not to kill Elang Kadek."

Bradshaw nodded slowly. "So, that kid was somebody important."

"That kid was the brother of Indonesia's preeminent underworld shot caller," the white man said. "If you can inject it, snort it, smoke it, or fuck it, chances are that he's got his fingers in it."

Bradshaw glanced between the two men. "So, what tipped you that the dot-gov story is bullshit?"

The white man shrugged. "You actually give a shit if the cops are honest, and you had no way to know the ones we killed were bent. That's not a man that murders four *honest* G-men for shits and giggles."

Bradshaw folded his arms. "Think you can put in a good word for me back home?"

The white man laughed and grinned. "No way in hell. You think I'd be here if I were in their good graces?" The grin faded, and he shrugged. "Then again, I'm not in the same spot you are, so I guess I should count my blessings."

"And all over some social justice warrior," the Asian said. His hands were stuck in his pockets and he shook his head slowly. "You know they're rotting your nation from the inside out, right?"

Bradshaw immediately disliked the Asian. "Gabriela Rivera's a good woman."

"I'm just saying, maybe she ought to cut the President some slack," the Asian said. "He's doing a lot for your country."

Bradshaw's scowl intensified. "Yeah, like letting his flunkies put bullshit warrants on my name and sending crooked cops to murder me in my fucking apartment. What a public service!"

The white man stood and positioned himself between the two men. "Easy, gentlemen. I'd say we have more pressing issues, wouldn't you?" He faced Bradshaw and extended his hand. "Danny Pace." Bradshaw accepted the gesture. Pace's grip was firm, dry, and calloused, a good sign. After the handshake, he gestured to the Asian. "This is Lucas Tan."

Bradshaw nodded to Tan but didn't extend his hand. "Judging from your name, you're not Indonesian."

"Nope," Tan said. "Singaporean."

"All right," Bradshaw said. He looked back to Pace. "You implied prior government employment. You already indicated you weren't in Warakas for me. What *are* you doing here?"

"Elang's brother," Pace said. "Suparman Guntur. He's the target."

"Guntur runs the Kuwat Syndicate," Tan said. "Old school *preman* group, goes back to the colonial days. They were on the verge of shifting out of the black market and following the rest of the groups into politics. Defense of Islam and nation, what have you."

"Old Suparman decided vice held more money than religion," Pace said. "So, he murdered the boss and his inner circle in a bloody coup. Took over the Syndicate, secured the necessary contacts in government to remain untouchable, and built himself a nice little fiefdom."

"And why are you involved?" Bradshaw asked. "Who's shepherding this op?"

Pace and Tan looked to each other. "We are. We're doing this for ourselves." Pace turned his eyes to Bradshaw. "Nobody's paying us to do this. We're doing it because this is the right thing to do. You've seen what they do to these girls when they round them up in the stable?"

"No, but I saw them try to kidnap one in broad daylight," Bradshaw said. "That's why I killed Elang."

"Then you know what we're up against," Pace said. "Guntur's too entrenched to rely on our usual MO of gathering intel, handing it over to law enforcement, and letting them do their thing. There are entire police divisions in Guntur's pocket."

"He's got somebody in each of the municipal Criminal Detective Units," Tan said. "Managed to turn an entire *Brimob* detachment into his own personal hit squad. That's who cornered you in Warakas."

"There's rumors he's even got contacts in *Kopassus*," Pace said, referring to the Indonesian Army's Special Forces Command. "He hasn't penetrated the military as deep as he has the police, but he's got a lot of money to throw around."

"I see," Bradshaw said. He scratched his beard as he thought.

"Yeah," Pace said. "He's a real piece of shit."

"And that's why we're going to put a bullet in his brain," Tan said.

Bradshaw pointed between Pace and Tan. "Who else is involved in your op?"

"Just us," Tan said. "We've got a network we utilize for legit jobs, but when it's time to wander off the reservation, we work alone."

"That sounds fucking suicidal," Bradshaw said. "That many guns on you, you're bound to catch a bullet."

"We'll be fine," Pace said. He paused a beat, then changed topics. "We've got access to a document guy. We can hook you up with some clean papers. You change your hair up a bit, you'll be clear to run. Should give you some breathing room before whoever you pissed off comes knocking."

That'd be the logical move, Bradshaw thought. *You need to worry about yourself.* At the same time, there was something magnetic about the pair. Very few soldiers enlisted as cynics, but many arrived there after seeing enough combat. There was a certain idealism about them that spoke to the young Ranger within him, the one that still believed whole-heartedly in what he was doing. With an audible sigh, Bradshaw made his decision.

"If you think I'll draw heat on you, I'll run," Bradshaw said. "Otherwise, I'd like to stay."

Tan's eyes narrowed as he studied Bradshaw. "Why?"

"Because I've got no love for sex slavers, either," Bradshaw said. "And I'm a man who pays his debts. You're gonna take on the Indonesian mob, you're gonna need every gun hand you can get." A wry grin crossed his lips. "Not like I'm doing shit else, anyway."

Tan nodded approvingly, then looked to Pace. "He *is* as far off the reservation as one gets."

Pace stared at Bradshaw. "Confirm for me. Where'd you serve, son?"

"Army. 3rd Battalion and Special Troops Battalion, 75th Ranger Regiment."

"What'd you do at Special Troops?" Pace asked.

Bradshaw smiled. "Ranger Recce."

"Yeah, he rates a shot," Pace said. He finally rose from the desk. "What you got in the duffel?"

"Took a patrolman's rifle and service weapon," Bradshaw said.

Pace nodded thoughtfully, then walked across the room to a duffel bag of his own. He dug through it until he found what he was looking for, then returned to Bradshaw with items in hand. "Bianchi leather holster, Kydex in-waistband mag pouches."

"Thanks," Bradshaw said as he accepted both. "Glad I didn't blow my nuts off, carrying *bandito*."

"I figured," Pace said. He looked to Tan. "Get that license plate switched out. I'm gonna scrounge up a corpsman's bag and patch up our friend."

"Rah," Tan said with a two-fingered salute before he left the room.

"Take a seat," Pace said. "We'll get you squared away, then bed down for the night. Tomorrow's gonna be busy."

Bekasi, West Java, Indonesia
14 March 2019
21:05 hours Golf (14:05 hours Zulu)

POLICE CHIEF COMMISSIONER Mega Nyoman held a manila folder in his left hand as he followed the pair of heavies through the foyer and up the stairs. At 1.76 meters, he stood taller than most of his countrymen. The wrinkled, off-the-rack suit was indicative of the honest portion of his income. The streaks of silver in his thick and otherwise black hair was premature for a man of his 40 years. Bags under his eyes were evidence of consecutive 18-hour shifts. As the commissioner of Jakarta's Criminal Detective Unit, he was one of the most powerful men on the island, but he was owned by the man who'd summoned him. Nyoman dropped what he was doing and heeded the call, and given the briefing he'd received before his arrival, he understood the urgency.

The guards escorted him to the study. One of the escorts opened the door and held it for Nyoman. The detective stepped inside and crossed the room, where Suparman Guntur sat at his desk, still dressed in a robe and downing another glass of Drum Green Label. Nyoman stood before the desk, his hands clasped behind his back as he watched the *preman* glance at a framed photo in front of him. Guntur smiled morosely, then turned the picture towards Nyoman. It was a photograph of Guntur and his brother, both of them flanked by several women, most of them Westerners.

"You know why I never gave my brother a high-ranking post in the Syndicate, Mega?" Guntur asked.

Nyoman shook his head. "No, sir."

"He was too impulsive," Guntur said. "He loved wandering the streets. He loved to fight." The smile grew wider. "He loved to fuck. Leadership wasn't for him. I doubt he'd have taken such a position if I offered it to him. All he wanted was to make money with me."

Nyoman nodded smartly. "Yes, sir."

"He wasn't even my full brother," Guntur continued. "Different fathers. But, he and I came up together."

Nyoman said nothing. He knew Guntur's upbringing, and knew that men had died for even the *perception* of bringing it up in a derogatory fashion.

Guntur raised his tumbler to the photo. "Here's to you, little brother. You lived fast and hard, the same way you died." He poured the double down his throat, then slammed the tumbler against the desk. Nyoman could smell the liquor stench on Guntur's breath from across the desk. Again, he said nothing.

After a moment, Guntur gestured for Nyoman to sit. When he did, Guntur said, "What have you found?"

Nyoman extended the manila folder across the desk. "Shook down the residents. Found out he works at the Port. Made some calls to the Port Company and to the Directorate General of Immigration." He took a deep breath. "Neil McCloud. Friends call him 'Ace.' Canadian from Rutland, Kelowna. No criminal contacts. By all reports, he kept to himself and was a hard worker."

Guntur held up the perpetrator's photo. "So, this is the motherfucker who murdered my brother," he said.

Nyoman nodded. "He's the only Euro-looking face in that neighborhood. Most expats steer clear of Warakas."

"And?" Guntur asked.

"In my experience, somebody who's willing to endure impoverished conditions when they have the means to reside elsewhere is trying to hide. I suspect McCloud is hiding something."

Guntur nodded slowly, then set the photo down. "It makes sense," he said finally. "He was able to fight off three people at once and he managed to evade your drag-net."

"That's another thing," Nyoman said. "I received the transcripts from the *Brimob* operation. They had McCloud dead to rights and were moving to apprehend him. The coroner says they were killed by a mixture of .45 and 9mm rounds from blind angles. The thing is, nobody heard the gunshots."

Guntur glared at Nyoman. "Silenced pistols?"

"Yes, sir," Nyoman said. "It seems that way."

Guntur's face darkened. "You think this was the Shadow Wraiths?"

"We can't rule out the possibility," Nyoman said. "If that's the case, this would be their first incursion into Java. It's likely they're planning something major."

"I agree," Guntur said. He closed the folder, exhaled, and pushed it back across the desk. "You put out an APB for this McCloud?"

"Yes, sir," Nyoman said. "Also reached out to the Canadian Embassy for any information they can provide. See if he has a motive for disrupting your business or some sort of military background."

Guntur pointed a finger, then pressed it against the desk. "The moment you find something, you bring it to me."

"Yes, sir."

"And I still want him brought to me, *alive*," Guntur said. His face twisted into a scowl as he forced an exhale past his lips. "He doesn't get to die quickly. That's too good for him. We're going to make an example out of him."

Nyoman nodded. "I'll take care of it, sir."

Guntur pursed his lips, his eyes still fixed on Nyoman. "See that you do, Mega."

CHAPTER SIX

Cengkareng, West Jakarta, Indonesia
15 March 2019
11:49 hours Golf (04:49 hours Zulu)

After Pace patched him up the previous night, Bradshaw had relinquished his blood-stained clothes to Lucas Tan for disposal. He'd showered and slept in a pair of running shorts and an A-shirt that he'd kept in his go-bag. After six hours of fitful sleep, Bradshaw gave up on rest and clambered out of his cot.

Bradshaw immediately noticed a pair of shopping bags and an Adidas shoe box on the floor. He recognized the company labels on the bags and surmised that either Pace or Tan had done their shopping in a South Jakarta department store that was frequented by American and Canadian expatriates. Given that the average Westerner was considerably taller and heavier than the average Indonesian, Bradshaw appreciated the intelligence behind the selection.

Before he could put on the new clothing, Bradshaw needed a change in appearance. A pair of clippers were left in the bathroom, and Bradshaw used them to reduce his chieftain beard to neatly trimmed stubble. He kept his hair longish, knowing that his Neil McCloud legend had him with shorter hair. Once his image started circulating, he needed to look as different from the official photos as possible.

A shower and a change of bandages followed the haircut, and Bradshaw put on his new wardrobe: a light button-down black shirt, khaki slacks, and black running shoes. Tan and Pace had sized him appropriately, and the clothes fit well. They also included another set of clothing to add to his bug-out bag, bringing his total number of outfits to four.

Things are looking up, Bradshaw mused as he made his way to the common area. Breakfast consisted of Powerbars, water, and coffee. Tan and Pace joined him shortly thereafter, and he toasted them with his Styrofoam cup.

"Cheers for the new threads," Bradshaw said.

Pace gestured to Tan. "Thank Lucas for that. He's been hustling all morning."

"Wrap that up," Tan said, pointing to Bradshaw's meager repast. "Gotta do a photoshoot."

Bradshaw finished eating and followed Tan past the living quarters to another room. It had been converted into a makeshift photo studio, complete with white lighting and a backdrop. Tan took several photos of Bradshaw with a digital camera, then inspected the shots. When he was satisfied, Tan said, "Good. I'll handle the rest."

Tan departed shortly thereafter, leaving Bradshaw and Pace to their devices. Pace said nothing in the interim, and Bradshaw sensed that the other man was opposed to dialogue. Bradshaw spent his time checking news updates on their ruggedized laptop, utilizing a VPN to mask their location.

Bradshaw abandoned the laptop when Pace finished cooking lunch. The meal consisted of beef *nasi rendang*, steamed rice, cabbage *gulai,* and green *sambal* from a local restaurant. The pungency would have done a number on Bradshaw's gastrointestinal tract when he'd arrived in December, but his body had acclimated to the local cuisine. Judging from the way that Pace inhaled his meal, his body was similarly adjusted.

You've been here a while, Pace, Bradshaw mused as he glanced at the man out of the corner of his eye. *What's your story?*

Despite Pace's earlier reticence, Bradshaw decided to risk conversation. He swallowed the food in his mouth and said, "You a Marine?"

Pace smirked, but his eyes remained focused on his food. "What gave it away?"

"Last night," Bradshaw said. "You said I 'rate' a chance. I've only ever heard that term from Uncle Sam's Misguided Children."

"You're perceptive," Pace said.

"At the same time, you're not just a grunt." Bradshaw scooped another forkful of beef and rice from his bowl and held it at chin level. "SOF background. You a Raider?"

Pace shook his head. "Before my time."

Bradshaw nodded with realization. "Force Recon."

"Before the Towers fell," Pace confirmed.

Bradshaw pursed his lips. "That doesn't explain your entire skillset."

"No, it doesn't." Pace set his fork down and fixed Bradshaw with a discerning stare. "You've got a lot of questions, Bradshaw. That's understandable. Understand this: I've just met you. I'm rolling the dice and betting you're a stand-up guy. Until I know for sure, know that I'll give you all the information you need. Nothing more, nothing less."

Before Bradshaw could respond, the laptop sounded off with a digital chirp. Pace left his food and went to the laptop to check on the alert's source. Tan and Pace installed surveillance cameras and motion sensors internally and externally when they had initially settled in the warehouse, and the noise meant that one of the security measures had been tripped.

Bradshaw joined Pace at the computer and glanced at the screen. The Toyota Alphard pulled to a stop, and Tan stepped out. Bradshaw noticed that the license plates looked different from the night before. Tan marched into the warehouse, and Pace and Bradshaw stepped out of the office to greet him.

"Costs top dollar, but it's worth it," Tan said. He extended the documents to Pace, who looked them over and nodded.

"This is good work," Pace said. He handed the documents to Bradshaw. "When we're done with Guntur, these should get you out of the country clean. Just try not to make a habit of flashing them about in the meantime."

The passport was black with silver leaves along the right edge, marked with the words "New Zealand Passport" in both English and Māori, and the New Zealand coat of arms beneath it. Bradshaw flipped it open and saw the photo that Tan had taken hours earlier. He looked at the name, scowled, and looked to Pace and Tan.

"Charles Edward Finley?" Bradshaw asked.

"Yep," Tan said, beaming with pride.

Bradshaw arched his eyebrows. "Do I look like Bruce Campbell to you?"

"You look like somebody looking the gift horse in the mouth," Pace said with a glower. "Had we charged you for that passport, we could clean out the rest of your bug-out fund."

Bradshaw pursed his lips, rebuked. "Point taken."

"Besides, Chuck Finley was a hell of a good player," Pace said. "Brought my dad in many a dollar with his talent. And now he's bringing you a hell of a value deal."

"I don't think he knows just how good of a deal he's getting," Tan said.

Bradshaw folded his arms. "Lay it on me."

"It's a brave new world in passport forgery," Pace said. "I got a look at the one you used to get here. Had you landed in a fully developed nation, you'd have been detained by customs. Your biometric chip was a sham, just for show. Of course, as the technology develops, so do the counterfeits." He tapped the chip embedded in the false passport. "This is coded to your biometric data, so when they scan it, it'll trigger a virus that seeks out any files matching your data and erases them. It also sends that data over their network to their central database, ensuring continuity across terminals."

"Hold on a second," Bradshaw said. "How do you trigger a virus unless it's already there..." His eyes widened as they fell on Pace, who gave him a nod and a smile.

"It's an amazing program," Tan said with a grin. "Project Spartacus."

"Spartacus?" Bradshaw asked.

"It started as a joke," Pace explained. "Theoretically, all three of us could be...I dunno, Mike Norgard or something. Lucas passes through. 'I'm Mike Norgard.' He clears with the Spartacus passport. Fifteen minutes later, I come through. 'I'm Mike Norgard.' The system clears me. Then you come through…"

"I get it," Bradshaw said. "Cute."

"Rah," Tan said with a grin.

"The guy who made the passport?" Pace said. "He and I go way back. One of his first assignments was writing the viral code and then infiltrating a tech company as an engineer to insert it into the software. Every major Western company which writes that kind of software was similarly infiltrated. About the only places you can't go are nations directly under the influence of Russia or China."

"Why's that?" Bradshaw asked.

"They use their own companies specifically to prevent that sort of infiltration," Pace said. "Not sure if we ever got somebody inside Russia. We did have code in place in China…when they cracked our comm firewall in 2010, we knew it was only a matter of time before they found out. Back in 2015, Langley's man inside Neusoft was finally compromised and thrown in Qincheng Prison. Three months later, China announced a revamp of their customs and immigration scanning software."

"You think they reverse-engineered it?" Bradshaw asked.

"It's likely," Pace said. "But, we used different embedding methods and virus codes for the Chinese op than for the Western ops." He pointed to the passport. "That system should still be intact."

"Isn't Indonesia within the Chinese sphere of influence?" Bradshaw asked.

"They're friendly," Tan spoke up. "But they're also friendly with the United States. Not friendly enough to share an extradition treaty, but you knew that." After Bradshaw chuckled, Tan continued, "All in all, they're pretty neutral. When they start to resemble a proxy state, that's when you've got to worry."

"Got it," Bradshaw said with a nod. "Thanks."

"Stash that with your bug-out bag," Pace reminded. "No reason to blow two covers in one go."

"Tracking," Bradshaw said. "Now that Tan's back, you said something about a job tonight?"

Pace woke up the laptop, typed in a few keystrokes, and brought up a Powerpoint presentation. A thin, tattooed man with a rat face and a greasy ponytail was in the photo, holding a cellular phone to his ear.

"Raja Wira," Pace said. "Owns a nightclub in South Jakarta, 'Batavia.' Caters to expats. Primarily peddles dope, but he keeps a small stable of girls on hand for those who lack the game to secure evening companionship."

"He's got two primary jobs," Tan said. "One is to organize the smuggling of the materials needed for narcotics into Indonesia, primarily opium from Myanmar, Vietnam, or Thailand and precursors from China. The second is to wash the money through Batavia and turn it into legitimate income. We snatch and download him, we'll start to develop a target deck."

Bradshaw folded his arms. "What's your source intel?"

"You're looking at it," Pace said.

"We were working on a *chao pho* group in Phuket," Tan said. "Watched Wira make a pickup. Once we got done with those guys, we made our way here and started to develop the situation."

"All right," Bradshaw said with a nod. "You know for a fact he's going to be at this club?"

Pace hit the arrow key on the laptop to change the slide. There were several surveillance photos of Wira in a club setting. One of them was a photo of Wira sitting with a man that carried himself with self-importance. Bradshaw pointed to that photo.

"I'm guessing that's our Kryptonian," Bradshaw said.

"Suparman Guntur," Tan confirmed. "That was our second confirmation that Wira's connected with something. Now we just need the raw intel to build a web."

Pace changed the slide. A series of blueprints filled the screen. "Here's Batavia's layout," he said. "Lucas and I have confirmed these specs are accurate." He pointed to a red circle superimposed on the blueprints. "This is Wira's office. We've got to get in, grab him, and get out with minimal friction."

Bradshaw's eyes narrowed. "Seems like a tall task for a three-man team," he said.

"Two-man team," Pace corrected. "I need you in the getaway vehicle. Too many eyes in the club. One of them recognizes you, they'll go to red. They don't know Lucas or me, so we'll handle it. You need to ensure a quick get-away."

Bradshaw sighed as he stuck his hands in his pockets. He didn't like it, but Pace made a valid point. "Roger. I'll cover outside."

"But I still want your input on how to conduct the snatch," Pace said. "Doesn't hurt to have a second opinion from somebody who'd seen through the looking glass."

Bradshaw smirked. "Or you're looking to verify my credentials."

Pace smiled coldly. "Or that."

"Well, you won't be ambushing me with a cup of cof-fee," Bradshaw chuckled wryly. He moved closer to the computer screen. "Tell me what you know."

Tanah Abang, Central Jakarta, Indonesia
15 March 2019
16:24 hours Golf (09:24 hours Zulu)

MAX SANTOSO SAT in his office, hunched over his desk. Held delicately in his fat, arthritic fingers was a lit Dji Sam Soe 234 *kretek* cigarette. Its distinct, full-bodied smoke carried its aroma throughout the office. On his computer monitor was a spreadsheet that was divided into three lists: one of articles that needed to go live on the company web-site overnight, one that could wait until the newspaper printed early in the morning, and those big enough that the articles would be published to both.

Santoso ashed the clove cigarette before he took another drag. At 65, he was one of the paper's old hands. He'd been around before the company *had* a website. Santoso had joined the paper at age 22, fresh out of college with a journalism degree in hand, eager to seek out the truth. Despite living under the corrupt Suharto administration, Santoso had entered the job brimming with optimism, hoping things could change.

He'd covered the uglier parts of Suharto's New Order. Santoso had reported on the mass graves filled with suspected "Communists," all done with the implicit approval of the American CIA. He'd covered Suharto's embezzlement throughout the autocrat's 30-year reign. His words brought light to war crimes committed by troops in East Timor, acting under Suharto's orders.

It wasn't a smooth ride. Santoso could have retired if he received a thousand *rupiah* for every time some government strongman had shook him down or threatened him if he ran a story. The Directorate General of Taxes had audited him more times than he cared to remember, hoping to find some sort of discrepancy in order to incarcerate and silence him. Once, Santoso had endured a beating from a gang of masked men that he was sure were off-duty National Policemen.

Still, in the end, Santoso didn't regret a single moment. He'd done a lot of good. Things were relatively peaceful, the economy was booming, and the government was far more accountable to its constituents than it had been at any other point in his life. Dealing with the steep technological learning curve seemed a small price to pay for a chance to see the fruits of his labor.

Santoso stubbed out the *kretek* cigarette in a glass ashtray and reached in his shirt pocket for another. He was short in stature, with bronze skin and a heavily receded hair line. What hair remained was jet black, with silver trim at the edges. Some of the younger kids likened him to

John Woo. He couldn't see it himself, but he wasn't bothered by the comparison. Woo was a master of his craft, as was Santoso.

A trio of knocks filled the room. Without looking up at the door, he said, "Enter."

Santoso heard the door open and close, then looked away from the computer screen. Kirsana Nirmala walked across the spacious room and took a seat in front of Santoso's desk. She wore a conservative pantsuit, and her hair was tied in a neat bun. Nirmala crossed her legs and brushed a loose strand of hair from her eyes.

"You wanted to see me, Max?" she said.

"Uh-huh," Santoso said. He pulled up the report sent to him by the social media team, then spun his monitor to face Nirmala. "These are the insights on the article you did last night. Best performing article this week. If these numbers continue, solid chance it'll be the best this month."

Nirmala shrugged. "I was in the right place at the right time."

"You were also following your instincts," Santoso said. "You were working the streets. You heard the rumors on young women disappearing from Jakarta slums. You concluded they held merit. Luck has a little to do with it, but so does intuition."

"I have a good mentor," Nirmala said with a smile.

"No," Santoso said with a wry grin. "You can't teach this. You've got your fingers on the national pulse. You can feel the people are fed up with the *preman* still working the drug trade. They're worried their wives and daughters are gonna get hooked on dope and forced to service some sleazy foreign businessman."

"It's hard to miss what people are saying," Nirmala said. "In the polls and on the street. You remember how they cheered when the government executed those two Australians a few years back?"

Santoso nodded slowly. "I remember."

"There's even people saying we're not going far enough," Nirmala said, leaning forward as passion crept into her voice. "They look to Duterte in the Philippines and say they want something like the Davao Death Squad. If groups like the Kuwat Syndicate are allowed to operate unchecked, somebody's going to capitalize on that sentiment and we're going to get a strong-man president. That benefits nobody." She leaned back, interlaced her fingers, and held her hands above her chest. "No. We take them down with the press. The people get to see the bad guys lose and the politicians don't resort to extreme measures."

A smile dawned on Santoso's face. "And that's something else I can't teach. Zeal. Love of your work. Giving a damn." He held up his hands and gestured about the office. "You're the person I want filling this office when it's my time to go."

"You've still got a few years," Nirmala said.

"I do," Santoso agreed. "Still, you're not affected by this generation's cynicism. You're not seeking clicks, likes, views, whatever. You're about finding the truth. At the same time, you're not a dinosaur. You don't need somebody holding your hand while you try to figure out technology." He pointed to her. "You're the evolution of my generation."

Nirmala smiled warmly. "You have no idea how much that means to me, Max."

The smile on Santoso's face faltered a bit. "I spoke it over with the board, and they're in agreement. I want you to follow this story. Do a full profile on the Kuwat Syndicate. Keep me in the loop on your progress." As Nirmala's face lit up, Santoso's darkened. "You need to watch your back out there. These *preman*...you threaten their meal ticket, they can reach out and touch you."

"They're overgrown children," Nirmala said dismissively.

"Often high out of their minds and loaded with firearms," Santoso said. "I'm serious."

"I'll be fine," Nirmala said. "I promise to be as safe as possible, and I'll keep you in the loop."

"Good." Santoso nodded. "Well, that's all I've got."

Nirmala smiled, then rose and walked out of the office. He sighed when the door closed behind her, then remembered the unlit *kretek* cigarette on his desk. Santoso picked it up, placed it between his lips, and fired it up with the flick of his Zippo. He'd never bothered to take a wife or sire children. His job had always come first, much to the disappointment of his late parents. What he missed in an opportunity for parenthood, he made up in his mentorship of Kirsana Nirmala. She was family, a continuation of his legacy.

As Santoso pulled on the *kretek,* he prayed to a deity in whom he wasn't sure he believed, hoping that Nirmala wouldn't have to endure the same dangers that he had.

CHAPTER SEVEN

Mampang Prapatan, South Jakarta, Indonesia
15 March 2019
22:44 hours Golf (15:44 hours Zulu)

Bradshaw sat in the Alphard's driver seat, parked across the street from the club. He wore a nondescript ball cap low on his brow to obscure his features. He glanced at the club through the passenger's window. Batavia was a two-story edifice with a long line outside that extended down the block. While Indonesia was the most populous Muslim nation in the world, the social conservatism usually associated with the religion was absent in Jakarta. Part of that was due to the large expatriate presence in the district—mostly Japanese and Korean, with a fair number of Europeans interspersed in the line—but there was also a considerable amount of local nationals present, as well. Exposed shoulders and midriffs, as well as uncovered and let down hair, were signs that Sharia was not enforced.

Bradshaw glanced at the sky. It had drizzled earlier, but the skies were clearing up. The crescent moon hovered above, the sole source of visible interstellar illumination. A wistful cloud lingered over Bradshaw's countenance, and Pace glanced over just in time to catch it.

"What's up?" Pace asked.

Bradshaw shook his head. "Back home, the U of A funds a lot of telescope facilities for astronomical purposes. Those brought on light pollution laws. If you're on the Tucson outskirts, you can stare skyward for a few minutes and the stars will come through real clear." He took a deep breath in through his nose and shook his head. "Just missing home. I'm good."

"Good, because I need your head in the game, Bradshaw," Pace said. "Get homesick later."

Bradshaw looked over to Pace, an unasked question in his mind. He mentally shelved it for later. Pace was dressed in a T-shirt, jeans, and sneakers. His face showed far too much mileage to pass for partying age, but it was possible that he could pass for an older man looking to re-capture the glory days.

"That's gonna be a long wait to get in," Bradshaw said, gesturing to the line.

Tan leaned forward from the backseat, a couple sheets of paper in hand. "That's why we've got these," he said. "Purchased VIP ahead of time."

Bradshaw looked to Tan. He wore a polo shirt, jeans, and Oxfords. In the States, Tan would have drawn all sorts of looks for his peculiar dress fashion, but in Indonesia, he blended in with the natives.

"Right," Bradshaw said. "You really think you'll be able to walk him out without a hassle?"

"If I make a big enough diversion," Pace said.

"Make too big a diversion, you'll land yourself in the drunk tank," Bradshaw said.

"I won't let it come to that."

Bradshaw looked back to Tan. "We never went over how you plan on convincing Wira to walk out with you."

Tan reached to his belt buckle, pushed a switch, and yanked outward. Attached to the buckle was a three-inch push dagger with serrated edges. "I put this to his throat and draw a little blood. He'll fold and walk."

Bradshaw nodded his approval. "Smart." He sighed. "Shame you guys didn't have a way to splice the camera feeds. I could play overwatch."

"This is the private sector," Pace said. "Technology's great, but sometimes you've got to get back to first princi-ples."

"Yeah," Bradshaw said, turning back to the road ahead of him and scanning his surroundings.

"I'm going in," Pace said. "Get a good radio check when I'm inside." He glanced over his shoulder. "Lucas, wait five minutes, then make your way in." He turned his gaze to Bradshaw. "When Lucas is in, get a radio check with him, too."

"You've got it," Bradshaw said.

Without another word, Pace accepted a VIP pass from Tan, got out of the minivan, and jogged across the street. Bradshaw watched him approach the bouncer, produce his pass, and receive a wristband before being granted entry. He chuckled as he looked the bouncer over.

"What?" Tan asked.

Bradshaw pointed to the window. "Earrings, ponytail, black shirt tucked into black slacks, tats…change the language, change the ethnicity, and you'll find the peculiarities remain the same."

"That's the global economy for you," Tan said. "Eschewing national identity in favor of pragmatism and capitalism. I love it."

Bradshaw nodded, then decided to make a play. "So, you've been working with him a while?"

"Yeah," Tan said. "About a year and a half."

"Singaporean…" Bradshaw said. "That means you're prior military."

"Conscripted, originally," Tan confirmed. "Turns out, I like soldiering. Not a whole lot of soldering to be done in Singapore, though."

"So, what? You decided to go hunting for sex slavers?"

"With a few steps along the way," Tan said. He grinned and arched his eyebrows. "You really are an amateur when it comes to gathering information. I'll give you a freebie: I'm a private investigator by trade. You're gonna need to try a lot harder to get me to open up."

Bradshaw pursed his lips as he pushed an exhale through his nostrils. "Half a world away and I still can't get away from the PI world," he muttered.

"Come again?" Tan asked.

"Don't worry about it," Bradshaw said. "Let's just hope this plan works."

* * *

Raja Wira stood at the edge of his office, his hands clasped behind his back. From his vantage point, he could see the entire club through its glass walls. This was *his* domain, the proof of his hard work and cunningness. His chest filled with pride as he regarded the customers below. He wondered if that pride was the same felt by Ken Arok, surveying the domain of his Rajasa Dynasty. Or it could be what Jan Pieterszoon Coen felt as he beheld the entirety of Batavia, the colony he had founded and the seed for what would become the Dutch East Indies.

Wira grinned wryly. *I'm sure Suharto knew this feeling as he flew overhead in helicopters and airplanes.*

The way Wira saw it, Suharto was responsible for the path that he'd traveled during his 48 years. His parents had been card-carrying members of the Indonesian Communist Party, and had evaded the political purges that had taken place five years prior to his birth. They never abandoned their ideals, and worked in secret to subvert both the Sukarto and Suharto administrations. Wira had faint memories of his parents. His father was a giant of a man, always with a smile on his face, and his mother embodied love, quick to scoop Wira up in her arms and shower him with affection.

That came to a head one dark night shortly after turning five. National Policemen kicked in the door while his parents hosted a strategy meeting in the family den. All the adults were marched outside and forced onto their knees. Without ceremony, a rifle-bearing officer had moved behind the line, pausing just long enough to fire his weapon at point-blank range. Some of the condemned held their heads high, while the less stoic amongst them trembled and wept in fearful anticipation. In the end, all died face down, their gray matter pooling from their skulls into the dirt.

Suharto had spoken at length about his New Order being designed to erase Sukarto's mark on government, but one thing carried over: Communism was illegal; its practitioners, subhuman scum that had to be eradicated.

Wira and three other children had been recovered by the soldiers and made wards of the state. That only lasted eight years. Wira fled to the Jakarta slums, where he tried his hand as a huckster. When that fell short, he became a pickpocket, and that eventually evolved into becoming a Kuwat *preman*. At first, Wira's wages were not exclusively from drugs. He viewed himself as a procurer, looking to meet market demand with supply. Wira was determined to be a better capitalist than those who had slaughtered his parents, and if it vexed the murderous administration, so much the better.

Drugs emerged as the most lucrative black market, and Wira cut his teeth as a smuggler. He made connections in Thailand, Vietnam, and Hong Kong for the necessary ingredients, and had a hand in the product's concoction. After Suharto left power, Wira continued plying his trade. Retirement wasn't in the cards. Criminality was all that he knew.

When Suparman Guntur seized the Syndicate's reins, he asked Wira to help him expand into prostitution, something that had previously been a niche market. Wira still primarily dealt in narcotics, but he would be lying if he said there weren't fringe benefits to prostitution, some financial and others carnal. He was promoted to management and given a crew, which meant no more nerve-wracking smuggling runs or bribery meetings with unsavory law enforcement officers.

The double door behind him opened, and a waifish girl of 17 wandered in, sporting a little black dress. Her eyes were glassy, likely from being administered a dosage of heroin to get her through the night. She approached him from behind and helped him out of his dark purple blazer.

As she knelt before him and started her shift, Wira allowed himself a wide grin at the reminder of another spoil of his posting.

* * *

IF DANNY PACE hadn't received a year of training from some of the world's foremost experts in tradecraft, he would have glared at the display. He had seen the teenaged prostitute enter Wira's office. He had to look away when she went to her knees. His expression remained neutral, despite the violent ideations that played out in his mind. Pace had no illusions about bringing the sex slavery trade to an end, but he never grew acclimated to seeing young women stripped of their autonomy and innocence, and reduced to pincushions for monsters who masqueraded as men.

Pace focused on his club soda as he took a deep breath in through his nose. The booming bass of the industrial track being mixed by the 20-something DJ at the dance floor's helm only made it harder to look like he was enjoying himself. Not for the first time on such an assignment, Pace considered throwing away nearly two years of sobriety to drown out the noise. He couldn't understand the music's appeal, unless the aim was to get high, drunk, or both, and then simply lose themselves to the rhythm.

As he glanced around the club, Pace honestly couldn't understand the popularity of clubs in general. Often, they were a nightmare example of a dearth of emergency preparedness. Hundreds of bodies in close proximity, dim lighting, and often only a single point of egress made it a tactical horror show. A bomb or an active shooter could easily accrue mass casualties with minimal effort. Pace knew the Syndicate employed armed security to protect their assets, so such an act would eventually be repelled, but there was no telling how many people would die in the process.

Pace looked at the front entrance in time to see Tan enter the establishment. He sipped his club soda as he returned his attention to his immediate surroundings. His eyes flicked from face to face in search of a suitable candidate. Pace needed somebody who looked volatile enough to serve his purposes, but not capable enough to do him much damage. After a few moments, Pace spotted a white man that was about his height, about 15 to 20 years his junior, with his shirt collar popped and wearing brown Oxfords with shorts and ankle socks. Just one look at the man's face immediately stirred feelings of dislike within Pace, and he decided he'd be the one.

With a sigh, Pace picked up his club soda and started making his way in the direction of the young man. As he grew closer, Pace saw that the man was with three others with roughly the same dress code, along with a group of local national women that were dressed to showcase. He adjusted his trajectory to be on a collision course with the chosen man. Pace took a few more steps, then made contact. The club soda spilled on the young man's shoulder and back, which elicited a gasp and an incredulous look.

"Oy, what the fuck, mate?" the young man said in Australian English.

"Yeah, what the fuck," Pace said, playing up the ugly American stereotype. "Drink's too goddamn expensive to spill. You need to watch where the fuck you're going, asshole."

"Oy, look at this," the man said to his buddies. They immediately ceased their pursuit of carnal knowledge and moved to encircle Pace. "This fuckin' seppo's got a big mouth on him, yeah?"

Pace glanced over his shoulders, then squared off with the leader. "Is this supposed to scare me, Crocodile Dundee?"

"Last chance, you fuckin' Yank cunt. Walk away."

Pace turned around and laughed, scratching his chin with his finger. He then spun on a dime, hocked a wad of phlegm, and launched it at the leader. It landed square on the leader's forehead and dribbled to the left of his nose.

"Eat a bag of dicks, you Bogan fuck," Pace rasped.

"You motherfucker!" the leader roared. Pace watched him telegraph the haymaker, and could have easily ducked underneath it, but that would ruin the cover of being a belligerent jerk neck-deep in a mid-life crisis. Pace braced himself as the fist made contact with his jaw. The strike was hard enough to smart, but not enough to cause any damage. Pace rocked with it, then pivoted and drove his fist into the leader's solar plexus. He pulled the punch at the last second, but it was clear the leader wasn't used to taking a technically proficient strike. The half-power blow was enough to fold the pompous windbag in half.

"Oy!" another called out. "Ralph's down!"

"You fucking drongo!" the other called, lashing out with a crisp left jab that stunned Pace. He followed up with a right straight, but Pace's muscle memory had taken over. The straight was blocked, followed by two fast and sharp left hooks to the assailant's ribs and a right uppercut.

Pace turned to search for the other man still standing, and found him just in time to get speared. He wrapped his legs around the aggressor and rode the attack to the ground, careful to tuck his chin to his chest to avoid injuring his head. When they made impact, Pace released the attacker, lifted his knee to his chest, and drove the heel of his foot into the attacker's groin. As he doubled over, Pace lashed out with a second kick to his face, taking him out of commission.

Not one to waste time, Pace scrambled to his feet and assumed his fighting stance. On cue, several bouncers weaved through the crowd, converging on his position.

Hurry up, Lucas, he urged mentally, steeling himself for the second onslaught.

THE GIRL HAD finished her job. Wira extricated himself from her, zipped his trousers, then walked to the right side of the room, where he fetched a washcloth. He returned to where the girl knelt and tossed the washcloth to her. Her reflexes were dulled, and the cloth hit her face and fell to the floor before her hands moved to catch it. She clumsily clawed at the floor before she picked it up and began to clean herself off.

"You're good," Wira said. "But, you've gotta put some effort into your performance."

"Effort?" the girl asked meekly.

Wira nodded and gave her a condescending smile. "This is your trade. Your craft. You should take pride in it. Your goal should be to make the client walk away on the verge of falling in love with you. We're in the business of selling fantasies. I'm the salesman, you're the fantasy."

The girl nodded and gave him a forced, practiced smile. "Okay."

Wira reached down to touch her, and she involuntarily flinched. No doubt, it was a conditioned action from the way Wira's lieutenants treated the girls. Some of them got off on inflicting pain on the merchandise. Wira allowed it within reason, but the rule was that there would be no visible bruising. The smarter ones carried plastic bags with them and relied on asphyxiation to gain compliance. It had been a while since one of them had flat out laid hands on the merchandise in anger. A bruised product was an unsellable product and a drain on profits due to the convalescence period.

"Here, stand up," Wira said, gently placing his hands on her shoulders and guiding her to stand upright. He looked deep in her brown eyes and proffered an oily smile. "You're a beautiful girl." His eyes wandered over her figure. "You could walk runways in Tokyo."

The girl smiled weakly. Apparently, she had no interest in being a glamour model. That was no surprise, considering where she was from, but Wira found it a shame that she couldn't appreciate her own beauty, or her potential to please a man. He reached out to touch her face and ran his thumb over her plump lips. His blood boiled hot once more, and he felt the stirring in his loins. Wira wondered if he should just keep the girl to himself for the night, begin to groom her for greater things.

Wira watched the girl's eyes widen slightly. As he started to ask what the matter was, a strong grip torqued his left arm behind his back, twisting the wrist to gain pain compliance. A split second later, Wira felt a blade pressed against his carotid artery. Warm breath hit his cheek, followed by rough but understandable Indonesian.

"Hello, Raja." After a short pause, the voice told the girl, "Go put your nose in the corner and don't move until somebody tells you otherwise."

As the girl scurried away, Wira swallowed nervously. "You're making a mistake."

The man pressed his knife harder against Wira's throat. "I didn't ask you to speak." He inhaled deeply and said, "Here's how this is gonna work. I'm going to place this blade against your spine. We're going to walk out of here quietly, utilizing your executive exit. Then, we're going to go for a little ride and I'm going to ask you some questions."

The man applied additional pressure to the wrist, and a squeal fell from Wira's lips. The interloper continued, "You alert your guards or do anything to jeopardize our safe passage, I'll slip this between your vertebrae. I'll leave you a cripple. Do you understand?"

Wira nodded nervously. "I understand."

"Good," the intruder said. "Now, *walk.*"

CHAPTER EIGHT

Mampang Prapatan, South Jakarta, Indonesia
15 March 2019
23:01 hours Golf (16:01 hours Zulu)

Kirsana Nirmala sipped on her Bintang Beer, set the bottle down, and dragged on her *kretek* cigarette. The music was some K-pop hit that utterly failed to hold her interest. She had dressed down in a sleeveless blouse with a plunging V-neck, a black pencil skirt, and five-centimeter heels. More than one drunken boor had taken a pass at her, but thankfully her nonchalance had put off the wishful suitors.

Her eyes flickered as she scanned her surroundings. The security was easily recognizable in their black-on-black attire, with some of them opting for matching blazers to conceal firearms and tattoos. They were converging on a fight across the club, which appeared to be a three-on-one. She rolled her eyes and averted her gaze.

Men.

Nirmala spotted more than one scantily clad woman that possessed the glassy-eyed look that suggested narcotic influence, but she couldn't be sure that they were prostitutes. Indonesia was neck-deep in a drug epidemic. It could easily be some middle-class office worker looking to escape the minutiae of their daily lives.

Movement registered in Nirmala's peripherals. She recognized the sleazy, ponytailed man with the reptilian eyes. *Raja Wira.* Her contact in the National Police said that he was a known drug and sex trafficker for the Kuwat Syndicate, and that Batavia was a front for laundering the proceeds. That he operated with impunity confirmed her theory that the Syndicate had people in high places who watched over them.

As Wira descended the stairs from his perch, Nirmala spotted a hand firmly on his shoulder. That piqued her interest, and she turned to face him. Wira reached the bottom step and button-hooked right. In that moment,

Nirmala spotted a smaller man behind Wira. There was something clenched in his fist and it was pressed against Wira's back. It was then that Nirmala noticed how stiff Wira was as he proceeded to a door that had been guarded by his bouncers just a moment earlier.

Oh, shit! Nirmala thought as she reached into her purse for her smartphone. *Somebody's snatching him!*

She hastily threw a wad of *rupiah* on the bar as she rose from her chair and slipped through the crowd. As Nirmala neared the stairs, she saw that the doors that Wira had approached were thrown open. Her heart pounded in her chest as she moved toward the door.

Theories raced through her mind: *is it a special police unit? A rival* preman *group? Vigilantes? Who would be so bold as to kidnap a Syndicate boss in his own club, right under his security's nose?*

WHEN HE HIT the executive entrance with Wira, Lucas Tan pressed the knife harder against his back to spur on the dope-pushing pimp. The two men broke into a jog as they traversed the 15-meter corridor. At the door, Tan tightened his grip on Wira's shoulder and pushed him against the wall.

"Wait," Tan ordered. "Hands behind your back, palms out, *quickly!*"

Wira complied, and Tan held the knife in place as his left hand reached into his pocket for a pair of flex-cuffs. Tan slipped them over Wira's wrists, cinched them down one by one, then slipped the knife back into his belt. Tan pressed the locked-down Wira against the door as he looked at the adjacent keypad.

"Gimme the code," Tan said. "You trip an alarm and I'll leave you here to bleed out."

"4-7-3-5," Wira said through clenched teeth.

Tan punched the numbers rapidly, and the keypad's indicator light flashed green. He opened the door, pushed Wira outside, then spoke into his Bluetooth earpiece. "Boy

Scout, this is Lionheart. I'm in the side alley. I pass jackpot."

"Roger that," Bradshaw's voice said through the earpiece. "Coming up now."

Thirty seconds later, the Toyota Alphard came racing into the side alley and screeched to a halt parallel to Tan and Wira. Tan threw the sliding door open, shoved Wira inside, then climbed inside and slammed the door shut.

"Let's go," Tan said.

Bradshaw glanced over his shoulder. "Where's Rusty?" he asked, using Pace's call sign.

"Irrelevant," Tan said. "He can take care of himself."

Bradshaw sighed angrily, then unbuckled his seatbelt. "Unacceptable."

"Whoa, whoa!" Tan said. "Where the hell are you going?"

"Keep the engine running," Bradshaw said as he disembarked. "I won't be long."

"Boy Scout!" Tan shouted as Bradshaw made his way around the Alphard's front. As he reached the door, Tan shouted louder. "*Boy Scout!*" Bradshaw disappeared into the executive corridor, and Tan took a deep breath in through his nose. As he exhaled, he muttered, "Goddamn it."

THE AUSTRALIAN QUARTET lay on the ground, clutching their injuries. They had been replaced in short order by a group of eight bouncers. Pace was a formidable fighter, but at the end of the day, he was still subject to the laws of probability, just like everyone else. He had started on his feet, doing his best to isolate a bouncer or two and put work in on them. In the end, however, they had swarmed him, and one sucker punch later, Pace was on the ground. At that point, all he could do was ball up, shield his vital organs, and take the beating. It wasn't the first he'd ever taken, and he was certain it wouldn't be the last.

The only problem was that if Tan had done his job and gotten the target off the X, the police would put two and two together. There would be no drunk tank for Pace. The National Police would likely slap him around in search for answers. If they didn't buy his story—and Pace doubted Suparman Guntur was in a mindset to accept a narrative at face value—they would likely hand him over to the *pre-man* for a more direct interrogation.

Pace knew there was a chance he wouldn't survive the encounter. In that case, he had made his peace and had spent his twilight years doing good. He was ready to face the verdict.

He heard a man yelp, immediately followed by a body hitting the ground. The beating stopped, and Pace could hear it clearer: a series of blows landing against flesh in rapid order. Enough bouncers diverted their attention that Pace was able to risk a peek past his arms. He blinked his eyes rapidly to bring his vision into focus. When he realized what he was watching, a scowl crossed his face.

What the fuck?

One of the bouncers had his arms wrapped around Bradshaw in a bear hug. Bradshaw lifted his knees to his abdomen, then push-kicked a bouncer square in the chest with both feet. When the restraining bouncer tried to stop the thrashing, Bradshaw threw his head back, cracking the bouncer's nose. He then stomped the guard's instep. With the grip loosened, Bradshaw stepped to the side and positioned his foot between the bouncer's legs. He half-squatted as he grabbed a fistful of the bouncer's pants in each hand, then exploded upward. The bouncer fell hard on his back, and Bradshaw fell on top of him. Once they hit the ground, Bradshaw scrambled to his belly, grabbed the bouncer by the throat, and drove his elbow into the bouncer's face repeatedly, leaving it a bloody, pulpy mess.

Another bouncer marched forward, his eyes on Bradshaw. Pace saw his leg, grabbed it, and yanked on it hard. The bouncer face-planted, and Pace crawled on top of him, bladed his hand, and drove the outer ridge hard into the bouncer's esophagus. As the bouncer clutched at his own throat and struggled to breathe, Pace scrambled to his feet in time to find Bradshaw on his six.

"What the fuck?" Pace snarled.

Bradshaw pointed over Pace's shoulder. Pace looked and found another four bouncers advancing. This group drew handguns from beneath their jackets as they made their way through the crowd.

"Bitch later," Bradshaw said. "Run now."

Bradshaw took off sprinting, Pace hot on his heels. A young man with slicked-back hair stood in Bradshaw's path. He pushed the man hard out of his way, knocking him to the ground and compelling several nearby onlookers to leap out of the way. The path to the executive corridor was clear. Pace and Bradshaw were nearly shoulder to shoulder as they bolted, the bouncers hot on their heels. Their breathing was short as they traversed the corridor and reached the open exit. The Alphard was still in position. Pace leapt into the shotgun seat, while Bradshaw climbed in the back and slammed the door behind him.

"*Go, go, go!*" Bradshaw bellowed.

Tan shifted the Alphard into gear and raced down the alley. A moment later, several figures emerged from the club. Bradshaw saw the muzzle flashes before he heard the reports. Wira was sitting in a seat, his hands bound behind his back. Bradshaw reached to grab Wira and drag him to the ground, but before he could make contact, the rear windshield cracked and Wira cried out. Bradshaw grabbed the *preman* and shielded him with his body as Tan reached the mouth of the alley. The Singaporean whipped the Toyota hard left, nearly tipping the minivan over, then floored the gas as he sought to put distance between them and the nightclub.

Bradshaw felt something damp beneath him, and he looked down as he lifted himself from Wira. A round had cut through the middle of his back, and blood gushed from the wound. Bradshaw immediately ripped off his own shirt and pressed it against Wira's wound.

"Wira's hit!" Bradshaw barked. He pressed two fingers against Wira's carotid artery, grimaced, then resumed putting pressure on the wound. "Pulse is weak!"

Pace whipped around in his seat, his eyes wide. "You keep that motherfucker alive!"

"I need a med kit!" Bradshaw said. "He's bleeding all over the fucking place!"

"We don't have one in here!" Tan shouted, his knuckles white on the steering wheel.

"Control that fucking bleeding, Boy Scout!" Pace rasped.

"*Goddamn it, I'm trying!*" Bradshaw snapped.

THE ARMED BOUNCERS lowered their pistols. One of them reached beneath his jacket for a cell phone and dialed a number from memory. A couple of seconds passed before he said, "Unidentified personnel have kidnapped Wira." The music in the club had been turned off, and people were being evacuated out the front. Yelling from the call's other party could be heard, but none of the words were discernible. The caller straightened up and forced an exhale out his nose. "Yes, sir." He then hung up the phone, then started pointing to his subordinates. "Go access the surveillance footage. Assess our casualties. We need to find these bastards, *now*."

As the bouncers retreated into the club, Kirsana Nirmala slowly edged her Samsung from around the corner. She killed the footage, then checked that everything had been captured. The one thing she'd missed was the actual loading of Raja Wira into the van, which was a shame. Still, with what she had, there was definitely a story at hand.

The most surprising element was the return of the mystery man from Warakas. He appeared Western, though he hadn't spoken in her presence, so she had no clue as to his nationality. Still, that made two events connected to the Kuwat Syndicate where he had made an appearance as a member of the opposing team. Her curiosity was whetted.

While she didn't adhere wholesale to the axiom "the enemy of my enemy is my friend," that the Syndicate wanted him dead was a sign that she should at least attempt to track him down and get his side of the story.

Nirmala slipped the smartphone into her handbag and began walking briskly towards the street. The ejected partiers had congregated and were slowly ambling away from Batavia. Nirmala seamlessly slipped into the crowd. She would follow them for a few blocks, at which point she would attempt to hail a taxi or a ride share. The thundering of her heart resounded in her warm ears, and she was certain the sensation wouldn't subside until she was safely at home, in her shower with a beer in hand.

"WE'RE LOSING HIM!" Bradshaw shouted. "He's going into shock!"

"*Give him chest compressions!*" Pace barked back.

"I can either stop the bleeding or I can do the chest compressions," Bradshaw said. "Pick one!"

Pace popped the glovebox open and rummaged around. He found nothing, then redirected his search to the center console. His hands rummaged through until he found a mostly-expended roll of duct tape.

"Hey!" Pace said. When Bradshaw looked up, he tossed the tape to him. "Tape him up, give him chest compressions."

Bradshaw ripped a strip away from the body and wrapped the blood-soaked shirt tight to Wira's body with precision. Pace looked over to Tan and asked, "How far out?"

"Still another 20 minutes, and that's if I'm redlining," Tan said.

Pace said nothing. He knew Tan's skill behind the wheel was unmatched, and that if he could move faster, he would. In the backseat area, Bradshaw had straddled Wira at the hips, interlaced the fingers of his left hand atop his right, and locked his arms out as he placed his palm on

Wira's sternum. The first compression was accompanied with the nauseating *snap* that announced the breastplate had broken. Under his breath, Bradshaw chanted the chorus to "Stayin' Alive" to attain the proper cadence for his compressions. After 100 compressions, he leaned over and hovered his cheek above Wira's blue lips. There was no rise in the chest.

"He's not breathing!" Bradshaw shouted as he resumed compressions.

Pace unbuckled his seatbelt and climbed into the backseat. He took a knee beside Wira as Bradshaw continued emergency aid. Pace pressed two fingers against Wira's carotid artery. The skin felt cold, and he couldn't pick up a pulse. He then reached behind Wira's back, found a wrist, and held his fingers in place. There was nothing. Pace produced a flashlight from his pocket, used his free hand to hold Wira's eyes open one at a time, and shone the light into each of them. The light was 400 lumens in brightness, and yet, the pupils did not dilate. Pace sighed through clenched teeth and clicked off his light.

"He's dead, Jack," Pace said quietly. He returned to the front seat and buckled up without a word.

Bradshaw sat back, his hands on his thighs as he breathed through his mouth. A sudden rush of fury seized him, and he picked up the duct tape roll and hurled it at the rear windshield as hard as he could.

"Damn it!"

CHAPTER NINE

Cengkareng, West Jakarta, Indonesia
16 March 2019
00:14 hours Golf (15 March 17:14 hours Zulu)

The remainder of the drive was silent. Tan focused on staying within speed limits and avoiding the toll roads. Pace brooded in the shotgun seat, his eyes scanning for any sign of the law. In the backseat, Bradshaw sat facing the rear windshield, his back pressed against Pace's seat. His elbows were on his knees and his hands were clasped together.

Once they arrived at the safe house, Pace looked over his shoulder and spoke quietly. "Search the body. Take anything of value."

Bradshaw nodded, then returned to the body. He produced a Google Pixel phone from Wira's jacket pocket, a billfold with a considerable stack of *rupiah* and some identification, and a couple of condoms. Bradshaw showed Pace what he'd unearthed.

"Ditch the condoms," Pace ordered. "Bring the phone and wallet." As Bradshaw climbed out of the Alphard, Pace told Tan, "Dump the body, burn the van, get us some new wheels."

"This is gonna set us back a bit," Tan said.

"Shit happens."

Tan nodded. "That, it does."

Once the Alphard's doors were closed, Tan peeled out and headed north. Bradshaw followed Pace inside to the living quarters. Pace pointed to a counter and said, "Set the shit there." As Bradshaw relinquished Wira's belongings, Pace produced a pair of black heavy-duty trash bags and extended one towards Bradshaw.

"Clothes?" Bradshaw asked.

Pace nodded. "Everything you're wearing. Clean up, then come see me."

Bradshaw nodded, accepted the bag, and made his way to the showers. He stripped down, placed every article of clothing in the bag, and secured it. He then turned on the shower and tested the water. The stream was strong, the water clear and odorless, and the temperature was somewhere between warm and scalding.

He stepped into the shower, finding a bar of generic soap on a dish and a travel bottle of shampoo. Ten minutes were spent attempting to scrub the dried blood from his face, hands, and arms. Once most of it was gone, Bradshaw lathered up. His body was lean and in fighting shape, though he had lost some of his muscle mass since leaving the States. There were no weights on the cargo ship, and Bradshaw found it prudent not to show his face beyond the bare necessities. Thus, he had resorted to cardio and calisthenics in the privacy of his home. He was still strong, but he looked closer to how he'd looked upon graduating the Ranger Indoctrination Program, as opposed to his physique during his heyday with the Regimental Reconnaissance Company.

Bradshaw rested his head against the tile and let the water run over his hair and down his back. He had spent the past six months in what was effectively a calm period. His guard never came down, but it had become routine to work, exercise, eat, sleep, and repeat. No worrying about remaining undetected from clients, or leading Rangers into the line of fire with the fear of bringing them home in a body bag. Having to clean blood out of his hair, off of his skin, and from his clothes twice in a three-day period was a stark reminder that the tranquil interval had come to an end. He should have known that the moment he signed up for the gig, but something hadn't quite registered until that point.

And why did you jump at the chance? a voice inquired from within Bradshaw's subconscious. *You don't know those girls. You don't have any real skin in the game. Is this really about bringing these slavers to justice? Or are you looking for somebody to kill?*

Bradshaw did his best to shut out the voice. He stood up straight and quickly hit every spot on his body with the bar soap or shampoo. Five minutes later, he shut off the water, grabbed a towel, and spent a few minutes drying off. Bradshaw wrapped the towel around his waist, walked across the room to the sink, and used his hand to wipe the condensation from the mirror.

He almost didn't recognize the man that stared back at him. Logically, he knew it was him, recognized the tattoos on each of his shoulders. The man Bradshaw saw had aged horribly since the last time he had bothered to study him. He immediately noticed the bags beneath his eyes, faint wrinkles on his forehead, and crow's feet at the outer corners of his eyes. Something about the stubble only added to the aged appearance.

You're not even 31 yet, Bradshaw thought. *Why are you so old? Where'd the time go?*

With a sigh, Bradshaw wandered back to his room and found his go-bag. Five minutes later, deodorant was applied, his ribs were rebandaged, and undergarments were donned. He clothed himself in a plain black T-shirt, grey cargo pants, and hiking boots. Bradshaw rubbed a bit of coconut oil gel into his beard and hair, and then combed both until they were neat and presentable. Satisfied with his appearance, he made his way back to the common area.

Pace had utilized a shower area at the opposite end of the hall, closer to his living quarters. He was now dressed in a sky blue polo, khaki slacks, and running shoes. Pace poured a pile of ibuprofen in his hands, scooped them all into his mouth, and chased it with several large gulps from a canteen. When he finished, he capped the canteen, set it on the counter, and folded his arms as he fixed Bradshaw with a hard glare.

"What the fuck were you thinking out there?" he asked in a quiet tone.

"I was thinking that we don't leave fallen comrades to fall into the hands of the enemy," Bradshaw said, a harsh edge to his voice. "Pretty sure I swore a creed to that effect."

Pace unfolded his arms as he advanced on Bradshaw, a move that immediately spurred Bradshaw to take a half-step back and prepare for an assault. "Goddamn it, Jack!" he erupted. "Can't you fucking see? We're not in the fucking military anymore! All that 'leave no man behind' bullshit doesn't fly here. There's only the mission, and you've jeopardized that with your sentimentality."

"Are you kidding me?" Bradshaw asked, pointing to Wira's effects. "We got his fucking cell phone, dude. Nine times out of ten, we'll learn way more mining data than we will trying to sweat the intel out of a captive. As far as I'm concerned, that's a win."

Pace threw his hands up, walked away a few paces, then marched back. "Did you hear what I just said? We're not in the fucking military. We don't work for the fucking government. It's you, me, and Lucas, and whomever we know that's willing to help." He pointed a finger at Bradshaw and said, "After that stunt, I'm not sure I want you around."

"Cool," Bradshaw said coldly. "I'll go pack my things."

"Good," Pace said.

Bradshaw took three steps, then turned back to address Pace. "Oh, by the way…for somebody obsessed with the mission, you sure seem keen to shoot yourself in the foot."

Pace scratched his head, turned around, and folded his arms once more. "How so?"

"I've got a way to crack the phone," Bradshaw said. He shrugged, then added, "But hey, apparently I'm too sentimental for your outfit, so I'll leave you to find your bullet."

"You've got no IC background," Pace said. "How do *you* have such a resource?"

"What do you care?" Bradshaw said. "You're the hot shit operator. I'm sure you'll figure things out."

Bradshaw made it another three steps before Pace called out to him. "Wait."

He turned around to find Pace with his hands on his hips, his eyes trained on the ground. After a moment, Pace spoke. "When you work out in the cold, the desire to suspend the mission to retrieve your fallen is dangerous. The missions are of greater strategic importance. You're operating without the safety net the military provides." Pace met Bradshaw's eyes and pointed at the ground. "Doing this? Being this far off the reservation? It's a black hole. You have less than zero safety net."

"Think about the tactical implications," Bradshaw said as he walked forward, his hands held at his chest as he employed a conciliatory tone. "You get captured, they realize we snagged their man. Only a matter of time before they realize you were in on it." He stopped a few feet short of Pace. "I get it. You're a tough guy. You'd have to be to get to this point. It's because you're here that you and I both know that *everybody* breaks. Had Tan and I left you behind, they'd break you down and roll us up. Mission failure." Bradshaw shook his head. "No. Retrieving you was the smart play."

"Okay," Pace said quietly. He folded his arms "So, let's say we use your plan. What would you need?"

"Your laptop, a charging cable, and the phone. I'll reach out, and if my contact's willing to help, they'll have something for us with a quickness."

"How do you know this connection?" Pace asked.

"I knew somebody who knows somebody," Bradshaw said. "Are you game?"

Pace nodded slowly and gestured to the counter. "Go for it."

"Thank you," Bradshaw said. He walked past Pace, grabbed the ruggedized laptop, and moved it towards the phone. His fingers flew over the keyboard as he recalled the email and password combination he had used six months earlier, when he'd needed intelligence on a Russian operative who had been passively surveilling him.

"Jack?"

Bradshaw looked over his shoulder at Pace. "Yeah, Danny?"

Pace's hands were jammed into his pockets. He nodded uncomfortably as he said, "Thanks."

"Think nothing of it," Bradshaw said. He dug in the laptop bag for a micro-USB cord and connected the phone to the computer. Five seconds later, the screen lit up as it began to siphon power from the computer. Bradshaw brought up a new email, left the recipient line blank, and typed "An Old Friend" in the subject line. He tabbed to the body and typed:

> I hope you haven't forgotten me. If you've got the time, I could use your help with a phone. I understand you're under no obligation to help me. I would be in your debt.

Bradshaw then saved the e-mail as a draft. He waited five minutes, refreshed it, and checked it again. There had been no change. Pace materialized behind Bradshaw, looking over his shoulder.

"What've you got?" Pace asked.

"Still waiting," Bradshaw said. He refreshed the page and saw the first line of the e-mail had changed. Bradshaw moved the cursor to the draft and clicked on it.

> Hello, old friend. I wasn't sure I would hear from you again. I don't normally do this sort of thing, but I'm aware of your situation, both at home and abroad. I've got a soft spot for underdogs. Check back in 24 hours and I'll have something. Tell your rusty friend he's doing God's work out there.

"What does that mean?" Pace asked.

Bradshaw unplugged the phone and pushed it off to the side. "They've already lifted the raw, encrypted data from the phone. They'll sift through it and see what they can find."

Pace scratched his chin, impressed. "Grey hat hacker?"

"Yeah," Bradshaw said. "I think they like me."

"I hope so," Pace said.

"I know they like what you're doing," Bradshaw said. "Should've warned you: when I access that email, they can lift pretty much anything connected to it. They've probably got a pretty good idea of who you are and what you and Lucas are doing."

Pace shrugged. "Well, if it helps us out, I don't mind." He sighed. "What now?"

"Now?" Bradshaw signed out of the email account and closed the laptop. "Now we wait."

Washington, D.C.
15 March 2019
13:45 hours Quebec (17:45 hours Zulu)

THE SPECIAL INVESTIGATION Unit's office was located on the second floor of the East Wing. It was housed there to keep it from the prying eyes of the media. The unit had been announced without fanfare, a point the unit's brainchild had emphatically stressed to the Man. If they wanted to bring down the whole house of cards, all it would take was a 3:00 AM Twitter rampage and only the most fervent of the President's supporters would remain at his side.

Jeremy Hawthorne walked through the hallways. He preferred to work in street clothes, but it was the White House. One did not march through the central hub of American political power in cargo pants and a T-shirt. The upside was that the unit's funding included a clothing allowance, which allowed him to commission a bespoke suit. If somebody were to witness him come or go from the East Wing, they would assume he was some sort of military staffer or a Secret Service agent. With his rugged good looks, muscular build, and neatly trimmed strawberry blond hair, he could pass for both roles. It didn't hurt that his background included both the military and federal law enforcement.

In Hawthorne's hand was a manila folder. He'd just returned from Arlington. The total round trip had taken an hour and a half, with a solid 40 minutes of that spent driving. He loathed D.C. traffic, but it couldn't be helped. The urgency to return to the White House had increased, and it all stemmed from the folder's contents.

The placard on the door read "Special Advisor to the President" in large print and "Gregory N. Lambert, Ph.D." in the smaller print. Hawthorne removed a keycard from his pocket and scanned it against the reader. When it beeped in the affirmative, Hawthorne entered the outer office. He marched past a series of empty desks and saw Patricia Walton, Dr. Lambert's secretary, seated at her desk. Hawthorne saw why Lambert had hired her: aside from her top-notch organizational skills and mastery of public relations, she was tall, blonde, and curvaceous, with a pair of legs that had spurred second thoughts within Hawthorne about his own marriage.

"The boss in?" Hawthorne asked.

"Yes," Walton said as she adjusted her black-rimmed computer glasses.

"Thanks," Hawthorne said with a polite smile. She nodded professionally and returned her attention to her monitor. Hawthorne stood in front of the inner office door, knocked firmly three times, and waited for an answer.

"Enter!" came the command.

Hawthorne opened the door, closed it behind him, and marched smartly to the desk. The office was sparsely decorated, with only a couple of photos and a handful of odds-and-ends on the desk as décor. The Dell laptop on the desk was open, and was marked with a red label which indicated that it possessed classified information. Hawthorne stood in front of the desk and awaited acknowledgement.

Greg Lambert looked up from the computer. Tall, handsome, with a shock of neatly-groomed dark hair and piercing blue eyes, he was the unit's founder, and the man whom had tapped Hawthorne as the field team leader.

Lambert nodded, then gestured to a chair. "Have a seat, Jer."

Hawthorne lowered himself into a seat, then leaned forward and set the manila folder on the desk. Lambert pushed his laptop off to the side, grabbed the folder, and opened it up. "What are we looking at?" he asked as he skimmed the contents.

"A contact at DSS reached out," Hawthorne said. "Bradshaw's in Indonesia."

Lambert cocked an eyebrow as he read. "Really?"

"Apparently, he's wanted for kidnapping and murder," Hawthorne said. "Offed two members of the National Police's special unit, then kidnapped a nightclub proprietor. Bureau of Intel and Research thinks they're connected with a local organized crime group, and the FBI LEGAT attached a memo agreeing with that assessment."

"How'd they get it?" Lambert asked.

"He was living on a false Canadian passport," Hawthorne said. "The Indonesians found that out and referred it to their Embassy in Jakarta. The Canucks searched and found nobody on their rolls under that name. Apparently, it'd already been flagged but it was low priority until the capital allegation got tacked on. It was forwarded to their International Ops guy in Kuala Lumpur, who recognized him from our press release."

"So, from the Indonesians, to the Canadians, to DSS, to us," Lambert said quietly as he continued to skim the documents.

"He's an amateur way out of his depth," Hawthorne said. "He's got no tradecraft training. We can spin up the boys and handle him."

Lambert's brow furrowed as he considered it. He shook his head. "No."

Hawthorne canted his head slightly as he looked at Lambert. "Gonna let our friends across the pond handle it?"

"No need," Lambert said. "And no point giving the opposition another link. Democrats have been froggy since retaking the House."

"Right," Hawthorne said. He knew that the House could launch problematic investigations all day long, but as long as the Republicans held the Senate and Supreme Court, they'd be shielded from most of the fallout. Still, it was prudent to tread lightly. "What then?"

Lambert tapped the papers with his free hand. "You said he pissed off a local crime syndicate?"

"Yeah," Hawthorne said. "They're pretty localized, but the consensus is that they've got friends in law enforcement and the government."

"Then it's simple," Lambert said. He closed the folder and tossed on the desk. "Give the Indonesians his file, as unredacted as possible without compromising operations, tactics, techniques, or procedures."

Hawthorne nodded slowly as the plan dawned on him. "You give it to State, State gives it to the Indonesians, and the Indonesians give it to the mobsters." The nodding increased as his mind made the connections. "They lock him down, disappear him…the biggest loose end from the Rivera op is dead and our fingerprints aren't within a grid square of the whole thing."

Lambert smiled. "You always were a quick study, Jer."

Hawthorne picked up the folder and rose from his chair. "I'll go call the Pentagon."

Lambert nodded. As Hawthorne approached the door, he said, "Jer?"

Hawthorne turned around. "Yes, boss?"

"How are we coming on restaffing the unit?"

Hawthorne pursed his lips and exhaled. "Working on it. Can't afford to bring the wrong men on-board. Not everybody understands the necessity of what we do."

"Of course," Lambert said. "And you've been doing phenomenal work with what you've got so far. I'd just like to get the unit back up to full capacity as quickly as possible."

Hawthorne nodded. "Womack and I will work over the weekend, reviewing files and setting up interviews."

"Very well," Lambert said. "Thank you, Jer."

"Aye-aye, sir," Hawthorne said as he departed.

CHAPTER TEN

Bekasi, West Java, Indonesia
16 March 2019
14:04 hours Golf (07:04 hours Zulu)

Setiawan Mahmud was escorted from the front door to the dining area. The first thing he noticed when he entered was the immaculate chandelier that hung centered above the finely polished Tasmanian oak table. Traditional Indonesian music played softly in the background as workers in chef coats and hats stood by along the wall adjacent the kitchen, their hands clasped behind their backs.

From the right of the entrance was a black marble bar area that would put most nightclubs to shame. It not only had a complete local selection, it was also well-stocked with international spirits. Directly past the table were a pair of bulletproof glass sliding doors, pristinely cleaned to near-invisible transparency. Beyond the dining room was a swimming pool and jacuzzi, and past that was a walk that led to the shore.

Suparman Guntur sat at the head of the table, dressed in a three-piece suit. He was remarkably coiffed, looking every part the businessman he believed himself to be. As Mahmud approached the seat to Guntur's immediate left, a waiter stepped in to pull the chair out. Mahmud undid the top button of his bespoke suit and lowered himself into the seat. From there, the waiter scooted it close enough to the table for Mahmud to be within reach of the meal to come, but not so close that he risked pressing himself against the table.

"I'm glad you could join me, Mr. Deputy Governor," Guntur said.

Mahmud gestured to the servants on standby. "A Cordon Bleu trained staff…" He pointed to the patio door with a bladed hand. "An amazing view." As his eyes met Guntur's, he smiled. "And I don't even have to spend a dime." He leaned forward and smiled conspiratorially.

"Are you sure you don't want to enter the restaurant business?"

Guntur smiled politely. "Perhaps one day. For now, let's eat." He looked to one of the kitchen staff and waved with two fingers. The master chef—a portly, serious man with a craggy face and gray hair—nodded curtly, then marched to the kitchen. The staff on standby fell in and followed without having to say a word.

Mahmud unrolled the napkin from around his utensils and spread it across his lap. "What's on the menu today?"

"For the entrée: bruschetta with Italian prosciutto, mozzarella Fio di Latte, heirloom tomatoes, mint, and aged balsamic vinegar," Guntur said. "Grilled rack of lamb with a parmesan crust, smashed potatoes, braised baby leeks, and port wine jus for the main course. Dessert will be mango and passion fruit cheesecake."

Mahmud salivated at the mere thought of the food. "That sounds absolutely amazing," he said. He smiled and said, "You certainly have a restaurateur's knowledge."

Guntur offered Mahmud another polite smile. "When you grow up impoverished, you learn never to take food for granted," he said. "I just happen to take it to another level. Perhaps in another life, I would have grown to be a chef. My master chef, Gunadi, is patient enough to tolerate my observing in the kitchen and occasionally participating in the cooking. He has taught me much."

Mahmud's lips broke into a wry grin. "Surprised he doesn't see that as a threat to his job."

Guntur chuckled and shook his head. "No, his job is secure. I am able to cook simple dishes under supervision, but beyond that...I'm afraid I am too old to be taught a new trade."

The master chef, Gunadi, appeared with a bottle of Chateau d'Esclans Garrus Rosato in his hand, and he poured enough for taste in each of the men's glasses. He disappeared into the kitchen with the bottle, and a moment later, he returned with a platter of bruschetta.

Mahmud smelled it before he saw it, and he closed his eyes to savor the aroma. When he opened them, the platter was on the table.

Guntur gestured to the platter. "Help yourself, Setiawan."

"I certainly will!" Mahmud picked up a piece. The bread was still hot. He blew on it to cool it off, then stuffed it in his mouth. As he chewed, the complement of flavors washed over his taste buds. Mahmud took his time before he swallowed, then chased it down with a sip of the Chateau d'Esclans. Mahmud looked to Gunadi and said, "Absolutely wonderful."

"Thank you, sir," Gunadi said with a slight bow. He looked to Guntur, who gave him a nod of approval, and then turned for the kitchen.

When the room was clear, Mahmud looked to Guntur, a serious expression on his face. "Before we talk business, I would like to pass along my condolences on Elang's passing. I know how much he meant to you."

Guntur nodded solemnly. "Thank you." He picked up a piece of bruschetta and stuffed it in his mouth.

"Is there anything I can do to assist you?" Mahmud asked.

Guntur shook his head as he chewed. Once his mouth was cleared, he said, "My people are handling it."

Mahmud's face darkened a notch. He searched for diplomatic words. "Suparman...our arrangement is that you are allowed to operate your businesses under two conditions: no kidnapping the Javanese, and discreet operation."

Guntur fought to keep the annoyance out of his voice. "I remember our deal."

"What was Elang doing kidnapping that girl in broad daylight?" Mahmud asked.

"She wasn't Javanese," Guntur said. "She was a whore who'd walked away from the bordello. I'd sent Elang and his team to recover her."

"Okay," Mahmud said. "I can accept that. That still doesn't explain your lack of discretion."

Guntur sipped on his wine. "How do you mean?"

Mahmud reached into his jacket for his Motorola Moto G6, unlocked it, and retrieved a saved article in his Chrome bookmarks. He extended the phone to Guntur, who accepted it. A moment later, a scowl grew on Guntur's face.

"That's the second article *Kompas* has put out about the Syndicate," Mahmud said. "Her articles are generating traction. Both times, she was there, recording your people."

Guntur set his wineglass down and returned the Moto to Mahmud as he glared icily. "Perhaps I ought to pay this cunt a visit and teach her to keep her mouth shut."

"*No*," Mahmud said forcefully. He leaned forward. "Attacking the press is the most surefire way to cultivate negative sentiment. It'll generate attention aimed towards our consortium."

Guntur slapped his hand on the table and hissed through clenched teeth. "Those motherfuckers kidnapped one of my senior lieutenants. They killed my *brother!* You expect me to sit back and remain silent?"

"No," Mahmud said, calm creeping into his voice. "I expect you to demonstrate a modicum of discrimination in your violence."

Guntur slouched in his chair as he reached for the wineglass and another piece of bruschetta. "If I had an identity and a direction to pursue, that would be possible."

"I might have something for you," Mahmud said as he accessed the files on his Moto. He handed the phone over once more. Guntur held it in front of his face and used his index finger to scroll the through the documents.

"What am I looking at?" Guntur asked.

"Received this from a contact at the Ministry of Foreign Affairs," Mahmud said. "Your 'Neil McCloud' from Kelowna is really John Bradshaw from Tucson, Arizona. Former member of their Army Rangers, served multiple combat deployments in Iraq and Afghanistan as a member of their special operations task forces. Bronze Star with

Valor and Purple Heart. Trained sniper. Expert in recon-naissance."

Guntur let out a long, slow breath as he read the file. "What is he doing here?"

"He's wanted for the murder of four federal agents back in the United States," Mahmud said. "This file was passed over from the US Department of State. There's no extradition treaty in place, so I think this is their way of washing their hands of the entire affair."

"I don't know," Guntur said as he continued to read. "It seems too easy."

"Sometimes, we get lucky," Mahmud said. He picked up another piece of bruschetta and bit into it. Once his mouth was clear, he said, "I would strongly advise handing this over to your friends in the National Police. Allow them to arrange a violent resistance to arrest."

"No," Guntur replied immediately. "I need to feel his blood on my hands and watch his life seep from his body."

Mahmud paused at the top of his inhale. "Okay," he said. "In that case, that information should allow you to be a bit more discriminant in your utilization of violence." He held out his hand and accepted the phone back from Guntur. "When I transmit this information to you direct, can I count on you avoiding any more escapades with the press?"

Guntur nodded slowly. "As long as Bradshaw is mine."

"He will be," Mahmud assured him.

Guntur forced an exhale past his lips, then returned to his pseudo-businessman persona. "Let's finish the entrée," he said. "We'll feast, and then we can resume business talk."

Mahmud smiled as he reached for another bruschetta. "With pleasure."

* * *

Damar, East Belitung Regency, Indonesia
16 March 2019
20:19 hours Golf (13:19 hours Zulu)

THE SMALL VILLAGE was uncharted on most maps and was located about 13 kilometers east of the shore. Its population was Malay and about 200 strong. The edifices within the clearing were constructed of bamboo with straw roofs. In the center of the village was a well, which pooled water from a reservoir that was built hundreds of years earlier. In turn, that reservoir largely collected rainwater during the monsoon, usually accruing enough to provide for the area for the duration of the dry season. Even as tourism picked up in the relatively more metropolitan areas along Belitung's coastline, the villages further inland continued their lives the way several generations before them had done so.

Sharif Aditya stood at the well, his hands resting on the buttstock of the Pindad SS1-V1 slung across his chest. His eyes traversed the line of young girls that his men had rounded up. Stifled sobbing could be heard from within the huts, along with the occasional gunshot. Whether his men were intimidating the locals into cooperation or simply putting down the troublemakers, Aditya didn't know or care. As long as the *preman* crew made their quota for the run, it was of no consequence.

Rainfall drizzled, most of it kept out of Aditya's face by the boonie hat worn low on his brow. Like the rest of his men, Aditya was clad in Disruptive Pattern Material fatigues, old school load-bearing suspenders and pistol belt, and jungle boots. The crew's constitution was a peculiar intersection between armed service veterans and previous occupants of penal institutions. Aditya was one of the latter, though he was smart enough to recognize solid methodology when it presented itself. The result was tactical proficiency with a penchant for quick escalation to violence.

When Aditya's eyes reached the end of the line, he traversed in the opposite direction. Most of the girls' eyes were seized by fear. A couple of them stared defiantly, their urges kept in check by the selective-fire rifle on his chest. The corners of Aditya's mouth tugged towards his ears. He wouldn't need to physically coerce the defiance out of them. All it would take was a sufficient dose of heroin. The withdrawals would be bad enough that they would practically beg to service a man for another fix.

Two more girls were dragged to the line, making the quota. Each of them was zip-cuffed behind their backs. Umar Pratama approached from Aditya's right, took a position next to Aditya, and sighed as he looked over the girls.

"What is it, Umar?" Aditya asked.

Pratama shook his head. "Nothing."

"Umar…" Aditya said tiredly. "You're my second-in-command. That alone means I should know you. That we survived Kerobokan together means I *definitely* know you. You're brooding."

Pratama sighed. He was a year older than Aditya, but was blessed with good genetics that made him appear much younger than his 35 years. Clean-shaven with short hair, Pratama could have easily been mistaken for one of the crew's military veterans. After a moment, Pratama looked to Aditya.

"I'll be honest, Sharif," he said. "I find this part of the business distasteful." When Aditya said nothing in response, Pratama continued, "If we remained solely in narcotics, Guntur would have more than enough money to live as a king for the rest of his days and still ensure the Syndicate's associates earn reasonable wages." He gestured to the entirety of the village. "This is only bound to draw undue attention. Eventually, the government will be compelled to action."

Aditya nodded slowly. "I can see your point of view. I also see Guntur's point of view."

"Which is?" Pratama asked.

"We're one of the few remaining *preman* organizations engaged in the black market. The others have become religious enforcers, and most of the other drug groups are individual crews, often foreigners. We have a corner on the market. Rather than rest on our laurels, we should press forward, expand our wealth."

"And when the people tire of our actions and demand a government response?" Pratama pressed.

"Look around," Aditya said. "The cash in my pocket probably exceeds the net worth of this village. The politicians won't give a shit what these peasants have to say."

A shout from one of the huts snapped Aditya and Pratama out of their dialogue. An older gentleman, his hair graying at the edges, rushed out of the hut, a machete in his hand. He let out a war cry as he rounded the girls and made a beeline for Pratama and Aditya.

Pratama immediately took a step forward, snapped his Pindad rifle to the ready, and rotated the selector to SEMI. His finger twitched twice, and a pair of 5.56x45mm rounds took flight from the muzzle. The bullets ripped through the old man's heart and punctured one of his lungs. It took another second before the man's body registered the damage, and he stumbled forward, his face impacting hard against the muddy soil.

As Pratama approached, the dying man's horrid gasps grew in volume. The man's lungs filled rapidly with blood, and the struggle to breathe only intensified. Pratama trained the muzzle on the man's head and pulled the trigger once more, putting him out of his misery. Pratama safed his rifle and turned back towards Aditya. As he did, he saw one of the girls trembling, her eyes reddening as tears mixed with the precipitation. Her mouth locked open to scream, but her vocal cords wouldn't cooperate.

Aditya sauntered over to Pratama. He studied the corpse, then turned his gaze to the girl on the verge of catatonia. Aditya clicked his tongue then said, "Hmm. Must have been her father."

"Yeah," Pratama said quietly. He looked back to Aditya and asked, "What do you want to do if she can't move?"

"We only need to get her to the trucks," Aditya said. "Then from there, to the boats. Short distances. She'll make it."

Pratama nodded slowly. "Right."

Aditya whistled loud to summon his crew's attention, then waved his left hand in a wide circle above his head. "Load 'em up! Let's move!" He then turned to Pratama and said, "Supervise them."

Pratama nodded. "You've got it."

As Pratama and the others began to stand the girls up and move them to the trucks, Aditya reached for a pouch on his web belt and produced a satellite phone. He dialed the number, hit CALL, and then held the phone to his ear. Two ringtones later, Suparman Guntur picked up the phone.

"Yes."

"Cargo's retrieved," Aditya said simply.

"Good," Guntur said. "Get them to the transport. I'll meet you at the pickup point."

"Got it," Aditya said. He terminated the call, placed the sat phone back in its pouch, and marched briskly to catch up with his men.

CHAPTER ELEVEN

Cengkareng, West Jakarta, Indonesia
17 March 2019
00:20 hours Golf (16 March 17:20 hours Zulu)

Pace and Tan flanked Bradshaw as he pulled up the browser window and logged into the email account. He used the trackpad to guide the cursor over to the Drafts folder, then left-clicked. Bradshaw smiled when he saw there was a new draft in the box.

"They came through," he said.

Pace nodded in approval. "Nice. Let's see what we've got."

Bradshaw opened the draft. Pace and Tan leaned in closer to read along.

> You, old friend, are a shit magnet. Most people in your predicament would be laying low, sipping beers on the beach, and going out of their way to avoid these kinds of folks. I would advise you to hand this off to your friends and get as much running room as possible…but I know you well enough to know you wouldn't listen, Boy Scout.
>
> So, here's what you were looking for. Use it wisely.
>
> Be careful out there.

"Aw, I knew you cared," Bradshaw said with a smile as he downloaded the attached .zip file. When it downloaded, he expanded it and found a PDF. He opened the document, and a moment later, an organizational chart filled the screen. Each box had a name and photo, where applicable, as well as a phone number and a brief data sheet with what the grey hat hacker was able to gather.

Pace let out a low whistle as his eyes traversed the chart. "Your hacker's got an IC background," he said. "That's a textbook target deck."

"Yeah," Bradshaw said as he scrolled through the document. "That match up with your intel?"

"Yeah," Pace said.

"More than that," Tan added. "It's an expansion. We were able to identify some of these targets on our own, but this is definitely a more comprehensive breakdown. It would have taken us days, maybe weeks, to expand our target deck to this level."

As Bradshaw continued to scroll, he found a map of Java with key points marked in both latitude/longitude and the Military Grid Reference System. He rolled the cursor over the points and found that the map was interactive. On a hunch, Bradshaw held the control button as he scrolled, and the map zoomed in. He guided it over to Java, where there were three points of interest.

"All right," Bradshaw said as he highlighted each of the points. "Looks like there's a whorehouse in Senen and a gangster clubhouse in Kembangan." His eyes narrowed as he reached the third point. "Hmm. That's interesting."

"Yeah," Pace said as he read what had caught Bradshaw's attention. "A training camp outside of Bagogog in West Java." He glanced over to Tan. "Didn't know they actually trained. Guntur's a straight convict."

"Doesn't mean he couldn't have decided to get smart, learn the way of the gun," Bradshaw said.

"Fair point," Pace said. He pointed to the terrain around the training camp. "Heavily wooded, some rolling hills…looks pretty suitable for an ambush." He turned his head towards Tan. "What do you think?"

Tan nodded. "It's doable."

Bradshaw held up his hand. "Whoa, whoa, whoa, whoa, whoa, let's slow down a bit." He pointed to the map. "Judging from the size of that compound, they've got to have at least 15 to 20 tangos on-site. Unless you've been holding out, the heaviest weapon in our possession is the Pindad rifle I took off of the cop the other day. How is this doable?"

"O ye of little faith," Pace said as he clapped Bradshaw on the shoulder, then reached into his pocket for his phone.

"Who you calling?" Bradshaw asked.

"A friend," Pace said. "Go ahead and bed down. Shit's gonna get busy."

Tanjung Priok, North Jakarta, Indonesia
17 March 2019
01:35 hours Golf (16 March 18:35 hours Zulu)

THE LIGHT DRIZZLE was still going strong as the Azimut 80 yacht pulled into the berth in the multipurpose terminal. Aditya and his crew had changed into civilian clothes once they were underway, then stashed the heavier weapons in various compartments within the yacht. While they did have guardian angels in Jakarta law enforcement, it was a point of courtesy and professionalism not to brandish the heavier weapons within the city proper.

As one of the crew moored the yacht, Aditya exited the bridge, made his way aft to the stairs, and descended to the lower deck. Suparman Guntur stood on the dock, flanked by his personal security detail. Aditya stepped onto the dock and shook Guntur's hand.

"How did we do?" Guntur asked.

"Twenty-five fresh bodies, as requested," Aditya said. He turned in time to see Umar Pratama leading the procession of girls off the yacht and onto the deck. Most of the girls kept their heads down and their eyes averted. The one that had been defiant back on Damar still hadn't lost her spirit, and she stared daggers at both Aditya and Guntur as she was marched past.

"Wait," Guntur said. He pointed to the defiant one. "Pull her aside. March the rest to the vehicles."

One of the heavies did as he was ordered, and a moment later, the girl was presented to Guntur. He grabbed her by the chin and jerked her head from one side to the other, inspecting her facial features. His eyes swept over her figure in an evaluative fashion. Guntur smiled as he met the girl's daggered stare.

"What's your name?" Guntur asked in Javanese. She said nothing. Guntur cocked back and delivered a vicious backhand to the girl's face. His voice remained even as he repeated, "What is your name?"

"Nari," the girl finally replied through clenched teeth.

"You have fire, Nari," Guntur said. He reached into his jacket for an oblong leather case. "I love it when we take girls like you." His grin flourished sadistic. "I love it because I know I will see you fall. I will break you. By the end of the week, you won't fight back when I jam my cock in your mouth. Two weeks from now, you'll beg to service me, all so you can get a little bit of this." Guntur waved the case in front of her face, watching her eyes lock onto it.

Guntur looked to the guard restraining her and nodded. Another guard stepped in to assist, holding Nari's arm locked out and in place while the other rolled back her sleeve. Guntur opened the leather case, produced a rubber tourniquet, and handed it to one of his hired guns. The tourniquet was cinched down just beneath Nari's bicep, and one of the thugs slapped the crook of her arm, bringing the vein to the surface.

Nari thrashed against her captors, and one of them delivered a brutal kick to the back of her leg, bringing her to her knees. Guntur squatted in front of her, set the pouch between his legs, and withdrew a bent spoon and a vial full of white powder. He sprinkled a small dollop of the powder on the spoon, capped the vial, and swapped it out for a portable butane torch. Guntur fired up the torch and held it beneath the spoon until the powder began to bubble. Once enough liquid was produced, the torch was substituted for a syringe. Nari's eyes were wide as she watched the syringe fill with brown liquid.

Guntur flicked the needle a couple of times, then grabbed Nari's forearm. He slipped the needle into the vein, pulled back to confirm the syringe had found its mark, then slowly depressed the plunger.

It happened almost instantaneously. The fight in Nari's eyes evaporated, replaced by glassy euphoria. As her pupils dilated, Guntur watched her resist the opioid's warmth. Once the syringe was empty, Guntur removed it from Nari's arm and smiled as he placed the expended syringe back in the kit.

"The sensation you're feeling is the opium latching onto your body's five major receptors," Guntur said. "They're spread throughout your brain, spinal cord, and other major organs. The beautiful thing about heroin from a sales perspective is that you will *never* again feel a high like your first. You see, the body develops a tolerance rather quickly. You have to keep increasing your doses until you finally overdose."

Guntur leaned in close as he watched Nari struggle to process him. Her jaw had gone slack, and a bit of drool leaked from the corner of her mouth. His lips brushed against her ear as he whispered, "The layman's term for what I've described is that I've just made you my bitch. I *own* you. Every piece of your body is mine for my pleasure. When I tire of you, your body will be for my profit. And eventually, when you're so strung out that you've exceeded your singular purpose…only then will I give you the final high that you crave."

He stood and waved sharply. The guards picked Nari up and dragged her to the vehicles. Guntur put the heroin kit back in his jacket as Aditya stepped closer.

"Has there been any signs of the Shadow Wraiths?" Guntur asked.

"Not since Batavia," Aditya said.

Guntur produced his smart phone, opened the file from Setiawan Mahmud, and handed it over to Aditya. "Our friend, the deputy governor, has produced a lead."

Aditya studied Bradshaw's file, then looked to Guntur. "His whereabouts have been accounted for. There's no way he's one of the Shadow Wraiths."

"Not initially," Guntur agreed. "I do believe he's working with them now. Whether it's an alliance of convenience or a recruitment remains to be seen, but I have an intuition. We find Bradshaw, we'll find the Shadow Wraiths."

Aditya nodded. "If you can send me that file, I'll circulate it to our people." He paused. "What about the one that escaped and caused this whole mess?"

Guntur smiled cruelly. "Oh, I'm not done with her yet. Soon, though. She won't hold out much longer."

"Of course," Aditya said.

"Make another run tomorrow evening," Guntur said. "You'll be compensated. Step up expansion of the stable. Then, when the time is right, we'll bring the press into it."

Aditya glanced back to Guntur. "You think they'll bite?"

"I think they'll be hungry enough to lash out that they'll ignore their sense that it's a trap," Guntur said. "Their sentimentality will drive them to ruin."

Setiabudi, South Jakarta, Indonesia
17 March 2019
08:45 hours Golf (01:45 hours Zulu)

PACE HAD INSISTED on the suits. Bradshaw had no clue where Tan and Pace had managed to procure a suit that fit him so well on such short notice. The charcoal slacks and blazer fit him in every conceivable fashion, and had enough room for him to store his Pindad P1 in a leather shoulder holster over his black button-down shirt without printing through the blazer. None of the trio wore ties. Both Pace and Tan wore khaki suits, though Pace wore a pale yellow button-down while Tan had opted for a form-fitting black cotton T-shirt.

Bradshaw glanced to Pace as the elevator continued its ascent. "I guess this contact of yours has a penchant for class," he said.

Pace nodded. "She certainly appreciates the finer things in life," he said.

Bradshaw arched his eyebrows. "*She*?"

Pace returned the gesture with a cocked eyebrow of his own. "What? You don't think women work the black market?"

"I didn't say that—" Bradshaw started defensively.

"Better you gaffed now than during the meet," Pace said. "Last thing I need you doing is tainting the atmosphere by getting caught staring at her tits."

"And trust me," Tan added. "You *will* look at her tits." His grin widened. "She's not a little SJW snowflake. She can handle a gawk."

Bradshaw suppressed the urge to roll his eyes. He focused on the door in front of him and took a deep breath. "What's the nature of the relationship?" he asked Pace.

"I'll leave that up to her to divulge," Pace said. "She's a very private individual. I know enough from my own research and my dealings with her that she's legitimate. Beyond that?" He shrugged. "I figure some things are better left unasked."

The elevator crawled to a smooth halt as it arrived at the penthouse level. The door opened slowly to reveal white tile with brown stripes that formed squares at set intervals. A yellow and white patterned wallpaper covered the corridors, and the lights were bright enough to leave no dark spots while dim enough to avoid a blinding effect. As soon as Bradshaw stepped onto the floor, he spotted the circular surveillance camera mounted high.

"Don't worry about it," Pace said. "She looped the cameras. They'll stay looped long after we're gone. She doesn't like being caught on camera any more than we do."

"Tracking," Bradshaw said with a nod.

The walk from the elevator to the front door was 15 meters long and involved a right turn. When they stood at the door, Pace raised his fist, rapped his knuckles against the door three times, paused, and knocked twice more. Fifteen seconds passed before the door opened, and

Bradshaw had to fight to keep his upper and lower jaws connected.

She stood barely above five feet tall and sported a flawless olive complexion. Her dark brown hair was slick with pool water, judging from the faint chlorine stench and slight redness to her warm, brown eyes. High cheekbones framed her face, and her small yet plump lips parted to reveal white, even teeth that would bring a dentist to tears. A black satin robe that stopped halfway down her toned thigh was all that she wore, and it clung to her curvature. The robe was parted from a few inches above her navel, and Bradshaw felt his eyes dropping before he forcibly redirected them upward. If she had noticed the slip, she didn't let on.

"Danny!" she said, leaping into Pace's arms. The two embraced, and she planted a kiss on his lips. "It's good to see you, baby!"

"You too, gorgeous," Pace said with a smile, the first genuine one Bradshaw had seen from him. He let her down gently, and she turned to Tan. "C'mere and give me a hug, weirdo."

"It sounds so charming when she says it," Tan said with a wide grin. The two embraced briefly, and exchanged a pair of cheek kisses. Only then did the woman face Bradshaw and look him from head to toe, her hands on her hips.

"You looking to trade hardware for the boy toy?" she asked Pace playfully with her eyes locked on Bradshaw. His cheeks immediately reddened, and Pace laughed.

"Jack Bradshaw, meet the Mermaid," Pace said.

Bradshaw cleared his throat as he extended his hand toward her. "A pleasure to meet you, ma'am," he managed to say without stammering.

"It's Milena," she said. "Milena Wright. Not 'ma'am.'" Despite her diminutive stature, her grip was firm and dry. "I have to say, you're *far* better looking than in your federal warrant photo. Ditching the mustache for a beard was definitely a good move."

Bradshaw ignored the comment on his dearly-departed Thomas Magnum-inspired mustache. A semi-stunned expression crossed Pace's face as he processed Wright's identity reveal.

"It took me nine months before you told me your name," Pace said.

Wright reached up and patted Pace gently on the face. "You were still a Company man, darling," she said. Her eyes traversed back to Bradshaw. "Him, on the other hand...I spent 18 years at Langley, and I've never seen them burn somebody like that to get them operating. If they had, I'd have heard about it." She flashed her brilliant smile at Bradshaw, then looked back to Pace. "He's truly out after dark on his own. He's lucky to have you."

"I wouldn't go that far," Pace said. "He's with us until we take the Kuwat Syndicate down. One thing at a time."

"Of course," Wright said. She motioned to the room's interior. "Come in, come in. I dunno if you've eaten yet. I ordered room service."

"I might take you up on that," Bradshaw said, earning a sideways glance from Pace.

"Danny, go easy on the young man," Wright chastised, her eyes remaining forward. Before Pace could say anything, she added, "Yes, I know you're giving him the stink eye."

"Show off," Pace muttered.

As they rounded the corner into the room proper, Bradshaw saw the spread to his right, with scrambled eggs, pancakes, toast, bacon, sausage, and fresh fruit. His eyes traversed left, and he caught a bikini set patterned after the Brazilian flag, hanging from a chair and dripping wet. He then looked towards the bed area and completely forgot about the food and the swimsuit.

It was a mobile arsenal. The pair of king-sized beds were covered from headboard to foot with an assortment of rifles, handguns, and shotguns. Machine guns were propped up on the floor at the beds' feet. In between were open Pelican cases that displayed an assortment of grenades. Along the wall adjoining the sliding balcony door were holsters, war belts, plate carriers, and camouflage fatigues. Directly opposite were cases of ammunition.

Pace caught a glimpse of the look in Bradshaw's eyes and chuckled. "Well, I've seen it all. First time I've seen somebody ignore a half-naked woman to gawk at a bunch of guns."

"When you said she was connected, I figured it was gonna be a couple of rifles and some magazines," Bradshaw said. "You didn't say she was on that *Lord of War* time."

"Danny's predisposed to understatement," Wright said. She folded her arms. "Though to be fair, I'm not strictly an arms dealer, per se. Think of me as a jill-of-all-trades." She smiled as she studied Bradshaw. "You see anything you like?"

"Oh, yeah," Bradshaw said. He made his way to the foot of the bed and took a knee beside an FN Minimi Para. He pointed the barrel to the ground, pulled the charging handle to the rear, pressed in the safety, and pushed the handle forward. Bradshaw then lifted the feed tray cover and feed tray to ensure it was clear, closed both, and tested the trigger to see if the safety held. Satisfied, he pulled the handle to the rear again, placed the weapon on fire, squeezed the trigger, and rode the bolt forward. Bradshaw tapped the squad automatic weapon and looked to Pace and Wright, a wide grin on his face.

"Yeah, you would've been a lifer," Pace said.

Wright giggled. "I think his enthusiasm is kinda cute."

"Don't encourage him, Mil," Pace groaned with an eye roll.

"We're gonna need this," Bradshaw said, before he stood and moved toward the backboard. He perused the rifles and said, "Where did you get these?"

"Some of them, I imported," Wright said. "Other places? Accounting errors. Sometimes, folks relinquish them when they no longer need them. In this neck of the woods, if it's available to the Filipinos, Malays, Singaporeans, or Indonesians, it's available to me."

Bradshaw met Wright's eyes. The playful manner was there, but there was a hard glint to her eyes. He recognized it for what it was, nodded, and rolled his lips beneath his teeth. With a click of his tongue, Bradshaw selected a short-barreled Colt M4. The fixed front sight had been removed and replaced with a flip-up sight at the front end of the top rail. Attached beneath the barrel was a local clone of an M203 grenade launcher. An Aimpoint Micro T-1 served as the weapon's optic. He tested the Aimpoint to ensure it was functional, then inspected the rest of the weapon.

"This seems my speed," Bradshaw said. "How much will all of this cost?"

"Nothing," Wright said. "A couple of lapsed Catholics need hardware, call it the St. Jude's Giveaway." When Pace glared at Wright, she shrugged and said, "What? It's written all over both of you. Besides, you'll be working together past this assignment."

"What makes you say that?" Pace asked.

Wright clasped her hands behind her back and offered a coy smile. "Call it intuition."

Bradshaw had moved over to the kit wall. There was an Osprey plate carrier that matched the DPM fatigues, along a variety of load-bearing options, both chest-rigs and direct MOLLE mount. He set those aside and looked around. "Gonna need some grenades…war belt…holster…" Bradshaw looked to Wright. "I'm pretty sure I'd marry you right now if you had a Glock 19."

Wright pointed to the bed closest to Bradshaw. "Check the middle."

Bradshaw marched over and glanced until he found what he was looking for. It was a Gen 4, with his preferred finger grooves. The only modifications to the pistol were the Trijicon Bright & Tough tritium sights and an extended, threaded barrel for a sound suppressor. He ensured it was unloaded, then pointed it towards an unoccupied wall, aimed down the sights, and squeezed the trigger. When the striker dropped, Bradshaw racked the slide and slowly let out the trigger until he felt the crisp *click* of the reset.

"You taking proposals?" Bradshaw asked.

"Maybe if you were Jason Momoa and I were interested in monogamy," Wright said with a smile. She looked to Pace. "You want your usual?"

"You know it," Pace said.

Her eyes shifted to Tan. "Lucas?"

Tan hefted a Knight's Armament SR-25 sniper rifle and beamed. "Rah!"

Wright turned back to Bradshaw, looking him over. "I really do hope you bring him by more often, Danny," she said. "Not worth betting half my shit, but he still looks fun."

"Oh, don't go breaking that poor boy's heart, Mil," Pace said. "You know he couldn't handle you."

"No, but he deserves the opportunity," Wright said, a wicked gleam in her eyes.

Pace rolled his eyes. "Let's get this stuff packed up. Still got a lot of work before we kick this thing off."

CHAPTER TWELVE

*5 kilometers south-by-southeast of Klapanunggal, West
Java, Indonesia*
19 March 2019
03:00 hours Golf (18 March 20:00 hours Zulu)

Jack Bradshaw lay in the prone beside Lucas Tan, both of
them clad in the British DPM fatigues they'd acquired
from Milena Wright. In lieu of a helmet, they wore nylon
head harnesses with an attachment point for the AN/PVS-
15 night vision binoculars. Boonie hats covered most of
their heads, with the front part of the flap jammed beneath
the harness's rhino mount. Their faces were covered in
camouflage paint, with the high points of their face painted
dark and the low points painted light.

Warm rain drizzled from above, cutting through their
fatigues and soaking their skin. Bradshaw could feel rainwater slosh between his toes, despite the moisture-wicking
socks he wore and the vent holes in his jungle boots. The
logical part of his brain told him to be wary of indigenous
land leeches and that he'd need to powder his feet and
change his socks at the first opportunity to prevent trench
foot.

On the other hand, Bradshaw's impulsive side rejoiced.
Minus a single overnight/day recce six months ago, he had
not truly soldiered in over a year and a half. That recce
was strictly an observation mission. This would be an
offensive mission, designed to inflict maximum casualties
on the enemy. The miserable conditions and the task
brought Bradshaw life in a fashion he wasn't sure that he'd
ever feel again.

Bradshaw and Tan had set up an LP/OP on a hill
overlooking the compound six hours earlier. They had
done a range card to detail what could and couldn't be
seen from the observation position, as well as taken notes
of the defenses. The Kuwat Syndicate established a

surprisingly respectable training compound. The perimeter consisted of a tall fence topped with concertina wire, as well as an outward-swinging front gate. While there were no guard towers, the men did maintain roving patrols. At the back of the compound was a rough but serviceable shooting range with a maximum distance of 50 meters. There was a tent village, with a mixture of small and large tents which were sure to be a mixture of residential and common areas.

At the same time, it was obvious the Syndicate weren't professional soldiers. White lights could be seen inside the tents, marking the insomniacs. The ones on duty knew not to use white lights, but they also relied solely on their body's natural night vision. Most held their weapons at the low ready, but some of them slung them on their backs. A couple congregated out of sight to engage in conversation as a means to combat boredom and fatigue. One of them actually was ballsy enough to light up a cigarette.

"I could kill that fool right now," Tan whispered. His NODs were flipped up, and his dominant eye was glued to the SR25's Leupold variable optic, enhanced by the AN/PVS-22 night vision sight mounted at the front. Through the optic, everything within the Mil-Dot reticle was lime green and crisp. The crosshair was centered on the man's chest, and Tan contemplated teaching the dolt a lesson.

"No," Bradshaw said quietly. He watched as the patrol rounded the front gate corner closest to them. "I'm going to go set up. Cover me."

"I've got you," Tan said, a hint of disappointment in his voice.

Bradshaw rolled his eyes as he set the FN Minimi Para's stock in the grass without a noise. *Dude's a character.* He backed away from the gun and rose to his feet. Bradshaw double-checked the heavy satchel slung across his chest and cinched tight to his side, then drew his Glock 19 from its Kydex holster on his war belt. His free hand snaked into the admin pouch on his Eagle Industries

Rhodesian Recon Vest and removed a SilencerCo Osprey9 sound suppressor. Bradshaw fastened the suppressor on the threaded barrel, ensured it was snug in place, and began his approach.

The initial movement was unhurried. Sudden motions registered in peripheral vision, particularly at night, and the same would cause him to slip and roll down the hill. Bradshaw walked sideways, knees bent, probing with the outer blade of his foot before shifting weight from the trail foot to the lead. He repeated the process all the way down the slope. His eyes traversed the terrain ahead, looking for any sign of deviation from the observed patterns. The Glock was held sternum-high at the ready. It was a last resort. If the Austrian pistol saw play before the trap was set, then Tan and Bradshaw were compromised beyond repair and their chances of successfully extracting would lessen considerably.

Bradshaw reached flat ground, and he picked up the pace from a crawl to a standard walk. He continued to scan laterally. At the back of his mind, he thanked the Lord that the Kuwat Syndicate's arrogance had led them not to build guard towers. If there were elevated spotters, the approach to the target site would have been far more difficult. That same part of his mind found himself wishing for the GPNVG-18 panoramic NODs that had been slotted for phasing-in when he'd left the Regimental Reconnaissance Company.

Win some, lose some.

The nearby sentinels had their backs turned to Bradshaw, and those in the distance were far enough away that they couldn't see him. The steady precipitation served as a form of concealment, limiting visibility. Bradshaw spotted the smoker in the background. His hand was cupped around the cigarette to keep it concealed—likely out of a desire to keep the tobacco dry rather than a sense of tactical awareness—but each time he lifted the smoke to his mouth, Bradshaw picked up a small but bright orb through his NODs.

Amateur.

Bradshaw had not been exerting himself on the walk, but by the time he reached the selected site, his heart pounded in his chest. He took a knee, stuffed the Glock as far into the holster as the suppressor would allow, and unslung the satchel. Bradshaw set the satchel in the grass in front of him, then reached to his Press-to-Talk button attached to his AN/PRC-48 MBITR radio.

"Lionheart, Boy Scout," Bradshaw said. "How we looking?"

"All clear from here, Boy Scout," Lucas replied, his voice coming through loud and clear over the headset.

"Roger," Bradshaw said. "I'm getting set up."

Bradshaw opened the satchel. He removed a thick, curved, olive drab rectangle with pair of prongs folded in on the bottom. Etched into the slick plastic on the outside were the words "FRONT TOWARDS ENEMY." Bradshaw rotated the scissor prongs on the M18A1 Claymore down and 90 degrees clockwise, spread the prongs, and then sunk them into the moist soil with the business end facing away from him.

With that in place, Bradshaw produced the roll of detonation cord that he had pre-measured prior to insertion. He located one end, then removed an M4 blasting cap from the satchel. Bradshaw carefully crimped the det cord around the blasting cap, removed the right fuse well plug, and fed the det cord through the plug and into the well. Once he was satisfied that the blasting cap was sufficiently buried in the mine, Bradshaw fastened the fuse well plug.

Bradshaw unrolled more of the det cord as he moved about five meters to his right. He stopped and removed a second Claymore from the satchel. It took three minutes for Bradshaw to feed the det cord through the mine via the pair of fuse well plugs. He then moved five more meters to the right and repeated the process.

"Lionheart," Bradshaw keyed up as he finished with the third mine. "SITREP."

"Looking good, but might wanna wrap it up, most ricky-tick," Tan said. "Our strolling couple is about half-way around the far side."

"Roger," Bradshaw said. "I've got two more and we'll be Gucci."

"Roger that," Tan said.

The Claymores were emplaced in an L-shaped for-mation. That guaranteed overlapping fields of fire and expanded the kill zone. Normally, an ambush of this nature would have been conducted with at least a couple of squads, but in the absence of additional guns, explosives and the element of surprise would have to do.

Bradshaw emplaced a total of six mines. On the final mine, he crimped a blasting cap on the other end of the det cord, fed it through the fuse well plug, and buried it in the mine. He then grabbed an electric firing wire spool and found the end that had a blasting cap attached. That was fed into the other fuse well and secured. From there, Bradshaw slowly unspooled the firing wire until he was halfway back to the base of the hill. He took the plug end and attached it to the clacker. Bradshaw knew both were serviceable as he had used a tester to ensure the circuit was functional. He set the primed clacker down and reached for his PTT.

"Lionheart, Boy Scout. We're set."

"They're walking around the corner now," Tan said. "Waiting on your go."

"Roger."

Bradshaw took a knee. He was grateful for the high grass, as it not only provided concealment for him, but it also made the mine emplacement easier, as he did not need to take additional time to conceal the mines or wires. Bradshaw drew the Glock, removed and put away the suppressor, then slipped the pistol back in its holster. He continued to observe his surroundings through the PVS-15s. The pair of sentries held their Pindad rifles at the low ready as they engaged in animated conversation.

Bradshaw took a deep breath in through his nose to quell his impatience. *Recce ain't sexy,* he reminded himself. Getting upset with their lack of alacrity wouldn't make them move any faster.

Five minutes passed before the pair rounded the corner, and another three before they were in range. *Finally,* he thought as he reached for his PTT. "Lionheart, Boy Scout. I'm initiating."

"Roger."

Bradshaw reached to his chest rig for the M48 stun grenade. It was almost identical to the M84 he'd used while on active duty, with the major aesthetic difference being the red-orange label marked with Hebrew print. Bradshaw thumbed away the grenade's safety, yanked the pin loose from the body, then cocked back and hurled the cylinder as far as he could toward the ambush sector. As the grenade flew, Bradshaw turned away, went prone, and covered his ears, doing his best to ignore the pain that stemmed from his bruised ribs.

The grenade detonated a split second after Bradshaw covered up, expending its brilliant and deafening combination of magnesium and ammonium nitrate. A moment later, Bradshaw turned back towards the kill zone, the clacker in his hand. He pushed the safety bale down, then keyed the PTT.

"Lionheart, Boy Scout. Talk to me."

There was a pause before Tan replied. "They're freaked out. A lot of lights just came on in the tents. Perimeter guards are moving to the source. Got a couple inside the perimeter moving to the front gate."

"Roger," Bradshaw said. "Please advise."

"The gate just swung open," Tan said. "You've got the six on the perimeter plus another eight to ten mobilizing at the front gate. Got more in the tent village that are gearing up."

Bradshaw's thumb moved along the clacker's operating handle. His pulse picked up in his chest, anticipating the break in the calm. *C'mon, you motherfuckers,* he urged mentally. *Walk right on in. Got something for you.*

"First three or four are in the kill zone," Tan said. "The rest are at the periphery. Almost there."

Bradshaw could hear hushed conversation as the gangster-soldier hybrids probed further. He couldn't make out what they were saying at that distance, but he could only imagine they were confused. Their footsteps were quiet, but beyond that, Bradshaw's sole point of reference was Tan's radio commentary.

"Boy Scout, you've got 10 in the kill zone," Tan said. "You can try to pull more in or you can initiate. Your call."

A long exhale fell from Bradshaw's nose as he resisted the temptation. "Holding what I've got," he said into his mic quietly.

An excited cry carried over the clearing, followed by hurried footsteps. The conversational tone returned to normal volume, though the voice sounded as if a discovery was made. Tan came back on the net.

"Boy Scout, you've got 12 solidly in the kill zone."

"How about the ones at the gate?" Bradshaw asked.

"Some walked in. The rest seem to be waiting in reserve."

Smart. "You'll need to keep their heads down."

Bradshaw could hear the grin in Tan's voice. "We going loud, Boy Scout?"

"Yep. Going loud." *Finally.* "Fire in the hole." He slapped the clacker hard three times with the heel of his palm.

The clacker sent an electric current through the wire, which detonated the attached blasting cap. That triggered the second cap in the last mine, which in turn ignited the det cord that ran through all the mines. Near-simultaneously, the C4 plastic explosive inside each of the six mines exploded. Each mine launched 700 3.2mm steel balls into the kill zone at 1,200 meters per second.

The 12 men inside the kill zone stood no chance. Between the explosion itself, the shockwave, and the crossfire created from the L-shaped formation, those trapped in the blast radius were instantly reduced to a bloody, pulpy mass. As the smoke cleared, what was a grassy clearing had transformed into scorched hell, littered with body parts. The acrid stench of charred flesh filled the air.

Bradshaw did not stick around to survey his work. He scrambled to his feet and bolted up the hill. Shouting from the background reached Bradshaw's ears as he reached the hill's halfway point. A second later, the *crack* of incoming rounds filled the air around him. The bullets went wide, but that knowledge did nothing to reduce Bradshaw's pucker factor as he gritted his teeth and pushed harder to crest the hill. The shrill report of suppressed 7.62x51mm rounds told Bradshaw that Tan had entered the fray, engaging targets with his SR25.

The incoming fire stopped long enough for Bradshaw to reach the hilltop, bank hard right, and bolt back to the overwatch position. He transitioned into a straight-leg slide that carried him within a foot of his Minimi. Bradshaw rolled onto his stomach, locked the PVS-15s in the upright position, and tucked the stock into his shoulder. He thumbed the safety to FIRE, used his support hand to clamp the skeletal buttstock with an overhand grip, and pressed his cheek to the stock. Once he acquired his sight picture through the mounted AN/PAS-13 thermal sight, Bradshaw shifted his body until he was focused on the front gate. A line of men had raced out the gate, illuminated in white-hot vision through the optic, their rifles at the ready

Bradshaw adjusted his point of aim to lead the point man, then squeezed the Minimi's trigger. The squad automatic weapon chattered as it let loose with a six-round burst, which Bradshaw timed by chanting under his breath, "Die, motherfucker, die." The point man walked right into two of the bullets and fell, and the man behind him caught a round. As they fell, the line froze, shocked at the death happening right before their eyes. Bradshaw pressed the advantage, sweeping the line right-to-left with another burst of six. As they fell, he shifted his aim downward and swept back rightward, dumping more rounds into the bodies to ensure they were out of the fight.

Beside him, Tan had shifted targets to inside the camp. He saw a target raising what appeared to be a scoped rifle. Tan centered the Leupold's crosshairs on the man's chest and squeezed the trigger twice. The target fell backwards, his rifle falling out of reach. On the second shot, Tan felt his rifle fail to cycle. He went off glass and tilted his rifle to the left, his eyes inspecting the ejection port. When he saw he had an empty chamber, he immediately reached to his chest rig with his left hand while his right index finger hit the magazine release.

"Reloading!" Tan called over the sound of the Minimi.

Bradshaw immediately shifted hard left to focus his fire on the camp. His time between bursts shortened as he compensated for a gun being out of the fight. If Bradshaw even thought he saw movement, he serviced the source with a six-round burst. Just as Tan sent the bolt home on his SR25 and fired the first round of his fresh 20-round box magazine, Bradshaw felt his Minimi's bolt lock forward.

"Reloading!" Bradshaw hollered as he rolled onto his side. He removed the empty 100 round soft pouch from its position at the bottom of the receiver, grabbed a fresh replacement from his chest rig and slapped it place. He then popped open the feed tray cover, brushed broken links from it, laid the start of the new belt onto the feed tray with the links facing upward, then slapped the cover in place and locked the bolt to the rear.

A group of six remained, and had broken down into two fireteams. One of them laid suppressive fire down on the hilltop while the others attempted to maneuver to Bradshaw's and Tan's right. Bradshaw focused his sight on the support-by-fire element and began to sweep their line with six-round bursts.

"They're flanking our three o'clock!" Bradshaw called out.

"Cover me!" Tan screamed.

Bradshaw increased his rate of fire to borderline cyclic, which served to keep the base-of-fire's heads down. Tan scooped up his SR25, leapt to his feet, and raced about 15 meters to the right of his original firing position. He took a knee and peered through his Leupold scope. Three shooters were doing their best to balance speed and security as they ascended the hill from about 150 meters away. Tan shouldered the SR25, placed the reticle to where it just about touched the point man, and squeezed the trigger. The 168-grain hollow point round made impact with the target's abdomen, creating a massive wound channel as it made its passage. As the first man fell, Tan transitioned to the second target and fired, this round making touchdown on the attacker's sternum. The third man froze, and Tan gave him a round to the chest as well. All three men were dead within four seconds of each other.

As Tan turned to jog back to the LP/OP, he heard Bradshaw's Minimi go silent. He stopped where he was, dropped to a knee, and scanned the perimeter through his optic. Tan's free hand went to his PTT.

"Boy Scout, you good?"

"I'm good," Bradshaw said. "I've got nothing on my end."

"Nothing from here, either," Tan said. "Let's pack up and roll out before reinforcements arrive."

"Roger that," Bradshaw said. "I'll hold for you."

CHAPTER THIRTEEN

Kembangan, West Jakarta, Indonesia
19 March 2019
03:45 hours Golf (18 March 20:45 hours Zulu)

Danny Pace blended in and stood out all at once. Being tall and white drew eyes to the few people who remained on the street. Nonetheless, he managed to remain unassuming, moving with an expat's confidence rather than a tourist's bewildered aura or a predator's gait. His red long-sleeved button-down shirt and khakis were soaked from walking in the rain, though his feet managed to stay dry. A messenger bag was slung across his chest and rested along his left hip.

The street was so narrow that the most it could accommodate was a compact car. Most of the vehicular traffic in the area consisted of motorcycles, motorized scooters, and mopeds, and that traffic was scant at zero-dark-thirty. The only people Pace spotted as he walked were people racing through the area to reach safer ground, and the ruffians who owned the turf. The latter eyed him up, saw he was aware of his surroundings but projected a non-threatening tenor, and left him be while keeping an eye on him.

Pace's eyes fell to the target ahead. It was a two-story building without markings. A pair of heavily tattooed, sinewy men stood guard at the entrance, pistols jammed down the front of their jeans. He took cover under an awning and behind a stand, pulling out his cell phone as if to check messages. Pace pulled up Google Maps and scanned the surrounding streets. The area in the target building's vicinity was completely congested, with no apparent side streets he could utilize to slip inside. It was looking more like he would have to mount a frontal assault, a possibility that held zero appeal to Pace. As trained and experienced as he was, the enemy's quantity of manpower would win the battle unless he exploited a weakness.

He looked back to the front entrance, then back to his phone. *Hmm,* Pace thought. *Might have to come back and hit this with the boys. Was really hoping for simultaneous hits.*

To punctuate the point, his phone vibrated in announcement of an SMS from Tan. Pace opened it.

Pass Terminator. 20+ EKIA, 0 FKIA/FWIA.

Pace automatically translated the message. "Terminator" was the code word for Bradshaw and Tan's successful neutralization of the Kuwait Syndicate's training camp. Over 20 enemies were killed in action, and neither Tan nor Bradshaw were killed or wounded in the process.

With a relived sigh, Pace pecked at the on-screen keyboard with his thumbs. *Rgr.* He hit SEND and put the phone away. An abort was looking likely. Even without hitting the club, demolishing the camp was a major victory. The Syndicate would feel the inflicted damage.

Footsteps cut through the rainfall, and Pace spun to address the source, his right hand snaking to his waistline for his Springfield MC Operator 1911. When he saw who approached, Pace immediately brushed his shirt back over his pistol and straightened up.

The man had to be well over 50, with silver hair tucked beneath a flat cap. He wore a short-sleeved button-down, jeans, and sneakers. In each of his weathered hands, he held large plastic bags. Judging from the bulges within, he was making a food delivery. He looked to be in good health for his age, and yet each step he took appeared weighted.

When Pace got a look at the man's dark eyes, he could see why. It was clear he was intimate with the painful ghosts that accompanied loss. That observation compelled Pace to wave the old man over on a hunch.

"Excuse me, sir," Pace said in gutter Indonesian. "I have a question for you."

"I speak English, young man," the man said in lightly accented English. "I only have a moment."

"A moment's all I need, sir," Pace said in his own native tongue. "Are you delivering to that club down the street?"

The old man glanced over his shoulders. "I don't want any trouble."

"No trouble," Pace said in a soothing tone. "Was just curious if you wanted to make any extra money."

"Money?" the old man asked.

Pace reached into his pocket for his billfold and produced a wad of *rupiah*. "Whatever they're paying you, I'll double it."

The man eyed the ground. "Double of nothing is still nothing."

Pace's eyes narrowed. "I don't understand."

When the man met Pace's eyes, the ghosts were more apparent than before, their strength growing. "Two years ago…my daughter worked for my food store. I didn't want her to make the delivery. Told her I could handle it. She insisted she would be fine."

"Oh, no," Pace breathed. He knew where the story was going, but allowed the man to tell it.

"After she was gone for a day, I went to the police. The next day, the *preman* came to my store. Trashed the entire place. Told me to stop asking questions. Forced me to agree to free food on call in exchange for 'protection.'" His voice grew brittle. "Nine long months passed before I received a call from the National Police." The man sniffled and gathered his breath. "My Intan had been found in a cargo container at Tanjung Priok. She was malnourished. Injection sites all over her body. Heroin found in her system. Blood tested positive for syphilis and gonorrhea."

"Son of a bitch," Pace rasped.

"The police ruled her death a suicide. I knew better. But, I have another daughter at college. I have a wife. I cannot revolt against them. If giving their thugs free food means they will leave my family alone, then it is what I must do. Do you understand?"

Pace nodded slowly. "I understand, sir. What is your name?"

"Eka."

Pace offered him the entire cash roll. "Ninety thousand *rupiah*. It's yours. You won't have to do anything out of the ordinary."

Eka's brow furrowed. "What do you mean?"

"When you approach, I want you to tell me if you see a fuse box outside the building. Then, when you're inside, I want you to give me a rough estimate of how many *preman* are inside the building. That's all you have to do."

Eka looked Pace over. "You are a soldier."

"Yes," Pace said. Years of conditioning told him to correct Eka and inform him he was a *Marine*, but he knew it was neither the time nor the place.

"You will kill them?" Eka asked. The look in Pace's eyes answered the question. Eka nodded slowly. "I will do this for free."

"You've done enough for free, Eka," Pace said. "Allow me to compensate you."

"You are compensating me," Eka said. "You are delivering something the police refused to grant: justice for my Intan."

Pace slowly placed the cash wad back in his pocket. "If you reconsider, the money is yours."

Eka grabbed Pace by the shoulder. "My decision is final, young man." With a smile, Eka moved from cover, purpose in his step. Pace peeked out and watched him, then glanced around to check if there were any eyes on him. When he found none, his gaze returned to the clubhouse. Judging from the body language, Eka's greeting to the doormen was cheery. They granted him access, and Pace slipped back behind the food stand.

Pace dug into his pocket for a pack of Marlboro Reds inside of a zip-locked bag. Keeping his cigarettes water-proof was a habit he'd picked as a young lieutenant in command of a line rifle platoon. He'd brought a pack to the field, went to smoke one after a particularly grueling movement, only to find they were soaked and worthless. From that point on, Pace made a habit of saving the beverage bags to store his cigarettes and a lighter. Once he left the Corps, the beverage bags became standard sandwich bags.

A sad smile crossed Pace's face as he lit the cigarette and took a deep drag. *A simpler time.*

Pace continued to scan his surroundings. The awning and the food stand provided ample shadows for him to remain hidden. Activity in that section of the street was virtually non-existent. One could smell the cigarette smoke coming from the location, but the closest people to Pace's position were the front door sentries, and neither one of them seemed concerned with the smell.

Five minutes passed before Pace heard footsteps approaching from the direction of the bar. A moment later, Eka appeared under the awning, his hands free. He stepped in close to Pace and spoke conspiratorially.

"The fuse box is in the alley to the right of the front door," Eka said. "Inside, you've got about seven or eight men that I could see on the ground floor, as well as a half-dozen captive women for...*entertainment.*" Eka spat out the last word venomously, the grief in his eyes intensifying. After a deep breath, he continued. "There is a set of stairs that lead to a second floor, and I saw two on the landing. Beyond that, I didn't get a chance to see."

"That's okay," Pace said. "You did great." He produced the wad of *rupiah* and held it up for Eka. "It's yours."

Eka put his hands on top of Pace's and gently pushed the money back. "I'm fine. Even with these leeches, I have enough money to support my family. What I don't have is my daughter." Eka gave him a steely glint. "Teach them the cost of their actions."

"Yes, sir," Pace said with a dutiful nod.

Eka turned and marched down the street. Pace waited until he was out of sight, then reached into the messenger bag to retrieve an IMI Micro Uzi. The barrel was shrouded by a Knight's Armament sound suppressor. Attached to the suppressor via a clamp was a vertical foregrip. A rail had also been mounted just forward of the rear sight to allow the mounting of a Trijicon RMR reflex sight. Pace would have preferred a short-barreled M4 or an H&K MP7, but he had learned long ago to make do with what he had. The Micro Uzi would be more than adequate once he got inside the club.

Pace slipped his head and right arm through the Micro Uzi's one-point sling, locked out the folding stock, then tilted the weapon to the left and pulled the charging handle back just far enough to see the glint of brass in the chamber. He let the Micro Uzi dangle by its sling, dug into the messenger bag, and removed a night vision harness with a set of PVS-15s attached. Pace donned the headset, ensured the NODs were functional, then rotated them upward. He gripped the Micro Uzi with both hands, moved the selector switch to SEMI, and forced an exhale past his lips.

Here we go.

Pace rounded the corner, the Micro Uzi at the ready. He advanced on the target building at a brisk pace, his knees slightly bent and his footsteps faintly exaggerated outward. The pair of sentries at the front door stood under a light. Pace trained the RMR's red dot on the closest sentry's head and squeezed the trigger. A lone 9x19mm Parabellum hollow point raced through the suppressed barrel and made impact with the target's skull with a juicy *thwock.* As he collapsed, Pace shifted aim to the second target, who had just started to react. He fired another round, and the second guard joined his comrade on the pavement, blood and gray matter gushing from the massive exit wound.

When he reached the front door, Pace put another round in each man's face to confirm the kills, then turned back for the alley. He pied the corner, exposing only his dominant eye and the submachine gun's muzzle as he side-stepped to gradually clear dead space. Once he saw it was clear, Pace pressed forward.

The fuse box was secured with a solid padlock, but the door itself was flimsy. Pace dropped the Micro Uzi on its sling and plucked his Cold Steel Recon Tanto from his pocket. He flicked the blade open, wedged it between the housing and the door, then gave the handle a solid palm strike. The door ripped away from the lock housing with a *pop*, and Pace put the knife away.

"Lights out, motherfuckers," Pace said as he switched off every fuse on the panel.

With the building power's cut, Pace grabbed his Micro Uzi and jogged back to the corner. He peeked at the front door and found only the pair of dead bodies. Pace rushed forward, reaching in his bag for an M48 stun grenade. He dropped the Israeli submachine gun on its sling, primed the grenade, then held it with his off-hand while he reached for the door with the other. Pace could hear shouts on the other side of the door, more aggravated than alarmed.

Pace threw the door open, hurled the grenade in with a high lob, and slammed the door shut. He heard the *clink* of the spoon separating from the grenade body, then felt the shockwave of the grenade detonating through the door. Pace lowered his NODs, flicked them on, and threw the door open. He raced over the threshold, trained the red dot on the closest target, and tapped out three rounds in rapid succession. As the *preman* fell, Pace transitioned to another and fired again. The 9x19mm hollow points tore through the target's breastplate, shredding through vital respiratory and circulatory organs as they made their transit.

The sound of a shotgun pump being worked triggered instinctive action. Pace dove to his right as a 12 gauge slug cut through the air where he had been a moment earlier. He turned to his left, finding a barkeep with a sawed-off in both hands.

Pace trained his sights in the shotgunner's general direction and squeezed the trigger as fast as his finger would move. Lead tore through the barkeep's pelvis, abdomen, and chest. He tried to raise his shotgun and get another shot on Pace, but his body surrendered and he fell out of sight.

Pace remained on the ground and transitioned to the prone. A trio of *preman* had reached in their pockets for their smart phones, using the flashlight feature in an attempt to locate their attacker. Pace shot the one on the left, shifted and serviced the middle man, then shifted once more and put three rounds in the one on the right. He worked his way back, giving each man another controlled pair. All three hit the ground within seconds of each other.

There was movement to Pace's right. He immediately spun to face the threat, only to find a trembling captive in slinky clothing. Even through the night vision's lime green amplification, Pace could see that her makeup had become tear-streaked. Along the right-hand wall were three more sex slaves, squatting and huddling, their eyes fearfully locked on Pace. He lowered his muzzle a notch, then motioned with his support hand towards the door.

"Keluar! Pindah! Sekarang!" Pace barked. *Get out! Move! Now!*

The first girl made for the door. When the others saw her reach the entrance without interference from Pace, they bolted after her. Before they could escape, gunfire rang out. Pace shouldered his Micro Uzi and charged forward, making immediate target acquisition on a pair of pistol-wielding *preman*. Pace alternated back and forth as he expended the remainder of the magazine, shredding the gangsters' innards and felling them.

Pace suddenly found himself on his back, the air knocked out of him. The pain spread rapidly across his chest. *Fuck...caught it in the vest...*

Back on task. He pushed through the agony, dropped the empty Micro Uzi on its sling, and drew his MC Opera-tor 1911 from its appendix holster. He raised the pistol with both hands and scanned the upper landing. A single *preman* searched for Pace, a pistol stretched out in front of him. Pace lined up the low-profile tri-dot tritium sights, centered them on the shooter's chest, and cranked off four quick rounds. The gangster danced as the .45ACP hollow points ripped through him. He stumbled backwards a few steps and then fell out of sight.

"Goddamn it," Pace wheezed, rubbing his chest where the round had made impact with the Level IIIA soft armor beneath his shirt. He took a deep breath and forced an exhale past his lips with a snarl. "Get up, pussy."

Pace struggled to his feet, grabbed a spare 1911 magazine from his belt line, and replaced it with the partially spent one in the weapon. He stuffed the half-empty pistol magazine in his back pocket, then replaced the empty Uzi magazine with a fresh one from his messenger bag. Pace racked the charging handle to put the weapon in battery.

Doing his best to block out the throbbing chest pain, Pace shouldered his Micro Uzi and advanced on the stairs. He hand-railed the wall on the left, his aim trained at the bannister. When he reached the landing, Pace made his way across to the mouth of a corridor. He remained behind concealment as he took a knee. With a sharp exhale to steel himself, Pace leaned around the corner to find a *preman* at the end of the hall, one hand holding his smart phone up as a lantern and the other gripping a pistol. Pace put four rounds into the man's chest and checked his work through his sights.

When the man fell, Pace searched left and right. There were two doors on each side of the hallway. A target exposed his head and shooting hand to crank rounds down the corridor. Pace rewarded his gall with a pair of 9mm lead pills to the forehead. He continued to scan as he formulated a plan. The set up was bad for Pace, no matter how he cut it. If Tan, Bradshaw, or both had come along, they'd be able to establish security to keep from being blindsided.

Fuck it, Pace thought. *Always forward.*

Pace moved into the hallway, his back to the left wall and his muzzle trained on the first right-side door. As he approached the edge of the first left-side door, Pace's free hand dug into his bag for another flashbang. He brought it up to his shooting hand, looped his middle finger through the pull pin, and yanked it free of the body. Pace strode to the door, gave it a solid kick just to the side of the door-knob, and tossed the stun grenade in through the crack. There was a shout just before the grenade detonated.

With a growl, Pace rushed the door, entering to find a sex slave and a *preman* both clutching their ears as they fought through the grenade's effects. Pace trained his sights on the *preman* and cut him down with a quartet of rounds. As he moved around the bed to check on the girl, Pace heard footsteps behind him. He spun, dropped to a knee, and snap-aimed the Micro Uzi just in time to find another *preman* rushing in. Pace stitched him from groin to face as he fired until he saw the attacker hit the floor.

Pace rushed back to the door and leaned out. A third *preman* charged the hallway, the pistol in his hand barking as he sprayed rounds. Pace knelt, aimed, and pumped the rusher with five 9x19mm rounds. The hollow point lead pills ripped through lungs, heart, and spine, immediately cutting the strings from the human marionette. Pace transitioned his aim to the fallen man's head and put one more round in his face to finish the job.

Whimpering emanated from Pace's six o'clock, and he spun to the source. The captive girl sat on the ground, her arms wrapped around her legs, rocking back and forth as her lip tremored. Pace went to the fallen *preman*'s weapon, picked it up, and stuffed it in his messenger bag. He didn't think the young woman would be a threat, but he couldn't risk her being Stockholmed.

It took Pace 90 seconds to clear the remaining three rooms. He encountered no resistance and no additional slaves. Pace thought to go back and comfort the victim in the first room, but he dismissed the notion. She had just witnessed him murder her captors, whom had more than likely impressed upon her that the sight of a man meant abuse and torture. He had given her a chance to escape by killing her slave masters. The rest would be on her, and hopefully any family or professional counselors to whom she had access.

"Intan sends her regards," Pace said to the cadavers.

He made his way downstairs, stashed the Micro Uzi and NODs in the messenger bag, and briskly exited the club. It was only a matter of time before the Syndicate's friends came to investigate, and Pace wanted to be well clear of the area before that time.

A part of Pace had entered the club in the hopes that the dark feeling in his chest would have dissipated after a righteous massacre, but as the rain resumed soaking his hair, skin, and clothing, he realized the notion was for naught.

The slavers had been put down. For the liberated, the horrors were far from over.

CHAPTER FOURTEEN

Kebayoran Baru, South Jakarta, Indonesia
19 March 2019
04:10 hours Golf (18 March 21:10 hours Zulu)

The sound of Adele hitting high notes tore Kirsana Nirmala from her fitful slumber. She turned over in bed, snatched her Samsung smartphone off the bedside stand, and glanced at the screen. Her brow furrowed at the display. It was a blocked number.

Nirmala was tempted to silence the phone, write it off as a telemarketer, and return to sleep. It had been a long and unfruitful night of wading through Kuwat Syndicate-controlled territory in search of a lead on the people who had kidnapped Raja Wira. She had to be up in four hours for work. At the same time, many of her confidential sources utilized blocked numbers to obscure their connection with her. With many of the circles Nirmala covered, being linked to the press was potentially deadly.

A sigh fell from Nirmala's lips. She slid her thumb across the screen to accept the call and held the phone to her ear. "Yes?"

"It's me."

The voice compelled Nirmala to sit up straight. Sampurno Lanti was an officer with the West Java Regional Police's Criminal Detective Unit. He had been a reliable source of information for several years. She knew Lanti wouldn't reach out to her unless it was important.

"What's going on?" Nirmala asked as she rubbed the sleep from her eyes.

"Check the drop," Lanti said. "It's bad."

Before Nirmala could respond, Lanti terminated the connection. She stared at the screen as if her gaze would produce answers. After a moment, Nirmala set the phone down and swung out of bed. She grabbed a T-shirt off of the ground and slipped it over her exposed torso before making her way barefoot across the wooden floor. Once she was seated at her home workstation, Nirmala opened her HP laptop and powered it up.

Four minutes later, Nirmala was logged into a G-Mail account to which only she and Lanti had access. It was a simple and anonymous method of information exchange utilized worldwide by intelligence professionals and terrorists. She made her way to the draft folder and found a new message. It consisted of several photographs and a brief narrative:

Massive firefight south of Bagogog. At least 20 personnel killed. Number cannot be positively affirmed due to use of explosives. Compound was known Kuwat Syndicate training camp. 5.56mm and 7.62mm shell casings found throughout the crime scene, both near the camp proper and on a nearby overlooking hill. Volume of 5.56mm brass with presence of M27 links suggest employment of a machine gun, potentially an Army-issued Minimi.

Nirmala opened the first image. It was a professional crime scene photo that depicted a massive crater, charred with burnt human remains. She immediately began to retch, and bolted from her chair. Nirmala barely made it to the toilet in time to empty the meager contents of her evening meal. Her neck and temples strained from the physical effort required to vomit, and her throat burned from the stomach acid's passage.

When she was sure she was finished, Nirmala stood and rinsed her mouth out with sink water. She followed that by brushing her teeth to rid herself of the taste, then splashed several handfuls of water across her face. Nirmala stared in the mirror as she ran a damp hand over her nose and mouth.

"Get it together," she told herself quietly.

With a deep breath, Nirmala returned to the computer and perused the remainder of the photos. They were more of the same, providing a visual for Lanti's terse narrative. The longer she stared at the photos, the more she forgot she was viewing images taken in her homeland. Nirmala was no stranger to covering violent stories, but she had never covered a war.

Before she finished analyzing Lanti's information dump, her phone sounded off once more. Nirmala made her way back to the bed and glanced at the screen. It was a text from another contact, a street vendor that lived in Kuwat-controlled territory. A video file was attached to the SMS without a caption. She tapped the thumbnail and expanded it to full size as she made her way back to her desk. Her mouth locked open as she took a seat.

The video showed a blurry figure rushing the front door of an establishment, wielding some sort of suppressed automatic weapon. The man killed two guards at the front door, threw some sort of grenade over the threshold, then rushed inside. Gunshots erupted, followed by silence. Time passed, and a group of young women bolted out, their high-heels in hand. There were additional gunshots, then a long period of silence. Finally, the man reemerged, his weapons hidden, and he disappeared down the street. The distance was too far to get a clear glance at the man's face, and she doubted that digital enhancement would help.

"Holy shit," Nirmala breathed. Given the video's vantage point, she surmised the vendor had taken it from inside his home, above his shop. If memory served Nirmala well, the featured establishment was a nightclub and brothel run by the Kuwat Syndicate. She checked the time stamps in Lanti's crime scene photos and compared them to the one in the mobile video. Both incidents took place within an hour of each other.

Coordinated...

Nirmala brought up her contacts, sought out Max Santoso's number, and hit the green send button. She cradled the phone between her shoulder and ear as she reached for a pack of *kretek* cigarettes on the table's corner.

Santoso picked up after the second ringtone. "Kirsana, it's four in the morning," he said groggily. "This better be worth it."

"It is," Nirmala said. "Gonna have a new piece just in time for the morning print."

"Okay," Santoso said. His tone invited her to elaborate.

Nirmala lit a cigarette and took a deep drag. "A Kuwat training camp in West Java was hit just over an hour ago. It's estimated that at least 20 *preman* were killed in the attack."

Santoso let out a long sigh. "Was it an Army raid? That'd be pretty ballsy."

"I haven't seen any press releases, but I just got this lead. I haven't had time to develop it." She paused. "That's not all."

"No?"

"No. Less than 30 minutes later, a lone gunman attacked a *preman* nightclub in Kembangan. I've got video of him emerging with what appear to be several sex slaves being ushered from within."

"Holy hell," Santoso murmured.

"Yeah," Nirmala agreed.

Santoso clicked his tongue. "That's not the *preman* methodology. They'd roll in with force. Same with the Army, or the police if they dared to bite the hand that feeds them."

"Right. They'd *definitely* not free the sex slaves, either. Either they'd claim them for themselves, or they'd murder them for violating Sharia chastity laws."

"That doesn't leave us with many plausible options."

Nirmala took a deep breath, preparing herself for a rebuke. "I have a possible theory."

"Oh?"

She quickly added a disclaimer. "Nothing firm to run in print, but something to keep in mind as the story develops."

"Kirsana, I know you well enough to know you won't go flying off the handle like an American internet blogger," Santoso said. "Give it to me."

Nirmala sighed, then accessed her browser's bookmarks page. As she pulled up the links, she said, "It goes back to the masked men in Warakas. I reflected on it after the Batavia incident. Both times, the people aiming to disrupt Syndicate operations conducted themselves in a professional manner."

"A professional manner?"

"Employing violence only when necessary. Avoiding civilians in the crossfire."

"They killed two members of the Regional Police," Santoso said. "I wouldn't call that discriminatory."

"Neither did I, at first," Nirmala said. "That's before I did some digging. In Warakas, those officers belonged to the Regional Brimob's Pelopor Regiment, Detachment C. A source of mine at the national *Propam* says that Detachment C has been under investigation for the better part of the past year."

Santoso grunted at the nickname for the Bureau of Internal Profession and Security, the National Police's accountability division. "Let me guess. They suspected them of being Suparman Guntur's paramilitary vanguard, but they can't prove it."

"Not for lack of trying," Nirmala said. "Several members of the unit had financial discrepancies. *Propam* kept digging, presented their findings, and wanted to do a sweep to see if they could flip anybody for something juicier. Orders from on high are to let the investigation die, and from the way it sounds, it was external pressure. Political."

"Okay," Santoso said. "You've convinced me. The mystery men are good guys and professionals. At the same time, they're not state actors. They don't care about the money or the product. They don't care about collecting evidence." He paused as he made the connection. "This is personal."

"Exactly," Nirmala said. "But the theory gets deeper."

"Tell me more."

Nirmala shifted the phone from her right hand to her left. "I figured that whoever these guys are, they didn't start here. At first, I started a search throughout Indonesia for any series of violent events that seemed professional and was targeted at the *preman* groups."

"And you came up empty," Santoso said.

"Yes," Nirmala said. "So, I expanded the search to southeast Asia. Starts with the Qizhongji Triad in Manila, October of 2017. Over the span of two weeks, 47 Triad associates were murdered in what was attributed to criminal warfare. The assailants remain unidentified. Philippine Red Cross also reports a spike of sex slaves seeking assistance after liberation from captivity."

"How was this not bigger news?" Santoso asked, his voice disbelieving.

"Another Triad moved in and picked up where the last left off," Nirmala said. "It was all for naught."

"What else?"

"Myanmar, February 2018. A human trafficking group based out of Myitkyina was dismantled after a week-long series of violent exchanges between them and unknown interlopers. During that week, 31 members of that group were gunned down."

The sound of Santoso scratching his chin carried over the line. "How many other incidents have you been able to ascertain as potentially linked?"

"Matching the methodology? Twenty incidents. If all of them are linked, this group is responsible for killing over 500 criminals over the past 18 months."

"God…" Santoso let out a low whistle.

Nirmala kept the phone pressed to her ear as she made her way to the kitchen. "The most recent one before now? A few weeks ago, a warehouse exploded and was initially believed to have caused 40 deaths. Additional forensics determined that some of the bodies showed signs of being deceased *prior* to the explosion. Gunshot wounds, mostly.

One was garroted. The warehouse was connected to a *chao pho* group known for opium production and smuggling of methamphetamine precursors out of China and throughout the region."

"Okay…"

"The kicker?" Nirmala filled a kettle with water and set it on her electric stove. "One of the *chao pho*'s clients is believed to be the Kuwat Syndicate."

"Wow…"

"Mmm-hmm." Nirmala paused a beat. "Apparently, the underworld has a name for these vigilantes: Shadow Wraiths."

"Shadow Wraiths?"

"Yes. Some believe they're some sort of secret army. Others believe they're a handful of vigilantes, former soldiers with special training. Nobody's been able to make a positive ID, but there's enough whispers, both here and abroad, that I can't dismiss it as superstition or hearsay."

"Okay, you're onto something," Santoso said. "I'm sold."

"Yeah, but it's all circumstantial," Nirmala said. "It's reasonable suspicion, not probable cause."

"Agreed. Run what you've got confirmed and keep working this angle up. You said you can crank this out before the morning deadline?"

"I can." Nirmala grabbed a box of tea bags and set them on the counter. "I'd like to work from home, though. I've slept like shit."

"That's fine," Santoso said. "Finish the article, then get some rest. Keep me in the loop."

"Thank you," Nirmala said. "I'll get back to you."

* * *

Bekasi, West Java, Indonesia
19 March 2019
06:00 hours Golf (18 March 23:00 hours Zulu)

IN THE JAPANESE martial arts, Suparman Guntur's morning routine would be known as a *kata*. There was not an equivalent term in Guntur's chosen style of *pencak silat*, but he liked having a term for it, so that was what he called it. Without fail, every morning, Guntur would saunter down to the beach, more often than not clad only in a pair of gray drawstring pants. He would stand on the beach, his arms at his side, the sand between his toes, taking deep breaths of the crisp sea air. In losing himself in his surroundings, Guntur filtered out the concerns of the temporal plane and found balance.

Once centered, the *kata* began. Its purpose was not power. That would come later, during his time on the heavy bag. The intent was to perfect one's form. Speed came from good form, and power came from speed. Even master practitioners religiously rehearsed their *katas* in order to reconnect with the fundamentals.

Guntur's daily *katas* were the recipe to his proficiency in the martial art. As a young man on the receiving end of savage physical persecution, Guntur had sought refuge in a school library, where he picked up a book that detailed the principals of *pencak silat*. Guntur taught himself the martial art, taking to heart the necessary meticulousness of the *katas*.

The bullied became the predator, exacting revenge on those who visited harm upon him and his younger brother, Elang Kadek. His skill grew to where he participated in cage fights. The thrill of physical combat and the unbridled release of pent-up rage kept him coming back for more, and the supplemental income was added incentive. Guntur's name was still murmured in the fight circuit with fear and reverence, as he had never tasted defeat in the chain-linked square.

It was those fights that had brought him to the attention of the Kuwat Syndicate, which became a home for Elang and him.

Guntur heard footsteps approaching from the rear. He kept his attention forward. There was only one man who would dare to interrupt him during the *kata,* and he would only do so if it were critical.

"What is it, Sharif?" Guntur said. He didn't break stride as he launched from a crawling tiger stance into a crisp rear snap kick.

"It's the Shadow Wraiths," Aditya said, his hands clasped at his waist. "They killed everybody at the training camp and the clubhouse."

Guntur let out a shuddering sigh as he ran through a circuit of hand strikes and blocks. "How many did we lose?"

"Thirty-six. Our man in the police can't make positive identification on a lot of them at the camp. It seems they lured our men into an explosives-based ambush."

"I see," Guntur said. He switched to a right-foot-forward side stance and lashed out with a snap kick. As he transitioned into his hand strikes, he said, "It changes nothing. Are the men ready for the run tonight?"

"They're ready," Aditya said.

"Good," Guntur said. He alternated punches. "Make the video graphic. We will manipulate their rage and their self-righteousness."

"Of course," Aditya said. He offered a small bow, then turned and marched back to the house.

Guntur's *kata* continued to accelerate. Grunts fell from his lips with every imagined blow. Finally, when he reached the end of the *kata,* Guntur lashed out with a right-cross as his mouth locked open to make way for a blood-curdling scream. When he finished, he remained in forward pose, his trembling fist locked out in front of him, breathing heavily through his clenched teeth. His eyes were wide and laced with fury.

* * *

Cengkareng, West Jakarta, Indonesia
19 March 2019
07:43 hours Golf (00:43 hours Zulu)

PACE PARKED THE maroon Toyota Rush in front of the riverfront safe house. The first thing he saw was a matching vehicle parked out front. A grimace crossed his face as he undid the seatbelt, the motion rubbing against his bruised chest. Pace grabbed his messenger bag and grunted with exertion as he climbed out of the vehicle. The rain had subsided, but the pavement was still slick with precipitation. Pace heard his footsteps splash as he made his way inside.

Just outside the common area, Pace found Bradshaw and Tan seated at a folding table. The Minimi was disassembled into its major groups. Tan ran a bore snake through the barrel, while Bradshaw worked a cotton swab into the receiver's nooks and crannies in search of carbon build-up. Tan's Samsung smart phone was connected to a portable Bluetooth speaker, and Johnny Cash's "The Man Comes Around" filled the room, growing in crescendo as Pace approached.

Bradshaw looked up from the weapon component to greet Pace, his hand continuing to clean. "Good to see you made it back."

Pace nodded, then looked to Tan. "Didn't know you liked country, Lucas."

Tan shrugged. "I don't, really. But, I ran through my GARNiDELiA list and he managed to only scowl in silence, so I figured it was only fair he gets to pick the next playlist."

"Nobody beats the Man in Black," Bradshaw said. "Though, I'm also down with some Kristofferson, some Willie, some Waylan, some Merle…"

"Outlaw country," Pace said.

"Outside that subgenre, George Strait is king, and I'm down with some Garth Brooks. The old school." Bradshaw returned his gaze to the task at hand. "Just spare me the Florida Georgia Line, Luke Bryan, Jason Aldean bullshit. That's just empty pop garbage with a Southern accent."

"I don't disagree," Pace said. "Mold-breakers. After that, it all kinda goes downhill." He folded his arms. "Same with rap. Started off as party music, became an outlet to air political grievances and give outsiders a glimpse inside hood life, and now it's mumbling and pill-popping." He shook his head ruefully. "It's a goddamn shame."

Bradshaw nodded slowly. In days past, he would have vehemently argued that rap was repetitive and glorified negative stereotypes. His best friend, Logan Fox, had once famously refuted that point during their first deployment to Iraq.

The time spent with Gabriela Rivera further broadened his horizons. He wouldn't drop money on a Jay-Z album anytime soon, but he did acknowledge there was more skill and diversity within the rap genre than he'd initially credited.

Gabby... Bradshaw exhaled and changed the subject. "How'd the hit go?"

"Could've gone better," Pace said. He winced as he removed his messenger bag and set it on the table. "Took one to the vest."

Both Bradshaw and Tan put down their work and wiped as much carbon off their hands as they could. Tan killed the music and rose from his chair, following Bradshaw over to Pace.

"You good?" Tan asked.

Pace held up his hand. "Yeah, I checked on the way back. Didn't over-penetrate. Bruised like a motherfucker, though." He poked a finger in the hole where the bullet had ripped past his shirt, then unbuttoned it and shrugged out of it. Pace removed the soft armor, grunting as he lifted it over his head, then set it on the table. Embedded inside of the Kevlar was a smashed bullet. Pace removed it and held it up.

"That looks like 9mm," Bradshaw said as he squinted.

"Probably," Pace said. "Thank God for DuPont."

"Yeah," Tan said. "Good thing we got extras from Milena."

"Yeah." Pace pulled his undershirt over his head, suppressing a grunt. A dark circle over the diaphragm marked where the bullet would have achieved penetration were it not for the vest. An immediate yellow ring encircled the mark, and gradually transitioned into shades of red, purple, and dark blue. The rings overlapped with the front of Pace's ribs and extended down to a couple inches above his navel.

Bradshaw and Tan cringed in unison. It wasn't the first time either one had seen the end-result of body armor doing its job, but it still wasn't pleasing to the eye.

"I'll get some ice," Tan said.

"Get me some Ranger candy, too," Pace called after him.

"How are your ribs?" Bradshaw asked.

"Probably better than yours," Pace said. "I can breathe all right. Just hurts to bend over or stretch, or do anything other than stand up straight or lay down. I'll ice and medicate it, take it easy during the day today. Tonight, we're right back at it."

Bradshaw nodded slowly. "Well, all things considered, guess you're lucky. The odds were against you walking out of that clubhouse alive."

"I had a little help," Pace said. "And they didn't have night vision."

"Fair point."

Tan returned with a bag of ice, a roll of ACE wrap, and a bottle of ibuprofen. Pace accepted the painkillers and cracked the bottle open as Tan applied the bag of ice to Pace's chest with a gentle touch. Pace winced at the contact but did not verbalize his discomfort. Tan looked to Bradshaw.

"Help me wrap him up," he said.

Bradshaw stepped in and accepted the wrap. Tan held the ice in place as Bradshaw layered the ACE wrap around the bag, cinching it tight enough to prevent movement but not so tight as to cause Pace undue distress. Pace held his arms up, pouring 3,200 milligrams of ibuprofen into his palm and pouring them down his throat without a chaser. Neither Bradshaw nor Tan blinked at the high dosage. Both men understood first-hand the practice of abusing ibuprofen to take the edge off of injuries and remain operational.

As he neared the end of the wrap, Bradshaw cinched it in place with a medical pin. "There. You're good."

"Thanks," Pace said. "Got some water?"

Tan produced a bottle from his cargo pocket and handed it to Pace. "Got you covered."

Pace gave Tan a thin-lipped smile. "Thanks, pal."

"Rah," Tan said.

Bradshaw folded his arms as he said, "So, I've been thinking."

"What have you been thinking, Jack?" Pace asked.

"How do we plan on getting the girls off the X?"

Pace and Tan exchanged a look, then looked to Bradshaw. "We're not getting them off the X," Pace said finally.

Bradshaw blinked, then edged his head forward. "Come again?"

"We don't have the resources to get them to safety, beyond ushering them out of the building," Tan explained. "We also lack the training and logistics to deprogram them and integrate them back into society. To put it bluntly, that's somebody else's problem."

"All we can do is kill the slavers," Pace said. "The rest is on somebody else."

Bradshaw's countenance darkened. "What's stopping the Syndicate from scooping them back up and taking our actions out on them? Or some other group from picking them up and tricking them out?"

"Nothing," Pace said flatly. He sighed. "Look, Jack. We're doing what we can, but we're working within the confines of reality. We're not a proper NGO. That brings advantages and disadvantages. We move lighter and in places NGOs can't go, but that means we can't really do much for the girls."

"Then what the fuck are we doing here?" Bradshaw asked.

"We make trafficking deadly," Pace said. "We make the slavers look over their shoulders. We keep hitting them. Take the slavers out of circulation permanently."

"Sounds like a giant game of Whack-A-Mole to me."

Pace stuck his hands in his pockets and arched his eyebrows. "You should be used to that, Jack. You played Washington's version over in the sandbox. Messy half-solutions should be right in your wheelhouse. Otherwise, I wonder how you lasted as long as you did in the Regiment."

Bradshaw dropped his head and inhaled deep through his nose. "Fair point."

"All right," Pace said. "Lemme get a shirt. We need to refit and rest. Got a long night ahead of us."

CHAPTER FIFTEEN

Senen, Central Jakarta, Indonesia
20 March 2019
02:55 hours Golf (19 March 19:55 hours Zulu)

Lucas Tan reached into the admin pouch on his Haley Strategic D3CR Heavy chest rig and removed a pack of caffeine pills. He ripped the packaging open, popped the pills in his mouth, and washed them down with water from his Camelbak. Were he shooting at distance, Tan would be concerned that the caffeine would induce trembling. However, it was only 16 meters from his position to the closer end of the target building. Tan had reduced the Leupold scope's magnification to its lowest setting, and he was still relying on his off-glass eye to spot the targets. At that range, the only way Tan could miss was with intent.

He had been in position on the rooftop for the past eight hours. Tan had gone ahead of Pace and Bradshaw, surveilling the neighborhood from behind the wheel of the Toyota Rush. He then parked his vehicle about a kilometer from his selected LP/OP and made his way to the site on foot.

Tan had climbed a 10-foot concrete wall on the back end of the residence he had selected to establish vertical dominance. When nothing had greeted him, Tan had made his way to a drainpipe on the building's right side and began to scale it. The ascent would have been a breeze were it not for his kit, the SR25 sniper rifle in a soft case on his back, and the portions of the pipe still damp with rainwater. Still, Tan managed the climb in a not-too-shabby five minutes.

Once he was on the roof, Tan had crawled to the edge, then slipped the case off of his back and got set up. He was covered in a burlap net to break up his outline. Some of the burlap had also been applied to the rifle, particularly around its sound suppressor, which was flush with the roof's edge. From there, Tan had situated his optics and opened an observation log. Every 15 minutes, he would radio his findings to Bradshaw and Pace.

After the first five minutes on glass, the greatest enemy became complacency. Inactivity presented the temptation of zoning out. As the advance element, it was Tan's job to let Bradshaw and Pace know what to expect once they were on-site. To combat the boredom, he fell into the habit of imagining what his targets were thinking or saying, or tracing patterns between targets as he scanned.

Tan's earpiece crackled, and his body stiffened as Pace's voice filled his ear. "Lionheart, this is Rusty."

Tan keyed his PTT. "Go, Rusty."

"I pass Kiltlifter," Pace said.

"Roger," Tan said. "I copy Kiltlifter. What's your ETA?"

"Five mikes."

"Roger. Lionheart, out."

Tan took a deep breath to keep his pulse under control. "Kiltlifter" was the phase line that indicated Bradshaw and Pace had disembarked and were moving to the objective on foot. The wait was coming to an end. The terrain looked brand new again to Tan as he began assessing targets.

Four minutes later, the radio crackled again. "Lionheart, Rusty."

"Go."

"We're 60 seconds out," Pace said. "Approaching from the east. Gimme a SITREP."

"Roger," Tan said. "You've got a couple on the ground level, outside the left door. No rovers on the streets. One on the rooftop. Still no sign of comms checks."

"Roger," Pace said. "Solid copy. Boy Scout and I will take the ones on the ground. Take the rooftop sentry. We'll advise when we're in position. You'll initiate."

"Roger," Tan said. He resisted the urge to glance to his left to check his teammates' progress. Instead, he centered the Leupold's reticle on the lone man standing on the roof. It was a straight 50-meter shot. Through the 3x magnification, Tan could clearly make out the man's facial features. The sentry was young, short, and thin, with wispy hairs that constituted a pale imitation of a mustache. Tan watched the man make love to his *kretek* cigarette, the cherry a glowing orb through the AN/PVS-22 mounted forward of the Leupold. As he watched, he slowly rotated the SR25's selector switch from SAFE to FIRE.

Tan found himself wishing that the rains would return. It was a clear and dry night, which was better for laying out in the open but worse for sound concealment. None of the windows or glass doors were open. They appeared to be locked in place with dense steel bars, and the glass looked thick enough that it might obscure the sound of the gunshot. Still, solid rains would have been an immense aid to noise discipline, and a lightning storm even more so.

If wishes were fishes…

"Lionheart, Rusty," Pace said, cutting through Tan's reverie. "On site."

"Roger," Tan said. He took a deep breath in, slipped his finger inside of the trigger well, and pulled the trigger straight back as he started to exhale. The sniper rifle bucked against Tan's shoulder, and his sight picture shook. Tan caught the movement of the rooftop sentry falling. He couldn't hear Pace's and Bradshaw's shots over the shrill *crack* of his suppressed 7.62x51mm round making its passage.

Tan scanned the windows and doors, starting at the third story and working his way to the ground floor. As he reached the bottom, he spotted the doorway sentries sprawled on the asphalt, blood pooling from their heads. He caught a glimpse of Bradshaw and Pace moving towards the door. Both men wore their night vision mounted to ACH-style helmets, as well as D3CR Micro chest rigs over their Osprey body armor, which they wore over black knit long-sleeved shirts. War belts, jeans, and combat boots constituted the remainder of their uniform.

Tan breathed a sigh of relief at seeing his teammates, then worked his way back up to the roof. When he came up empty, he reached for his PTT.

"Rusty, Lionheart. You're clear."

PACE KEYED HIS PTT. "Solid copy, Lionheart. We're going in." He stepped out from cover, reached down, and grabbed Bradshaw by his chest rig. Pace pulled up, which was Bradshaw's signal to rise to his feet and move forward. Bradshaw took up the left side while Pace moved to the right. Both men advanced towards the sheet metal door. When they arrived, Bradshaw dropped to a knee, lowered his suppressed Micro Uzi's muzzle, and reached for the doorknob with his support hand. Pace remained out of the fatal funnel, his muzzle trained at the doorjamb. The two men met eyes, then shared a nod.

Bradshaw twisted the knob, pushed the door open, and raised his Micro Uzi. Pace traversed his muzzle left to right, up and down.

"Got a hallway, right," Bradshaw murmured.

"Stairwell, straight ahead," Pace said.

"How do you wanna play it?" Bradshaw asked.

"Clear it floor-by-floor," Pace said. "Take our time, keep it quiet. Locate the girls, scatter them to the four winds, kill anyone else we find."

"Tracking," Bradshaw said.

"Cover the stairwell," Pace said. "I'll take point."

Bradshaw shifted his point of aim to the stairwell. Pace button-hooked into the hallway, took up real estate in the middle, and walked slowly. Once Pace was committed, Bradshaw made entry, keeping his Micro Uzi trained on the stairwell until he was in the hallway.

At that point, Bradshaw picked up rear security. He moved by taking a large step back with his strong side leg, sliding his support leg backwards until he had resumed his natural shooting stance, and repeating the process. That ensured stability that would have been absent had he simply walked backwards.

The temptation to rush was strong. Pace and Bradshaw had enough close quarter battle experience to know they were in a nightmare scenario. One look at the target building made it clear that hallways and stairwells would be in play. Their only cover were their submachine gun muzzles, and that would only come in 30-round intervals. At the same time, they knew to work with what they had on-hand, and that rushing with their vastly inferior numbers increased their likelihood of being cut down in a blaze of lead. Thus, they each took up a 180° sector and moved with deliberation.

"Door left," Pace said, just loud enough for Bradshaw to hear. He stopped just short of the door and waited. Bradshaw took a step to his left and continued to walk backwards. Once he was clear of the door, he lowered his muzzle and moved to the opposite side. Bradshaw's gaze flickered down the hall one more time as Pace took a knee and grabbed the doorknob. They met eyes, exchanged nods, and Pace threw the door open.

Bradshaw rushed inside and to the left while Pace broke right. When they saw the room was dark, they lowered and powered on their NODs. The PVS-15s amplified the low ambient light, which enabled them to search their respective sectors through their red dot sights. The room was lined with cheap metal racks full of cleaning materials. Vacuums, buffers, and other tools cluttered the middle. Bradshaw glanced back to Pace and flashed him a thumbs-up. When the gesture was returned, both men returned to the doorway. They raised their night vision from their eyes as they reentered the hallway.

There were two more rooms on the ground floor, both of them storage. The second room had bedsheets, pillows, and toiletries. Contraceptives and sex toys made up the third. As they left the last room and continued to the end of the hallway, Pace keyed up his radio.

"Lionheart, Rusty."

"Go," Tan replied.

"Ground floor's clear," Pace said. "Bunch of storage rooms. Ascending west stairwell to the second floor."

"Roger that. You're clear out here. Stay frosty, gents."

"Always."

Pace led the way to the corner and held his position. Bradshaw took a couple more steps, turned and stacked on Pace, and put his hand on Pace's shoulder. When he felt Bradshaw squeeze, Pace rounded the corner, moved to the right side of the stairwell, and trained his Micro Uzi above the bannister. Bradshaw took up the left side and kept his muzzle trained straight ahead. They proceeded slowly up the steps. When they reached the midpoint landing, Bradshaw spun and continued to aim straight ahead, while Pace went wide to cover the left side.

Bradshaw and Pace stopped short of the top stairwell. Pace waved to Bradshaw to get his attention, pointed to him with two fingers, brought the fingers towards his own eyes, and then gestured over his shoulder with his thumb. Bradshaw nodded, then moved to the corner and took a knee, with Pace taking a step back to give him space. He let the Micro Uzi hang by its sling, reached into his chest rig's admin pouch, and removed a telescopic inspection mirror. Bradshaw put his back to the wall and edged as close to the corner as he could while remaining hidden. He extended the mirror's pole, locked it at a 90° angle, and then slowly edged it around the corner.

The hallway's setup was the same as the ground floor, with the exception of doors that presumably led to rooms on the north side of the hall where there had been cargo doors on the ground floor. Bradshaw spotted one sentry walking towards the east end of the hall, a rifle held at the low ready. A second was posted at the hallway's midpoint, his face focused on the smart phone in his hand.

Bradshaw brought the mirror back behind cover, collapsed it, and put it away. When his submachine gun was back at the ready, he reached back, tapped Pace's leg, and made eye contact. Bradshaw held his left hand upside down with his thumb and index finger extended, making the hand signal for "enemy spotted." He then pointed down the hallways to indicate their direction, and held up two fingers. Pace acknowledged with a curt nod, then gestured with his head towards the hallway.

A moment later, Bradshaw entered the corridor, his Micro Uzi shouldered and the RMR's red dot trained on the roving sentry's back. Pace moved to the left side of the corridor and filled his sight picture with the stationary sentry. Bradshaw waited until he was within five meters of the moving target, then tapped out a four-round burst that ripped through his target's spine. As soon as Bradshaw fired, Pace opened up on his target with two rounds at center mass, then shifted his aim a notch upward and drilled a third round through the *preman*'s skull. Bradshaw's target fell forward, while Pace's slid into a slumped, seated position, a blood streak along the wall marking his descent.

Pace immediately spun around to cover their rear, while Bradshaw froze in place and scanned for emerging threats. They stood and searched for 15 seconds before Bradshaw broke the silence.

"We gonna search these rooms?"

Pace pushed an exhale past his pursed lips. "Limited penetration. Silent and quick. We see something of interest, make entry and clear. We see nothing, we move on."

Bradshaw nodded. "On you."

Pace led the way back to the first door. He took up real estate on the far side, while Bradshaw stacked opposite of him. Pace reached for the knob, threw the door open, and trained his weapon on the right side of the room. Bradshaw aimed left, and both slipped inside the room and just offset of the fatal funnel.

If it weren't for their training and experience, what they witnessed would have brought them to their knees and emptied their stomachs.

A series of lights encased in metal shrouds provided just enough illumination to render NODs unnecessary, but were dim enough that Bradshaw's and Pace's eyes required adjustment. The first thing that struck both men was the stench. It was a repugnant fusion of feces, urine, and rotting flesh. There were crudely constructed triple bunk-beds that lined both sides of the room. In front of each bunk were a trio of large clay pots. Neither Bradshaw nor Pace could see a lavatory within the room, which led to the surmise that the vessels were chamber pots.

Heads poked out from the bunks, their eyes wide with fear. Their gazes jetted back and forth between the pair of foreign interlopers and something in the room's center. Bradshaw and Pace couldn't see what the object was, so they lowered their muzzles and advanced with trepidation, their heads remaining on a swivel as they proceeded further.

Bradshaw was the first to see what the room's center held in store. He saw bare feet, and his heart plunged into his stomach. Bradshaw clenched his jaw and closed on the person. As he turned towards the body's front, he lost all the color in his face. A moment later, Pace spotted the same, and his mouth locked open in shock and disgust.

The girl was stripped naked. There was no rise or fall to her chest. Her wrists were bound by handcuffs, and in turn those handcuffs were looped around a hook, suspending her six inches off of the ground. Dried blood streaked from her wrists where the restraints broke skin, as well as down her face and body. Bradshaw couldn't see an inch of her that wasn't tarnished by blood, bruises, or open welts.

Both Bradshaw and Pace instinctively made the sign of the cross, and Pace murmured, "Dear God in Heaven." Bradshaw's attention remained on the girl. He took a step closer and studied her face. Her left eye socket was swollen shut and her lips were chapped, but there was enough of her face unswollen for Bradshaw to recognize her.

"Citra…"

Pace looked at Bradshaw. "You know this girl." It wasn't a question.

"Yeah," Bradshaw said quietly as his eyes took in the room's every detail and subconsciously stored it for future nightmares. He closed his mouth, cleared his throat, and said, "Yeah. I know her. Suparman's kid brother tried to snatch her. I killed him for it." Bradshaw clenched his jaw and a heavy breath fell from his nostrils. "Looks like he caught up with her."

Pace put a hand on Bradshaw's shoulder. "We need to go."

"Not before we get her down," Bradshaw said as he slung his Micro Uzi. "I'm not leaving her like this."

Pace knew that it was a tactical error to divert from the mission, and also knew that certain things superseded tactical sense. He stepped back towards the door and kept his weapon at the low ready. "Make it quick, Boy Scout."

Bradshaw moved to Citra's body, took a half-squat, and wrapped his arms around her waist. He hefted until he heard the handcuff chain slide off of the ceiling hook. Her arms remained locked above her head. Bradshaw's forensics knowledge was limited, but he recalled reading that rigor mortis set in a few hours after death and lasted a couple of days, which provided him a rough time frame as to when Citra had passed. There was no telling how long she'd been tortured prior to that point. Rage boiled within Bradshaw's chest, clashed with his wave of sorrow, and threatened to overtake him. It took several deep breaths to keep the wrath in check.

There will be a time, he told himself. *There will be a place. Now is neither.*

With Citra's corpse in his arms, Bradshaw carried her over to an empty bed, lowered himself to a knee, and laid her down on the right side. He yanked the left side of the sheets downward, then hefted Citra and set her down on the other side. Bradshaw covered her body with reverence. He made the sign of the cross once more, then did something he hadn't done in a long time.

"Lord," he said quietly, "Citra was likely not one of Your faithful. She wasn't administered the Last Rites. She was still one of Your children. Watch over her as she travels to the next world, Lord."

Bradshaw closed his eyes, hung his head, then looked at Citra's outline beneath the blanket. His next words were directed at her.

"I'm sorry."

CHAPTER SIXTEEN

Senen, Central Jakarta, Indonesia
20 March 2019
03:10 hours Golf (19 March 20:10 hours Zulu)

Pace looked over his shoulder. "Hey, Boy Scout," he said. "We need to roll."

Bradshaw rose from where he'd laid Citra, cleared his throat, and grabbed his Micro Uzi's pistol grip with his strong hand. The sorrow had subsided entirely to make way for his tightly controlled rage, which was etched into every line in his face. He rejoined Pace at the middle of the bay.

"I'm ready," Bradshaw said.

Pace nodded, then switched his tongue to rudimentary Indonesian. "We are not here to harm you. You are liberated. Quietly walk down the stairs and out of this building. Outside, walk right from where you face and keep walking until you find *Kramat Raya* Road. From there, take a left and walk about half a kilometer. You will find a police station. Tell them what happened. You will be safe." *Hopefully,* he didn't add.

The girls quickly gathered their meager possessions and scurried into the hallway. Bradshaw counted 20 of them. He looked to Pace and said in English, "Hope that precinct isn't under Suparman's control."

"I'm banking on Guntur knowing when to cut his losses," Pace said. "A drove of malnourished young women is bound to attract attention, and attention attracts the press. Not a guarantee they'll be safe, but it's all we can do."

"Yeah," Bradshaw said. "Better than nothing."

Pace reached for his PTT. "Lionheart, Rusty."

"Go," Tan said on the net.

"How we looking out there?"

"All clear on the southern front."

Pace nodded and said, "You've got about 20 girls on their way out now. We're gonna keep sweeping the objective."

"Roger that," Tan said.

After the girls cleared out, Bradshaw stacked on Pace, who led them into the hallway with the squeeze of a shoulder. They moved across the hall to the second room, made limited penetration, and found another 18 girls. Pace repeated his speech, ushered the liberated sex slaves out of the room, and reported the progress to Tan. The next two rooms in the hall were a repeat of the first two, with another 42 freed captives joining the initial 38.

The final room on the left only served to add to the fury. That room was full of cages, just tall enough for an average-height Indonesian adult female to squat or sit. There were three girls locked inside of cages, rooting in their own waste matter. There was a table in the center of the room. Upon that table were whips, chains, cat o' nine tails, and various other instruments of pain. In that chamber, their purpose was singular: forced compliance.

Bradshaw marched to the nearest occupied cage. "Move back," he said in Indonesian. "I am going to break this lock." The girl scooted to the rear of her cage. Bradshaw grabbed his Micro Uzi by the muzzle and the folding stock, reversed it, and struck it against the lock. On the fifth strike, the shackle broke from the body. He knelt, ripped the broken lock free, and opened the cage.

"You need to go," Bradshaw said. "There are others at the bottom of the stairs. Follow them. You'll be safe. Go!"

The girl did not move at first. Bradshaw backed well out of reach, then gestured towards the door. "C'mon! You've got to go!"

Only when the girl thought she was safe did she scramble out of the cage. She could not stand up straight and only managed to move at a quick hobble, but she made her way to the door and out of sight. In that time, Pace had liberated the other two, who joined Bradshaw's liberated charge at the door.

"We're burning candlelight," Pace said. "C'mon. One more door."

Bradshaw and Pace moved across the hallway. The door was locked. Pace dug his Micro Uzi's suppressor hard against the wood to the right of the doorknob, then pulled the trigger twice. With the locking mechanism ruined, all it took was a boot to the door to throw it open. Pace and Bradshaw entered the room, and for the second time in the past few minutes, both of them lowered their weapons and took in their surroundings. That time, though, it was astonishment and not horror that had gripped them.

There were five 3'x3' pallets in the middle of the room. Each of them was stacked five feet high with legal tender. As Bradshaw circled around the right side of the pallets, the most remarkable thing he noticed was that there wasn't a single *rupiah* in sight. The majority of it were American greenbacks and various-colored Euros, along with a respectable amount of what appeared to be Chinese *yuan* and Japanese *yen.*

"Well, well," Bradshaw said in a quiet voice. "Looks like we found one end of their money train."

Pace looked to the nearest wall, where he found a folding table, chairs, and several bill counters. He pointed to the table and said, "Looks like they count it by currency and denomination, store it here, and likely pick it up and move it to a central location. More than likely a Syndicate-owned cash-only business to turn it into reportable income and keep them seemingly above-board."

"Yeah," Bradshaw said. He scowled at the American tender. "I get that the dollar's the world reserve currency, but I have a feeling that's not why we're seeing so many Benjamins."

"Traveling to southeast Asia to take advantage of the lax protections against sex slavery is popular amongst affluent American pedophiles," Pace said. "You hear more about this kind of thing in Thailand or the Philippines, but it's not non-existent in Indonesia."

"Motherfuckers," Bradshaw rasped. His eyes drifted beyond the pallets and spotted several empty duffel bags strewn about the floor. The gears in his mind started turning, and the scowl on his face turned into a wicked grin. He looked to Pace and said, "How'd you like to really piss Suparman off?"

"I'm listening," Pace said.

"This is easily several million dollars in currency," Bradshaw said.

Pace pointed to the nearest pallet full of American dollars. "This one right here is probably a couple mil alone…three of those. The ones with Euros are equally as valuable."

Bradshaw walked over to the duffel bags, grabbed two of them, and returned to Pace. He extended one of the bags. "Let's load these up."

It was Pace's turn to scowl. "You're thinking of looting? After what we've just seen?"

"You're goddamn right," Bradshaw said. "You're the one that keeps telling me that we don't work for the government anymore. That means we've got to handle our own logistics. Even if we part ways after we get done with Suparman, you and Lionheart are gonna need capital to keep your operation going. Why not use the devil's money against him?"

Pace pursed his lips as he shifted his jaw laterally. "There's no way we're gonna be able to carry all of this out."

"So we don't," Bradshaw said. "We take one each. We fill it up, that'll be maybe 40, 45 pounds. We can hump that and still clear out the rest of this bitch."

"That still leaves Guntur plenty of cash," Pace said.

Bradshaw smiled as he reached into his admin pouch and produced a pound of C4, a blasting cap connected to a device with an antenna, and what appeared to be a miniature radio. "This oughta singe his piggy bank on the way out."

That tipped Pace over the fence. "Get to it."

As Bradshaw began to set up the charge, Pace keyed up the radio. "Lionheart, Rusty."

"Go," Tan said.

"Short halt on the second floor, east end, south room. Will advise when we're oscar mike."

"Roger. Everything good?"

"Too long. I'll explain when we exfil."

KIRSANA NIRMALA SAT in the back of the taxi, consulting her note pad. The first half of her day had consisted of squeezing every source she had in order to develop a list of brothels utilized by the Kuwat Syndicate. Some of her sources flat out froze her out and refused to budge. The brunt of her efforts were spent on those sitting on the fence, and they paid off. She had a list of five locations spread throughout the city: three in North Jakarta, one in Central Jakarta, and one in West Jakarta.

Once Nirmala had her list, she reached out to Banyu, a cabbie she kept on standby. When Banyu received her call, he would turn off his meter and be her chauffeur. It was a semi-regular gig, with the middle-aged, salt-and-pepper haired cabbie being party to many of her stories. He knew the routine: drop her off, drive in circles with his phone on and charged, and come running if things got hairy. She paid him thousands of *rupiah*, covering the fares he would have missed and then some.

Banyu had watched one too many American movies involving taxi drivers, and it showed in his sense of fashion. He adjusted his flat-bill cap and glanced in the rearview mirror as Nirmala studied her notes.

"You find what you're looking for yet?" Banyu asked, his voice raspy from decades of smoking.

Nirmala shrugged. "One of those looked abandoned. The other one had heavy security. No way I was gonna get close without attracting attention. The third one was also bullshit. Just an empty building full of squatters." A sigh fell from her lips. "I'm really going to have to reevaluate my sources. They fed me nonsense."

Banyu gave her a sad smile. "I'm sorry it hasn't panned out for you yet."

Nirmala returned the smile. "The night's still young, Banyu."

Banyu's eyes returned to the road, and his eyes went wide as he hit the brakes. Nirmala was thrown forward, her seatbelt keeping her face from making hard contact with the seat back. She glanced around and immediately saw why Banyu had brought the taxi to a screeching halt. Nirmala's eyes widened as she took in the girls. Some of them wore nothing but rags. Others wore nothing at all. All of them showed signs of malnourishment and abuse.

"Hold on," Nirmala said as she unbuckled her seatbelt. She threw her door open, her Samsung in hand and recording video. A few of the girls recoiled at the smartphone's bright light. Nirmala waved the phone slowly up and down the line, getting as much of the procession as possible. Thirty seconds later, she ended the video, and began to snap as many photos as possible.

The end of the line drew near. Nirmala put the phone back in her purse and stepped towards a girl clad in a large, raggedy shirt. The girl recoiled and screamed, and Nirmala held up her hands to placate her.

"I'm a friend!" she said. "I'm a friend. I'm here to help. Where did you come from?"

The frightened girl turned back and pointed to the intersection from where the line appeared. "A big house over there," she said. "There were dead bodies at the door."

"Where are you going?" Nirmala asked.

"The two foreigners…they told us this leads to a police station," she said. "They said we would be safe. We could go home."

Oh, shit, Nirmala thought. *The Shadow Wraiths.*

"They were right," Nirmala said. "Go. Join the others."

As the girl jogged to catch up with the line, Nirmala bolted to the Prius and knocked on the passenger window. Banyu rolled it down as Nirmala produced her notepad, found a blank page, and furiously scribbled a name and phone number.

"Get these girls to the police station," Nirmala said. "Call this number. He's with the Criminal Detective Unit. We can trust him. You watch those girls and don't let a single person move them until either he or I arrive. If he gets to the station before I do, come back to this intersection and call me."

"Where are you going?" Banyu asked.

"To the whorehouse," Nirmala said. "My story's there."

BRADSHAW AND PACE both had duffel bags slung on their backs and cinched down tight to keep them as immobilized as possible. Each bag was about 40 pounds, as Bradshaw predicted, but the weight was awkward, with a fair amount of it being focused on the back of their left hips. Still, their range of motion wasn't critically compromised, and they emerged in the hallway and made their way to the east stairwell.

"Rusty, Lionheart," Tan said on the radio.

Pace keyed up, held it for a moment, then released the button. That was his non-verbal method of letting Tan know that he was danger close and that maintaining noise discipline was critical.

"Roger," Tan said. "Just figured you wanted to know that the girls got away safely. Still got clear eyes and clear skies out here."

Pace keyed up twice, letting Tan know that he received and acknowledged the message. His support hand returned to the Micro Uzi's foregrip as he and Bradshaw reached the landing.

As Pace went to move wide around Bradshaw, a *preman* in a soccer jersey and jeans materialized at the top of the stairwell, a *kretek* cigarette in his mouth. The gangster's eyes went wide when he saw Pace and Bradshaw, and he scrambled for the Pindad pistol stuck down the front of his jeans. Bradshaw and Pace engaged the man simultaneously, their suppressed 9x19mm Parabellum rounds cutting the man down where he stood.

A moment later, a shout in Indonesian filled the corridor. "*Holy shit!*"

"Fuck!" Pace hissed. "Go loud!"

Pace and Bradshaw took the stairs two at a time and reached the third floor. They stopped short of the corner, and Pace leaned out from behind cover. He immediately ducked back, the *preman* at the end of the hallway letting loose with his Kalashnikov rifle. Bradshaw took a knee, leaned out, and cranked off five quick rounds, forcing the *preman* to hit the ground. Pace rejoined the fight in time to see the sex slaver holding a radio to his lips and speaking frantically. Bradshaw and Pace lit the target up, with bullets tearing through his chest, throat, and face.

"He got his call out," Bradshaw said between breaths.

"Yeah," Pace said as he reached for his PTT. "Lionheart, Rusty. We're compromised. One of the tangos got the call out. Expect a QRF, most ricky-tick."

"Got you covered," Tan said. "Advise you make haste and *di-di-mau*."

"Read you Lima Charlie, pal," Pace said.

Pace and Bradshaw made their way down the hallway, both of them facing forward. Every few seconds, Bradshaw would check over his shoulder to ensure nobody was flanking them from the rear. Pace reached the door, fished an M48 from his admin pouch, put his back to the door, and booted it hard with a back kick. The prepped flashbang was lobbed high in the room, and Pace took refuge on the other side of the door.

When the flashbang detonated, Bradshaw and Pace rushed into the room. A portly Japanese man immediately extricated himself from atop a sex slave and held up his hands in surrender. Pace glanced at Bradshaw to see what he would do, and Bradshaw responded by firing a single round into the man's head. As the body fell, Bradshaw lowered his Micro Uzi and waved frantically to the girl.

"Get your clothes!" he said in Indonesian. "Go! *Hurry!*"

As she gathered her clothing and scampered out of the room, Bradshaw glanced back to Pace. "He's a rapist. A bullet was lenient."

"No argument from me," Pace said. "Fuck 'im. Let's move."

TAN'S PULSE PICKED up as he heard the flashbangs detonating on the top floor. His focus was on the street level, in search of the enemy response that was guaranteed to come. He scanned left and right in search of targets. A lone figure from the east end of the street caught Tan's attention, and he trained the crosshair on the figure. At the last second, he held his fire as he saw it was a woman, holding up her smart phone. His brow furrowed as he tried to ascertain the purpose of her actions, but he abandoned the notion and continued scanning. The important thing was that she was unarmed, and thus was not an immediate threat.

The purr of an engine from the west reached Tan's ears, and he adjusted his aim in time to see a trio of Land Rovers pull up in front of the building. He scowled, wishing he had brought along one of the M4/M203 platforms they had acquired from Milena Wright. Instead, Tan's hand snaked to his PTT.

"Rusty, Lionheart. You've got 12 tangos rolling in hard, time now."

"We just cleared the top floor," Pace said. "Walking the last group of girls out now. Need some breathing room, Lionheart."

"Say no more," Tan said. He traversed his crosshair until it settled on the back of the first target, then squeezed the trigger. The round made impact between the target's shoulder blades and tore through his spine and heart. Tan immediately made acquisition on a second target and fired, catching him in the ribs. He shifted to his left, found a third target, and squeezed the trigger. The *preman* spun, stumbled, and fell to the street.

"*Sniper!*" one of the survivors called out. A few of them returned fire in Tan's general direction while the rest scrambled for cover. Tan cranked off another round. It narrowly missed its mark as the target dove behind the Land Rover's engine block.

Tan clenched his PTT. His microphone perfectly captured the carnage of inbound gunfire as he spoke. "Rusty, four down. Eight left standing. They're focused on me."

"Roger that," Pace said. "We'll take it from here."

PACE TURNED BACK to the six girls in the line behind them and held up a hand. "Stay here," he said in Indonesian. "Cover your ears and stay low."

As the girls complied with Pace's instructions, Bradshaw reached to his war belt for an M67 fragmentation grenade. He pushed away the thumb safety, then looped his middle finger through the pull ring and looked to Pace, who had prepared his own grenade. They exchanged a nod, yanked their pins from their grenade bodies, then let the spoon loose. Bradshaw and Pace stepped toward the door, lobbed their grenades towards the Land Rovers, then ducked back inside. A *preman* saw the grenades and opened his mouth to say something, but the fuses reached their ends first.

The Composition B ignited, spraying shrapnel outward in all directions. The Land Rovers slumped forward, their front tires punctured. Engine oil caught fire, and the conflagration spread as the oil leaked onto the asphalt. All eight of the enemy shooters were well within the grenade's 5-meter kill radius.

Pace took point, stepping outside and sweeping both ways with his Micro Uzi at the ready. When he saw nothing, he keyed his PTT.

"Lionheart, how we looking?"

The response was delayed a couple of seconds. "You're clear. Nobody else yet, but I'm sure that'll change when the initial QRF fails to respond."

"Then let's bounce," Pace said. "Go ahead and exfil."

"Roger that," Tan said. "See you back at the pad."

Pace looked over his shoulder to find Bradshaw walking the last six girls out. The former Marine waited until they were even with him, then looked each of them in the eyes as he pointed to the west.

"Head that way," Pace said. "Hit the main road, hook a left, and keep going until you find the police station. The rest of the girls should be there. Go, go!"

The girls did not need a second invitation. They took off as quickly as their weakened legs would carry them. Once they were out of sight, Pace looked back to Bradshaw.

"Hope your ruck legs are still good, Boy Scout," Pace said. "We've got a bit of a hump back to the trucks."

"Oh, I'm good," Bradshaw said as he reached into his admin pouch. "But first...a little 'fuck you' for Suparman." He produced the radio detonator, turned it on, and extended the antenna as far as it would go. He lifted the button cover, held the detonator at head-level, and pressed the button.

The ground rumbled, and a loud roar filled the air as the C4 explosive detonated. All of the second-floor windows shattered, along with one on the ground floor. Bradshaw and Pace were just far enough away to avoid the glass rain, and their electronic ear protection/radio headsets filtered out the explosion's deafening report.

"I wouldn't call that 'little,'" Pace said.

"I would," Bradshaw said. "He's got a hell of a lot more coming."

"Amen, brother," Pace said. He clapped Bradshaw on the shoulder. "Lead us out."

NIRMALA REMAINED HIDDEN behind the pair of trash cans, peering through the gap between the two as she watched the pair of men speak to each other. They were dressed in a similar same fashion as the Western special operations troops she had seen in *Kompas's* international affairs sections, as well as when they covered stories regarding joint exercises between the West and Indonesia's *Kopassus* unit. They had large duffel bags on their backs, which puzzled her.

Was this a robbery? she wondered. If it was, then Nirmala could look the other way. By her count, they had freed at least 50 girls, if not more. As far as she was concerned, they were more than entitled to the slavers' spoils.

Nirmala strained her ears as the men continued to speak. She could only hear bits and pieces of their conversation, but what she did hear quickened her pulse.

English…they're Americans.

The pair of soldiers jogged west down the street, and Nirmala made herself as small as she could as she waited for them to pass. Their footsteps grew in crescendo, reached peak volume, then faded into the background. Nirmala got video of them running away, then hit the STOP button. She held her phone up and checked that she'd gotten all of her intended footage, then brought up her contacts. A moment later, she held the Samsung to her ear as it dialed Banyu's number.

"I heard explosions," Banyu said when he picked up. "Are you all right?"

"I'm fine," Nirmala said quickly. "Are the girls all right?"

"Yeah," Banyu said. "Your detective friend just arrived."

"Tell him he's got six more coming to him from the same location, then come pick me up. I'll be at the intersection in a couple of minutes."

"What's going on?"

"Change of plans," she said. "I'll fill you in when you get here."

Nirmala terminated the call, rose from her position, and walked to the west. She attempted a balance between speed and silence. She had a gut feeling that they wouldn't kill her if they discovered her, but she hadn't made it as long as she had as an investigative journalist by being careless.

CHAPTER SEVENTEEN

Senen, Central Jakarta, Indonesia
20 March 2019
03:35 hours Golf (19 March 20:35 hours Zulu)

The Micro Uzis, body armor, chest rigs, helmets, war belts, and duffel bags were safely stashed away in the back of the Toyota Rush. All that Bradshaw and Pace kept handy were their pistols—concealed beneath their shirts—and a single MBITR, which was switched to speaker mode. As Pace guided the Toyota down the street, Bradshaw ran his hands over his sweat-slicked hair and pushed a long exhale past his pursed lips.

"That was close," Bradshaw said.

"Yeah," Pace said. He checked the rearview and side mirrors, then returned his eyes to the road.

Bradshaw glanced over at Pace. "You have any other intel for us to work off of?"

Pace shook his head. "I was hoping to develop more from Raja Wira, but I doubt he knew more than what his cell phone revealed."

Bradshaw shrugged as he looked forward. "We could have a chat with my old boss down at the Port. Maybe there's something he knows isn't right and is keeping to himself to avoid rocking the boat."

Pace glanced at the rearview again. "That's a bit of a risk, don't you think? He's just as likely to turn you in as he is to spill something useful."

"Maybe." Bradshaw peered out the window and exhaled audibly. "I don't know. I'm just spitballing. Best to press the momentum while it's in our court."

Pace eased the Toyota right at the intersection. As they proceeded down the road, Bradshaw's eyes flickered to the rearview mirror. His brow furrowed as he sat up in his seat, studying the car trailing back about 50 meters.

"Hey," he said. "Not wanting to sound paranoid, but I'm pretty sure that taxi took the same three turns we just took."

"You saw it too," Pace said approvingly. "Yeah. We picked up the tail right after we started rolling."

"You think it's Suparman's pipe hitters?" Bradshaw asked.

Pace shook his head. "They wouldn't be using a taxi, and they'd be rolling a hell of a lot deeper than one Prius."

Bradshaw looked to Pace. "You wanna find out who they are?"

"Yeah," Pace said. "Canisius College is about a klick from here. The parking lot's a solid interdiction site. Just gotta make sure Tan's in position."

"I'm on it," Bradshaw said as he hefted the MBITR. "Lionheart, Boy Scout."

A moment later, Tan responded. "Go."

"What's your current position?"

"Just passed Satumedia TV," Tan said. "What's up?"

"How fast can you get to Canisius College?"

There was another pause. "About five minutes. Why? What's up?"

"We picked up a tail," Bradshaw said. "Need you to set up a vehicle interdiction. Let us know when you're set."

"You've got it," Tan said. "Oscar mike."

"WHERE THE HELL are they driving?" Kirsana Nirmala asked Banyu.

"I don't know," Banyu said. "If I had to guess? Maybe they're making sure that none of the *preman* followed them."

Nirmala frowned as she watched the Toyota Rush make a left turn. A few seconds later, Banyu followed them onto the next street. The Rush was still there. While there were other vehicles on the road at that time of night, the roads were far less congested than during the daytime.

"If they know we're following them, then they're not making any effort to lose us," Nirmala said.

"I don't think they know we're here," Banyu said.

Nirmala shook her head slowly. She pulled out her phone and accessed her Samsung Cloud app. Nirmala checked the latest backup to ensure all of the photos from the Senen bordello had successfully reached the cloud. She was certain she was just being paranoid, but in the off-chance that she was wrong about the vigilantes and they got their hands on her phone, she wanted to make sure her proof wasn't destroyed.

"They're turning left again," Banyu announced. "Headed on *Arif Rachman Hakim.*"

"They're breaking pattern," Nirmala said.

"Must figure they're safe," Banyu said. "Probably finally headed back to wherever they're staying."

Nirmala leaned forward. "When they get there, you can drop me off and head home. I don't want you mixed up with these people. If I'm wrong about them, there's no need for you to get involved."

"Nonsense," Banyu said. "You paid me for the night, I'm yours."

"But what about Diah and Puspita?" Nirmala asked, referring to Banyu's wife and daughter, respectively. "You've got people expecting you home at the end of the night."

"And you've got a story that needs telling," Banyu said. "I won't leave you on your own. I go home after I drop you off at yours."

Nirmala started to speak, but she watched the Rush veer onto *Menteng Raya.* "Headed south now."

"I'm on them," Banyu said.

The Rush drove for another 45 seconds, then turned right. Nirmala's face twisted in confusion. "The university?"

"Perhaps they're meeting somebody," Banyu said. "Follow them?"

"Yeah," Nirmala said with more confidence than she felt.

Banyu guided the Prius into the large U-shaped parking lot in front of the university's entrance. As they committed, Nirmala saw the Rush parked perpendicular in the middle of the parking lot, blocking their path. A moment later, a second Rush raced into the lot, parking behind the taxi and boxing them in.

Shit, Nirmala said as she reached for her phone. *It's a trap!*

Before she could get her phone out of her purse, she heard a tap on the window. Nirmala glanced to see one of the two men from the brothel. He had discarded the military gear from before, but he wore the same clothing. The pistol in his hand was trained directly at her forehead. Wide-eyed, Nirmala held up her hands.

A voice outside the car shouted in rough Indonesian, "Turn off your vehicle, remove the keys, and toss them out the window! Do it slowly!"

Nirmala looked forward and discovered a second man standing between the Rush and the Prius, his pistol extended in front of him. She swallowed nervously, then looked to Banyu and nodded.

"Do what he says, Banyu," she said quietly, keeping her hands at head-level.

Banyu rolled down the window, removed the keys from the Prius's ignition, and tossed them out. He held his hands up and kept them in sight.

"Unlock the car," the man in front said.

Banyu did what he was told. The nearest gunman opened Nirmala's door, reached in, and pulled her out. He shoved her roughly against the car, relieved her of her handbag, and tossed it to a third man, who had presumably driven the second vehicle.

"Search that," the man said in English. He turned his attention back to her and said, "Hands on the roof."

"I'm a reporter—" Nirmala tried to say.

"Hands on the car," the man reiterated.

Nirmala complied. The man's search was thorough. He patted down each arm down to the armpit, swiped a bladed hand between and under each of her breasts, searched both sides of her torso, and searched each of her legs all the way up to the pelvis. The manner in which he searched her was professional, but the feeling of violation was still very real. She clenched her jaw and pushed an exhale through her nostrils. Her eyes flittered to the front of the car, where Banyu endured the same treatment at the hands of the man up front.

When the search was done, her captor took a step back. "Slowly," he said in Indonesian. "Turn around. Keep your hands on your head, fingers together."

"I speak English," Nirmala said.

The man gave her a curt nod, then switched tongues. "All right. You with Suparman Guntur?"

Nirmala's face contorted with disgust. "Hell no! I made sure those girls you rescued made it to that police station safely and had an honest officer waiting to receive them! You took a huge risk leaving it up to the police to reunite them with their families. You know that?"

A hint of guilt flickered across her captor's face. "Keep your voice down," he said. "Why were you following us?"

"You're the vigilantes," Nirmala said. "The ones they call Shadow Wraiths. You kidnapped Raja Wira, took out the Kuwat Syndicate training camp in Bagogog, and hit the club house in Kembangan. You're taking the war to the *preman.*"

Nirmala's captor exchanged glances with Banyu's captor. Neither one lowered their weapons. The third man broke the silence.

"Hey, Boy Scout. She's got press credentials. Kirsana Nirmala with *Kompas.*"

Nirmala's captor, Boy Scout, looked to the one up front. "Rusty?"

"Guy's name is Banyu. Mononym. He's a licensed cabbie. Meter's not running, though."

"He runs favors for me," Nirmala explained. "I pay him in advance, he drives me around while I chase leads."

"What do you wanna do?" the third man asked his partners.

Nirmala looked at Boy Scout. Her eyes narrowed with recognition. She tried to conceal her epiphany, but Jack Bradshaw caught the look.

"She knows who I am," he said quietly. "Saw me on the news."

"Shit," Rusty said.

"Now what?" the third man asked.

Nirmala decided to speak up. "I can help you."

Bradshaw studied her. "How?"

"I've been running down leads on the Syndicate for the better part of a year," she said. "You guys were the spark that got my editors to greenlight my findings. I want those bastards taken down just as badly as you."

Bradshaw chuckled mirthlessly. "Oh, I doubt that. But that doesn't answer the question. How do you plan on helping us?"

"Let's find some privacy and talk shop," Nirmala offered.

Bradshaw deferred to Rusty. From the front, she heard him say, "You ride with us, blindfolded and zip-cuffed. Your cabbie goes home and doesn't breathe a word of this to anyone. We see any cops, we toss you out of the moving car. That arrangement doesn't work for you, we'll drop your keys and cell phones a mile down the road."

"Deal," Nirmala said without hesitation.

Rusty looked to Bradshaw and said, "Get her ready."

Bradshaw looked to the third man. "Lionheart, you've got her?"

Lionheart moved until he stood next to Bradshaw. "Got her."

Bradshaw holstered his weapon, then jogged back to the Rush. He returned a moment later with a gag and a pair of prepared flex-cuffs. "Turn around," he ordered. "Backs of hands together at the small of your back."

Nirmala did as she was told and heard the signature *zip* of the cuffs being cinched before she felt the hard plastic against her wrists. The strip of cloth came next, thick enough to cover both her eyes and the bridge of her nose. Once the blindfold was securely in place, she felt one hand on her shoulder and another on her left wrist.

"Walk with me," Bradshaw said. They made their way to the car. He tightened his grip when they arrived, her indication to stop. She heard the door open, then heard him said, "Duck your head and watch your step." Once she was situated in the backseat, Nirmala felt Bradshaw lean in over her. A moment later, she heard the *click* of the seatbelt being fastened.

The door slammed shut without another word from Bradshaw. Nirmala closed her eyes beneath the blindfold, took a deep breath in through her nose, and pushed the exhale past her closed lips.

I really hope I don't regret this.

Tanjung Priok, North Jakarta, Indonesia
20 March 2019
04:14 hours Golf (19 March 21:14 hours Zulu)

THE DRIVE WAS quiet. Suparman Guntur watched the scenery shift from rural tropical to Asian metropolitan. It truly was a border between worlds for Guntur. In the former, he enjoyed the fruits of his labor, the spoils of his struggle. In the latter, he metamorphosed into the sort of man necessary to defend his fiefdom.

Guntur contemplated the scenery as his mind mulled the news delivered 45 minutes earlier. In contrast to his reaction to the camp and club attacks, he had been more subdued. He'd summoned his personal security detail and placed two phone calls while they prepared. The first recipient tiredly complied without argument. The second had to be cajoled into agreeing to the meeting.

Sharif Aditya waited at the designated dock as the Land Rover convoy arrived. As the vehicles slowed to a halt, the bodyguards dismounted. Unlike the Syndicate's rank and file soldiers, Guntur's PSD wielded Micro Galil carbines, equipped with Meprolight M21 reflex sights. They dismounted and scanned the surroundings, acknowledging Aditya's crew. Once they were sure the area was secured, the one closest to Guntur's door opened it and stepped aside.

Guntur dismounted and took a deep breath of the shore air. Mother Nature had given Java a reprieve from the rain, and Guntur savored every moment. It was not bound to last, with weather forecasts predicting additional rain in the next 48 hours.

As Guntur approached the dock, he adjusted the Heckler & Koch MK23 in its vertical shoulder holster beneath his left armpit. The pistol had been given to him by a contact within *Kopassus*. Guntur had fallen in love with the massive German hand cannon at first sight, and though it had taken hundreds of hours of practice, he had mastered its operation. It embodied the one thing closest to Guntur's heart: sheer, unadulterated power.

Aditya's lieutenant, Umar Pratama, marched past Guntur with the girls in tow, not bothering to look him in the eye. Pratama had always been an odd one, but Guntur wondered if Pratama harbored doubts about the organization's actions. Aditya had vouched for Pratama, with the two men enduring the horrors of Kerobokan Prison together. Still, time changed men, as Guntur knew all too well.

Guntur and Aditya met on the dock, with the former crossing his arms and staring at his subordinate. "How did it go?"

Aditya nodded. "We did as you asked."

"Show me."

Aditya fished his phone from his cargo pocket, brought up the gallery, hit play on the video, and turned the screen towards Guntur. The video lasted 90 seconds. Sobs, pleas, blood-curdling shrieks, and gunfire took flight from the phone's speakers. When it ended, Guntur nodded and clapped Aditya on the shoulder.

"Well done, Sharif," he said. "Well done." Aditya nodded, and Guntur said, "Come." As they marched towards the cargo truck where the girls had been gathered, Guntur asked, "Were you briefed on what happened?"

"Received the radio traffic on the way in," Aditya said. "It's definitely the Shadow Wraiths."

"They're emboldened," Guntur said. "In the past 48 hours, they've killed 54 of our men. They're responsible for the destruction of millions in profits that were awaiting transfer to our central hub. If we don't take them out of play, they're going to dismantle us."

"What are you saying?" Aditya asked.

"The video itself may not be enough to lure them out," Guntur said. "They're more capable than I'd originally credited. We need to whip them into a rage."

"Will we be making another video?" Aditya asked.

"No," Guntur said. "We're going to need something a bit more...visceral."

Guntur and Aditya reached the gathered girls. Each of them stared at the pair of men. There were no bold ones in this group. All were thoroughly cowed. Guntur's eyes traversed the crowd in search of his sacrificial lamb, the one who would serve as a message to those who dared threaten his domain. He met eyes with one, a little on the thin side and who couldn't have been a day older than 16 years. A cold smile spread across Guntur's face, and it sent a shiver down the girl's spine. Her eyes betrayed that every fiber in her body told her to flee, but fear held her in place. Guntur fed on that fear. He welcomed it. Craved it.

"Company approaching," one of Guntur's PSD members announced, breaking his reverie.

Guntur turned to see the inbound four-vehicle convoy. The PSD stood by with their weapons at the low ready, simultaneously relaxed and alert. They were expecting the newcomers.

The jet black Toyota Avanzas pulled to a halt about 15 meters from where Guntur and his men were gathered. The men of Detachment C, Pelepor Regiment, Greater Jakarta Regional Brimob disembarked, their Pindad rifles held low as they secured their end of the venue. Once the special purpose officers gave the go-ahead, two men in suits stepped out and approached.

"Chief Commissioner," Guntur greeted. "Deputy Governor."

Mega Nyoman said nothing as he planted a *kretek* cigarette between his lips. Setiawan Mahmud, on the other hand, let his annoyance show. "This had better be damned good, Suparman."

"Last time I checked, it's my money that fills your off-shore accounts, Setiawan," Guntur said quietly. He pointed a finger at Jakarta's deputy governor. "I'm not seeing a whole lot of return on my investment. But that's about to change."

"Oh?" Mahmud crossed his arms. "How's that?"

"As of this moment, John Bradshaw is a member of an up-and-coming *preman* group with connections to the Triads in Hong Kong. You will make him the sole priority of both the regional and national police forces."

"Nobody's going to believe that the Chinese are letting a *bule* run their businesses," Mahmud said. "*Especially* here."

"That's why we're going to give them something to believe," Guntur said.

Nyoman pulled on his *kretek.* "What's that?"

"A young woman's body, dumped in a high-visibility area," Guntur said. "Beaten, raped, mutilated, and strangled to death."

Mahmud paled and shook his head. "No," he said. "You're insane. This is your mess. I want no part in this."

Guntur drew his MK23, thumbed back the hammer, and trained it on Mahmud. The C Detachment shooters raised their rifles, and Guntur's PSD did likewise. Nyoman slowly edged away from the line of fire while continuing to pull on his cigarette. Incredulity spread across Mahmud's face as he turned around and stared down the H&K's barrel.

"Is this how you wish to proceed?" Mahmud asked quietly.

"No," Guntur said, "but you leave me little choice. I don't think you appreciate the gravity of the situation. When the body turns up, you *will* report it the way *I* tell you to report it. Otherwise, you're of no use to me."

Mahmud scowled. "There will be repercussions," he said.

Guntur laughed. "No, there won't," he said. "Otherwise, I'll let your account information leak to the press. You'll be disgraced, your name forever tarnished in politics. Your trophy wife will leave you, as will your mistresses. When you have nothing remaining, you will see this again." He bobbed the H&K vertically for emphasis. "The difference is, when that time comes, I'll put a bullet in your face, and nobody will miss you."

Mahmud took a deep breath and straightened his posture. "Fine. You'll get your bullshit story."

Guntur nodded, then looked to Nyoman. "That will give you the resources to turn over every stone in search of Bradshaw and his Shadow Wraiths. You bring him to me alive, there will be a bonus. You have to kill him, then bring me his head as proof."

Nyoman nodded meekly. "Fine."

"The sooner we eliminate Bradshaw, the sooner life returns to normal," Guntur said. He decocked the MK23 and slid it back in its holster. His PSD lowered their weapons, and C Detachment reluctantly followed suit. Guntur sighed and held out his hands in a conciliatory fashion.

"We've had an excellent working relationship for many years," he said. "We can have that again. All that we need to do is eliminate the threat to the Syndicate." He looked to Nyoman. "I assume you want to go back to being paid a handsome amount to do essentially nothing?"

"Of course," Nyoman said flatly.

Guntur looked back to Mahmud. "And I assume you wish to be governor someday. Or perhaps a senator. Maybe even president. You stay the course, Setiawan. We can make that happen."

The change in Mahmud's eyes was subtle. Indignation gave way to raw Machiavellian aspiration that was translatable in any language. While the deputy governor would not leave smiling, he would leave as a willing participant in the plan.

"Yes, all right," Mahmud said.

Guntur nodded, then waved towards the other convoy. "Go."

Nyoman and Mahmud slowly made their way to their Toyotas. Once both men were inside, the paramilitary Regional Policemen mounted their vehicles. A moment later, the convoy raced off into the distance. Guntur sighed, then looked to his sacrificial lamb.

"Bring her to me," he said. She tensed as two of his men hefted her by her shoulders and dragged her towards Guntur. He looked to the others and said, "Load them up and ship 'em out!"

As the crew kicked into motion, Aditya looked at Guntur. "Do we want to take her back to your place?"

Guntur shook his head, his eyes locked on his prey. "No, we'll do it here. It'll be a closer drive. Besides, nobody will hear us." He reached out and grabbed her arm, which made her body tense and tremble simultaneously. Guntur gave her his most reptilian grin as he said, "It'll be an intimate affair."

Cengkareng, West Jakarta, Indonesia
20 March 2019
04:30 hours Golf (19 March 21:30 hours Zulu)

THE BLINDFOLD WAS removed from Kirsana Nirmala's face. She blinked rapidly as her eyes adjusted. She was seated in the middle of an empty warehouse, with her hands still bound behind her back. The men she knew as Lionheart and Rusty stood in front of her, their arms folded and their eyes locked on her. She heard footsteps to her left, and turned in time to see John Bradshaw moving to her back, a pair of wire cutters in his hands.

"Relax," Bradshaw said. "I'm just going to cut your restraints." He took a knee behind her, slid the wire cutters between her left wrist and the flex-cuff, and applied pressure until the latter snapped. Bradshaw repeated the process on her right wrist, then removed the restraints from her hands. She moved her hands to her front, rubbing her wrists as she eyed the men before her.

"You said you could help us take the fight to Suparman Guntur," the one known as Rusty said. "What do you have in mind?"

"I have sources in both the regional and national police," Nirmala said. "Honest officers and detectives that are tired of the corruption and want something done about it."

"They don't sound like they'd be very useful if they're honest," Rusty said.

"They keep their ear to the ground," Nirmala said. "I've also got sources in prisons, slums, political offices...my net is wide."

"Okay," Bradshaw said. "So, what's in it for you?"

"Being the one whose journalism breaks Guntur's empire," Nirmala said. "Ridding my nation of a scourge. Does it seem that absurd that I would want the same thing as you?"

"Not absurd," Lionheart agreed. "Just concerned you'll make us focal pieces in your next story. We don't want publicity."

"I can keep your name out of it," Nirmala said. "I've also got something else you could use."

"What's that?" Rusty asked.

"Contacts inside of social services. I've studied your work. Your MO tends to be liberating the girls and hoping for the best. Some of them slip the orbit. Others get picked back up by the slavers when you leave, or worse, acquired by competitors. I could give those girls a fighting chance as far as getting out and *staying* out."

Bradshaw glanced at Rusty. She saw that had won her points with him. Rusty and Lionheart remained unconvinced. "Sounds like you're selling a miracle," Rusty said. "Learned a long time ago not to get my hopes up when it comes to happy endings."

"And yet, you keep doing what you do," Nirmala said. "If you were simply looking for a fight, you'd join a private military company. You wouldn't be operating in the gray, risking life and limb for next to nothing. That makes you ideological."

Rusty and Lionheart exchanged another look. Lionheart stepped forward, his hands clasped behind his back. "If we were to take you up on this offer, how would it work?"

"I keep my ear to the ground," Nirmala said. "I hear anything, you get it first. Give you lead time to work with it before it hits the press. If you recover any more girls, you let me know where they are, and I'll arrange pickup."

"That seems to be a violation of journalistic neutrality," Rusty said.

Nirmala smiled. "Sometimes, you've just gotta pick a side. Look at your Matthew VanDyke, who found himself embroiled in both the Libyan and Syrian civil wars. Or look at Grant Cogar."

Rusty's eyes narrowed. "Huh?"

"Fictional Chicago journo, womanizer, and shit magnet," Lionheart said. "Cult thriller hit. I like those books."

"Whatever," Rusty said. "I've done some research on you, Ms. Nirmala. You've built a hell of a reputation over at *Kompas*. Seems out of character to rub shoulders with us."

"Desperate times call for desperate measures," Nirmala replied. "And if you were plugged into Jakarta on the information side, you'd have ditched me once I told you I was a journo. Yet, here you are. That tells me that you're looking for your next target and could use a nudge in the right direction. I'm that nudge."

Bradshaw glanced to Rusty and Lionheart as if to say, *I told you so.* Rusty hung his head, adjusted his footing, then met Nirmala's gaze again. "I'm going to have to talk it over with my partners."

"All right," Nirmala said. "I'll be here."

WHEN THEY WERE in the common area and out of earshot, Danny Pace scowled at Bradshaw. "Your poker face sucks donkey dick."

"What?" Bradshaw asked, genuinely perplexed.

"It was so fucking obvious that you're on board with what she was selling," Pace said. "No attempt at neutrality, no effort to remain detached."

"That's because this is what we need," Bradshaw said. "You know she's a good journo. She managed to piece together our hits and stumble onto us. I think she'll deliver."

Pace shook his head, then looked to Lucas Tan. "What do you think?"

"I think it can't hurt to try," Tan said. "I also think that regardless of what we pick, we're going to need to fall back to another safe house. This one's burned."

Pace drummed his fingers against his bicep as he let out a prolonged sigh. Bradshaw decided to make another pitch.

"Think of it this way. Us three? Yeah, we're doing damage. We're pissing Suparman off." Bradshaw pointed back to where Nirmala sat patiently. "She can turn the whole nation against the Syndicate, give them a reason to demand action. With her pen and paper, she can do far more damage than we can with our hardware."

A moment passed before Pace let loose with a frustrated sigh. "Fine." He pointed to Tan. "Give her a burner phone, head out, and drop her off. By the time you get back, we'll have the gear loaded up and ready to roll."

Tan nodded. "I'm on it."

As Tan returned to Nirmala, Bradshaw turned to Pace. "You're making the right decision."

Pace's eyes remained locked on Nirmala. "We'll see."

CHAPTER EIGHTEEN

Menteng, Central Jakarta, Indonesia
20 March 2019
07:35 hours Golf (00:35 hours Zulu)

The rain clouds had returned to deliver a light morning drizzle. Traffic was already approaching peak congestion, with commuters beginning another day of pursuing their livelihood. Thunderstorms and heavier rains were forecast for later in the day, which was sure to worsen the vehicular obstructions.

Brigadier First Class Bagus Soleh sat under the awning at the south end of the Hotel Indonesia traffic circle's Selamat Datang Monument. The 28-year-old Padang native had relocated to Java when he enlisted in the Army, doing four years based out of Badung with the 312nd Infantry Battalion. While he enjoyed shooting guns and playing in the jungle, Soleh wasn't a fan of the irregular schedule, and had separated at the end of his enlistment. He'd worked Imperium Strategic Security for about a year before he was picked up by the National Police. After the academy, he'd landed a posting with the Greater Jakarta Metropolitan Regional Police.

Soleh's motivation and optimism had been high coming out of the academy. He had aspirations for joining *Brimob* or perhaps working his way into the Criminal Detective Unit. Those goals were quickly tempered within his first year working the streets. Between groups of officers running their own protection rackets and those who acted as enforcers for *preman* groups, Soleh found that the police force's political landscape was a minefield.

By the end of his first year, Soleh had married and had hopes for a child. His *modus operandi* became ignoring as much of the badged criminality as possible, collecting his paycheck, and going home every night. The reputation he'd developed in his precinct was one that wouldn't file paperwork with *Propam*, but who also wanted nothing to do with the rackets. Soleh's fellow officers left him be, and that was exactly how he wanted it.

His assignment to the motorcycle division and posting at the HI traffic circle came with perks: a promotion to First Class, excellent working hours, and—most importantly—he worked alone. It was relatively safe, with his duties usually including the issuance of traffic citations and detaining vagabonds that would urinate in the Selamat Datang Monument's pond. It was a complacent life, and one Soleh was sure he could maintain for another 20 years if necessary.

Soleh's thumb worked his iPhone's screen as he perused the article on the *Kompas* app. He'd gone to bed with nothing of import for the news, and had woken up to reports of a massive firefight in Senen. Nearly 50 females—many of them hovering around the age of consent of 15, with some beneath it—had been held in captivity in a bordello. The report—masterfully written by Kirsana Nirmala and accompanied with photographs and videos—alleged that it was the Kuwat Syndicate that had been responsible for the females' enslavement. At least 10 purported *preman* were killed when the slaves were liberated and reported to the nearest police station. The Criminal Detective Unit and social services were caring for the girls.

Interesting times, Soleh thought. His wife, Ningsih, continued to urge him to walk away from the National Police entirely. Her father was the owner and manager of two franchise locations of the South Korean-based Lotte Mart, and had offered to connect Soleh with a position as a security manager. The pay would be considerably higher than his law enforcement salary, and there would be none of the corruption. The only thing that stopped Soleh from taking it was wanting to earn his own way. With the news headlines indicating a street war had started in Jakarta, that reservation was rapidly fading.

Soleh closed the *Kompas* app. He caught a glimpse of his background photo before he locked his phone. It was a picture taken with the Java Sea as the backdrop. Soleh and Ningsih stood by by side, with their daughter, Mlathi, in her arms. He and his wife wore wide, natural smiles, and the photographer had waited until Mlathi—seven months old at the time of the photograph—smiled with her eyes wide before taking the photo. It was the daily reminder of why he put on his gun and badge every day, why he bothered to keep his khaki-on-brown uniform crisply pressed and his high boots polished to a mirror sheen.

A loud screech grabbed Soleh's attention. He looked up in time to see a white third-generation Mitsubishi Delica pull up to a fast halt. Two men hopped out carrying something, but Soleh could not ascertain what as the monument at the center of the pond obstructed his view. Even over the sound of traffic, Soleh heard a loud splash, followed by the two men hopping in the Delica and slamming the sliding door shut. As Soleh grabbed his motorcycle helmet and stood to get a better look, the Delica peeled out, cut off several vehicles, and raced north on *M.H. Thamrin.*

What the hell? Soleh thought as he jammed his helmet on his head and made his way to his Yamaha XJ900S. He climbed onto his bike, revved the engine to life, and turned on his lights as he pulled out of the parking spot and circumvented the traffic circle. His intuition told him that what he had witnessed was seriously off, but his imagination couldn't immediately fathom what it could be.

Thirty seconds later, Soleh was on the north side. He parked his Yamaha, kept the lights on, and dismounted his bike. His hand snaked to his right hip, undid the leather holster's flap, and wrapped around the butt of his Pindad P1 sidearm. As Soleh walked to the edge of the pond, his skin grew pale and his stomach churned.

The young woman couldn't have been a day over sixteen. She was stripped bare. Dark splotches marked her skin where she had been savagely beaten. A jagged hole had been cut in her throat, with caked blood on both sides of the laceration. There was a dark, bloody circle where her left eye had been. Toes on her right foot were missing, the stubs charred black from where they had been cauterized to stave off hemorrhage.

A pair of *jiǎnhuàzì* characters were carved into her stomach, with the blood cleaned off so that they could be clearly read.

Soleh could not hold back any further. He turned away, bent over at the waist, and emptied his stomach on the asphalt. When his stomach ran empty, he continued to dry heave as he struggled with hyperventilation. Soleh secured the holster flap, then fought to compose himself as he reached for his radio. As he constructed the message in his head before transmission, Soleh decided that this was the sign to walk away. He would speak with Ningsih's father, and hand in his resignation by the end of the week.

Bagus Soleh considered himself a man of stern constitution, but he couldn't be around *this* kind of evil and still be the man that his family needed.

FOUR AND A half hours had passed since Bagus Soleh put the call out on the police net for medical personnel, a supervisor, and detectives. In that time, the press had gotten a hold of the story, and they had milked it for every ounce of coverage they could get. On the various news stations, forensics experts, retired investigators from the Regional and National Police, and human rights advocates had been called in for interviews.

Some takes were grounded in reality, saying that the investigation was young and proposing grounded theories as to motive and perpetrator. Others launched into more sensational tirades, blaming everything from the tolerance of secularism to Western influence on what had killed the girl. The latter proved to rake in higher ratings and generate more watercooler conversation. That carried the networks to 11:00, when Deputy Governor Setiawan Mahmud announced that he would hold a press conference in an hour.

The Governor's Residence was located just a kilometer to the east-by-southeast of the Selamat Datang Monument. The Press Briefing Room was located in the residence's west wing. Its decoration was spartan, with cream-colored walls and light blue carpet floors. At the front was a short stage, upon which was a podium flanked by the flags of Indonesia and Jakarta. The podium itself bore Jakarta's coat of arms. Mounted on the wall, to the right of the podium, was a large, flat-screen television that bore the coat of arms and the title "Governor of Jakarta" beneath it.

By 11:25, the room was packed from reporters from all of the national and local services. Reuters, the Associated Press, and the BBC had also managed to get correspondents into the briefing. In the age of mass media, local stories became national spectacles, and national-worthy news spread into international rallying cries. There was plenty of interest to be had in a dead and desecrated teenaged girl dumped at a national monument. For the press corps members present, it was about covering the story and discovering the truth. Their corporate sponsors, on the other hand, wanted the ratings, since truth wasn't a reliable mode of income.

At 11:50, the Deputy Governor's press secretary—an ebullient 20-something female sporting a black pantsuit and a white *hijab*—marched smartly into the Press Briefing Room and stood at the podium.

"May I have your attention please?" she said. Once all eyes were on her, she said, "The Deputy Governor will be here in about 10 minutes. He will make a brief statement, and then turn the briefing over to the police representative. The Deputy Governor will not take any questions. Thank you."

In the backstage area, Setiawan Mahmud stared at a wall, his hands clasped behind his back. Light makeup had been applied to conceal the bags beneath his eyes. The knowledge of Suparman Guntur's pending machinations had robbed him of sleep. When he received the news from the Greater Jakarta Metro Police, his heart had plunged into his stomach. He'd declined to see the photos. Mahmud was already having doubts about if he was on the proper path, and wondering how he had reached this point.

Mahmud possessed a realistic assessment of his morality. The truth was that he found the term to be subjective. There were plenty of self-righteous crusaders that wished to dictate how others lived. Mahmud was not one of them, but he also realized that there were certain realities that had to be respected in order to progress in politics. People expected him to be a family man, so he found a woman willing to tolerate him enough to give him a son and keep her infidelities to herself, as he did. Mahmud also realized that backroom deals were the fuel for the political machine, and rubbing shoulders with unsavory types was the way things were done.

When Mahmud had entered into an alliance with Suparman Guntur, he saw it as political expedience. The money being donated to his campaign coffers notwithstanding, Guntur was plugged into the underworld. He had a commodity more useful than sex, weapons, or narcotics: information. It was Guntur's knowledge of the political party leadership's vices that had earned Mahmud the mayorship of Central Jakarta, an administratively appointed position. In turn, that gave him his chance to shine and made him a shoo-in for the deputy governorship when the incumbent resigned to run for vice president.

Another thing of which Mahmud had no illusions was his thirst for power. He had his eye on the Jakarta governorship. The incumbent president had used the billet as a launch pad for national power. Mahmud saw no reason why he couldn't replicate that path to the highest office.

Simultaneously, Mahmud thought of his plays as harmless. Sure, some people's livelihoods were ruined, but they were still alive to pursue other methods of subsistence. It was no different from when he had been the CEO for the rubber company that his father had founded. It was a healthy, harmless exercise in sociopathy.

That "harmless exercise" had led to a girl lying on a slab in the medical examiner's office, her body defiled in every fashion possible, and the knowledge that her dese-crator had Mahmud firmly in his pocket. He would remain there until he ceased to be useful or Guntur died. Mahmud had the power to give the police a nudge in the right direction to make that happen, but Guntur had thoroughly infiltrated the National Police. There was no telling who would tip Guntur off, and the cost of that betrayal would be lethal.

Mahmud took a deep breath as he stepped over to the mirror and looked himself over. Not a hair was out of place on his head. His black two-piece suit was pressed, his shoes shined, and his Indonesian/Jakarta flag lapel prominently displayed. Mahmud tried to dispel the cloud hovering over his aura, then decided against it. The people wouldn't be looking for charisma. They would want to see he was troubled by the events, show that he was human, but to complement that with a stern determination to bring the perpetrator to justice.

Footsteps echoed from behind, and Mahmud spun around. Mega Nyoman entered, a *kretek* hanging from his lips. His posture seemed more slouched than usual, though his suit appeared to fit better than it normally did, no doubt due to somebody with fashion sense forcibly applying advice. Still, the absence of a baggy, off-the-rack suit only seemed to shift Nyoman's appearance from "haggard, unmotivated detective" to "funeral home director."

"You look fine, Setiawan," Nyoman said. "You don't need to keep inspecting yourself."

"Yes, I do," Mahmud said. "You ought to check your-self, too. We're going on TV. We have to sell this."

"We won't have to sell it hard," Nyoman said. "You recall public reaction to the Bali Nine?" Mahmud nodded. "The people crave law and order. All you have to do is point out this foreigner is looking to disrupt that. You'll have them eating from your palm." He finished his ciga-rette, and extinguished it in a nearby ashtray. "I'm guessing you'll have little resistance from the press and virtually none from the people."

Mahmud studied Nyoman. "Never took you for a student of the human condition."

Nyoman shrugged. "I dabble in detective work."

Mahmud smiled at the deadpan joke. "C'mon. We're up."

CHAPTER NINETEEN

Menteng, Central Jakarta, Indonesia
20 March 2019
12:00 hours Golf (05:00 hours Zulu)

"Ladies and gentlemen, Deputy Governor Mahmud."

Kirsana Nirmala watched as Mahmud and Chief Commissioner Mega Nyoman marched on stage. Mahmud took his place at the podium, while Nyoman stood in the background. Rudi Irwan, Nirmala's photographer for official events, lifted his Nikon digital camera and snapped away, leaving Nirmala to focus on the briefing. She held her Samsung in her hand with the voice recorder running for later recollection of comments.

Nirmala observed Mahmud as he got settled in. He was a handsome man and a rising star in the Greater Indonesia Movement Party, transitioning to politics after a successful business career and a brief stint in the Demokrat Party. Despite being aligned with the center-right, Mahmud was known to reach across the aisle and work with Democratic Party of Struggle, the center-left opposition and the President's political party. Mahmud championed Indonesian exceptionalism, advocated fair tax reform, was tough on crime, and was a supporter of the President's "a thousand friends, zero enemies" diplomatic platform.

In short, Mahmud analyzed popular opinion and tailored his policies accordingly. It made him a successful politician with a bright future. It also made Nirmala inherently suspicious. His cinema-star good looks were lost on Nirmala, which left her with the clarity to study his political motives. She couldn't tell if it was his attempts at perfection or some sort of intuition that told her something was off with Setiawan Mahmud, but she was convinced there was something hidden beyond the façade.

"Gentlemen," Mahmud said. "Ladies. At approximately 07:30, a young woman's body was found by Greater Jakarta Metropolitan Regional Police in the Selamat

Datang Monument Pond." He reached for a clicker on the podium, pointed it towards the television, and paused. "I should warn you that the images you are about to see are graphic."

Nirmala's jaw clenched as she saw the first crime scene photo. The victim's breasts and genitalia were censored, but the rest was left for the world to see. Several audible gasps filled the room. Nirmala's eyes shifted away from the images and back to Mahmud. She noticed his eyes were on the crowd rather than the presentation, and watched him try to suppress a nervous swallow. Her eyes narrowed. *What's that about?*

After a moment, Mahmud said, "As you can see, she was badly beaten, mutilated, and murdered." He hit another button, and a new image of the same woman on a medical examiner's slab filled the screen with similar censorship. "Carved into her stomach are the simplified Chinese characters for the word 'whore.'"

Nirmala caught Mahmud gauging the audience again, which raised an immediate red flag. Even the most cynical of politicians knew it was bad form to be obviously more worried about reactions than the event at hand.

Mahmud clicked to the next slide and looked at the screen for the first time. When Nirmala saw the slide, she fought to suppress a grimace, and her hackles stood high on end. She inhaled deeply through her nostrils and let the breath out quietly past her lips.

"This is John Bradshaw," Mahmud said. "He entered the country four months ago illegally under the alias 'Neil McCloud.' He is an American citizen wanted for the murder of four federal agents in his home nation. In Indonesia, he is wanted for over three dozen murders, including the murder of two members of the Greater Jakarta Metro *Brimob* Pelopor Regiment. DNA from seminal fluid was found linking Bradshaw to the heinous rape and murder of this young woman.

"*Baintelkam* believes that after fleeing the United States, Bradshaw sought the employ of the Shui Fong

Triad, based in Macau and Hong Kong," Mahmud continued. "Our working theory is that the Triad took interest in the skills developed through his military special operations background, and is using Bradshaw to expand their drug empire into Indonesia, which has thus far remained untouched by the scourge of major organized crime."

Mahmud met the eyes of each member of the press corps. "I call upon the great Indonesian people to help bring this foreign menace to justice. Bradshaw is armed and extremely dangerous, so please do not approach him. If you see him, or any suspicious foreigner, contact your Regional Police precinct and report the sighting. With your help, law enforcement can bring this monster to account for his reprehensible misdeeds." He nodded dutifully, then said, "Thank you." Mahmud then marched off the stage and out of the room, ignoring the shouted questions from the press corps.

"Allow me to have your attention," Mega Nyoman said, surprising the room with the force with which he said it. The press corps had been so focused on obtaining further comments from Mahmud that they failed to notice Nyoman approach the podium. As the room quieted, he exhaled heavily. "The Deputy Governor touched on the major points of our investigation thus far. Through the Criminal Detective Unit, I have command of the investigation, and I am coordinating with regional and national law enforcement assets, as well as the American legal attaché to try and bring Bradshaw to justice before he is allowed to take another life. I'll now take any questions."

Nirmala was the first on her feet, her hand held high above her head. Nyoman's face remained impassive, but the flicker in his eyes betrayed that he recognized her. That didn't surprise Nirmala. Her extensive journalistic catalogue contained several pieces on the corruption and lapses in professionalism within the Indonesian National Police. She knew on that basis alone that Nyoman would want to yield the floor to anyone else. Nirmala also knew how evasive it would look if Nyoman ignored her. She suppressed a smile as Nyoman caved and gestured to her.

"Yes," he said.

"Kirsana Nirmala, *Kompas,*" she said. "First, allow me to say that this is a national tragedy, and that we appreciate all that the National Police and the Deputy Governor are doing to keep Jakarta safe."

Nyoman nodded dutifully. "Thank you, Ms. Nirmala." The expression on his face broadcasted his immunity to her flattery, so she shifted her approach.

"The body was dumped around 07:30," Nirmala said. "I imagine that time of day, traffic being what it is in that part of the city, the response time was somewhere between 30 minutes to an hour. I presume that standard crime scene procedure was not to touch the body until crime scene technicians, a supervisor, and an investigator from your office arrived to accept custody of the body."

"Ms. Nirmala, please get to your point," Nyoman said evenly.

Nirmala gave him a polite smile and said, "My apologies, Chief Commissioner. I'll come to my point. Did you have Bradshaw's DNA on file beforehand?"

"No," Nyoman said. "We acquired it from the Americans when Bradshaw murdered two of my men."

"That's an impressive expedition of the bureaucracy," Nirmala said. "We all know the Americans can't move anything without permission forms signed in triplicate from four different departments. Something must have changed."

"Yes," Nyoman said, fixing her with a penetrative gaze. "What changed is that he's killed law enforcement officers just doing their jobs in two different nations, and is allying with a transnational criminal syndicate."

"I'm just curious," Nirmala said. "Returning to my previous point...if we're to take you at face value that you already obtained the DNA sample from the Americans, that sample had sufficient time and opportunity to be contaminated. How can you be so certain that the DNA found on that body belongs to Mr. Bradshaw?"

Nyoman's eyes narrowed. "What are you insinuating, Ms. Nirmala?"

"I'm not insinuating anything, sir," Nirmala said. "I'm simply seeking clarification."

"Allow me to provide you some," Nyoman said. He leaned forward, gripping the podium. "Advances in medical forensic technology allowed us to salvage enough usable specimen to make a 99.99% match to Bradshaw. That has given us a target to focus on bringing him to justice."

Nyoman scooped the clicker off the podium and moved to the next slide. Two men filled the screen, clad in National Police dress uniform and sporting dark blue berets upon their heads. He paused to study the photo, then looked back to Nirmala. When he resumed speaking, his voice brimmed with raw emotion.

"Police Brigadiers Joyo Dumadi and Vikal Kersen. Both of them proud Army veterans. Both of them tenured members of the Greater Jakarta Metro Regional Police. Volunteers for the *Pelepor* Regiment. They acted under orders to arrest Mr. Bradshaw for murder. He replied by gunning the both of them down."

"With two different caliber weapons, if memory serves me well," Nirmala said. "No return shots fired."

"A testament to Bradshaw's skill in murder," Nyoman said. "It is utterly disgraceful that instead of doing your patriotic duty to help bring Bradshaw to justice, you're wasting your time attempting to paint law enforcement in a negative light."

"The only duty I have, sir, is to the truth," Nirmala said. "If I find inconsistencies in the official government narrative, it is my job to explore them, not to mindlessly pass them on to my readers as gospel."

"I invite you to say that to their widows," Nyoman said. He scanned the room. "Next question."

* * *

Beltsville, Maryland
20 March 2019
02:30 hours Quebec (06:30 hours Zulu)

DIANA FAIRCHILD SAT at her dining table, her favorite gray microfleece robe wrapped around her body. Her dyed red hair was pulled back in a messy bun. Designer glasses shielded borderline bloodshot pale blue eyes which bore the burdens of fatigue beneath them. She cradled a Darth Vader mug with lukewarm Earl Grey in one hand while the other held her Google smartphone. The longer she studied the article, the more her eyes hurt.

Goddamn it, she cursed internally. *Why couldn't he have gone to ground somewhere closer to home?*

Fairchild knew the grousing was irrational. From memory, she knew there were 81 nations and nine disputed territories that lacked extradition treaties with the United States. The vast majority of those were in Africa, the Middle East, or in the former Soviet Union. Out of all the places to land, Indonesia was the natural choice. It was populated, with a healthy expatriate community, which provided social camouflage. More importantly, it was outside the immediate influence of both the United States and Russia.

She knew this because once upon a time, she lived in constant fear that she would have to utilize a similar plan of her own. In retrospect, the danger notwithstanding, it had been a simpler time. All she had to do was work and avoid being caught. That was all before she gave the scam known as marriage a try, sacrificed her autonomy, and emerged on the other side traumatized, divorced, and with two children to raise on her own.

Nope, Fairchild told herself. *Not going there right now.* She returned to the Jakarta Post article. Proverbial storm clouds had formed on the horizon, and action was demanded.

He couldn't run forever, she mused. A half-smile spread across her lips. *Still, not bad for somebody without the proper training.*

Fairchild set her phone and mug down, removed her glasses, and rubbed her temples tiredly. The past day had been long enough. A 12-hour work day coordinating assets 7,000 miles away, a parent-teacher conference, and helping Jared and Raven with homework, all before factoring in the off-the-books assignment that had started nearly two years earlier and grown in crescendo.

It was that side job that had disturbed Fairchild's sleep, by way of the shrill news alerts she had programmed into her phone. It was responsible for her sipping tea and reading international news in the early morning hours. She had a feeling that it would be a very long time before she got a solid night's rest, at least at the rate things continued to develop.

Fairchild closed the browser and opened the Wickr application. She knew better than most how unsecure standard messaging was, particularly on social media. The majority of her extracurricular activities were debriefed face-to-face for that reason, but an instant communication method was necessary for emergencies. Fairchild certainly qualified the current situation as such.

When she found her intended contact, Fairchild entered the pin to access the message thread. She held the phone in both hands and tapped out a message:

You see the news?

A half-minute after Fairchild sent that message, she received a response:

No. Something wrong?

Despite the message's encryption, there was no way Fairchild was going to communicate her thoughts over a digital line. Both parties agreed from the onset that Wickr was only to be used sparingly, and they would assume their targets had found a way to breach the communications security.

I'll tell you at the usual spot.

The response came a moment later:

OK

Fairchild closed Wickr and checked the time: *02:34.* She'd need to drop the kids off at school early if she wanted to make the rendezvous in time to avoid a schedule interruption. If she fell asleep immediately, she could potentially rest another three hours before the day started.

Not for the first time, Fairchild exhaled tiredly and said to herself, "I should have been a fucking lawyer."

Menteng, Central Jakarta, Indonesia
20 March 2019
13:45 hours Golf (06:45 hours Zulu)

"CAN YOU BELIEVE the *nerve* of that son of a bitch?" Nirmala said once she was safely in her company-issued car and on her way back to *Kompas* HQ. They were gridlocked in traffic, and it was shaping up to be at least an hour before they returned.

"Yeah," Rudi Irwan said off-handedly, his focus on checking the photos he had taken.

"He sells us that load of shit and expects us to lap it up, ask for more?" Nirmala's knuckles grew white as she gripped the steering wheel tightly. "Their story doesn't match up, and once the questioning grew too intense, they thumped the patriotic drum and expected us to fall in line. *Fuck* him!"

"You think there's more to that story?" Irwan asked.

Nirmala chuckled darkly. "I *know* there's more to that story, and I have half a mind to think that Mahmud and Nyoman are up to their necks in that girl's murder." She shook her head. "This has something to do with Suparman Guntur. I can feel it in my bones."

"So, what's your next move?" Irwan asked.

Before Nirmala could respond, her phone announced the arrival of a new email. She reached to where it was suspended in the dashboard mount, navigated the menu screens to the email, and saw that the sender was j5140248@nwytg.net, with the subject line being "Abductions."

"What the hell is this?" Nirmala asked as she opened the email. She returned her eyes to the road and said, "Rudi, read that for me."

Irwan set the camera in his lap and looked at the email. "That's a burner email," he said immediately. "I've seen those before. You set up the email, use it to defeat spam-bots or remain untraceable. That domain will only be valid for the next few minutes, then it's completely erased."

That piqued Nirmala's interest. "Okay, read it to me."

Irwan squinted as he read. "The men who murdered the girl this morning have committed other atrocities. Over the past month, dozens of young women have been abducted from Belitung and forced into the employ of the Kuwat Syndicate. The fountain girl was one of them. This is video evidence of her abduction, along with others from her village. They are planning to make another run to the island tonight and will return to the Port of Tanjung Priok around 03:00 tomorrow morning. That will be your best chance to catch them in the act and expose them for what they are." He looked at the bottom of the email. "There's two attachments. An MPEG-4 and a PDF."

Nirmala glanced to double-check that the auxiliary cord was plugged into the Samsung's headphone jack, then said, "Play the video."

Irwan tapped on the attachment and watched while it loaded. Fifteen seconds later, the screen went black.

Nirmana's eyes shifted between the road and the video. She saw men in military-style equipment sporting automatic weapons. The camera panned over a line of girls who had been forced on their knees, their wrists restrained behind their backs. One face caught her eye, and she pointed at her phone.

"That's the girl," Nirmala said. "That's proof that their narrative is bullshit."

"That's just proof that she was abducted," Irwan countered. "Nyoman will probably spin it as those gunmen being Triad soldiers."

"Damn it," Nirmala growled.

In the video, a voice said in Indonesian, "Move them out!" Several of the soldiers stood the girls up and began marching them off-screen. Once the girls were gone, a group of families—men and women, some of them younger, others middle-aged—were pushed forward and driven to their knees. The soldiers that remained lined up in front of the families, and a tight sensation gripped Nirmala's chest as she knew what came next.

"No…" she whispered.

The cameraman shouted, "Fire!" The next instant, the firing squad held down the triggers to their Pindad rifles. It was all over in the span of 10 seconds. Twenty bodies lay in the mud, their blood seeping from their wounds. A low wail sounded off in the background and grew in crescendo, only to be silenced off-camera by a single pistol shot. The video ended there.

Nirmala took deep breaths in through her nose and out of her mouth. Her blood boiled, and her heart ached. It was not the first gratuitous act of violence she had witnessed as a journalist, and she was certain it wouldn't be the last. Still, the pain was there all the same.

"Holy hell," Irwan said. He closed the video, pulled up the PDF, and cleared his throat. "So, the PDF…it has a dock location for where the Syndicate is supposed to be dropping off their next shipment." He glanced over to Nirmala. "What are you going to do with this?"

Nirmala knew exactly what she would do, but she refused to tell Irwan. It would be safer for the both of them if he didn't know.

"We need to get back to headquarters," Nirmala said. "Once we're there, I can run digital forensics on the email and its attachments. When I have a better working knowledge of what we've just been given, I'll be in a position to better call the next move."

CHAPTER TWENTY

Cakung, East Jakarta, Indonesia
20 March 2019
17:12 hours Golf (10:12 hours Zulu)

The new safe house was another warehouse on the east side of the city. At one point, it had been a logistical storage site, but the tenant company had decided it was cheaper to abandon the property. It had been listed at a dirt-cheap price when Pace and Tan began their operational preparation of the battlespace. The purchase was a no-brainer.

Bradshaw ran his final stack of bills through the counter. When the machine finished its task, he secured the bills with a rubber band and set it with the rest of the counted cash. His eyes fell on the pile in front of him, then traversed the new living quarters, landing first on the other two cash piles. Four tedious hours had gone into accounting for their newly-gotten gains. His gaze then traversed to Tan and ended with Pace, each of them sharing the same exhausted look in their eyes.

"One million, six hundred thousand," Bradshaw said with a sigh.

Pace wiped his brow with his forearm. "Eight hundred thousand."

"Eight hundred thousand," Tan echoed. His fingers were interlaced as he twiddled his thumbs.

Bradshaw eyed the ceiling as he added the figures in his head. "As long as my math's not fucked up, that's $3.2 million, American."

"Yeah," Pace said. "Sounds about right."

"That's enough for you to continue your fight and for me to go off-grid after this is all said and done," Bradshaw said.

Tan wagged a finger at Bradshaw. "Gotta say, Jack. Didn't think you had a criminal mind about you."

"I've got a survivor's mindset," Bradshaw corrected. "Nothing happens without the green. This ought to keep me off the grid for a while. I pick the right country, I can live like a king in relative anonymity."

Pace eyed the ground as he rubbed his hands together. "Let me address the elephant in the room. I sure hope you didn't join up with us hoping to make a quick payday."

Bradshaw's face darkened. "Fuck you, Danny."

Pace held up his hands. "I'm not doing this for the money. Neither is Lucas. Put yourself in my shoes, Jack. How does it look?"

"Put yourself in mine," Bradshaw shot back. "Your own government tries to murder you. You go off-grid and try to lay low. You pop up on the radar. Your government then leaks your file to the world, inviting anyone and everyone to take a shot at you. I've got no support system. My bug-out funds were depleted during the voyage out here. Think I'm gonna get by on thoughts and prayers?" He shook his head. "I got into this because I saw what they were going to do to Citra. I'm *in* this because of what they did to her. That doesn't mean I can't stop thinking of my next move. The bad guys sure as shit are thinking about it."

"Fair enough," Pace said quietly. "I believe you." He looked to Tan. "Actually, we were thinking about having you come onboard full-time."

Bradshaw's eyes widened. "What?"

"You're battle-tested," Tan said. "Quick thinker. We've seen you make calls on the fly. And you just passed the last test. You believe in the mission. We'd love to have you on board."

Bradshaw hung his head as a sigh fell from his lips. "I really want to say yes." He looked back up to Pace and Tan. "The truth is...every second I'm around you, I'm putting you both in danger. The people who want me dead, they're banking on Suparman to get the job done. The minute they find out he's failed, they'll come looking for me. Your operation is centric to this region. That'll give them a set search area to find, fix, and finish me. If you're with me when that happens, they'll kill you, too." He shook his head. "No. The best thing I can do for the cause is make tracks after we put that piece of shit Suparman in the dirt."

Tan nodded his head. "That makes sense, and I appreciate that."

"Me, too," Pace said. "It's a shame, though. Thought we had a third shooter locked in for sure."

Bradshaw smirked. "What, like the Mod Squad?"

"Nah," Pace said. "None of us is black enough to pass for Lincoln, and as pretty as he is, Lucas ain't no Julie Barnes."

Bradshaw snickered. Tan rolled his eyes and said, "Yeah, you *ang mo* fucks are just hating that I don't age until I'm 62."

"Oh, I hate nothing about it," Bradshaw said. "I'd love to have you as my Ranger buddy on a field problem. We can spoon under my woobie and stargaze."

Tan's facial expression was genuinely perplexed. "Woobie?"

Pace's cell phone buzzed. He reached into his pocket and said, "Either you know, or you don't. Can't teach you the way of the woobie if you haven't lived it, brother." As he checked the incoming SMS, his face darkened. "Hey, Lucas, get the laptop, will you?"

"What's going on?" Bradshaw asked as Tan set into motion.

"Just got a text on the burner phone," Pace said as he tapped out an email address. "Apparently, she just got an anonymous tip on the Syndicate's operations."

"What kind of tip?"

Tan returned with the laptop in hand. He took a seat on his cot, and Pace and Bradshaw hovered around him. A moment later, Tan accessed the burner email they'd set aside in case there were files too large to send via text. The email was a forward, with a small note from Kirsana Nirmala:

The email was a temporary address. It's disappeared. Ran metadata forensics on the video. Geotag confirms the video was shot on Belitung. Still...something is off about this. Be careful.

-KN

Tan launched the video. When it ended, each man wore a hardened scowl on their faces. Bradshaw took a deep breath and attempted to compartmentalize the rage for later.

"Kirsana's got good instincts," he said to break the silence. "This smells like a trap."

"You think so?" Tan asked.

"If you're a dope-peddling, sex-slaving scumbag dealing with a merry band of moralistic crusading pipe-hitters, the best way to break them is to get under their skin. Get inside their head. PsyOp. It's no different than a street fight. You get your opponent angry, they let their rage take the wheel, they'll get sloppy."

"I can't discount that possibility," Pace said. "We also can't discount that maybe somebody in the Syndicate grew a conscience, saw her coverage of events, and decided she was a safe bet for reaching out."

"Sure," Bradshaw said. "But at the same time, err on the side of caution. We're high and dry for a lead, and this drops in our laps?" He folded his arms and shook his head. "I don't like it. It's too clean."

Pace continued to rub his palms. Finally, he said, "Jack, you're familiar with the port, yeah?" Bradshaw nodded, and Pace continued, "We'll run recce from a distance. It looks clear, we'll move in on the girls. We see something we don't like, we'll record what we see, exfil quiet, and get the footage to Kirsana. Let her see what she can do with it."

Bradshaw rolled his lips beneath his teeth. "Better than charging in blind."

"If it is legit, we could use Kirsana's connects to get the girls to safety," Tan said.

"Not an opportunity we get regularly," Pace said. "Agreed." He tossed Tan the phone. "Set up a meet. You'll run that end. Jack and I will run the recce."

"Tracking," Bradshaw said.

"Got it," Tan said.

"All right, then," Pace said as he rose from the cot. "Let's get the cash put away and refit."

McLean, Virginia
20 March 2019
07:50 hours Quebec (11:50 hours Zulu)

As Diana Fairchild navigated the parking structure, her eyes scanned the ceiling. There were more cameras there than in most corporate buildings. Given the structure's location, it didn't surprise her. When Fairchild had started working out of the headquarters building, the sheer volume of cameras unnerved her. Her training had specifically geared her to see surveillance as the enemy. After a while, she'd tuned them out, but with the beginnings of the side job, old habits reemerged.

Fairchild guided her Ford Escape to the fourth level. She saw her handler standing beside a black Mercedes-Benz parked one slot over from a pillar. Fairchild parked her vehicle in the empty slot, killed the ignition, and dismounted. On her way out of the vehicle, she snatched up her gray blazer from the passenger's seat.

The meeting site was selected as it was one of the few blind spots inside the garage. As long as they didn't take too long and there were no witnesses on-site, the meeting would go entirely undetected. Coworkers holding conversations in the structure was a regular occurrence. The only reason that discretion was required was that her handler was upper-middle management. Being seen with

Fairchild when they were separated by more than a few layers of bureaucracy would raise eyebrows.

Fairchild's eyes fell on her handler, and she couldn't help but feel a pang of envy. Sharon McBride looked two decades younger than her 60 years. With her raven hair straightened and cut short, she looked every bit the manager that she was. Her black pantsuit and sky-blue blouse perfectly complemented her runner's physique. McBride's intense brown eyes fell on Fairchild as the latter approached her between the parked vehicles.

"You're cutting it close," McBride said, her arms folded.

"Traffic on the Beltway was hell," Fairchild said as she slipped into her blazer.

"So what's going on?"

Fairchild slung her handbag on her shoulder, then dug into it for her phone. Once it was unlocked, she pulled up the Jakarta Post article and handed the phone to McBride without comment. It took her 30 seconds to scan the article. When McBride returned the phone, a glower adorned her regal face.

"Shit."

"This is Lambert's work," Fairchild said.

"No doubt," McBride said. "They're hoping the Indonesians can unwittingly tie up their loose end."

"What'd your asset say about the situation?"

A sigh fell from McBride's lips. "That Bradshaw's call sign fits. Apparently, this mobster's brother tried kidnapping some girl in broad daylight, and Bradshaw killed him for it."

Fairchild nodded silently. Her professional side chided Bradshaw for breaking cover over something that was trivial in the grand scheme. Conversely, her human side applauded the action, and was jealous that he got to act where she would have been told to stand down.

"That's not all," McBride continued. "Jakarta Chief of Station called me last night, right before you reached out. Danny Pace entered the country about a week ago on an

Australian passport. We only caught it because he slipped up. Used an alias from his time in Ground Branch."

Fairchild made the connection. "You think Pace recruited Bradshaw to go on the offensive."

"It's a fair bet," McBride said. "Thing is, Pace's gonna get him killed. He's good, but it's just him, Bradshaw, and his Singaporean asset. The full force of their government is gonna come crashing down on them. They've got the LEGAT involved, too. His best chance was to run. That's gone now."

Fairchild pursed her lips as she interlaced her fingers at her waist. She inhaled deeply right before she spoke. "What if you activate your asset? Could help him kill the mob boss and take off some of the heat."

McBride's eyes narrowed. "You know how hard we worked to infiltrate the *preman* groups? That's specifically a counterterror initiative. It's going to draw heat if we tell him to go proactive."

"I'm not seeing an alternative, ma'am," Fairchild said. She glanced around before she proceeded. "We agreed that if Bradshaw survived out in the cold, he'd be our best bet at taking down the President's Men. He's proven to be resourceful and self-starting."

"That's more Pace's involvement than anything," McBride said. "Bradshaw's a shooter, not an operative."

"Then we should recruit Pace, too," Fairchild said. "Have him teach Bradshaw the ropes. Pace's already established that he's a sucker for lost causes. We show him what we know, tell him Bradshaw will need him to stay alive, we can bring him around."

McBride rolled her lips inward as she contemplated the proposal. "We can't read in the Chief of Station. I don't trust our asset to handle this himself, and even if I did, they wouldn't believe it, coming from him."

Fairchild nodded in understanding. "What, then?"

A heavy sigh fell from McBride's nose. "I know D/NCS has been meaning to meet with his opposite number in the BIN regarding ISIS's franchising in the region."

Fairchild nodded at the mention of the *Badan Intelijen Negara,* the State Intelligence Agency. "I'll convince him to let me go there to hold the meeting and to see if we can assist with the Bradshaw situation. We'll use that as cover for recruitment. That'll give me an excuse to borrow you and bring you with."

"That sounds solid, ma'am," Fairchild said.

"We'll need a familiar face to approach Danny," McBride said. "He's careful. He's likely to put a bullet in our asset's face, especially if he's a known quantity. We roll in deep on him with a GRS element, it's likely he'll mistake it for a hit and come out shooting."

"You have an idea?" Fairchild asked. "Somebody in Jakarta Station he knows that we can read in?"

"No," McBride said after a pause. "But, there is somebody else we can use." She looked at Fairchild. "Leave that to me."

Fairchild nodded. "And as for activating the asset?"

McBride hesitated a moment before she continued. "He's already been having doubts about the organization. Says Guntur's been going off the rails. Kuwat's more plugged into vice than terrorism, anyway. We'll activate him, then give him his severance package."

"You want me to handle that, ma'am?" Fairchild asked.

"Discreetly," McBride said. "I'll give you the contact protocols. You can't do it from your work station."

Fairchild nodded. "Understood." She took a deep breath. "So we're doing this."

"Yeah," McBride said. She eyed the ground and shook her head. "I just hope this doesn't blow up in our faces. We're sticking our necks out enough as it is."

CHAPTER TWENTY-ONE

Tanjung Priok, North Jakarta, Indonesia
21 March 2019
02:55 hours Golf (20 March 19:55 hours Zulu)

A plain black kerchief was crudely fashioned into a bandana around Bradshaw's hair, keeping the sweat from dripping into his eyes. He laid flat atop of a shooter's mat, positioned at the top of a stack of Conexes. The SR25 was tucked into his shoulder, its bipod legs deployed and held in place with small sandbags. The port's ambient lighting meant that Bradshaw didn't need a night vision attachment to enhance the Leupold variable power optic.

The stay in precipitation held through the night, something for which Bradshaw was grateful. It wouldn't have been the first time he'd been soaked to the bone while manning an observation post, which only made him all the more appreciative for the calm weather. It was a balmy 80°F with negligent wind, which rendered the blue windbreaker unnecessary. The air was thick and humid, but that was just an environmental reality.

Bradshaw alternated between searching the dock for signs of hostile activity and scanning the horizon for the inbound vessel. He had wanted to be the one on the ground and argued his previous employment as a stevedore made him a natural choice. Pace's rebuttal brought that idea to a halt: if Bradshaw was discovered by one of Guntur's men or even a dock worker, there'd be no chance of playing it off. On the other hand, Pace was unknown to Guntur and was not the subject of a nationwide manhunt.

That left Bradshaw on overwatch, which was just as well. Bradshaw had graduated both the Sniper School and the Special Forces Sniper Course during his Army enlistment and had confirmed kills in his jacket. He was just as comfortable on-glass as he was up-close and personal.

Bradshaw's Peltor headset crackled and Pace's voice filled his ears. "You got anything, Boy Scout?"

He adjusted his microphone and reached for his PTT transmitter. "Negative, Rusty. It's dead as shit."

"They're cutting it close," Pace replied.

"Or Cronkite was right and this is a set-up," Bradshaw said, using their agreed-upon call sign for Kirsana Nirmala.

"I hope not."

Bradshaw surveyed the container yard. If he hadn't known where to look, he wouldn't have seen Pace's crouched form, his Micro Uzi at the low ready. He held his point of aim well above Pace's head. The rifle's safety was on and Bradshaw's finger was off the trigger, but he still felt uneasy laying the crosshairs directly on a teammate, even if only to confirm the latter's position.

After a moment, Bradshaw keyed up again. "Lionheart check in?"

"No," Pace said. "Should have heard back by now."

Bradshaw frowned. "How many comms windows has he missed?"

"Two. One more and we're aborting."

Shit. Bradshaw keyed up as he returned his point of aim to the dock. "Roger that. Still have nothing on the horizon." As he let go of the PTT, Bradshaw caught movement to his left. He worked the Leupold's throw lever to increase the magnification to its 10x limit. Bradshaw made out a yacht making good speed and moving in a straight line towards the dock.

"Rusty, I've got something."

"Go," Pace said.

"Inbound vessel, just under five klicks out. Looks about the right size to move pax."

"ETA?"

Bradshaw made rough calculations as he watched the vessel grow in his optic. "They're moving at a pretty good clip. I'd say…two minutes, maybe three."

"Roger," Pace said. "Just reached out to Lionheart again. He doesn't get back to us in 60 seconds, I'm pulling the plug."

Bradshaw let out a long exhale through his nose before he replied. "Roger." His eyes didn't waver from the boat. As it filled his point of aim, Bradshaw's free hand came up to the throw lever and gradually reduced the magnification. He searched the bow and found a figure on the port side, the familiar outline of a rifle in his hands.

"Rusty, this is Boy Scout," Bradshaw said on the net. "Confirmed tango on the bow, port side. I think this is it."

"Break, break, break," Pace said, his voice strained. "Tidal Wave. Tidal Wave."

Bradshaw's blood ran cold. "Tidal Wave" was the mission's emergency evacuation code, where enemy compromise was either imminent or on-going. He began to pull back from the rifle when he heard the faint *creak* of rusted metal. Bradshaw tightened his grip on the SR-25 and scanned the area beneath him.

He almost missed it. The Conex in question was roughly 100 meters away. Its door was barely cracked open. Bradshaw trained his crosshairs at the opening and maxed out his magnification. It was hard to see, since most of the figure was obscured by the Conex. He was able to make out a rifle muzzle and what appeared to be the outline of a ballistic helmet. That was more than enough for Bradshaw.

"Hold, Rusty," he said as calmly as possible. "We've got hostiles in the Conexes. I'm going to guide you out."

DANNY PACE'S HEART pounded in his chest. With Bradshaw's announcement of enemy soldiers lying in wait, things threatened to spiral out of control. He inhaled deeply through his nose and continued to scan his surroundings, his Micro Uzi held at the low ready.

One thing at a time, Danny Boy.

Bradshaw's voice filled his ears. "Rusty, walk east 200 meters and hold."

Pace spun around in place and raised his weapon. He walked at a steady rate, scanning laterally and vertically as he went. When he reached the hold point, Pace pressed himself against a Conex, took a knee, and keyed up.

"In position."

"Roger," Bradshaw said. "Stand by."

Sweat trickled down Pace's face and soaked through the gray T-shirt beneath his windbreaker. He wanted to ditch the jacket, but he figured he'd need it now more than ever if he managed to clear the dragnet. Pace took another deep breath in an attempt to lower his pulse and concentrate on the task in front of him.

"You're clear," Bradshaw said. "Another hundred meters due east." Pace hadn't made it more than 15 paces when Bradshaw returned to the net. "*Hold.* Enemy squad emerging from the Conexes. Take cover."

Pace narrowly squeezed between a pair of containers. A moment later, the sound of boots scuffling against concrete reached his ears and rose in volume. His grip on the Micro Uzi tightened as he willed himself into invisibility. The footsteps rose to a thunderous sonority. Indonesian was spoken in hushed terms. From the tone and the words he was able to decipher, Pace determined they were tactical commands.

Bradshaw returned to the net. "The boat's docked. *Brimob*'s swarming the container yard. I'm also seeing a couple of APCs posted outside the yard as a cordon. They were expecting us."

Pace keyed up once without speaking, his way of acknowledging the traffic while announcing that the enemy was danger close. He heard the footsteps fade away, and a moment later, Bradshaw spoke.

"Rusty, you're clear. Hit that intersection and turn south."

With a relieved exhale, Pace poked his head out from concealment and glanced both ways before emerging into the aisle. When he reached the corner, he put his back against a container to the south and cleared the dead space. There were no visible enemies. Pace then stepped away from the Conex, turned around, and slowly pied the corner. When he was greeted by empty space, Pace pushed forward.

"Enemy buddy team about to cross you," Bradshaw said. "Take cover."

Pace ducked between a pair of containers and waited. After a moment, Bradshaw said, "They appear to be alone. They're out of visual range of the outer cordon. I can either walk you past them or we can drop them. Your call."

Killing the pair of corrupt officers would have been the fastest way. If they punched through the cordon, they could clear the scene sooner and figure out what had gone wrong. At the same time, if the *Brimob* officers discovered one of their own dead, they would lock down the port. Even if they stuck to cover and concealment and their positions weren't fixed, neither Pace nor Bradshaw had enough ammunition to fend off a heavily armed and specially trained paramilitary platoon. Shooting had to be an absolute last resort.

With a frown, Pace reached for his PTT and keyed up twice. Bradshaw was on the net a second later.

"Yeah, that's what I would have gone with, too. Walk west between the Conexes about a hundred meters, then look for a way to break south."

Pace moved quietly between the containers, careful not to bump into either side. He held his Micro Uzi against his body with the suppressed muzzle down. When he guesstimated that he'd walked 100 meters, Pace looked for a break in the containers. A few steps later, he located a gap and entered it, facing south once more.

"I see you," Bradshaw announced. "Good news: you're almost out of the yard. Bad news: there's a *Brimob* APC positioned almost directly in front of the containers, on the other side of the fence. They took all their dismounts and drivers with them and left gunners in the turrets. We're going to have to take them out."

Pace keyed up. "The minute you put that long gun into play, somebody's gonna suspect something. Ambient noise isn't gonna cover that shot."

"I know," Bradshaw said. "Gonna have to hope that our outer cordon isn't really an inner cordon."

"Fuck," Pace said off the net. He pressed his PTT. "How spaced out are they?"

"About 15 meters between each vic."

"I could take all three of them. It'll be quieter than the long gun."

There was a pause before Bradshaw came back on the net. "All right. I'll cover you."

"Roger."

Pace exhaled, readjusted the stock in his shoulder, and pressed forward. As he approached the last row of Conexes, he slowed his gait. An electric surge of anticipation and anxiety coursed through his body. Pace halted just short of the edge of the Conexes, took a knee, and glanced to his right. He could see another APC parked further down, its turret gunner faced away from him. His hand snaked for his PTT.

"In position," he said quietly. "Going to take them west to east."

"Roger," Bradshaw said. "On your call."

Pace trained the Trijicon RMR's red dot on the turret gunner's face. He shifted the point of aim just beneath the target's Kevlar helmet. Judging from the outline, the *Brimob* officer was wearing the Advanced Combat Helmet that was standard US Army issue and spread to its allies through security agreements. It was rated to stop 9mm bullets, which meant all of his shots had to be beneath the helmet.

He thumbed the Micro Uzi's selector to the semi-automatic position, then inhaled. As Pace let the breath out, his finger took up slack on the trigger. At the bottom of his exhale, the trigger broke, and a lone round raced through the suppressor-shrouded barrel. Pace saw the *Brimob* gunner's body jolt as the 9x19mm Parabellum round made impact with his forehead and cut through skull and gray matter. The gunner's body slumped on the Pindad SPM2 machine gun's stock, driving the muzzle skyward.

Pace rounded the corner and found his next target. The second gunner was close enough that Pace could see the surprise in the man's eyes. He centered the red dot on the center of the man's face as the SPM2's muzzle began its rotation in Pace's direction. The Marine was faster than the *Brimob* officer, and the Micro Uzi coughed. A lone bullet cut the gunner down.

One more, Pace thought as he stepped further around the final Conex. He saw that the final machine gunner had already trained his weapon downrange. Pace rushed and squeezed off a pair of rounds. Both of them made contact with the officer's helmet. He watched the gunner rock back, then rush to get back on his gun.

Shit!

A shrill *crack* resonated through the dock. Pace recognized it as a suppressed supersonic 7.62x51mm round. The final gunner's head snapped back, then his body slipped torpidly inside of the turret. Blood and brain had been propelled through the back of the helmet and stained the underbelly of the turret hatch.

Bradshaw's voice was strained as it filled Pace's ComTac III headset. *"Run!"*

BRADSHAW SCRAMBLED DOWN the back of the Conex stack. His hands alternated downwards along the line of door handles, and his feet leap-frogged each other in a sort of vertical backward crawl. The *thud* that resounded each time his boot made impact brought a cringe to Bradshaw's voice, but it couldn't be helped. The moment he squeezed the SR25's trigger, a countdown had started. If he and Pace didn't slip the net before the time ended, they'd be dead.

When he was 10 feet above the ground, Bradshaw pushed away from the stack and fell. He landed on the balls of his feet, then allowed gravity to carry him onto his left side, making contact with the asphalt on his calf, thigh, and back. Bradshaw turned the modified parachute landing fall into a shoulder roll, then bolted to his feet. His left side stung, but he pushed the sensation from his mind.

Bradshaw's hand snaked for his Glock as he raced out of the container yard. He maneuvered past the open gate, dashed between the APCs, and made his way toward the front office. Just ahead, he watched Pace slide across the hood of their Toyota Rush. By the time Bradshaw arrived at the compact SUV, Pace had fired up the engine and thrown the passenger door open. Bradshaw jumped inside and slammed the door as Pace floored the gas. He scanned forward and right for any sign of inbound *Brimob* officers or Kuwat *preman* before glancing to Pace.

"What the fuck happened?" he growled.

"Not now," Pace rasped. He gripped the steering wheel with white knuckles as he guided the Toyota back to the city.

"COMMISSIONER!" A *BRIMOB* officer called. "Up here!"

Mega Nyoman's knees ached as he ascended the ladder. He'd never considered himself a real athlete. His parents had insisted he play soccer in school, and there had been the daily calisthenics/aerobic regimen when he had been a Naval Military Policeman. At the end of the day, there was a reason he had chosen the detective and command career paths rather than the life of the hard-charging *Brimob* paramilitaries. Brainwork was preferable to physical exertion.

With that said, Nyoman knew law enforcement came with a level of physical effort. He wasn't the young man he'd once been, and by the time he reached the top of the container stack, sweat had formed along his brow. Nyoman patted himself on the back for dressing down.

The climb would have been far more uncomfortable in his standard duty Oxfords than in the combat boots he wore beneath his cargo pants.

Nyoman walked over to where a pair of *Brimob* officers stood. His eyes fell on what had gained their attention. It was an SR25 sniper rifle, similar to those used by the armies of Singapore, the Philippines, and the United States. If memory served Nyoman well, it was an expensive weapon, which suggested the Shadow Wraiths were well-connected.

"There's a single shell casing here," the same *Brimob* officer said, indicating with a pointing finger. Nyoman grimaced as he squatted beside it. As he studied the casing, the *Brimob* man said, "We can search for other casings."

"No point," Nyoman said. He placed his hands on his thighs and grunted as he pushed and rose to his full height. "The shooter had discipline. Knew that the suppressor would mute the sound at distance and hide the muzzle flash, but once he fired it, he'd be compromised. They knew that it was better to lose a rifle than to be boxed in." He rested his hands on his hips and nodded. "They're professionals."

"Yes, sir," the *Brimob* officer said.

Nyoman walked to the opposite corner of the Conex and dug into his pocket for his Sony smartphone. Once it was unlocked, he accessed his call log and tapped the most recent call. Nyoman held the phone to his ear as he waited two ringtones for the other party.

"Do you have them?" Suparman Guntur said when he picked up.

"No," Nyoman said. "You were right, though. They took the bait."

"Of course I'm right," Guntur said, irritation laced in his voice. "What happened?"

"I don't know," Nyoman said. "They left in a hurry. Killed three of my men on the way out."

"What does that mean?" Guntur snarled.

Nyoman pursed his lips. "The only reason why I can see them abandoning a chance to liberate a stable is they saw they were compromised. My men stayed hidden right up to the moment that your yacht pulled into dock."

"What are you saying?"

After a deep breath, Nyoman pressed forward. "I think you've got an informer in your camp."

"Impossible," Guntur scoffed. "My men are loyal. They wouldn't sell me out to some *bule*."

Nyoman shrugged. "I'm just giving you my opinion. You've got one of theirs in custody. Why don't you ask him?"

"*Why don't you stop fucking up and go find the mother-fuckers who keep fucking with my shit?*" Guntur shouted.

Before Nyoman could reply, the connection died. He looked at the phone's screen, then shook his head. Nyoman pocketed the phone and grabbed the Motorola radio clipped to his rigger's belt.

"Nyoman to all points. They couldn't have gotten very far. Put the alert out to all local stations. I want Bradshaw and his compatriots found."

CHAPTER TWENTY-TWO

Bekasi, West Java, Indonesia
21 March 2019
03:20 hours Golf (20 March 20:20 hours Zulu)

Suparman Guntur resisted the urge to throw his phone across the room. His fingers clutched the phone, threatening to crack the body. After a moment, Guntur inhaled deeply through his nostrils, then placed the phone back in his pocket. He turned to face Sharif Aditya, who stood waiting expectantly.

"Bradshaw escaped," Guntur said.

Aditya maintained an impassive mien. "How?"

"Nyoman thinks that somebody tipped him off." Guntur interlaced his fingers and rested his chin in the crook formed by his index fingers and thumbs as he thought. "He's searching for them now."

"Do you think his theory holds any validity?" Aditya asked.

"I'm not sure," Guntur said. He tapped the pads of his index fingers together, then extricated his hands and spun on a dime. "Follow me."

They left Guntur's study, made their way down the corridor, and descended the stairs. When they reached the ground level, they hooked a left into the first hallway. A sentry armed with a Micro Galil stood post by the wine cellar entrance. When Guntur and Aditya approached, the sentry opened the door and stepped aside.

Guntur led the way down the stairs. His eyes fell on his impressive collection of racked wine bottles. The racks were positioned between rows of oak casks stacked on top of each other and against the wall. Other racks and casks were positioned in the center of the cellar and evenly spaced out.

The end destination was between the second and third cask/rack blocks. The man was shirtless, strapped to a chair, his hands bound behind his back. His pant legs had been rolled just beneath his knees, his socks and shoes had been removed, and his feet were placed in a short, wide metal pail half-filled with water. Beside the man was a set of jumper cables connected to a large car battery. A pair of armed guards stood on each flank, Micro Galil rifles at the low ready. Guntur stopped about five feet in front of the man, folded his arms, and looked at him pitifully.

"It was easy to find out who you were," Guntur said. "Made a few calls. A contact in Singapore reached out. Good for me. Unfortunate for you…Mr. Tan."

Lucas Tan glared at Guntur through his left eye, his right purpled and swollen shut. He said nothing.

Guntur clasped his hands behind his back as he paced. "Given what I was able to learn about you, I was surprised we were able to effect your capture. Two years in the Commando Formation. Five years in the Special Operations Force. Another three as a contractor with Sharp End. Somebody with your skills…I figured you'd have gone down with more of a fight."

He paused mid-stride and looked at Tan. The Singaporean offered no reaction. Guntur nodded and resumed, his Brogue shoes making muted *clicks* with every step. "If it makes you feel any better, we weren't watching you. Ms. Nirmala was our primary objective. You became a target of opportunity. We figured you might be one of the vaunted Shadow Wraiths."

Guntur reached the center, stopped, and moved his hands to his belt buckle. "I'm not going to mince words with you, Mr. Tan. You've inflicted too much damage on my organization to walk away from this unscathed. You're going to die today."

Tan spoke his first words. "*Rah.* Let's get this over with."

Guntur's eyes narrowed. "Come again?"

"Kill me," Tan said. "I'd rather get waxed than keep hearing you speak. Let's do it."

Guntur chuckled, then wagged a finger in Tan's direction. "Not so fast." He paused. "With how quickly you were captured, there was no time for you to warn your friends. Yet, they knew we were coming and managed to slip away." He took a step forward. "You tell me who helped you, I'll make it quick. Alicia and Marcus will remain unharmed."

Tan's expression chilled, his eyes piercing. He held up his chin and pushed an exhale out of his nose.

"On the other hand," Guntur said, "I've got all the time in the world. Maybe I'll send some associates to Singapore. Bring your family here. Flail your son. Force your wife to service my security personnel." A sinister gleam dawned in his eyes. "Have you ever seen a woman raped to death? I have. It isn't a pleasant way to go. I reserve it for ill-behaved merchandise. I may make an exception for Alicia."

A cold smile crossed Tan's face, which caught Guntur off guard. The Kuwat boss took a step back, a scowl on his face. "What are you smiling about?"

"You won't get to lay a hand on my family," Tan said. "By now, my friends have put two and two together. They know where you live, Guntur. They'll be coming to get me. Either I survive, or I won't. It won't change the fact that you won't live to see another sunrise."

Guntur smirked mirthlessly. "Whatever you have to tell yourself to get by," he said. He looked to one of the guards and nodded. The guard slung his rifle on his back, approached the car battery, picked up the jumper cables, then looked back to Guntur for direction. "Work him over a few more minutes, then give him a break. We don't want to let him off the hook too early."

With a nod, the guard opened the clamps, touched them to Tan's burned nipples, and held them in place. Tan's body convulsed, his eyes going wide as the electric current surged throughout. Guntur turned away, approached the other sentinel, and grabbed him by the arm. They walked out of earshot, then Guntur spun to face him.

"Who's been down here since we last spoke with the prisoner?" Guntur asked.

"Only Umar," the sentry said. "You sent him to check on the prisoner's wounds. He slapped the prisoner around a bit for getting defiant."

Guntur nodded slowly. "I see. Resume your post."

"Yes, sir."

When the guard returned to his post, Guntur slowly faced Aditya. "Did you order Umar to inspect the prisoner?"

Aditya shook his head. "No."

Guntur gestured toward Tan's guards with a nod. "They seem to be under the impression that I issued such an order."

Aditya's eyes narrowed. "There has to be a misunderstanding. Umar's one of my most loyal men. He saved my life more than once in Kerobokan."

"If it's indeed a miscommunication, he will have a chance to plead his case," Guntur said. He snatched a Motorola two-way radio from his belt and held it to his lips. "This is Suparman. This is a directive to all security personnel. I want Umar Pratama located and detained. Anyone with a visual is to contact me *immediately*."

Cakung, East Jakarta, Indonesia
21 March 2019
03:43 hours Golf (20 March 20:43 hours Zulu)

BRADSHAW HAD TRIED three times more to get Pace to talk. Each time, Pace shot him down and forced him to focus on scanning for inbound threats. After a circuitous drive that served as a surveillance detection run, they arrived at the safe house. Pace threw the Toyota into park, killed the ignition, and leapt from the vehicle. Bradshaw was hot on his heels, his frustration peaking.

"Hey, this shit won't work if you're gonna clam up," Bradshaw said. "What the fuck is going on?"

Pace said nothing as he crossed the expansive gap between the parking lot and the warehouse's common area. Bradshaw growled beneath his breath and picked up his pace.

"I swear to fucking God, Danny, talk to me or I'm fucking walking."

"Then walk," Pace snapped. "Or shut the fuck up."

"What the fuck's gotten into you?" Bradshaw barked.

Pace continued to march forward. He reached the entrance to the common area and threw the door open. Bradshaw caught the door before it closed, slipped inside, and jogged after Pace. Before he could catch up, Pace ducked into what had once been a conference room. Bradshaw bolted through the door and closed on Pace.

"Listen here, motherfucker—"

Bradshaw's threat was cut short by the presence of another in the room. He turned to face the interloper, and his eyes widened.

"Milena?"

Milena Wright stood at the other end of the room, her hands interlaced in front of her. She wore a plain green T-shirt, beige cargo pants, and hiking boots. A large revolver was strapped to her waist in a leather cross-draw holster. The playfulness that had graced her visage in their previous meeting was completely absent.

Pace slowly rounded the table and approached her, his voice menacingly low. "The evac code didn't come from Lucas's phone. It came from a burner. *Your* burner."

Wright nodded. "That's right."

"Help me make sense of this," Pace said.

"Lucas was grabbed when he went to meet with Ms. Nirmala," Wright said. "My people checked on her. She's safe, in her home. She has no idea how close she came to getting snatched. I've got a low-vis detail in place. Nobody will harm her."

"And Lucas?" Pace asked, an edge to his voice.

Wright took a deep breath. "Taken to Guntur's residence in Bekasi."

Bradshaw beat Pace to the punch. "There's no way Tan got the evac code out to us if Guntur has him locked down."

"Correct," Wright said. "Langley has a man inside the Kuwat Syndicate, part of a larger program to monitor the *preman* groups and ensure they didn't morph into jihadist franchises." She shifted her gaze to Pace. "They know our history, Danny. They knew you wouldn't believe it if it came from their asset. You'd believe it if it came from me."

"*Langley?*" Pace's eyes widened. "What do *they* have to do with this?"

Wright looked to Bradshaw and pointed. "They want to talk with him." She saw the panic spread in Bradshaw's eyes and added, "Calm down. If they were going to rendition you, they wouldn't have hired me to tell you. Not at my rates." She looked to Pace and smiled pleasantly. "They would have sent some of Danny's friends to snatch you off the street."

Bradshaw glanced back to Pace. "You were Ground Branch."

Pace ignored the declaration. "This changes nothing. I have a man in enemy hands. We need to pull him out."

"I agree," Wright said as she folded her arms. "I've got a soft spot for the little shit. As it turns out, we've got a two-for-one." Pace raised his eyebrows, and Wright carried on. "Langley doesn't want their asset pissing in the wind. Three objectives: pull out the asset, pull out Tan, kill Guntur."

A reptilian flicker filled Pace's gaze. "That's more like it."

"My contractors are waiting down the street," Wright said. "They're ready to go when you are."

"Wait," Bradshaw said. Pace and Wright looked to him. "Are you talking about assaulting a fortress blind? We don't know Guntur's defenses. We don't know the layout of his compound. We bum-rush this blind, we'll die."

Wright held up her phone. "It's not my first rodeo, Jack. I've got those details. We'll brief en route."

"Who's coming from Langley?" Bradshaw insisted.

"Sharon McBride."

Pace's head snapped to face Wright. "You serious?"

Wright nodded. "En route as we speak."

Bradshaw looked between the two. "Who's Sharon McBride?"

Pace's voice was barely audible as he spoke. "Deputy Director, National Clandestine Service."

Wright fixed Bradshaw with another smile. "You've impressed somebody, baby boy. Not every day the number two shot caller in covert ops hops on a plane to meet a fugitive."

"We're wasting time," Pace said impatiently. "Let's get a move on."

Wright nodded and gestured to the door. "After you."

Bekasi, West Java, Indonesia
21 March 2019
03:58 hours Golf (20 March 20:58 hours Zulu)

UMAR PRATAMA NEVER would have entered an alliance with the Americans had he knew it would end like this. At that moment, he was hidden in a guest bedroom, frantically erasing portions of his call and text log. He'd been blinded by the money they'd dangled in front of him: 846 million rupiah per year, about three times the national median income. The work had been pitched as simple: give the Americans a heads up if Guntur decided he'd rather slaughter whores for God and Muhammad than sell them for silver and gold.

Over the past three years, Pratama had watched Guntur's cruelty grow to intolerable levels. He wanted an exit strategy, a means to support himself when he no longer had the stomach for the work. The last thing he would have imagined was that the Americans would leverage his work for them and what remained of his conscious against him, placing him in the line of fire.

There was no walking out of the compound. The opportunity passed when he remained on-site to pass Lucas Tan's evacuation code to the American woman, along with security configurations and a layout of the building. Shortly thereafter, the word had gone out over the radio: Pratama was to be detained and handed directly to Guntur. Having done Guntur's dirty work on a regular basis, he knew what waited him on the receiving end.

All Pratama could do was stall for time. Empty call and message logs would arouse suspicion. That left filtering through each entry, searching for the burner numbers he'd used to pass information to the Americans, and deleting them. He'd combed through the messages and was half-way down the call log.

A series of knocks reverberated through the door. "Umar!"

Fuck. He scrolled down, found another burner entry, and deleted it from the log. *Goddamn it, Umar, why weren't you deleting these as you went?*

Because you didn't think you'd get caught, you stupid piece of shit, he answered himself.

The men at the door pounded on the door again. "*Umar!*"

Out of time. Pratama deleted one more entry, locked his Samsung, and emerged from the room's lavatory. He kicked off his shoes, peeled his shirt from his torso, and pulled back the sheets. Pratama stuffed the smartphone in his pocket, ensured the radio clipped to his belt was shut off, and walked to the door, rubbing his eyes as he went.

"I'm coming, I'm coming," he said in his best impersonation of a man awakened. He undid the lock and pulled the door open, finding himself on the business end of a pair of Micro Galils. Pratama raised his hands and back-pedaled. "What the hell is this?"

The riflemen stepped in, followed by Guntur and Aditya. Pratama noticed the disbelieving look in the latter's eye.

"Why'd you tell the men assigned to Tan that I told you to check his wounds?" Guntur asked, crossing his arms.

"I thought that's what you wanted me to do," Pratama said. The look on Guntur's face said that he believed it as much as Pratama did, which was not at all.

Guntur extended his hand towards Pratama. "Your cell phone."

Pratama was committed to playing dumb. He adopted a confuse look. "Huh?"

Guntur gestured to one of the riflemen. The closest one drove his muzzle into Pratama's midsection, then un-clipped Pratma's radio from his belt and searched his pockets. A moment later, the heavy had Pratama's cell phone in hand and extended it towards Guntur.

"Why didn't you answer your radio?" Guntur asked.

"It was off," Pratama said. "I was taking a nap."

"In one of the guest bedrooms?" Guntur asked.

"It was too loud in the security quarters," Pratama said. "They were hollering and playing their video games. I came up here for a nap." He could see Aditya considered the excuse. Then again, Pratama knew Aditya wanted to believe that he hadn't turned.

Guntur extended the phone towards Pratama. "Unlock it."

After a moment's hesitation, Pratama reached out and placed his thumb on the indicated portion of the screen. The phone recognized his thumbprint and granted access. Guntur pulled the phone back, opened the messages, and scanned through them for anything untoward. Pratama fidgeted in place, but did his best to remain indignant.

"What's this all about?" he demanded.

Guntur held up a finger in warning as he continued to scroll. He couldn't find what he was looking for, so he closed the messages and opened the call log. Guntur scrolled for 30 seconds. All eyes remained locked on

Pratama, searching for a tell that the accusations held merit. As the wait grew, Pratama figured he might have gotten away with it, that Guntur would believe his story.

That was when Guntur stopped scrolling. His eyes widened as his thumb tapped the screen. He studied the display, then turned the phone towards Aditya. Pratama stared at Aditya, his pulse pounding in his reddening ears. Aditya shook his head slowly, then fixed Pratama with a glare that was equal parts hurt and enraged.

I'm made.

Guntur turned the phone's screen toward Pratama. "Who's this?"

"A girlfriend," Pratama said.

"The call lasted seven seconds."

"I was asking her if we were still on for that night."

Guntur nodded slowly, then turned and handed the phone to Aditya. "You know," he said, "I have trouble remembering specifically what I did a couple of days ago. I find it amazing that you know exactly what you were doing on a specific evening three months ago without me even telling you the date." He smiled cruelly. "You're quick-witted, Umar. A little too quick-witted for your own good."

Pratama tried to swallow on a parched throat. "Suparman—"

Guntur addressed his next comments to the gunmen. "Take him to the cellar and get him ready. I'll be there soon."

Pratama tried to turn and plead his case to the sentries. One of them responded by reversing his Micro Galil's stock and driving it into Pratama's diaphragm. As Pratama doubled over, gasping for air, the pair of guards grabbed him by his arms and dragged him past Guntur and Aditya.

The last thing he saw before he was hauled over the room's threshold was Aditya's intense, reproaching stare.

CHAPTER TWENTY-THREE

Bekasi, West Java, Indonesia
21 March 2019
05:50 hours Golf (20 March 22:50 hours Zulu)

Bradshaw sat in the back of the gray Suzuki ER-V. Nerves coursed through his body and outwardly manifested in the form of a constant foot tap. The knowledge that the CIA was coming to speak with him weighed on his mind. While Milena Wright had a point that they wouldn't have warned him if their goal was to snatch him, Bradshaw was hardly sanguine about what would happen at the meeting.

He'd heard stories from Ranger buddies who had gone on to work for the Global Response Staff, the group of former SOF contractors responsible for case officer security. Assets were only useful so long as they continued to produce actionable intelligence. The minute that was no longer the case, the asset was more than likely on his own. The most optimistic scenario Bradshaw could formulate was that they wanted to recruit him. A cop-killing fugitive would make for a hell of a deniable asset. He wasn't even a spook and he saw the ingenuity behind it, as well as the likely conclusion.

Bradshaw forced himself to inhale deeply and clear his mind. *Get on task.* The trek from the safe house in East Jakarta to Guntur's compound in Bekasi was a two-hour drive, and Wright didn't have access to helicopters on such short notice. That placed their launch time just after sunrise. Bradshaw didn't argue the point because he knew the longer they waited, the less chance Tan or the Agency asset had of a successful extraction. Still, there was a reason why most military forces opted for nighttime assaults.

Look at the bright side, Jack, he thought wryly. *Can't get extorted by spies if you're dead.*

Bradshaw glanced around the Suzuki's interior. The windows had been replaced with metal panels, and the stock seats had been torn out and exchanged for larger after-market substitutes that faced the vehicle's center. Bradshaw could feel the vehicle riding low, which implied that it had been up-armored.

Wright's "contractors" turned out to be a buddy team. The first man was introduced as "Dado." He was 5'5" and powerfully built, with brown eyes and close-cropped black hair. Peeking from beneath Dado's short shirt sleeve was a circular tattoo. Bradshaw thought he could make out a pair of 1911-style pistol grips and the hilt of a dagger. Dado caught Bradshaw looking and simply gave him a polite smile and a nod.

The other man, Baz, was Dado's polar opposite. He stood an inch shy of six feet tall, with wrinkles etched into his face and hardened, arctic blue eyes. Baz's shoulder-length ashen hair was pulled back into a bun, and his thick circle beard matched in color. It was clear that he was at least in his mid-50s, if not older, and yet he exuded an air of competence and mastery. Baz had certainly taken care of his body, with the fabric of his long-sleeve knit shirt taut around his muscles.

Wright had equipped Dado, Baz, Bradshaw, and Pace with the same kit: Crye Jumpable Plate Carriers, Crye High Back Blast war belts, Safariland MOLLE-mounted holsters, and OpsCore maritime-cut FAST helmets with rail mounts for their Peltor comm headsets. Instead of the weaponry that Bradshaw and Pace had initially obtained from Wright, the four shooters in the van's passenger area held Heckler & Koch HK416 D10RS carbines. The German AR-derivatives were equipped with EOTech EXPS3 holographic sights, Surefire SOCOM sound suppressors affixed to 10.5" barrels, and Geissele Super Modular quad-rail handguards.

Sitting in silence in the van, Bradshaw almost forgot his predicament. He was back at home, in his element, in a fashion he hadn't felt during the *preman* training camp ambush or the assault on the sex slave stable. It was apparent that he was still deadly, but could he operate at

his former peak capacity? Bradshaw's co-occupants had
clearly been engaged in non-stop controlled violence for
years. On the other hand, he had taken a year off to play
private investigator, and then another six months as he fled
and kept his head low on the docks.

Guess there's only one way to find out.

Bradshaw double-checked that his carbine's safety was
engaged, then pulled back on the charging handle until he
saw brass glimmer from the ejection port. There hadn't
been time to conduct proper Pre-Combat Checks and
Inspections. While the gear looked squared away on first
glance, Bradshaw would have felt better had he assembled
it himself.

Wright turned in her seat and faced the passenger area.
She was outfitted in a similar fashion to her shooters, and
cradled an HK416C in her hands. The weapon was a
smaller version of the carbines the others held, with the
barrel an inch and a half shorter, the buffer tube shortened,
and the standard stock replaced with a retractable wire
stock. Wright's weapon was also suppressed and ran an
EOTech optic.

Her eyes fell on Bradshaw and she beamed. "I like your
attention to detail, but you don't gotta worry, baby," she
said. "I'm not gonna give you fucked-up kit."

Bradshaw forced a smile and nodded briskly, flexing
his fingers as he gripped his carbine. Wright glanced
around the van and said, "Listen up. Enemy situation: on-
site security is estimated at between 25 and 30 tangos,
equipped with rifles. Expect body armor. OPFOR is either
prior Indonesian Mil/LEO or trained by the same. Last
report was that Tan was being held in the wine cellar, one
level beneath the ground floor."

Pace spoke as he inspected his EOTech. "I'm assuming
you've got a plan that doesn't involve five shooters kicking a hornet's nest."

Wright met his gaze and simpered. "My original plan
was to gather a bunch of rival *preman* groups and have

them launch a diversionary raid that would cover our insertion."

Bradshaw's eyes widened. "You were going to arm a bunch of religious fanatics?"

"Not with anything they couldn't get on their own," Wright said. "Seems their principles took precedence over pragmatism. They didn't want to deal with a woman." She shrugged. "Their loss."

"And then?" Pace asked.

Wright's grin grew wicked. "I put myself in Guntur's shoes. He's not the only one with government shot-callers on speed-dial."

A LONG EXHALE crept past scowling lips as Suparman Guntur stood in the corner of the wine cellar, arms folded. Part of the facial expression was the stench that had seized the room, but that was negligible compared to the sight before him and what it represented.

Umar Pratama was stripped naked, his arms and legs spread apart and secured to an A-shaped frame. A padded garment was secured around his waist and ended mid-thigh, with a window that exposed his reddened and welted buttocks. Pratama breathed heavily, attempting to suppress his whimpers and steel himself for the next round.

Guntur had ordered a caning on only one other occasion. One of his *preman* had aspirations to dethrone him and turn his considerable resources over to one of the more religious like-organizations. On a whim, knowing the perpetrator hailed from the Islamic semi-autonomous province of Aceh, Guntur had ordered the caning as a form of interrogation. The man broke and divulged all that he knew before he was put out of his misery with a bullet to the face.

As Sharif Aditya approached Pratama for the next round, Guntur was glad he had the mental clarity to realize he was not the ideal person to carry out the caning. The betrayal-fueled rage simmered just beneath the surface. He knew he would skip the questioning and swing the cane until exhaustion. On the other hand, despite his personal connection to the accused, Aditya was utterly calm and detached, focused on the task of information extraction.

Aditya cradled the blood-slicked rattan cane. It was just over a meter long and 1.25 centimeters in diameter. Outside of Aceh, it was the preferred method of state-sanctioned corporal punishment in Malaysia, Brunei, and Singapore, a cultural remnant of British colonial rule. Most offenses ranged between 10 and 24 strokes, enough to inflict pain and leave scars but not enough to break the subject.

The previous round had concluded with the 50th stroke.

Pratama shuddered, tears streaming down his face, the ropes digging into his wrists and ankles as he fought against the restraints. Out of desperation, he glanced over his shoulder and met Aditya's gaze. Pratama's eyes were bloodshot, and perspiration coated his entire face.

"Sharif," Pratama blubbered. "Brother. You must believe me. I would never betray you."

Aditya remained aloof. Guntur felt a pang of envy. He knew he would not have been able to remain objective in that position.

"Tell us who you work for and this will end," Aditya said flatly. His voice was completely emotionless, his glare long and dead.

Pratama's body deflated as he gave up hope of swaying his former prison comrade. He turned away and hung his head, his voice barely audible. "Do what you must."

There was no hesitation. Aditya swiftly raised the cane above his head and brought it down on Pratama's buttocks with force. The *crack* of the rattan meeting flesh echoed throughout the cellar. Pratama's entire body shuddered as he yelped, his nails digging into his palms and threatening to draw blood. Aditya paused a beat, then struck again. Blood flowed down the backs of his legs and had begun to pool at his heels.

The strokes were consistent in timing and power. There was not as much as a flicker on Aditya's countenance. To grant his personal feelings entry into his action would only serve to damage Pratama beyond repair and send him into shock, which would render him useless in the realm of acquiring information.

As Aditya reared back to deliver the iteration's seventh blow, the ground trembled beneath them. Guntur immediately crouched and scanned his surroundings for the source, while Aditya dropped the cane and drew his Pindad P1 from beneath his shirt. The sentries inside the cellar raised their Micro Galils, but kept short of a high ready posture, mindful of muzzle awareness.

"What the fuck was that?" Guntur asked.

Another sentry emerged from the stairwell, a Lenovo high-definition tablet in his hand. "Sir!" he called out as he closed in on Guntur. When he arrived, the guard proffered the tablet. Guntur snatched it from his subordinate and held it a few inches from his face.

Surveillance camera feeds filled the screen. The front gate guard shack was charred and in flames, body parts strewn throughout the vicinity. A Pindad Komodo armored personnel carrier took up real estate where the front gate had been minutes earlier, and a camouflaged soldier manned an FN MAG machine gun in the vehicle's turret. Flashes leapt from the machine gun's muzzle. Dismounted soldiers marched forward on either side of the Komodo, M4 carbines held at the high ready.

"*Kopassus*," Guntur snarled. "SAT-81. Setiawan must have sent them." He shoved the tablet back to the reporting sentry and balled his fists. "*Motherfucker!*"

Aditya placed his hand on Guntur's shoulder, the other sentries moving to form a protective perimeter. "We need to get you to your study," he said. "We can harden defenses and repel the assault."

"Let's go," Guntur said through clenched teeth.

* * *

WRIGHT'S DRIVER HAD taken the van down to the beach. Bradshaw was tapped to take point, and he'd led the way up towards the mansion. They were halfway to the target building when the Indonesian Army Special Forces Command's SAT-81 counter-terrorism unit had initiated their assault. Bradshaw surmised from the signature howl that they had used a Carl Gustav recoilless rifle to breach the front gate and eliminate the guard post. The volume of 5.56x45mm rounds suggested that resistance was heavy, as predicted.

As Bradshaw kept the line moving, Wright managed command and control via her pair of AN/PRC-148 MBITR radios. The ComTac III headset was a dual-comm model, which had a wire running from each of the ear pieces and allowed her to monitor two nets at once. One radio was set to the team's internal comms, while the other was patched into the *Kopassus* net. They had a limited window to make entry before the Kuwat soldiers realized that the *Kopassus* shooters were acting as an outer cordon, which would force them to assess their flanks.

Bradshaw closed on the building, with Pace, Baz, Wright, and Dado in tow. He hand-railed the Olympic-sized swimming pool and closed on the rear patio door. His carbine was raised and he scanned the windows and third floor balcony for any sign of movement. Bradshaw continued to search above him until he slipped into a blind spot. Each person in the line did likewise, then stacked outside the patio door.

Once they were in position, Bradshaw tapped the top of his helmet with an inverted fist. Baz broke from the stack. The others closed ranks as Baz knelt beside Bradshaw, reaching to an abdominal pouch that dangled from his plate carrier. Baz removed a roll of breaching tape, then glanced through the patio door to check for movement. When he was sure he was clear, he ran a length from the door's top-left corner to the bottom-right. Baz tore the strip at the bottom, stuffed the roll back in the storage pouch, and retrieved a blasting cap. That was buried in the middle of the strip, and Baz unfurled a wire as he moved the stack away from the door. They reached the safety distance, and Baz connected the wire to a clacker-style detonator.

"We're set," he said.

Wright nodded, then switched her PTT to the *Kopassus* net and keyed up. "*Kopassus*, this is Mermaid," she said in fluent Indonesian. "We are making entry. Shift fire. I say again, shift fire."

Dado's weak hand rested on Wright's shoulder. He gave it a squeeze to let her know he was ready. In turn, given her diminutive height, she squeezed the right side of Pace's torso to pass along the message. Pace passed the signal to Bradshaw, who then gave it to Baz. Once Baz felt the squeeze, he slapped the clacker hard three times in rapid succession.

The ground rumbled as the strips of detonation cord embedded in the tape ignited, shattering the bulletproof glass. Before the smoke cleared, Bradshaw stepped around Baz, a CTS 9-Bang stun grenade prepped in his hand. He hurled the black cylinder through the opening and ducked back into the stack just as the 1.5-second fuse expired. Unlike a standard flashbang, the 9-Bang contained nine charges of magnesium and potassium nitrate, which created greater disorientation and gave entry teams additional time to gain a foothold within a target.

As the ninth explosion resounded, Baz rushed through the entrance, Bradshaw hot on his heels. A pair of *preman* clutched their eyes and ears, their Micro Galil rifles suspended around their necks by slings. Baz and Bradshaw each lined up their EOTech reticles with a target and squeezed their triggers in rapid succession. A swarm of 5.56x45mm rounds cut the gangsters down. Baz took the left side of the dining room, while Bradshaw moved right. Pace and Wright went with Baz, while Dado joined Bradshaw.

Dado palmed a 9-Bang grenade as he stacked behind Bradshaw at a door. Bradshaw opened it, and Dado tossed the grenade high. After the detonations finished, Bradshaw rushed in, encountering a professional kitchen. Chefs and wait staff grabbed at their own eyes and ears, grappling with the 9-Banger's effects. Bradshaw and Dado assessed the group through their EOTechs. Their hands were clear, and none of them appeared to be harmed.

Bradshaw took point, his HK416 remaining at the ready. "*Go!*" he barked in Indonesian. "*Go! Get the fuck out of here!*" He closed in on the first wait staff, grabbed them with his off-hand, and shoved them toward the door. "*Hands on your head! Move!*" As they started to flee, Bradshaw keyed up his radio.

"Mermaid, this is Boy Scout."

"Go," Wright said.

"You've got about one-five noncombatants making their way out the back. Kitchen staff."

"Roger. Solid copy."

One of the wait staff stumbled and nearly collided with Dado. He used his off-hand to grab the young man beneath his armpit, pull him up, and shove him out of the kitchen door. Once the kitchen appeared to be clear, Dado took up the left side while Bradshaw took the right. They made their way forward, checking their corners for anybody they had missed. As they reached a second entrance, Bradshaw looked to Dado.

"Clear," he said.

Dado nodded, then keyed up. "All points, this is Bull-dog. Friendlies coming out the kitchen, white-end."

"Come out," Pace replied on the net.

Bradshaw led the way out, his HK416's muzzle traversing laterally. Out of the corner of his eye, he spotted Pace, Baz, and Wright stacked up on a wall, just short of a stairwell. Movement registered from the stairs, and Bradshaw spun 90 degrees to his left and squared off with the inbound enemy pair. He fired a round into the one on the left, drove the carbine to the right target, cranked out four more bullets, then returned to the first and fired until the *preman* dropped. Both bodies skidded down the stairs, staining the tiles with their blood. He assessed both targets, then raised his muzzle to the top of the first flight.

Using his left hand to key up, Bradshaw said, "I've got you covered. Move."

Pace launched himself forward. As he rounded the corner, another trio of *preman* lay in wait, their Micro Galils at the ready. Pace narrowly ducked back in time to keep from being perforated by the oncoming lead cloud. Baz had already prepped a 9-Bang grenade by the time Pace returned to cover. The graying veteran operator stepped out of the stack, trained his aim on a hallway wall, and hurled the grenade hard. It banked off the wall and caught the enemy shooters' attention as it detonated.

When the grenade expended its package in full, the stack rushed the hallway. Pace took the right side, Baz took the left, and Wright filled the middle. Their suppressed weapons spoke as they gunned down the *preman* trio, the bullets finding skulls, throats, breastplates, and abdomens. As the bodies hit the floor, Wright spotted the door they had been guarding. She extended a bladed hand in that direction.

"That's the door," she said. "On me."

"Friendlies on your rear," Dado's voice said through the ComTac headsets.

Baz and Pace collapsed behind Wright on the left side of the hallway, just short of the cellar entrance. A moment later, Dado stacked behind Pace, with Bradshaw bringing up the rear. Pace yanked the pin free from a 9-Bang's body and held the spoon tight in place. The non-verbal ready signal was sent down the line, and Wright threw the door open. Pace tossed the stun grenade inside and stepped back.

Wright led the way down the stairwell, her HK416C's stock tucked tight into her shoulder. Pace moved at her side. The others filed in behind them. As they reached the cellar, Wright took the left side and Pace moved right. Dado and Baz fell in with Wright and Bradshaw moved with Pace.

A pair of *preman* stood in the center of the cellar, fighting the 9-Bang's effects. Wright's weapon spoke first, stitching her target from sternum to throat. A split second after she opened fire, Pace joined her, multiple rounds tearing through his target's lungs and heart. Both men collapsed to the floor, blood pooling across the cement.

That was when the stench assaulted their noses. A moment later, Pace found the source. His mouth dropped open and his eyes widened.

"No."

He slung his HK416 on his back and bolted forward. Lucas Tan was strapped to the chair, his feet in the pail, the car battery and jumper cables on the floor beside him. His chest was marked with burn scars, and the crotch area of his pants were soiled. Pace took a knee beside Tan, ripped off one of his gloves, and pressed two fingers to Tan's carotid artery. The skin was cool and clammy. Pace pressed harder into the throat. There was no pulse. He lifted Tan's head, used one hand to force an eye open, and grabbed a flashlight with his free hand.

"C'mon, buddy," Pace breathed as he turned the flashlight on and shone it in Tan's eye. The pupil was wide and didn't react to the light. He switched the flashlight to his other hand and checked the other eye. When there was no reaction, Pace slowly lowered Tan's head. He lowered his chin to his chest, let out a long sigh, and pursed his lips as he fought to keep the raging swell of wrath and grief in check. His eyes burned as he fought back tears.

"I'm sorry, buddy," he said quietly.

Across the room, Wright watched as Baz and Dado cut Umar Pratama down from the A-frame. The backs of his thighs were caked with blood, and the skin on his buttocks had been all but whipped away. As soon as Pratama's feet made contact with the ground, an otherworldly shriek escaped from his lips, compelling Baz and Dado to hold him up. Wright moved in, grabbing her medical kit from her war belt.

"I didn't talk," Pratama gasped.

"Honestly, wouldn't matter if you had," Wright said. She broke out a can of disinfectant spray and said, "This is gonna hurt."

Pratama clenched his teeth and nodded briskly. "Do it."

Wright popped the cap and held down the spray button. Pratama growled, his neck muscles bulging against taut skin as he fought the pain. Once the wound was disinfected, she put the can away and broke out a pair of Israeli bandages. As she placed the first on his left buttock and began to wrap it around his leg, Wright glanced up at him.

"You know where Guntur went?"

Pratama nodded as he winced. "They said something about holing up in the study. They're waiting for *Kopassus* to make entry."

"I'm gonna lay you down," Wright said. She nodded to Baz and Dado, who then gently guided Pratama to a prone position. "Baz, dress his wounds."

As Baz picked up where Wright left off, Dado took a step forward and raised his carbine, pulling security. Wright walked to where Bradshaw and Pace stood over Tan's body. When she looked Pace in his eyes, she saw the tightly controlled fury that had taken over.

"Pratama's good," she said. "Guntur's on the third floor."

Pace nodded curtly. Bradshaw straightened up and adjusted his grip on his HK416, a steely glint in his eyes as he spoke to Wright.

"You get Pratama to the vehicle. We'll get Guntur."

CHAPTER TWENTY-FOUR

Bekasi, West Java, Indonesia
21 March 2019
06:10 hours Golf (20 March 23:10 hours Zulu)

"Don't fucking tell me you don't fucking know about this," Suparman Guntur said, spittle flying from his mouth. His hand was wrapped around his phone, knuckles white. "You've got the connections in Cilangkap. This has your fingerprints all over it!"

"Calm down, Suparman," Setiawan Mahmud replied. "Take a moment and think about it. You're smart enough to take measures against this kind of play. If you go down, then I go down, too. Why would I put myself in that position?"

Guntur stopped pacing about his study and took a deep breath. "They're at my front door. They're at my *house!* I need these motherfuckers *gone!*"

"I'll reach out to my friends at the Defense Ministry," Mahmud said. "Find out who gave the order. When I know, you'll know."

Guntur killed the connection without salutation and looked to Sharif Aditya, who stood with his three best men. "His answers were too perfect," Guntur said. "I still think he's got something to do with this."

"Or maybe he's telling the truth," Aditya said. "He's not one to rock the boat. He's too worried about his reelection. We're his meal ticket."

"Then *who* ordered this?" Guntur barked.

"One thing at a time," Aditya said soothingly. "First, we repel the assault. Then, we'll find who ordered the hit and make an example of them."

The laptop computer on Guntur's desk sounded off with several beeps. He marched to it, spun the computer to face him, and studied the screen. Some of the surveillance feeds were offline due to damage, but most of the interior cameras were still active. Guntur noticed the bodies of several of his men strewn throughout. He spotted movement on one of the screens, and he enlarged it with a double click.

A pair of men retreated away from the wine cellar entrance. Both men were ethnic European, and their equipment looked too advanced to be *Kopassus* issue. One of the men briefly glanced overhead, looking directly into the camera. Guntur's heart lodged in his throat.

"Bradshaw…" he murmured.

Aditya glanced over to the desk. "Come again?"

"It's Bradshaw," Guntur said, louder that time. Realization dawned on him. "The Shadow Wraiths. Somehow, they managed to convince SAT-81 to launch this assault. It's the only explanation that makes sense."

Aditya's brow furrowed. "Everything we received from BIN and the Americans suggested that neither Bradshaw nor the Shadow Wraiths have the necessary resources."

"Then they're *wrong!*" Guntur barked. His eyes remained glued to the screen as Bradshaw and the other man approached the ground floor stairwell. "Get some men down there to intercept them!"

BRADSHAW'S SUPPRESSED HK416 cracked shrilly as it spat another three-round burst. The 5.56x45mm rounds found its target's center mass, critically damaging the heart and lungs. As the lead exited the body, the target fell to the ground, joining four of his comrades that had been killed in the preceding moments.

At the edge of the stairwell, Pace opened up with his carbine. A *preman* attempting to charge the stairs absorbed a quartet of bullets, spun around, and fell to the stairs. Pace continued to scan. They had probably killed most of the resistance on the first and second floors, if Wright's intelligence was correct, but he wasn't going to leave it to chance.

Bradshaw took cover by the edge of the hallway and said, "Reloading!" He pressed the magazine release, dropping the spent magazine as he fished a fresh one from his plate carrier. The magazine was placed in its well. He concluded by gripping the well and thumbing the bolt release to load a round into battery.

"I'm up!" Bradshaw said. He turned and scanned the hallway. It was a series of doors on both sides. "Looks like a bunch of rooms. You wanna clear 'em or press on to Guntur?"

"Press to Guntur," Pace said. "If they're hiding in the rooms, they'll either flee when we move or try to flank our six. We'll be ready for 'em."

"All right," Bradshaw said as he spun around. "Let's go."

"On your six."

Bradshaw moved to the left side of the stairwell, his muzzle alternating between what was directly ahead of him and just above the bannister. Pace pulled up the rear, scanning left to right, taking each step slowly while hunched forward to minimize his chance of falling. As they ascended, their ComTac headsets crackled in their ears.

"Boy Scout, Rusty, this is Mermaid," Wright said. "We've got Whitey back to the insertion point. You need backup?"

Pace answered. "Negative. Stand by."

"Roger that. Standing by. Good hunting."

They reached the midpoint landing without incident. Bradshaw took another step forward, then paused and threw his arm up at a 90-degree angle, his fist clenched. Pace looked over his shoulder and froze in his tracks.

"I hear something," Bradshaw whispered. "Switch me."

Pace moved alongside the wall, and Bradshaw went wide. He held his HK416 at the ready, keeping each step noiseless. As he reached the top step, Bradshaw took a deep, preparatory breath, then lunged out from behind cover. His eyes went wide as he saw a line of muzzles trained in his direction. He leaped back in the stairwell just as the line opened fire, the 5.56x45mm rounds whizzing through the air where he had been a moment earlier. Bradshaw slipped and skidded down the stairs, his tailbone taking the brunt of the abuse before he stopped just above the landing.

"Motherfucker," Bradshaw rasped as he bolted back to his feet. He pushed a long breath past clenched teeth and rushed back to join Pace. When he arrived, he watched Pace replace the partially spent magazine in his HK416 with a full one. The removed magazine was placed into the pouch where he'd fetched the replacement, with the rounds facing upward to indicate it wasn't full.

Bradshaw glanced to Pace. "How do you wanna play this?"

"Flash 'em," Pace said. "When the 9-Banger's done, hang left and use your muzzle for cover. I'll be right behind you."

"Tracking," Bradshaw said. He moved along the stairwell's left wall, double checked he had a fresh magazine in the rifle, then pulled back the charging handle to confirm a round was chambered.

Pace primed the 9-Bang stun grenade and held his breath as he approached the top step. He cocked back, leaned around the corner, and hurled the black cylinder as far as he could. As Pace ducked back, panicked shouts filled the hallway. They were cut short quickly, the 9-Bang running its course.

As soon as Bradshaw heard the final *bang*, he button-hooked left, raised his weapon, and lined up his EOTech's reticle on his first target, 50 meters down hall. The Hecker & Koch carbine spoke, the recoil barely noticeable as four rounds traveled the distance in an instant and cut the man down. He traversed left, found a second target, and fired again. Bradshaw's aim was true, and the man's lung and aorta were perforated with bullets.

Pace was on-line with Bradshaw, his carbine chattering in his hands. Movement at his feet drew his attention, and Pace lowered his HK416 long enough to put a single around in a wounded *preman*'s face. He snapped his

246| STEVEN HILDRETH, JR.

weapon back to eye-level and found a *preman* halfway through a reload. Pace executed a textbook failure drill, putting two rounds almost on top of each other through the sternum, lifting his sights a notch, and administering a fatal lead pill between the target's eyes.

A burning sensation registered on Pace's left deltoid. He sucked air through his teeth as he shifted to the source, finding a gangster with his Micro Galil at the ready. Pace was a half-second faster on the trigger, pumping five rounds into the *preman*'s chest. The gunman danced as the bullets made passage, took a step forward, and collapsed in a heap.

One *preman* remained. Bradshaw tagged him first with a round to the hip. The gangster's leg gave out, and he fell hard on his side. Bradshaw tracked him to the ground and put another controlled pair in his chest. The Kuwat soldier continued to fight through his injuries and attempted to raise his rifle. Bradshaw picked up his rate of fire and dumped the rest of his magazine in the target's chest, throat, and head. By that point, Pace had joined him, focusing his fire on the criminal.

Bradshaw surveilled the body as he dropped his empty magazine and reached for a fresh one. Several entrance wounds marked the last *preman's* forehead, and one of them had ripped through his right eye. Half of his lower jaw was gone. His throat had been chewed into a massive, gory crater, and his chest had been turned into mincemeat. The body twitched for a couple of moments, and then finally went still.

He looked up to Pace. Blood dripped from the Marine's left arm. Bradshaw finished his reload, then marched over.

"You're bleeding," Bradshaw said.

Pace glanced at his arm. "Yeah. Suppose I am. Just a graze."

Bradshaw checked the wound. The blood was slow, oozing, and dark colored. "Yeah, it'll hold until we're clear. You good everywhere else?"

"Yeah," Pace said.

A radio attached to a *preman's* hip crackled before Suparman Guntur's voice boomed through the speaker. "What's going on out there? Are they dead?"

Bradshaw glanced at Pace. "Let's finish it."

"Yes," Pace said coldly. "Let's."

THE STUDY DOOR burst open. Aditya and his men immediately raised their Micro Galils. A small black cylinder flew into the room, and Aditya recognized it for what it was a second too late.

"*Grena—*"

The 9-Bang stun grenade's vibrancy blinded the room's occupants as its explosions set off, one after another. Aditya and his three men never saw Bradshaw or Pace make entry, nor did they hear the gunshots that ripped through their torsos and felled them. As his eyesight faded back into focus, Aditya saw the pair of Westerners standing over his men, their suppressed carbines trained downward. A single round each rendered them out of the fight. Aditya saw Pace's boots advanced towards Guntur out of the corner of his eye. Bradshaw stood over him a moment later, his HK416 trained on his face.

A second later, things went black, the result of a lone bullet punching between his eyes and scrambling his brain matter.

Bradshaw stepped over Aditya's corpse and aimed his carbine at Guntur's face. His finger rested along the magazine well. "I've got him."

Pace slung his HK416 and moved on Guntur. The *preman* boss had drawn his hand cannon, but in the confusion caused by the 9-Bang, he'd only held it at his side. Guntur kept it there, knowing that to raise it would result in Bradshaw cutting him down. A moment later, Pace was at his side, yanking the massive pistol from his hands.

"SOCOM pistol." Pace turned the pistol from side to side, then dropped the magazine, racked the slide to empty the chamber, then tossed the pistol away. "You know nobody uses those, right? They sit on armory shelves, collecting dust, because they're too goddamned big." He pointed to Guntur. "Seems you were so damn determined to use it that you found a work-around."

Guntur swallowed nervously but kept his head held high. "So, are you going to kill me?"

Pace chuckled icily. "Oh, you're goddamn right, Suparman."

He closed his eyes and exhaled. "All right. Let's get this over with."

"Uh-uh," Pace said. "You don't get a bullet. Not after you *butchered* my friend." He took a menacing step towards Guntur, who remained frozen in place. "You see, I can set aside my personal feelings and recognize that he was a dead man the moment you took him. We attacked your business. Mercy isn't a strength in your line of work. I get it. Had you killed him quickly, it wouldn't have saved you, but it would have extended you the same courtesy."

Pace stopped and looked at Bradshaw. "Boy Scout. Gimme the knife."

Bradshaw dug into his pocket for the karambit he'd used to kill Elang Kadek, walked around Guntur with the rifle's muzzle still trained on his head, and extended the blade to Pace with his off hand. Once Pace accepted it, Bradshaw made his way back around Guntur to where he had stood.

"You're going to butcher me?" Guntur asked.

"Yes."

Guntur scoffed. "Doesn't that violate some sort of protocol in American society? Isn't this where you hand your guns off to Mr. Bradshaw and demand we fight?"

"This isn't a movie, dickhead," Pace said as he continued to approach.

"You butcher me, then you're no different than me," Guntur said. "You'll just be a monster with piss-poor business acumen. A populist slaughterer. End of the day, you still take joy in killing and brutality." He smiled wickedly. "So, go ahead. Do it, then. Get your rocks off, motherfucker."

"I don't rape," Pace rasped. "I don't kill people that don't have it coming." A cruel grin spread across the Marine's face. "As for business acumen, there's $3 million of your blood money sitting in a warehouse. So, while I ain't doing this as a business, I guess I'm doing something right."

He paused inches from Guntur, the karambit reverse-gripped in his right hand. "You are right about one thing, though, Suparman."

"What's that?" Guntur asked.

"I *am* going to enjoy this."

Pace grabbed the back of Guntur's neck, brought his blade hand to his opposite shoulder, then plunged it into Guntur's midsection. He twisted the blade as deep as it would go, then pulled hard across the body, sawing through Guntur's skin and abdominal wall. A sewer-like stench filled the room as the karambit penetrated Guntur's large intestine. Guntur began to shudder as the blade traversed his navel and stopped short of the left side of his torso. The intestines and stomach splashed as they hit the floor.

As Guntur neared the end of his death throes, Pace left the karambit sticking out his side and leaned in close. His lips hovered above Guntur's ear.

"His name was Lucas Tan, you son of a bitch."

Pace gave Guntur a push. The Kuwat Syndicate boss fell backwards, his entrails stretching from the wound to where they had initially hit the floor. His body shook a few seconds more. Bradshaw walked around the desk and stared Guntur in the eyes.

"Citra sends her regards," Bradshaw said. He hocked a wad of phlegm and spat it on the gory pile at his feet. Guntur's last breath escaped his body and he fell still. Bradshaw lingered on the sight a moment more, then took the long way around the desk and began to open drawers.

"What are you looking for?" Pace asked.

Bradshaw pushed a laptop across the desk towards Pace. "Grab that."

"We don't need to do SSE," Pace said. "Wasn't planning on follow-on ops without Lucas."

Bradshaw looked up at Pace. "This isn't for us. It's for Nirmala. She stuck her neck out for us in a big way. This will give her what she needs to break the story wide open."

Pace nodded. "Yeah, she's earned that. And, she can clear your name."

"Yep," Bradshaw said. He found a Samsung smartphone, then held it up for Pace to see. "Jackpot."

"Good," Pace said. "Just one thing left before we roll."

Bradshaw glanced at Pace. After all his lecturing about no longer being in the military, Bradshaw was comforted to see that Pace's martial sense of honor hadn't been completely erased by hard-bitten pragmatism. He gave the Marine a slow nod.

"Let's do it."

WRIGHT GLANCED OVER her shoulder, her HK416C held at the low ready. Dado was in the van, kneeling beside Pratama as he administered pain medication. Baz stood by her side, scanning the area for any sign of the enemy. Wright checked her watch impatiently, then glanced back towards the mansion.

"They should have come out by now," Wright said, the tension heavy in her voice.

Baz kept his eyes on the objective. "You want me to go back in?"

Wright considered the offer. "We'll hold a couple more minutes." She glanced back to the van's interior. "How's he looking?"

"He'll live," Dado said. "He'll be on his belly for a few weeks. Gonna be scarred all to hell. But, he'll live."

"Never figured Guntur to be one for caning," Wright said as she clenched her jaw. She was no stranger to the violent methods authoritarians utilized to control their populaces, nor was she unaccustomed to the techniques criminals used to enforce loyalty and compliance. Still, she never grew used to seeing the end results.

Before anyone could respond to Wright's comment, Bradshaw's voice filled their ComTac headsets. "Mermaid, this is Boy Scout."

Wright's hand snapped to her PTT. "Go."

"Coming out," he said. "We'll be at your position in about one mike, over."

"Roger." She stepped to the front passenger's door and glanced at her driver. "Fire it up."

"Yes, ma'am," the driver said, turning the key in the ignition.

A moment later, a pair of figures emerged, approaching briskly. Wright trained her gaze on the pair. As they closed in on her position, she saw that Bradshaw walked point, his HK416 at the low ready. Pace walked a couple of steps behind and offset of him. In his arms was a body, wrapped in a sheet.

When Pace reached the van, he climbed inside and gently set the body beside Pratama. He then stepped back out and looked at Wright.

"You got somebody who can fetch us about two-dozen bags of ice?" he asked.

Wright immediately understood the nature of the request. "I'll make the call en route."

"Thank you," Pace said quietly.

CHAPTER TWENTY-FIVE

Cakung, East Jakarta, Indonesia
21 March 2019
10:00 hours Golf (03:00 hours Zulu)

Danny Pace sat in a folding chair. The room had been an office during its tenure with its previous owners. Its floors and walls had been stripped bare when the property was liquidated, leaving nothing but concrete and drywall. Pace wasn't sure if that made it better or worse as a temporary storage area for Lucas Tan's body.

When the team returned from Bekasi around 08:00, Wright's people had already set up the room. A large bathtub was placed in the center of the room. Tan's clothing was cut away and discarded, and his naked form was lowered into the tub. Pace, Bradshaw, Wright, Baz, and Dado had all helped to break apart the ice bags, tear them open, and pour their contents upon Tan's body.

Forty-five minutes after arriving at the safe house, Tan's body was fully immersed in ice. It was a temporary measure. If his family wanted an open-casket funeral, he'd need to be transported to Singapore by the end of the day. Wright had assured Pace that she would pull every string with every Indonesian customs official on her payroll to make that happen.

The others had left the room, presumably to clean gear and develop exit strategies. Pace sat in the room by himself, elbows on his thighs and fingers interlaced, his clothes sweat-drenched and bloody. He stared at the tub, at the pool of ice, his eyes wide and unblinking. There was no well of tears behind an emotional dam, no dialogues with cadavers, no emotion to fight.

The only thing Pace felt was…numb.

Logically, he understood the numbness. He'd spent his entire adult life in combat, the latter half on shadow battlefields without a safety net.

After the loss of the first few comrades, the weeping was harder to come by, if not outright impossible. The irrational self-recriminations stopped.

The normal traumatic coping process had been shattered. Rather than store the grief for a more appropriate time, he locked it away completely and never returned to address it. Pace wasn't sure which was worse: being overcome with emotion or the incapability to feel it.

He heard the footsteps behind him, but did not turn to address them. Jack Bradshaw materialized at his side and folded his arms. Like Pace, Bradshaw hadn't changed since the Bekasi hit, aside from removing his overt tactical kit. Both men stared at the tub in silence, neither one sure of what to say.

Finally, Pace broke the silence. "Your hacker friend reach out?"

Bradshaw nodded. "They broke it pretty quickly. It's more than enough to lock up a chunk of Jakarta's government and law enforcement. Kirsana's gonna love it."

Pace nodded, his gaze still on the tub. "Good."

Another silent moment passed before Bradshaw spoke. "How long'd you know him?"

A sigh fell from Pace's nose. "Just short of two years."

Bradshaw nodded. "You meet in your Agency days?"

Pace shook his head. "Lucas was part of a series of events that saved my life," he said. "I was burned out when I left Ground Branch. Had an ex-wife who wanted nothing to do with me. Two daughters who call some other man 'Dad.' I just had nothing left in the tank. Eating my gun wasn't an option, but neither was starting over.

He rubbed his palms together slowly as he continued. "So, I wandered. Burned through my savings. Stumbled from bars, to brothels, to hostels, to the next bus or train station. Started in the UK. Made my way through the Balkans. Hit northern Africa. Rolled through India. Ferry-hopped through southeast Asia."

Pace's hands stopped moving as he took a deep breath. "I landed in Thailand. I got nice and liquored up, then I went to a brothel, looking for some overnight company. I walk inside. It's run by this grandma-looking madam. She asks me if I want some of the special selection. I'm intrigued, so I ask what's that entailed." Pace's eyes glassed over with rage as he recalled the memory. "Girls. *Children.* There was one, I'm not even sure if she was 12, man.

"I walked out, pissed off. The shit's commonplace there." Pace glowered, his jaw clenched. "Folks don't even bat a fuckin' eye that a bunch of foreign rich pricks come rolling in to rape kids. Shit sobered me up *real* quick. I needed to do something."

"What'd you do?" Bradshaw asked.

"Got myself a pistol from a black marketer," Pace said. "Went back to shoot the place up. It was Lucas who intervened. Stopped me from going off half-cocked. He was working a K&R gig for a Singaporean tech guy whose daughter got snatched and sent through the pipeline to Bangkok. That gig was on the up-and-up, back when that was all he did. Worked with the Royal Thai Police for the recovery. Lucas convinced me to work with his task force, and I ran recon in the brothel for the raiding party.

"We liberated 50 children," Pace said. "That's when I was reminded of two things: what sobriety feels like, and what purpose feels like. Quit drinking cold turkey, linked up with Lucas. I sold him on veering into the gray, operating semi-legally."

Bradshaw crossed his arms. "You knew him better than me, but I got the vibe that you wouldn't have to sell him too hard. He seemed to like the juice."

"Oh, he *loved* the juice," Pace said. "No contention about that. The man was born to soldier. Still, he was worried about the legalities. He didn't want to expose his wife to a criminal lifestyle. Turns out, she was down with it."

"Yeah?"

"Lucas got into this line of work because a childhood friend of his got snatched a few years back. She was whored out, then killed when the slavers deemed her of no further use. From being a PI, it was only a few more short steps into vigilante territory."

Bradshaw hung his head and shook it. "Shit."

"Yeah," Pace said. "Alicia knew her well. She was fine with Lucas taking the fight to the slavers. Anything to put those monsters down." He sighed again as he interlaced his fingers. "I've got to tell you…I'm not looking forward to breaking the news."

Bradshaw took a deep breath as he slipped his hands in his pockets. "Yeah. I wouldn't be, either."

"Yeah." Pace bit the inside of his lower lip. "If I'm being honest…I'm not sure what to do now."

Several footsteps resounded in the hallway, which drew Bradshaw's and Pace's attention to the door. A moment later, Milena Wright entered the room, also still in her sweat-drenched raid clothing. Her eyes fell on the ice-filled tub and a heavy sigh fell from her nose. She then met Pace's gaze.

"I've touched base with my man in Customs," she said. "We'll have Lucas on a flight to Singapore in a few hours. Don't worry about the funeral. I've already allocated the necessary funds."

Pace looked to the tub and nodded slowly. "I owe you, Mil."

"No, you don't. Even if you did, I don't keep count. Not with friends." She walked to Pace, wrapped her arms around him, and held him close. "I'm sorry. I really liked Lucas."

Pace leaned into the embrace, closed his eyes, and exhaled. "He liked you, too, a lot. You were definitely one of his favorite people."

Wright cupped Pace's face and stroked his cheek with her thumb. "If you need to talk before you roll out…"

"I appreciate it," Pace said. His voice was flat, but the look in his eyes conveyed sincerity.

Wright planted a firm, brief kiss on Pace's lips, patted his cheek, then extricated herself and approached Bradshaw.

"Watch yourself around McBride and Fairchild."

Bradshaw's eyes widened at the second name. "Fairchild?"

Wright folded her arms. "Diana Fairchild. You know her?"

"Yeah." Bradshaw barely managed to push the words past the lump in his throat. "I worked with her on Omega in Afghanistan."

Wright shifted her weight from her right foot to her left. "I shouldn't speak out of turn, but I like you, Jack. I want you to know what you're getting yourself into." She nodded in the direction of the conference room where the CIA officers waited. "That's an asset recruitment. Whatever they've got in mind for you, that's what you'll be to them: a deniable asset. If it comes down to protecting the nation and themselves or protecting you, they'll cut sling load in a heartbeat. Watch yourself. Ask questions. Demand answers."

Bradshaw nodded slowly. "I appreciate the heads-up."

Wright opened her arms and motioned for Bradshaw to approach. He closed the distance, and she wrapped her arms around him, holding him tight. When they separated, Wright tapped Bradshaw's chest gently with a pointed finger.

"If you need information or equipment, look me up. Danny knows how to get a hold of me."

"Thank you," Bradshaw said. He half-smiled. "Hopefully, the next time we cross paths will be under better circumstances."

"I doubt that, baby," Wright said with a mirthless grin. "I don't make my living selling flowers."

She patted his cheek, gave him a supportive smile, then turned and left the room. Bradshaw watched her leave and stuck his hands in his pockets. He let out a long, soft whistle, then looked back to Pace.

"You need a minute?"

Pace slapped his thighs, then pushed himself to his feet. "No. Let's get this over with." As he and Bradshaw entered the hallway, Pace added, "Everything Milena said is on point. Ask for the fine print. They've got an objective. You're a tool to accomplish that. They're not going to have your best interests at heart."

Bradshaw shrugged. "That's nothing new."

Pace stepped in front of Bradshaw and looked him in the eyes. "No, it's not, but these are salesmen. Worse than recruiters. I don't know Fairchild, but I do know McBride. She's made some real cold-hearted calls. Brace yourself for that."

Bradshaw nodded attentively. "Roger that."

Satisfied that the message had gotten through, Pace led the way to the conference room. Posted outside were two men in civilian clothing. Their loose-fitting button-down shirts managed to conceal the low-profile body armor well enough to fool the casual observer, but Pace could make out faint printing. Each of them held a Heckler & Koch MP7A1 personal defense weapon at the low ready, equipped with an EOTech holographic sight and a sound suppressor. Both Bradshaw and Pace made them as former special operations types, most likely members of the CIA's Global Response Staff. That was supported by the presence of the pair of Agency officials, as GRS's mission was case officer security in hostile environments.

One of them—a short, stocky black man with close-cropped hair and a goatee—held out his off-hand to stop Bradshaw and Pace from entering the room. "Gotta search you," he said. There was no malice in his voice, but the tone more than implied the consequences for non-compliance.

Bradshaw and Pace looked to each other, then the latter spoke. "If it's all the same, I'd rather keep my piece."

"It's not all the same," the other man said. That one was taller than the first GRS contractor, lanky, and with an olive complexion that broadcasted his Hispanic ethnicity. "No weapons."

Pace pointed to the room. "There's at least four of you in there. There's no way either one of us can draw without getting cut down."

The first one shrugged. "If that's the case, then there's no reason not to disarm."

Pace looked to Bradshaw. It was clear that the contractors weren't going to budge. He gave Bradshaw a nod, then the both of them removed their pistols from their waistlines in tempered, deliberate movements. The handguns remained in their holsters as they were extended to the contractors, butt-first. Each pistol was taken one at a time by the contractors, ensuring that one of the pair had effective security on Bradshaw and Pace at all times. Once the pistols were stashed in the contractors' waistlines, the Hispanic man pointed to the wall.

"Oh, c'mon," Pace said, rolling his eyes.

"Hey, man," the contractor replied, "you know you'd do the same in my shoes."

Pace pursed his lips but did not press the issue. He and Bradshaw planted their hands on the wall. The black contractor stood offset with his muzzle down and his eyes on the vigilante pair while the Hispanic thoroughly frisked them. Once the pat search was done, the Hispanic man stepped back and the black man cleared the way, gesturing for Bradshaw and Pace to enter.

When he entered, Bradshaw saw that Pace's assessment was accurate. There were four more men in the room, two posted to the left and two posted directly behind the pair of case officers. The L-shaped configuration allowed maximum coverage of the room and minimized the danger for the principals. Bradshaw and Pace glanced at each other, seeing they shared the same uneasiness. After a moment, both approached the table and took seats directly in front of their visitors.

The older black woman, Sharon McBride, spoke first. "I see age hasn't slowed you down one bit, Daniele." She pronounced the name with an Italian inflection.

Pace shrugged. "The same could be said of you," he replied.

McBride smiled, then looked between Bradshaw and Fairchild. "I assume you two already know each other."

Bradshaw nodded. "We've met, ma'am."

McBride's smile widened. "Oh, Sharon is fine. Figure this meeting alone places us past formalities."

"Okay." Bradshaw glanced between McBride and Fairchild. The former had the pleasantness of a young-spirited grandmother while carrying herself with the confidence of a corporate executive. On the other hand, the latter stared intently at Bradshaw, her designer glasses doing nothing to dampen her piercing gaze. Bradshaw felt himself start to shift uneasily beneath the stare. He thought he'd caught himself, but Fairchild smirked.

"What's wrong?" she asked. "Not what you expected?"

"Nobody expects the Inquisition," Bradshaw answered.

Fairchild's smirk turned into a full-on grin. She looked to McBride. "The man's cultured."

McBride pursed her lips, arched her eyebrows, and shrugged. "No, Mr. Bradshaw, this isn't an inquisition. It's a proposal."

"Regarding?" Pace asked.

Fairchild looked back to Bradshaw and pointed to him. "Doing something about the after-action review he handed me two years ago."

Bradshaw's blood temperature plunged. It took a moment for him to realize he'd been holding his breath. He forced himself to exhale, then inhale deeply to slow his pulse. Pace glanced over, his brow furrowed.

"What is she talking about?"

"COP Walker," Bradshaw said quietly. "Afghanistan. Ground zero."

CHAPTER TWENTY-SIX

Cakung, East Jakarta, Indonesia
21 March 2019
10:45 hours Golf (03:45 hours Zulu)

Danny Pace leaned back in his chair, one arm draped over the back. Disbelief was etched into his face as he processed Bradshaw's story: the discovery of Russians advising the Taliban, the Russians' subsequent covert co-opting of a white nationalist militia to spark a race war, and the four federal agents being sent to murder Bradshaw after securing the release of the Russian operative.

The story initially struck Pace as apocryphal. As he glanced between Sharon McBride, Diana Fairchild, and Jack Bradshaw, he found no trace of falsehood in any of their body language. Disbelief gave way to despair, and his chest deflated as he let out a long exhale.

"Holy shit," he murmured. "You're dead serious. This is real."

McBride nodded. "This is real."

"I knew there was more behind the story than what ran in the press, but…" Pace shook his head slowly. His gaze shifted to Fairchild as he pointed to Bradshaw. "How'd you know he was innocent?"

"I knew something was off when he changed his after-action review," Fairchild said. "His rough draft lacked signs of exaggeration or embellishment. I saw the body. We took photographs. There was no reason for the change. I held onto my copy and started digging."

"What'd you find?" Pace asked.

"He declined to reenlist when his career path indicated he'd be a lifer. After he got out, I heard whispers through the grapevine that he'd been declared persona non grata from government and private contract work. It wasn't until I talked to a Ground Branch guy who came over from DEVGRU that I found out they'd twisted his arm over tuning up Mukhtar Abu-Zar Noorzai."

Pace glanced at Bradshaw. "What'd you do that for?"

"Motherfucker had a tea boy," Bradshaw spat, referring to Afghanistan's widespread practice of pederasty.

Pace nodded slowly. "Okay, I get it. And they were gonna turn you in for that?"

"If I didn't remove references to Russian advisors embedded with the Taliban during the firefight, yes," Bradshaw said. "Figured it was some political consideration, not wanting to cause a ruckus with Moscow."

"That's right," Fairchild said. "And even after last year's dustup in Deir-al Zour and the public confirmation that the Russians have been arming the Taliban, the Army was content to let sleeping dogs lie. Doesn't help that your friend, Colonel Garrett, is now the J2 at JSOC."

"Fuck that guy," Bradshaw snarled. "Spineless piece of shit."

"Garrett's predecessor stuck by the falsified narrative," Fairchild said. "He's now one of the Assistant Commanding Generals at JSOC. Garrett's maintaining the party line. But, that's a tertiary detail."

"What's the primary?" Pace asked.

Fairchild set her briefcase on the table, entered the combination, and popped it open. She reached inside, produced a file, and slid it across the table. Bradshaw and Pace scooted closer together and opened it while Fairchild narrated.

"That's Colonel Stanislav Vadimovich Egorov, the D.C. GRU *rezident*." She paused, then added for Bradshaw's benefit, "Bureau's counterintel guys make a habit of following foreign intelligence types working under official cover. Look at the third photo."

Bradshaw flipped to it. He clenched his jaw. "I know this guy," he said, pointing to Egorov's companion in the photo.

"You should," Fairchild said. "Dr. Greg Lambert, self-made millionaire, political TV staple, and Special Advisor to the President." Bradshaw looked up at Fairchild with wide eyes, and she held up her hand to stop his thought. "This is hardly evidence. These meetings didn't come with audio, and making the accusation would just result in Lambert saying he was conducting a back-channel meeting on the President's behalf. What's of import are the time stamps."

Bradshaw's eyes fell to the corners. The photograph in his hand was stamped 20170612. The second was stamped 20170620.

"Holy shit," he murmured. He tapped the first photo. "This had to be right after my initial report made its way up the chain." Bradshaw set his finger on the second photo. "This was right after I'd redacted my AAR."

"Extremely suggestive," Fairchild said. "Not enough of a hill to die on, though. I'll save you some time and cut right to the chase. There's another photograph in there, a few months later. Soon after that meeting, the 'Mark Gerald' identity started hitting our systems.

"Mark Gerald?" Pace asked.

"Kazimir Merkulov," Bradshaw said. "Russia's man in the White Resistance Movement." He looked at Fairchild. "Was that enough to take it to the FBI?"

"No," she said. "So, I called an audible."

"What do you mean, 'called an audible'?"

McBride and Fairchild exchanged a glance, and then locked on Bradshaw. Fairchild spoke. "I personally hired private investigators to tail Lambert. They're retired Agency types we use for this sort of thing."

"This sort of thing?" Bradshaw asked.

"The Agency isn't allowed to operate on American soil," McBride explained. "When a subject's outside our reach and beneath the legal criminality threshold, we nudge our private investigation network. They're fully licensed where they work. Whatever they find, they pass onto the Justice Department. The federal investigators are covered to use the information under the Good Faith Doctrine, but there'd be a shitstorm if it ever hit the press."

"It's called parallel construction," Fairchild said. "Obtain the information through less-than-legal means, pass it through a conduit, and make it legal after the fact."

Bradshaw took a deep breath. "That's shady as hell."

"It's necessary," Fairchild said, an edge to her voice. "You don't get how difficult it is to catch someone in the act of spying for a foreign nation. It's even harder when you're a political appointee and your boss is friendly with the foreign nation in question."

"What did you find?" Pace asked.

"We focused on Lambert," Fairchild said. "As the surveillance expanded, so did our findings, and what we found wasn't pretty."

Bradshaw scratched his chin as he looked at the photographs. "Like?"

Fairchild took a deep breath. "The President has three special advisors. His son-in-law handles foreign policy. His domestic policy advisor started back on the campaign trail, brought on by the President's former chief strategist. It's the third, Lambert, who has a particularly niche role. Initially, it was to stem the leaks coming out of the White House.

"To that effect, the President gave him the authority to form a special task force and appropriate whatever resources he deemed necessary," Fairchild continued. "That task force is officially known as the White House Special Investigations Unit." She produced another set of files and handed them to Bradshaw and Pace. "It's a seven-man unit led by HSI Special Agent Jeremy Hawthorne."

"Let me guess," Bradshaw said as he read. "The four G-men that tried to murder me were under his command."

Fairchild nodded. "Secret Service Special Agent Bruce Kilgrave, Deputy US Marshal Philip Jones, HSI Special Agent Lucas Wilson, and HSI Special Agent Garrett Bryce. All of them were inaugural members of the SIU. All of them were former Navy SEALs that either served with Hawthorne or at the same time as Hawthorne."

"Holy shit," Pace said under his breath as he studied the files. "Seven SEALs. That's a boat crew…"

"That's actually the nickname we've taken to calling them," Fairchild said. "The Boat Crew, for that very reason."

"I assume they didn't start this far off the reservation," Bradshaw said.

"No," Fairchild said. "Initially, their goal was solely plugging leaks, investigating staffers. From what we were able to develop through our off-book network, mission creep set in fast. It expanded to shaking down journalists who were going to air news embarrassing to the President, digging up dirt on political and social rivals, and coordinating with local law enforcement under the guise of national security to catch Presidential critics in compromising conditions."

"Essentially," McBride interjected, "The Boat Crew inherited the mission of their Nixonian namesake. They're out to protect the President at all costs. But, it doesn't stop there."

Fairchild sighed as she produced another file. "A series of seemingly unconnected events. Difficult journalists having their past resurface to discredit them. Political rivals caught with kiddie porn or drugs. The Administration's most outspoken critics suddenly having their financial histories called into question." She paused. "You plot the Boat Crew's deployments, each one can be matched to a political scandal. The thing is, not all of them are aiming to protect the President."

"Who, then?" Pace asked as he continued to read.

"We don't know," Fairchild said. "We've been tracking the Boat Crew. We know about Lambert. Beyond that? We haven't had a single hit."

Bradshaw rolled his lips inward and tapped the bottom of his fist against the table. "Damn."

"We're going to continue working it from our end," McBride said. "But, we have another angle to pursue…and that's where you two come in."

Bradshaw's brow furrowed. "Come again?"

"I want you to take the war to the Russians," McBride said. A sly smile danced on her lips.

Bradshaw's eyes pressed up against their sockets. His hands gripped the chair's arms. A storm brewed in his mind as logic and emotion clashed over the proposition.

Pace chuckled and looked back and forth between Bradshaw and McBride. "I knew you were a Yalie, Sharon, but I didn't think you were about taking it back to the 50s with hairbrained schemes."

McBride waved her hands over the table. "Okay. Break it down for me. What's crazy about it?"

"We don't have the necessary logistics or connections," Pace said. "Money, safe houses, equipment, assets—"

"You've got the Mermaid," McBride said. "We know how far and wide she can reach. Why do you think we used her to get to you?" When Pace lacked a response, McBride continued. "She can get you up and running while you and Jack build your network. I know you've got access to Spartacus passports, so crossing borders isn't an issue." She pointed between Pace and Bradshaw. "You two can feed off each other. You've got the know-how, and Bradshaw's got the drive."

"The drive?" Bradshaw asked.

"One of the targets you hit, the whorehouse in Senen…according to Mr. Pratama, they had a room there where they'd store cash for pickup. He said that you'd set explosives in there, destroying about $10 million in cash. A few of the girls you rescued gave your description to the National Police. Said it was two Euro types with American accents, one older, one younger, both in military gear…each with a large duffel bag on their backs."

"You're well-informed, as usual," Pace said.

"My men found those duffel bags on the way in," McBride said. "You're millionaires. Even if you split it two ways, that'd be enough for Danny to continue his mission here for a while, and for Jack to stay off the grid indefinitely, if he plays his cards right." She focused on

Bradshaw. "You'll be looking over your shoulder the rest of your life, wondering if we're coming for you, or Lambert and his crew, or the Russians. But, survival is possible."

"Or?" Bradshaw asked.

"Or," McBride said, "you give that cash to the mermaid. She stores it offshore in a secure account only you two can access. You use it to establish safe houses, buy gear, and develop assets. You pursue the Russians. You pilfer their resources. If needs be, you target any other black market element. Dope runners, gun traffickers, sex slavers, blood diamond salesmen, whatever. Steal their money, and then use it to disrupt Russian intelligence operations on a global scale."

"To what end?" Bradshaw asked.

Pace caught on. "We become a pain in their ass, they'll have to send their A-team. We capture one of them, we can either bag somebody in a position to give us the intel we need on the President's Men, or we get ourselves one step in the chain closer to somebody who can."

Bradshaw shook his head. "That's suicide. We're just two shooters."

"Then you'll have to recruit more," McBride said. She sighed. "Look, it's not gonna be easy. Yeah, you might not succeed. Might even die along the way. But, if you want to take these bastards down, this is the only way." She interlaced her fingers and set them on the table. "If you want to clear your name, Jack? To come home? There's only one way there, and it's through the Russians."

Gabriela Rivera's visage flashed before Bradshaw's eyes. He blinked the image away, exhaled audibly, and looked to Pace. "Danny?"

Pace's eyes rested on his own thumb and pointer finger drumming on the table. He shook his head. "I don't like any of this. I'd heard the rumors about a PI network being used for parallel construction, but I thought it was a wives' tale. That almost lends credibility to the accusations about a 'deep state.'"

Fairchild broke in. "That's not even the same damn thing, and you know it."

Pace ignored her rebuttal and pressed forward. "At the same time...I'd rather have to worry about cleaning up in-house than have a wolf in the paddock. What you've discovered is...troublesome." He looked over to Bradshaw and smirked. "And I guess somebody needs to be Race Bannon to this guy's Jonny Quest."

"You'll need some more gray in your hair before you can claim that title," Bradshaw said with a grim smile.

McBride cleared her throat, bringing the attention back to her. "I'm glad to have you on-board." She rose and buttoned her blazer. "I'll let Ms. Wright know to come back and pick up the funds. Ms. Fairchild will be your point of contact. If you're killed, you're fugitives whose criminal ways have caught up with them. You're captured, we'll emphatically deny we had any hand in your activities."

She paused and shrugged. "If you're successful, your name's cleared, you come home, and you fade into obscurity. Regardless of the outcome, we won't meet again." Her eyes fell to Bradshaw. "Good luck, Jack." She looked to Pace and said, "Daniele. Always a pleasure."

"Sharon," Pace said with a nod.

McBride and two of the GRS contractors exited the room, closing the door behind them. Fairchild removed a manila folder from her briefcase, set it aside, and then collected the documents she'd handed out to Bradshaw and Pace.

"We don't get to keep these?" Bradshaw asked, looking puzzled.

Fairchild scoffed. "Hell no. You get caught with these, you'll burn the whole house down. Besides, that's just to prove that we know the government's narrative regarding your fugitive status is bullshit." Once the other documents were safely in her possession, she slid the folder across the table.

"What's this?" Pace asked as he opened it up.

"A fresh Spartacus passport, directions for an e-mail dead drop, and two tickets under your cover identities. One-way to Yaoundé, from Singapore, a week from now."

"Only one passport?" Bradshaw asked.

"As I recall, you've already got one in your possession," Fairchild said. "A New Zealand passport, if I recall correctly."

"What's in Yaoundé?" Pace asked.

Fairchild closed her briefcase, locked it, and stood. "When I meet you there in a couple of weeks, you'll find out. Until then, keep a low profile."

Without another word, Fairchild scooped up her briefcase and left the room. Footsteps emanated from the hallway and faded in decrescendo. Bradshaw looked at the manila folder, then stared at Pace with anxiety and anticipation.

"We're doing this, aren't we?" Bradshaw asked.

Pace nodded. "We're doing it."

CHAPTER TWENTY-SEVEN

Toa Payoh, Central Region, Singapore
29 March 2019
19:45 hours Hotel (11:45 hours Zulu)

Alicia Tan sat down on her couch, a glass of ice water in her hand. She hadn't changed out of her black dress, though she had ditched the heels at the door. Both her and Lucas's families had immediately come together when the news arrived. Alicia's father had offered to handle the funeral costs, as he could afford to do in his position as a bank manager. However, when her father went to pay the funeral home director, he'd found that a mysterious benefactor had already footed the bill.

Lucas's mother was the one who actively planned the funeral alongside the home. Various extended relatives came by and helped with watching Marcus, her 2-year-old, as well as doing housework and taking care of bills. They were aided by Tan's coworkers, as well as his friends from his Army and contracting days.

Overcast skies and a light drizzle had set the tone for the funeral day. Lucas was not particularly religious, but his family and Alicia's were all Presbyterian, so the funeral was held at the Tabernacle Bible Presbyterian Church, a short distance from their apartment building. The pastor who had presided over Alicia's congregation growing up opened the ceremony, quoting appropriate scripture and speaking in general but eloquent terms.

Lucas's father spoke next, wearing his dark blue Singapore Police Force dress uniform. His tone was stoic as he spoke of his love for his son, the pride he took in his son's military service and dedication to others, and that he died pursuing his convictions. Tears trickled down the man's weathered face, but never once did his voice crack or waver.

In contrast, his mother was a tearful mess. She recalled through her sobbing that, as early as she could remember,

Lucas split his time between burying his nose in every book that he could find and playing war with friends outdoors with weapon-shaped sticks. She focused on his being a quiet, thoughtful man with an underlying competitive streak, which came out most obviously in secondary school, where he engaged in student political debate and was a star forward in Fajar Secondary School's football club. She knew her son would love the Army during his national service, and was not surprised when he went into security contracting and private investigations. Her pride faltered, and she broke down as she wept. She eventually had to be helped back to her seat, where her husband wrapped his arm around her and held her quietly.

That was when it was Alicia's turn to speak. Most of what she had to say was expected: spending lunches with him at Fajar Secondary's cafeteria, working with him on school projects, realizing that she loved him when he shipped out to his basic military training, being a soldier's wife, and staying by Lucas's side when he tried his hand in the private sector. She kept her composure throughout the speech, right up until she traced her memories to the present.

"Lucas was my love," she had said. "He was my best friend...the father of my child...he was the model for which I want Marcus to aspire as he grows into a man." The tears started as she sniffled and battled in futility to keep her voice from breaking. "I have to raise him on my own...and I don't know where to start..."

Alicia ended the speech prematurely, rushing outside to get some fresh air. Her father and Lucas's father jogged after her to make sure she was okay. She had fallen to her knees outside the church, her body heaving as the sobs seized her body. They attempted to pick her up, but she became dead weight as she allowed her sorrow to consume her. It took a single, high-pitched, soft-spoken voice to snap her out of it.

"Mommy?"

Marcus had wandered out on his own after his mother. Alicia had beckoned Marcus over to her, brought him into her embrace, and held him close as she tried to calm herself. Marcus had rested his head against her chest, wrapped his arms around her, and patted her back with a gentle touch.

"It's okay, Mommy," he said. "Daddy told me to take care of you while he's gone. I'm here, Mommy."

That had brought on another burst of tears which dissipated as quickly as it had arrived. Her son in her arms reminded her that she could not afford to indulge her grief. Marcus needed his mother now, more than ever. Alicia had composed herself, rose to her feet, scooped her son in her arms, and walked back into the foyer with her father and father-in-law on her flanks.

The rest of the afternoon had been a blur. The pallbearers consisted of Lucas's father, her father, and a combination of Lucas's Army comrades and private investigator friends. After the casket was loaded in the hearse, the procession began. It was a 12-minute drive from the church to the cemetery. Lucas's father had secured a police escort. The pallbearers accompanied the casket from the hearse to the grave, and then gently lowered it into the ground. Each member of the immediate family took their turn tossing a rose each into the grave.

When Alicia reached the grave, she held her head high and paused. Her lower lip trembled as she fought to maintain her equanimity. A pair of tears slipped past the dam, and Alicia allowed them to make their trail along her cheeks. She inhaled deeply through her nose to center herself. Lucas would have wanted her to be strong, to mourn in private. As she exhaled, her fingers released the rose, and her eyes locked on as the flower made its descent. It made impact with the coffin, and Alicia quickly turned away to rejoin her family. It was all that she could do to keep from breaking down once more.

At the following reception, Alicia lost track of faces and names. It was a long string of condolences and promises to render aid if needed. She barely touched her dinner plate, and numbly went along with the proceedings. After dinner, the gathered trickled out, and her father gave her and Marcus a ride home.

Alicia had carried her sleepy son to his bed, tucked him in, and gave his forehead a tender kiss. That had led her to the couch. As she sipped her ice water, her mind still struggled to process all of what had happened. The worst part was, she knew the official story was a lie, and couldn't say a word about it. Lucas had given her enough details to sate her curiosity, but not enough to where she knew the ins and outs. Those details didn't jive with the official cause of death, but she had held her peace.

A trio of knocks resounded through the door. Alicia set the glass on her coffee table, crossed the living room, and peered through the door's peephole. She exhaled as she saw who it was, then undid the locks and pulled the door open.

Danny Pace stood in the doorway, dressed in a black rain jacket, gray T-shirt, jeans, and boots. His hair was slick from the rain, and his face was burdened with trepidation. His hands were in his pockets. Alicia stood back and folded her arms.

"Yes?" she asked tiredly.

"Alicia," he said. "May I come in a minute?"

Her eyes flittered to the hall, then back to Pace. "Only a minute. And be quiet. Marcus is sleeping."

"Of course, of course."

Alicia stepped aside and allowed Pace inside. She closed and locked the door behind her. Pace wandered into the living room and surveyed it. Photos of Lucas and Alicia adorned the walls. One of them was a photo of them with Marcus in a park, all of them smiling.

"This is cozy," Pace said. "I like it."

Alicia folded her arms again. "What do you want, Danny?"

Pace sighed as he looked back to her. "Look, Alicia, I'm sorry—"

Alicia held up a hand to stop Pace. "I appreciate what you're trying to do, but please, don't. For starters, I don't blame you."

"You should," Pace said. "I roped him into this whole thing."

"Lucas ran towards the gunfire," Alicia said. "He always has…" She took a deep breath before she corrected herself. "He always *did*. Any suggestion to the contrary detracts from his memory, so please. I understand the desire to place the blame upon yourself, but don't use me to assuage your guilty conscience."

Pace nodded as he bit his lip. "Fair enough." He cleared his throat as quietly as he could. "Look, I wanted to pay my respects."

"And so you have," Alicia said. "I don't blame you, but I'll be honest: seeing you is only reminding me of what I've lost." She stepped to the door. "So, please, if there isn't anything else—"

"There is," Pace said. "Lucas's folks are solid people, and I know your old man's secured. Neither one of them will let you and Marcus go hungry, naked, or homeless."

Alicia nodded. "Yes. They're good people."

"Well, I'd like to help, too," Pace said. He pulled out a slip of paper and extended it towards Alicia. She glanced at the paper, then back to Pace.

"What's this?" she asked.

"It's a bank account, registered with your father's branch," Pace said. "There's about $2 million Singaporean in there. It's legit and taxed. That money is yours."

Alicia's countenance darkened. "Where did you get this money?"

"Stole it from one of our targets," Pace said. "Like I said, it's clean, and the taxes are paid. Nobody'll question where it came from. We were going to use it for follow-on jobs, but…" His chest rose and fell with a deep sigh. "Truth is, I'm out of that racket. I got picked up for another job."

"What job?" Alicia asked.

"Another thing I have to do," Pace said. The look on his face transmitted the rest of the message.

"Right," Alicia said. She put her hands on her hips and looked off to the side. "Can't tell me." Her eyes locked back on Pace. "How about telling me how he *really* died? Because this nonsense about a rock-climbing accident is exactly that: nonsense."

Pace gestured his agreement with a nod of his head. "He was captured by our targets. He died bravely. His killer is dead."

The tears flowed freely. She lifted her hand to her mouth to stifle a sob. When she spoke, her voice quivered and broke. "That doesn't bring Lucas back."

"No, it doesn't," Pace said. He gently shook the slip of paper. "On the other hand, this pays off your flat. It gives you space and time to lock in a career. It pays for Marcus's education. It clears the deck so all you have to worry about is raising your son and allowing yourself to heal."

Alicia reluctantly accepted the paper. She unfolded it and read the details. As she read, Pace pointed to the slip and narrated.

"That's the account number, phone password, and web-site password. The name and number at the bottom is an accountant that'll continue to handle finances and taxes. He's solid, and I'm covering the costs. If you wish to go with someone else, let me know and I'll handle payment."

Alicia folded the paper and held it in her fist. "Thank you. Now, go. Please."

Pace paused at the top of his inhale, pursed his lips, and nodded as he saw himself out. When the door shut behind him, Alicia allowed the tears to flow freely, careful to keep her sobs silent as to avoid waking Marcus.

PACE MADE HIS way to the elevator. He thumbed the down button, stuck his hands back in his pockets, and let out a long exhale as he waited for the doors to open. It was a 20-second ride from the fifth floor to the lobby, and after that, another two-minute walk from the lobby to the parking lot. Jack Bradshaw waited behind the wheel of the jet-black Mitsubishi Lancer they'd rented upon landing in Singapore.

Bradshaw looked over to Pace as the latter climbed inside the car and closed the door behind him. "You good?" Bradshaw asked.

Pace nodded. "Yeah."

Bradshaw rolled his lips inward. "Sorry you have to go through that, man."

"It was the right thing to do," Pace said.

"Yes, it was," Bradshaw said. He shifted into reverse. "C'mon. We've got a flight to catch."

Kebayoran Baru, South Jakarta, Indonesia
29 March 2019
19:30 hours Golf (12:30 hours Zulu)

KIRSANA NIRMALA SAT cross-legged at the edge of her bed, clad in an oversized shirt and fitness shorts. She held a box of *mie goreng* with grilled chicken and peanut sauce in one hand and a fork in the other. It had been a hectic week. She had cranked out one article after another in an exposé series. The information she had received from Bradshaw and his compatriots had proven to be a damning treasure trove. Protestors had taken to the streets, demanding immediate action. The national government was involved, and grievances were filed by affected tribes, demanding reparations. *Div Propam* was designated the lead investigative element, and they quickly set out to verify everything in the information dump she had sent to them shortly before publishing her findings.

Nirmala scooped the last of the food from the box, deposited it in her mouth, and set the fork and box between her legs as she chewed. She grabbed the bottle of Bintang that was just behind the empty food box and lifted it to her lips, her eyes on the television as the *KompasTV* weather anchor finished the week's forecast.

"And in other news, the Kuwat Scandal continues," the perfectly coiffed male anchor said. A picture of Setiawan Mahmud was the inset photo, and the word "CORRUPTION" in bold print was positioned beneath it. "Today, federal investigators officially filed charges against Setiawan Mahmud, the former Deputy Governor of Jakarta."

The image changed to footage of Mahmud walking into a courthouse, his hands restrained in front of him, a *Div Propam* investigator on each side, holding his arms. "Mahmud has been charged with tax evasion, engaging in a criminal enterprise, racketeering, kidnapping, drug trafficking, and sex trafficking. The former Central Jakarta mayor and Gerinda Party figure was remanded to Cipinang Penitentiary Institution's pre-trial unit, where a federal judge has ordered he be held without bail. If convicted on all charges, Mahmud faces the death penalty. Mahmud's lawyer released a statement earlier today, saying that the charges were patently false, and that the facts would exonerate him."

Nirmala swallowed her mouthful of beer and chortled. "Fat chance of that, Setiawan," she muttered.

After another screen change, Mega Nyoman was shown in a courtroom, wearing an orange jumpsuit marked "148" on the left side of the chest, as well as a pair of handcuffs secured to a Martin chain around his waist. The look on his face was particularly dour, which brought no small satisfaction to Nirmala.

"Mega Nyoman was arraigned today. The former Chief Commissioner of the Regional Jakarta Metro's Criminal Detective Unit has been held without bail on similar charges, along with criminal activity under color of authority. His trial is scheduled for late next month. Nyoman, a 19-year veteran of the Regional Police, faces the death penalty if convicted.

"In other news," the anchor continued, "the charges against Jack Bradshaw for the murder of two members of Greater Jakarta's Pelopor Regiment have been dropped, in light of the news that C Detachment of the local regiment have regularly acted as an enforcement squad for deceased *preman* Suparman Guntur. The United States Ambassador released a statement today, warning that Mr. Bradshaw was still a very dangerous international fugitive, and that any tips regarding his whereabouts should be reported to the United States Embassy."

The talking head began to segue into remarks made by the Governor regarding this scandal, but the Samsung smartphone by her hip rang. She transferred her beer bottle from her right hand to her left, scooped up the phone, and looked at the screen. A smile spread across her lips as she swiped up to accept the call.

"Hi, Max," she said cheerily.

"Kirsana," Max Santoso said, "you watching the news?"

"Yes, I am. Mahmud and Nyoman in cuffs is the best thing I've ever seen. Would have loved to see Guntur in an orange jumpsuit, but I suppose we can't get everything we want."

Santoso's tone darkened. "From what I've heard, Guntur did not go peacefully into the night."

Nirmala took a deep breath. While she was grateful for the information from Bradshaw and his compatriots, her contact inside West Java's Criminal Detective Unit had shown her the crime scene photos from the Guntur estate. His killing was committed with a warlike brutality, and it had chilled her to the core.

"No," Nirmala finally said. "He did not." She took a deep breath. "Still, if anybody deserved it, it was him."

"What about the girls?" Santoso asked. "I heard you made arrangements for them with the Red Crescent and the Human Rights Council."

Nirmala let out another heavy sigh. "Yes, I did. I've already written a piece focused entirely on that. It's sitting in the queue."

"Doesn't sound optimistic," Santoso said. "Gimme the rundown."

"They'll try and reconnect the women with their families," Nirmala said. "They'll also provide them with as much physical and mental health care as possible. Some of these families might take them back. Others might reject them, blame them for being assaulted. Even with a lifetime of love and support, there's no guarantee that they'll recover. Suicide rates amongst rescued sex slaves are high. Recidivism is also high. Most of them are battling drug addictions, too." She let out a long, drawn out breath. "It's not pretty."

"Well, you're bringing awareness to it," Santoso said. "That's the first step."

"Yeah."

Santoso inhaled deeply. "On a more positive note, I've had a talk with the editors. They've contacted the Asia Society in New York. We're going to submit your series for an Osborn Elliot Award."

Nirmala's brow creased. "Wasn't the submission deadline for that two weeks ago?"

"The board's got some friends. They've managed to convince the Society that your series is impactful enough to warrant an exemption."

Nirmala sat up a little straighter. "That's going to be some rough competition. I'll be going up against international reporters."

"Don't sell yourself short," Santoso said. "You've exposed massive criminal corruption in the largest regional government. This is big. You've got a fighting chance."

"Thank you, Max," Nirmala said. "I owe you."

"You don't owe me a thing," Santoso said. "You put in the work. It's hard earned. Have a good night."

"You too."

Nirmala killed the connection, set the phone down on the bed, and allowed herself a small smile. With all the stories she'd covered, all of the bad endings on which she'd reported, her heart couldn't help but fill with hope.

For a change, the good guys had won one.

Washington, D.C.
29 March 2019
08:30 hours Quebec (12:30 hours Zulu)

GREG LAMBERT HAD entered his office an hour earlier. The other members had demanded the meeting, but Lambert was determined not to let it interrupt his morning schedule. After he had dismissed the previous night's sexual pursuit, Lambert had put in an hour and a half at the gym. Fox News had a short blurb about Jack Bradshaw being exonerated by Indonesian authorities, but it was merely filler. The Fox & Friends anchor was quick to move onto the latest budget fight, and the President clashing with the new Democratic majority in the House. That was another issue on Lambert's plate, but he'd tackle that after the meeting.

Lambert showered and changed at the private gym, then drove his Mercedes-Benz to the White House. The uniformed Secret Service agent took a cursory look at his identification before waving him to the employee parking lot. It was a short walk from his prime parking spot to the East Wing entrance. Lambert opted for the stairs, as it gave him a chance to work out the lactic acid he'd accrued during his leg workout.

Upon arriving, Lambert saw Patricia Walton was already at her desk. He'd given her a smile and said, "You work too hard, Trish."

"You work hard," Trish said. "I've gotta work harder to keep you on your A-game."

Lambert smiled. "I've got a teleconference meeting. Hold all my calls until 9:00 AM."

"You've got it."

As Lambert stared at the Wire contacts screen, his thoughts lingered on Walton. He'd maintained professionalism out of the principle that he shouldn't defecate where he feasted, but the qualities that made her a solid secretary also elicited arousal. Plus, Lambert would be lying if he hadn't mentally undressed her once or twice. He contemplated the notion right up to the time that the shrill digital chirping erupted from his speakers. He guided the cursor over to the ACCEPT button and left-clicked.

Twelve faces filled the screen. Each one of them was ethnic European. The youngest would turn 50 that year. Only one was female. Their combined net worth was in the billions of dollars. They shared a common interest: protecting the President and executing his agenda, at all costs.

"Gentlemen," Lambert said. "Let's bring this meeting to order."

The Congressman from California interjected. "What do you know about what's happening in Indonesia?"

Lambert suppressed a sigh. "Our sources indicate that Bradshaw was able to find, fix, and finish Guntur."

"Then the plan has failed," the same Congressman said. "Bradshaw's still an untied loose end."

"I don't know why we haven't deployed the Boat Crew to deal with this," the senior senator from Kentucky said. "Or at least leaned on the Russians. If you can't use your channels, I've got an in with Deripaska."

"That's the wrong move right now," Lambert said. "We're under the microscope. The Marxists have taken over the House, and they're out for blood. We give them any excuse to lash out, they're going to take it. The last thing we need is to be seen trying too hard to close the book on Bradshaw." He took a deep breath. "He's just jumped from one debacle to another. If he's smart, he'll lay low and stay off the grid."

"And if he doesn't?" a Congressman from Iowa pressed.

"Then we let the Russians handle it," Lambert said. "They want him dead, too. They've taken point by lobbying for a red notice to be filed with Interpol. It's only a matter of time before the request is processed and approved. They may have lost the election, but they still hold a lot of clout within the organization."

A little-known billionaire entrepreneur spoke up, his voice soft. "So you're saying that we're secure."

"Absolutely," Lambert said. He took a deep breath. "Don't worry about Jack Bradshaw. He's the least of our present concerns. We need to be focused on turning the political tide before all of our hard work is undone. The election is in 19 months. That's where our energies must be directed. Agreed?"

Each of the members verbalized their assent. Lambert sighed and said, "All right. Let's move onto other issues."

The other members of the committee launched into a discussion, and Lambert watched with detached indifference. There was a nagging feeling in the back of his mind that told him that he'd undersold the threat that Bradshaw posed.

Lambert pursed his lips as he dismissed the notion. Jack Bradshaw was one man who lacked the necessary skills to survive alone in the cold. He would be handled, one way or another, and the committee could press forward with their ultimate objective: the preservation of the United States.

Don't miss the next pulse-pounding entry in the series…

FORSAKEN

VERMILION BOILING

After narrowly escaping Indonesia with their lives, Jack Bradshaw and Danny Pace have arrived in Africa.

Their task: locate and rescue a deep-cover CIA operative in possession of critical information about Russian influence in the Central African Republic.

Working hand-in-hand with a convict-turned-Foreign Legionnaire and a disgraced US Army helicopter pilot, Bradshaw and Pace fire their opening salvo in their shadow campaign against the Russians.

Amidst the tested convictions, heinous atrocities, and shifting alliances of the Central African Republic's blood-drenched civil war, a specter will rear their menacing head…

COMING SOON TO AMAZON.COM!

Sign up for Steven Hildreth, Jr.'s mailing list:
https://tinyurl.com/HildrethMailList

And follow him on social media:
https://linktr.ee/stevenhildreth

Authors (especially independent authors) live by word-of-mouth recommendations. If you enjoyed this book, please consider leaving a review on Amazon, Goodreads, or both. Every review helps immensely. Thank you!

70263734R00174

Made in the USA
Columbia, SC
20 August 2019